P9-CRD-473

TELL ME MORE

TELL ME MORE

JANET MULLANY

For Sandy

Janet Mullany

Spice   *Enjoy!*

If you purchased this book without a cover you should be aware
that this book is stolen property. It was reported as "unsold and
destroyed" to the publisher, and neither the author nor the
publisher has received any payment for this "stripped book."

TELL ME MORE

ISBN-13: 978-0-373-60558-3

Copyright © 2011 by Janet Mullany

Recycling programs
for this product may
not exist in your area.

All rights reserved. Except for use in any review, the reproduction or utilization of
this work in whole or in part in any form by any electronic, mechanical or other
means, now known or hereafter invented, including xerography, photography and
recording, or in any information storage or retrieval system, is forbidden without the
written permission of the publisher, Spice Books, 225 Duncan Mill Road, Don Mills,
Ontario M3B 3K9, Canada.

This is a work of fiction. Names, characters, places and incidents are either
the product of the author's imagination or are used fictitiously, and any resemblance
to actual persons, living or dead, business establishments, events or locales is
entirely coincidental.

For questions and comments about the quality of this book please contact us
at Customer_eCare@Harlequin.ca.

Spice and the Colophon are trademarks used under license and registered in
Australia, New Zealand, Philippines, United States Patent and Trademark Office
and in other countries.

www.Spice-Books.com

Printed in U.S.A.

In memory of Macheath who always fell over for me.

1

"I'M HERE FOR MY SKIS."

I looked at him lounging against the doorway. He'd rung the doorbell, an exercise in futility or good manners—I wasn't sure which since both door and screen were open to catch the late-afternoon sunlight. Hugh was quite the lounger, particularly in others' beds. Searching for a snappy comeback, I said, "And how's the stick insect?"

"Flowyr's fine."

Flowyr. I'd been betrayed for a woman called Flowyr.

"My skis, Jo."

I stepped back. "You know where they are."

He straightened himself and ambled into the house, accompanied by a few yellow leaves. I tried not to watch. There was something about Hugh in motion, any sort of motion, that still did things to me, a sort of knee-jerk hot-wire to desire. My body was in no hurry to change its habits.

I heard him go into the basement. "Hugh, while you're down there, would you look at the traps?"

"I thought that was what your fucking cat was for." Banging and thumping noises accompanied his words.

"He can't empty mousetraps."

After a while Hugh came back up the stairs carrying his ski gear. "Nothing."

"Was the peanut butter still on them?"

"Christ, Jo, I don't know." He dropped his skis, poles and boots on the hardwood floor with a loud clatter. "I didn't look that close, okay? It's dark down there. Do you have my Ken Burns DVDs?"

I gestured toward the living room. "Feel free."

I followed him in anyway, telling myself it wasn't for the pleasure of seeing his ski-and-tennis-toned body drop to a squat, only to make sure he didn't take the Firth-Ehle *Pride and Prejudice*. He liked Jennifer Ehle and her astonishing elevated breasts; I liked all the astonishingly unfettered penises waving around inside the men's pants.

"So," he said, catching me gazing at his thighs, "the thing is, Flowyr and I aren't together anymore. I told you it was a onetime thing. An accident."

"An accident? You rear-ended her?"

"Don't yell, honey, you don't want to go on the air sounding hoarse—"

"Don't call me *honey*."

He stood—without a tremor, quads in great shape—clutching a stack of DVDs. "Jo, I'm—"

"I bought *Shaun of the Dead*," I said, seeing it in his hands.

"For my birthday, so it's mine. Jo, I'm sorry."

I'm sorry. The words you never expect to hear from a man. But was his apology for letting Flowyr run his red light or for depriving me of one of my favorite movies?

"I'm sorry," he said again.

I dropped to the couch, putting myself at eye level with a relatively unfettered penis uncurling behind his khakis.

He had apologized.

If only a moment could be bronzed. Hugh dropped to his

knees, laid the DVDs on the floor and shuffled forward. His hands landed on the couch on either side of me. "Sorry. I've been so unhappy. I know you have been, too. I was dumb. I…"

This was all too familiar; Hugh making himself available, those lovely toffee-colored eyes with the long lashes, his mouth and a slight dusting of late-day stubble, all within easy reach— all the above-the-neck parts I found sexy and irresistible. And he'd apologized, although I suspected it was pretty meaning- less— Had the man no shame? Did he really want to keep *Shaun of the Dead* that badly? Wasn't I intending to kick him out of my life (again) with no happy or unhappy returns?

Well, yes.

But.

A quick calculation. When did I think I was next going to have the chance of brainless sex with someone who knew what he was doing and knew what I liked? Shouldn't I be stocking up for the long famine ahead?

A whiff of eau de Hugh wafted into my brain, or crotch, or somewhere.

One of his hands moved to cup my hip.

Our heads swayed, angled.

His lips were slightly chapped. I hadn't been around to re- mind him to carry his organic hemp lip salve, and however much mindless screwing he'd had with Flowyr (*Flowyr!*)—well, that slut wouldn't be concerned about his lips. Or she might like it rough. Rough skin, that is, rasping on…

Oh, my God. We were kissing and for a moment it was poi- gnant and lovely before it became something equally lovely, but hot and driven. Hands delved into clothes, pushing up, aside, unbuttoning; the press and trail of fingertips, palms, as we became reacquainted with each other's skin. My T-shirt was up around my collarbone, my bra unsnapped and his tongue in my mouth, on my neck. I had to push him away so I could get rid of my clothes. As I struggled through the dark folds of

T-shirt and disentangled my bra, his hands went to work on my jeans, and I lifted my hips to help him get them off me.

"Santa's come early this year," he commented at first sight of my panties.

Well, I did need to do laundry, it was true. I watched as his fingers splayed over the faded jolly old elf, and dipped under the elastic, where things were getting very wet.

I lunged at his shirt, unbuttoning, pushing it off him. "Get your pants off."

He stood to undo his khakis. His cock sprang free, waving around a bit as though just woken and taking a look around. *Hmm, nice day, nice warm temperature, glad to be out of those boxers, and is that a pussy I see before me?*

I touched my clit through the cotton of my panties, while he shoved pants and boxers down, and toed off his sneakers and socks. I'd taught him that: *always get your socks off, Hugh. There's nothing as dumb as a guy with an erection in a pair of socks.*

He watched my finger, my middle finger, the one I always used. "Dirty girl," he said softly. "Such wet panties, too."

I spread my legs a little more. "I can't think how that happened." I slid my finger beneath the elastic, where his finger had tickled and stirred. My clit was hard. I wanted to come. I wanted him to watch me. I wanted him inside me, that shiny pink cock all ready for me. I wanted his finger and tongue tickling me in rude and naughty places.

"I want—" I said, and Hugh shoved his cock into my mouth. Obviously that's the sort of thing you did to a dirty girl who played with herself in front of you, and hadn't had the foresight to put on her special lace or silk panties, but sported her Christmas cottons (slightly grayed and ragged ones at that) two months early. Besides, I was right at crotch level, with my mouth half-open while I considered taking an orgasm before he obliged.

I made a sound of mingled surprise and appreciation and

clapped my hands to his nicely toned butt, my nose squished into his pubic hair, and swirled my tongue around his cock. I knew how he loved that, how he would groan and thread his fingers through my hair, and mutter a filthy stream-of-consciousness litany as he rocked in and out of my mouth.

"Oh God yes oh God baby that's right oh yes oh God yes oh yes like that keep doing that oh God Jo oh God baby make me come oh yes come in your mouth oh yes oh yes…"

And as dumb as he sounded, it made me hot. Made me squirm against the sodden crotch of my Santa panties and groan along with him, while reminding myself that absolutely no way was he going to have the privilege of coming in my mouth, not when there was work to be done below. My hands were busy with him, sliding to stroke his balls and thighs, to probe and tickle and pinch. Now and then one of my nipples would rub against his thigh, bounce off muscle and wiry hair and send an unmistakable signal to my clit—*get ready for takeoff*—but all I could do was wriggle and rub myself against the roughness of the sofa upholstery.

I pulled free. *Now.* We were so attuned to each other that I didn't have to say it, but Hugh, in a brilliantly executed choreography of lust, lunged for his pants on the floor and pulled a condom from his wallet.

A series of reactions rushed through my mind as he ripped it open.

He brought a condom.

What the hell, I want him to fuck me.

But he came prepared.

Very sensible, given the stick insect.

Or does he always have them in his wallet?

Oh, look at him slide it over himself. So sexy to see him handle his cock. I should have asked him to do it for me more often.

Did he always have condoms, even when he was living with me?

But he came here meaning to fuck me. Or fuck someone sometime—

"Hugh," I said, and he took it as an invitation, which in a way it was—an invitation to stop me thinking.

The Santa panties hit the floor and Hugh reared over and in me, my butt on the edge of the sofa, legs over his shoulders.

"Nice?" he panted. "Nice for the little lady?"

"Oh, yes. Nice." The little lady was being serviced, no question, fucked and screwed and impaled and penetrated and all the rest of it.

So good, so familiar, so very rude, in the middle of the afternoon with the front door open and me still wearing my socks (actually a pair of Hugh's but I didn't think he'd want to claim these fraying relics with a hole in one heel).

He bent his head to suckle one breast and then the other, sending me a notch higher. And higher, so that I stopped thinking about socks and DVDs and random condoms, everything except Hugh's mouth and cock and his fingers on my clit.

And I was there, torqued up to the breaking point and then breaking and flooding as I came, while Hugh kept me there as long as he could. Then he gathered himself and plunged away in his familiar oh-my-God-I'm-going-to-come home run, short staccato stabs that—other than postorgasm—didn't do a thing for me. He collapsed with a groan on top of me, folding me up like a pretzel.

"Nice?" I stroked his shoulder, damp with sweat.

He gave a primeval grunt.

"Uh, I can see this isn't a good time. Would you like me to come back later?"

At the sound of the unfamiliar Irish lilt, we both froze.

Then Hugh leaped to his feet. "Who the fuck are you? What the hell are you doing here?"

I grabbed Hugh's shirt to cover myself as I remembered, too late, the appointment I'd made. "Patrick…someone?"

Patrick someone, standing at the front door, smirked and blinked behind steel-rimmed glasses.

"Ah, I'll leave you to it, then," Patrick said. He glanced at my panties on the floor. "Merry Christmas."

"Jesus Christ!" Hugh spluttered.

I tried to restrain a giggle at Hugh, standing outraged, cock deflating and wobbly; a giggle did escape as the condom dropped to the floor with a splat.

"Who was that—that *leprechaun?*"

"He can't help being Irish. He was here to look at the apartment."

"Why?"

"Because I can't carry the mortgage on my own."

For an economist, Hugh was sometimes pretty stupid.

"But—but, you won't be on your own. I'm moving back in." He paused. "Aren't I? I mean, after...this."

"Hugh, you came to get your skis and DVDs. A fuck doesn't give you permission to move back in." I retrieved panties, T-shirt and jeans, and dressed.

Hugh, apparently realizing nakedness gave him no advantage, grabbed his clothes. "Jo, at least we should talk about it. I mean, we love each other. I'm sorry about...you know. Everything."

"No."

Brady, tail aloft, trotted into the living room and sniffed at the condom on the floor as though discovering some delicious edible.

"You fucking cat," Hugh said as Brady wound around his ankles, purring. Early on, Brady had decided that Hugh was his best friend and answered to *fucking cat* as an alternative to his real name.

"Who are you going to get to empty the mousetraps?" Hugh said with despicable cunning.

"I'll handle it. I've been handling it for the past three weeks."

I picked up the pile of DVDs and handed them to him. "I'll pack the rest of your stuff and let you know when you can come get it. I have to go to work now, Hugh."

"We need to talk about this," Hugh said, looking obstinate and ruffled in a way that pre-stick insect would have melted my heart.

"No, we don't. But Hugh, one thing. When did you start carrying condoms around? I mean, do you let them fall out of your wallet at faculty meetings to impress the Chair or something?"

I could just imagine the Economics Department snickering and high-fiving—*You get lucky this weekend, Hugh? You da man, Hugh!*—under the benign gaze of the Chair, a dead ringer for Alan Greenspan, horn-rimmed eyeglasses, wrinkles and all.

"Don't be ridiculous." Hugh picked up the condom from the floor and headed out of the room.

"Not in the toilet. You'll block it."

He stopped and turned to me, suspicion on his face. "How do you know that?"

"I just do." Virtually anything blocked up the downstairs toilet. It was strictly off-limits to males and menstruating women.

"You bitch," he said, and to my surprise he looked really upset. He flung the condom into the wastebasket in the corner of the room and flung himself and his DVDs out the front door. The effect was spoiled by his having to stomp inside the house again to get his skis. I sat on the couch, Brady kneading my legs, and listened to his car start and reverse out of the driveway and the sound die away with an awful sort of finality.

I cried a bit, then, thinking how tired I was of crying, but that you couldn't let three years of your life go without some grieving. Brady purred and allowed himself to be hugged with a friendly tolerance that implied an empty food dish.

The bright fall day was fading now, but before I could go to work there was something I had to do. I went into the kitchen and armed myself. Knife, peanut butter, barbecue tongs (Hugh's, and I might just forget to wash them afterward), rubber gloves, flashlight. Pants tucked into socks, in case anything was alive, and (aargh) panicked.

I didn't need a man for this. Or for anything much else in my life.

"You sound just like the lady on the radio," the woman in the store said. "We've got a new brand of organic peanut butter in. Would you like to try a sample? It's really good."

I am the lady on the radio. "No, this will do fine. Thanks."

Sometimes, if I'm feeling sociable, I'll admit to it, but then what usually follows is a disbelieving look, and a strange comment. *I thought you were taller...older...younger...blonde. I hate your fundraising drives. Why do you play so much Tchaikovsky? Why don't you ever play any Tchaikovsky?*

Once, inexplicably and with great indignation, *I thought you were black.*

I packed my mousing supplies and my sandwich and soup and fruit for the night in my backpack and started putting on my bike gear again—gloves, the sort of knit hat favored by hunters and rapists, helmet and a scarf to fill the gap between the hat and my lightweight down jacket. Around me, at the checkout, others were doing the same, some with huge backpacks full of organic goodies.

In this pristine Colorado college town you wouldn't dare *drive* two miles to work. I cycle.

Neither, of course, would you dare to do anything other than humanely trap rodents and release them into a gorgeous wilderness setting. Never mind that they'd have a matter of minutes to appreciate their new home before they became someone else's dinner—it would be *natural*. It's my deep, dark secret, sending mice to Nirvana on a delicious peanut-butter fantasy (and they certainly weren't getting the organic stuff;

my sentimentality only goes so far, and besides my concern was with ending, not enriching, their brief rodent lives).

Fall was definitely in the air now, crisp and wood-smoke-scented. Any day now we'd have some snow, and then I'd cross-country ski to the radio station. Funny how I never thought that the difference between Hugh and me could be so clearly defined by our choice of winter activities. He favored the mechanical assistance uphill and the short flashy burst of excitement of the downhill run, over in mere minutes. I enjoyed the diddling around with wax (oh, okay, I admit it—I have actually attended wax workshops…I am a certified cross-country geek). You can indulge in a slow, lazy plod uphill, savoring Mother Nature, or depending on your mood, bound athletically up—either way, you have the long, delicious glide down.

Not that it had anything to do with our sex life, which was pretty good, or more than good most of the time. Quite often I'd prefer the short flashy sessions on the kitchen counter or in the shower or… I wriggled around on my bike seat, wondering if it really was possible to have an orgasm by going over bumpy parts of the bike path, and whether it would be safe to do so. I could imagine myself hearing the local news, to my shame, from a hospital bed.

A massive, multibike pileup on the Douglas Pine Bike Trail resulted in several injuries today. The alleged perpetrator, Jo Hutchinson, a local radio personality who is neither blonde nor tall, showed signs of recent sexual arousal at the hospital. A spokesperson for the police department commented, "This sort of irresponsible behavior is something we take very seriously…."

I unlocked the back door of the radio station and wheeled my bike inside. Other bikes were still there; I was early tonight. The news was on and I listened to it briefly as I peeled off my bike gear. I had an hour before going on air, and later, in the wee hours of the morning, I planned to indulge in another of my deep dark secrets, one that did not involve the untimely demise of mice.

In my own way, I had been as unfaithful as Hugh, and with someone whose name I didn't even know.

2

AT PRECISELY SIX MINUTES AFTER MIDNIGHT MY time was my own, with the last of the news headlines delivered from faraway Washington, D.C. I chatted briefly on air about the weather, a chilly night but with another perfect fall day in store for tomorrow, and the likelihood of the aspens peaking. I brought music swelling into the studio, and checked the dance of the monitor. All was well.

As I switched the mic off the phone rang.

He's early.

I turned down the studio speaker and removed the head-phones. My heart pounded as I answered the phone.

"Jo, honey, what are you doing Friday night?"

"Kimberly!" Despite my initial disappointment I was glad to hear from my best friend, a displaced Texas blonde who ran the station fundraising; a workaholic with a busy social life, she was often awake at odd hours—my hours.

"I have someone for you to meet. A man." *May-un,* her voice dipped suggestively.

"Oh, for Christ's sake. I don't want to meet any men."

"You should for the sake of the environment. All those electrical devices buzz buzz buzzin' away in your bedroom. You're your own little brown cloud."

The studio door opened. Jason, the assistant station engineer, stood there, buckling his bike helmet under his chin.

"Hold on, Kim." I turned to him and smiled, for the sake of seeing him look adorably shy and give me a dazzling smile in return. "Hey, Jason. What's up?"

"Hey, Jo. I just wanted to tell you I'm going home, so you're on your own."

"Thanks. Good night."

He closed the door.

"Ah, the delectable Jason," Kimberly purred. "You and him alone in that big ole radio station. Why, if it was me I'd eat him up."

"You'd terrify him." The thought had crossed my mind, too. Lovely, lean Jason, all of twenty-one (young but legal!), with the obligatory ponytail, faded jeans, hiking boots, single earring, stubble—oh, my God, he was a walking cliché—shy and sweet and good enough to eat, as Kimberly so often pointed out.

"You don't think he's gay, do you?" Kimberly asked, as though preparing to revise her list of potential bedmates.

"No, but I wonder about hidden piercings."

"Me, too. All the time. Now this man, he's interested in the station, too, so this way I kill two birds with one stone. He's very eligible, Jo."

"For me or the station?"

"Both, and honey, I know you can get a volunteer in for your shift Friday, so you'll find a ticket to the symphony in your mailbox tomorrow."

I imitated her Texas accent. "I just luuurve a man with a bulgin' billfold."

"Oh, me, too, honey." But the fundraiser in Kimberly was in full swing now. "With the ticket you'll find a list of the people we'll be meeting. Memorize their names. Prepare to be charmin'. You can borrow my black taffeta skirt again."

"And the killer heels?" I asked hopefully. I loved that skirt, its suggestive rustle and the way it flipped around above my knees. Kimberly had an extensive designer wardrobe, as befitted a former Dallas debutante who married an oilman in the days when oilmen made real money.

"You bet. Hey, maybe you could invite him to sit in when you're on air."

I don't think so. "Maybe."

We chatted a little more—as usual, these days, I assured her that life without Hugh was progressing as well as could be expected—and after I hung up I realized I hadn't told her the story of the peeping leprechaun. A pity—she would have appreciated the comedic side of it—but then I would also have had to admit that I'd made the grave mistake of letting Hugh drop his pants.

And that reminded me that soon I'd have to make a decision about renting the apartment.

I'd deal with that later. I fired off an email to my roster of substitute announcers asking for a volunteer for Friday night, and looked at the clock. Half an hour to go on *Scheherazade.*

He'd better call soon.

I walked around the radio station, checking that the lights were off and the outside doors locked; also that Jason and everyone else had really left. I returned to the studio, the quiet space with its white walls and racks and racks of CDs, the gleaming console and monitors.

When the phone rang and I saw the screen announce "no data" I let it ring five times, despite my admonitions to the on-air staff to always, always answer the phone within two rings (unless you were on air, of course).

I picked the phone up and answered with a hint of yawn in my voice.

"Jo?" That voice, warm and dark.

"Yeah?" I pretended not to know who it was while my insides melted away and my nipples protruded through my T-shirt.

"This is a wonderful recording."

"I'm glad you like it." Now I felt shy, aroused, nervous. I, who put thousands of listeners at ease, now wanted one of them to assure me that I was safe—safe and loved—in his presence.

We chatted for a little while about the music—we both stopped to listen to the silvery flute ascent and descent, a magical, simple motif, and argued whether that, or the violin solo that represented Scheherazade's voice, or the push and pull of the waves, was the most spine-chilling part of the work.

"Have you read *The Arabian Nights?*" he asked. "No? Oh, it's a marvelous thing, Jo. Stories within stories within stories, like a maze. Sexy, too, although translators censored it, until the most recent editions."

As he spoke, I tried to place his accent. Boston or possibly someone who'd once lived in England; he had that clipped precision and diction of a Boston blue blood…some of the time.

A pause, and the sound of movement. "Sorry. I'm putting another log on the fire. It's chilly tonight."

"I bet the aspens are pretty from up there."

He chuckled. He wasn't to be caught that easily. "Yes, I believe you said during the last break that they would be peaking. Nice try. How are you? I hope that bastard Hugh hasn't been giving you any grief."

I told him the story of Hugh's visit and the leprechaun invasion, or at least a censored version—I used the term *in flagrante*…and heard him laugh with pure delight.

"How long do you think he'd been watching?"

"I don't know. It could have been from the beginning."

"Would you have liked him to watch?"

"I don't know." I lay back in my chair and watched the sound waves break and dance. We were moving into new territory here. We'd flirted, we'd talked about past relationships, but this—this was getting…well, kinky.

I cleared my throat and attempted to sound dispassionate. "Do you mean would I have liked to have known he was watching, or would I have liked to have found out afterward that he had watched? Oh. Damn. Mr. D., I have to go. Give me twenty."

Mr. D. I called him that after I'd tried to find out more about him and he'd hinted he was quite a bit older than me ("Decades, my dear. Don't ask." I wasn't sure whether I believed him) and old school. He called me *Miss Hutchinson* for at least the first dozen calls. It did sound sort of perverted to me—like I was letting him tie me up and spank me or something, or I was wearing a maid's uniform, or both, but I liked that formality, the Mr. Rochester/Miss Eyre suggestiveness. I knew he was in the station broadcast area, somewhere, and a substantial donor to the station, but through a foundation. I loved his voice, the way he talked about books he'd read and places he'd traveled to and the joy when we found an author we both liked. We shared a passion for mountains, for high, remote places.

For the past six months, as Hugh and I began that painful slide away from each other, Mr. D. had been a constant. A friend. Someone I could tell anything.

There was the possibility we might both disappoint each other if we met. That this relationship could only exist at a distance while we both polished who we wanted to be. And yet he made me yearn for what I didn't have—adventure, new experiences, the desire to become a sort of modern, land-bound female Sinbad, exploring and learning that one story could lead to another and another…

On the air again, with the pulsing red light outside the studio casting a warm blush into the studio through the glass window, I repeated the information about the last recording, and what we were to hear next, time and temperature… *Hope your evening is going well. A little later, we'll hear music written to put its patron to sleep, Bach's* Goldberg Variations *in their entirety, but leading us up to that, a short piece by Stravinsky…*

The next time the red light turned on, it was one in the morning. I talked briefly about the national morning news show, which we would interrupt a few times an hour with local news and weather. I hoped that those awake now—lonely lovers, people with insomnia or babies, or students with examinations to study for—would be asleep in four hours when the news began.

The Bach began—music to put you to sleep, but music that had always made me want to get up and dance.

The phone rang right on time.

"Forty minutes of genius and you," Mr. D. said. "Where were we? Ah, yes. Him watching."

"I don't know that he would have found it that sexy."

"Oh, he would have."

"Do you like to watch people fuck?" Well, that put us clearly into the sexual, and I was the one who'd asked.

Mr. D., with his usual mastery of deflecting questions, chuckled. "Merry Christmas." A pause. "I presume you've changed your underwear. Tell me about it."

"You want me to tell you what I'm wearing?" I was surprised. That seemed a little unsophisticated, not what I would have expected from Mr. D. I wondered if he'd jerked off already and was looking for a quick arousal. I was almost shocked, although our increasing intimacy, our shared secrets, our stories, our mutual voyage, had led us here. I knew also, without either of us having to say anything, that we could back off from this awkward moment, and return to our usual friendly banter. Back to the familiar port as if we had never even started our journey.

"I believe it's a standard approach," he said.

A standard approach. "That's one way to describe it."

He said, his voice hesitant, "I've never done this before. I'm embarrassed, to be honest."

So was I. I was also turned on, wild and slightly frightened, my hands cold, a little sweat on my forehead. I pressed the speakerphone button and laid the phone in its cradle. "Okay. It's okay. I'm wearing a black T-shirt. Was. I've taken it off. My skin looks very pale because it's almost dark in here. My jeans, now. Can you hear the zipper? I never wear shoes in the studio, and now I'm pushing my jeans down, and they're off."

"I can hear the sound of the denim rustling. But denim doesn't rustle, does it? I can't think of the right word."

"I'm wearing red lace underwear."

"The truth, Jo. Don't humor me." He sounded stern and sad. "I know men are all alike but...please, be honest."

Tears pricked my eyes. "I am telling you the truth." I swallowed. I sounded like a scolded child. "I—I always wear nice underwear for you. I want you to want me."

"Always?"

"Since, oh, the first couple of times we talked. When I realized that you wouldn't tell me who you are. It was all I could give you."

"I'm sorry. Thank you. That's an extraordinarily generous gesture." His voice was even deeper, slower. "Tell me about this red lace underwear."

"The bra is a half cup. My nipples are hard. I'm touching them." I winced. I didn't want to sound like a hooker but I didn't know what I should say.

"Go on."

"The panties...they're called boy panties—you know what they are? They have little legs, and they come up to just below my navel. Even so, you can see a bit of hair curling out at the top of my thighs. And you can see my pubic hair through them, because they're lace."

"Your pubic hair must be dark. I've seen your picture on the station website."

I giggled. "That picture doesn't show my pubic hair."

He laughed, too, and for a moment we were comfortable together. "I've imagined it. You look bright and intelligent and lively in that picture. And sensual. A smallish, slender woman, that's how I see you—quite athletic, from riding your bike. What color are your eyes?"

"I'm stripping off for you and you want to know the color of my eyes?"

"Ah. Please, don't make me beg. I'm already humiliated enough."

"I'm sorry. I keep getting nervous and saying dumb things. My eyes are gray. They change color with what I'm wearing so sometimes they look blue or green."

"Tell me what your breasts look like. Please."

I sat in my chair, my legs spread. "They're not very big. Although I'm dark-haired my skin is pale and the nipples are pink. I don't tan easily. My breasts are very sensitive. My nipples get erect easily. I like to have them caressed. Kissed."

I listened to him breathe.

"May I touch you?" he asked.

"Yes. Where?"

"I'm closing my hands over your breasts, squeezing them. Your nipples push against my palms. They're very hard."

"I love that. May I unzip you now?" I was pretty sure he was unzipped, stroking himself, pants spread open, my unknown man in his dark cabin. Did he gaze at his cock and hand, or were his eyes closed? Did he smile or grimace?

"Later. Let me give you pleasure. Stroke my way down your body. Ah, here's your navel, that sweet little crease. Take off your bra…good. I'm holding your breasts, squeezing them, feeling their weight. I want to lick them."

I licked my fingers and pinched my nipple. "I can feel it in my clit." *Oh, God, I'm so crude.* Heat spread over my face.

"I think your clitoris needs some attention, don't you? Are you wet yet? Take off those pretty panties, darling. I'm kissing the inside of your thighs, where the skin is so soft and silky. I can smell you. Yes, you're wet. Soaking. Dripping for me. You're swollen with desire. Your clitoris is as hard as your nipples."

My skin glimmered in the light, my pubic hair a dark mystery, my hand delving, playing.

"Taste yourself." His voice was hoarse against the artful spin of Bach.

I slipped my fingers inside myself, then into my mouth and tasted my arousal, my salty musk. I imagined his hand pumping, the flex of his forearm as he jerked off.

"I wish I could put my fingers into your mouth. Feel you suck them, lick between them. And I'd like to lick you. Your lips, your chest, your cock, all over. I want to make you come."

"I want you to come, too. I want to hear the sounds you make. Down between your legs, darling. Play with yourself. I'll play with your nipples. A little pinch, some fingernail—is that what you like?"

My toes gripped the edge of the console.

"Come for me," he whispered. "Come for yourself. Do it now."

I came so hard it almost hurt, ratcheting me upward. I abandoned the attention to my breast and clutched at the arm of the chair, terrified that I would fall, alarmed by the intensity of the orgasm, yet not wanting it to end. I subsided, sobbing for breath.

"Lovely." His voice was a whisper. Had he come?

"Did you…" I hoped he hadn't. I wanted to share the moment with him.

"No. I'm sorry."

"Let me help you." Maybe he was still shy.

"Your pleasure isn't enough?"

I could see him, a sprawled dark figure, face hidden, his stroke slowed to accommodate my needs, fingers curled loose around his cock. Sliding. Wetness, a very little, gathered and dribbled over his fingers.

"So." He cleared his throat. "What happens next?"

3

AT THE END OF AN AIR SHIFT, IT'S CUSTOMARY
to tidy up for the next person on air.

After I signed off for the night—the station is dark between
two and five in the morning—I made sure there were no embarrassing damp pieces of underwear lying around.

I reshelved compact discs and pulled the first few for my
morning announcer.

I took the last transmitter reading of the night.

I set the satellite for the morning news feed. I knew Gwen,
our local host, would do it anyway, but it was what I always
did as a courtesy to her.

I checked my email for the last time, and found two new
messages. One from Julie, a serious, earnest music major, saying
she could do Friday night, but wanted to be home by midnight.
Good enough. I could come in for a couple of hours.

The other was from the leprechaun, as Hugh had called
him—he looked ordinary enough to me, no dumb hat or buckled shoes. I had a vague impression of a shortish, slender man
with wild coppery hair, steel-rimmed eyeglasses and a strange

patch of beard on his chin. I remembered the amusement in his voice and the lilt of his brogue.

I'm still interested in the apartment if it's available. Please let me know when I may view it.

What a gentleman. No mention of Christmas or underwear or your future landlady having her ass screwed off on the sofa.

Lights off, bike gear on, alarm turned on and I was out into the cold night, a splendor of stars above me.

Could Mr. D. see those stars from his cabin or was it buried deep in trees? I was sure he lived in a cabin, high up in the mountains, although most of us in town had hardwood floors and woodstoves.

I pushed off, cycling hard up the hill, forcing myself. I wasn't afraid of cycling in the dark—at any time of night in this environmentally conscious town there were cyclists on the road. As I rode, I thought about renting the apartment, the mice in the basement…domestic trivialities.

Anything to stop me thinking about what Mr. D. had proposed.

After I'd emailed Patrick, telling him to come—an unfortunate word choice I changed to *stop by*—anytime after three the next day, I couldn't sleep. I wandered around the house, now too empty without Hugh. I couldn't put it off any longer. Had I made the right decision regarding Mr. D.? It had to be, since there was no going back.

To my surprise, the man who had proved so elusive for many months now wanted to meet me. One orgasm—mine, if he had told me the truth, and I wasn't quite sure he had done so—and he had a complete change of mind?

And I was embarrassed and angry. I had touched myself and talked dirty and moaned, broken my phone-sex cherry, I guess. I had shared this most intimate of pursuits with someone who hadn't reciprocated. I had performed without knowing it. Now I was not in a mood to be cajoled.

"But of course we should meet."

"No," I'd said.

"I've never been more intimate with a woman. Not even when I was married—"

"You don't know me. I'm a fantasy for you. You're a fantasy for me. It should stay that way."

"Don't push me away, Jo. I understand that you're feeling wounded by what Hugh did, but—"

"How do you know I didn't make Hugh up?" I was angry now. "And this isn't about Hugh. It's about you and me. Think about it, Mr. D. I don't even know your name. You haven't exactly been open with me, have you?"

"My name? You want to know my name? It's—"

"Stop!" I was panting as though I'd ridden a bicycle uphill. "Don't tell me."

"Jo, what do you really want?" His voice was gentle, sad.

I don't know. You. Maybe.

And then I thought of the men I'd loved, the men who claimed to love me back, the mistakes and infidelities, the withdrawal into indifference. I remembered pushing Hugh away in bed because I felt smothered; I remembered too how I'd reached out for him, when I was overcome with loneliness and regret, and his impatient grunt as he shook off my hand.

Did it happen with every relationship? I didn't want that familiar path anymore. I didn't want to take that journey—not yet anyway. Eventually I knew I could take the risk, but not now, still worn out and disillusioned by Hugh's infidelity.

I took a deep breath. "I don't think this is right for me. I'm sorry. We should say goodbye."

So it was done.

His last words to me echoed in my head. "Very well. I'm sorry, Jo."

A click and silence.

I had lost a friend.

Patrick had pretty much decided he'd move into the apartment on Yale Drive if Jo Hutchinson offered it to him, which he thought she probably would. It turned out she knew one of his references, a good sign.

The apartment was small, built over a garage; what Americans called an efficiency and he'd call a bedsit, one large room with a minimal sort of kitchen arrangement and a bathroom. There was a staircase up from outside and a door leading into the house and Jo offered him use of the washer-dryer in the basement and, if he had ambitious cooking plans, he could use her kitchen.

He told her he might well be inspired to bake a half-dozen loaves in that fancy high-tech oven, and she looked at him in a way that suggested she didn't know whether he was joking or not.

He liked her. She was a bit eccentric, and there was some awkwardness, mostly on his part, that he'd seen her naked.

She spent the first five minutes of this meeting staring at his chin and then told him that taking the beard thing off was an improvement. Given what she was doing the day before, he thought he should be flattered that she'd even noticed his facial hair. He launched into a long rambling explanation of how he tended to sideswipe the beard thing while shaving so it lost definition, but the silent subtext of his monologue was that he wished he'd got a better look at her breasts when she was naked.

Today she wore some sort of blue shapeless dress thing—her legs and feet bare—probably made of hemp or tofu or compost like everything else in the town. He liked her slender body and waifish short dark hair in a ragged sort of style that either cost a lot of money or was a mistake, he couldn't tell.

She didn't look the way she sounded on the radio; she was younger than he would have thought, about his age, late twenties. But her voice was sexy in real life, too, and he told her he liked the music she played even if he didn't always understand it.

"Do you like being a DJ?" he asked.

"I'm music director. I decide on the music programming. The on-air work is only a small part of what I do."

He felt he was being corrected. For someone who had a geeky sort of job, though, even geekier than his, and looked fey and otherworldly, she was right on the button when he asked about insurance and security and cable access.

By this time they were back in the kitchen, where she poured him a cup of coffee and examined his application. "It says here you're a web designer."

"Yeah, I'll be working from here."

"That's fine. We won't see much of each other because I sleep mostly during the day." She refilled his coffee mug. "I have a Mac, a laptop. I really like it."

"I use Macs, too. Three of them and six screens. I'll show you my setup if you like." He stopped, because it sounded as though he was boasting, or as if he'd waved his dick at her to prove it was bigger than her boyfriend's. (It was.)

He told her the brief, bare facts of his divorce, of how he was moving out until his soon-to-be ex-wife had finished her master's and they could sell the house. She nodded sympathetically and he had the urge to tell her how depressed and horny he was but instead he told her he was stable and financially responsible and so on.

He embarrassed himself trying to look down the front of the blue shapeless thing and musing on how he could persuade her to bend over so he could look up it. He wondered, not for the first time, if women spent as much time and energy, for instance, looking at men's flies or up the legs of their shorts. Elise had told him once that men were natural sprawlers and it was no big effort to spot, or ignore, a dangling penis in warm weather.

At one point, mildly exciting, Jo stood on one leg with the other foot against her knee in a sort of yoga pose—in this town you had to do yoga or pilates or else risk social ostracism, but he did neither. He suspected there was a crack squad of yoga police who would break down your door to make sure you had your foot in your ear.

Great legs, he noted.

They shook hands and she said she'd let him know.

As he drove away, he decided he absolutely had to forget that he'd seen her naked and stop thinking about what she'd be like in the sack (pretty good, he suspected). It was an honest mistake. He'd heard the moaning and groaning and thought someone was in pain, and looked around the open door and the first thing he saw was her pair of Father Christmas knickers on the floor, the crotch sopping wet.

After that, it was less of an honest mistake. He must have stood there for a good five minutes watching that unimaginative fuck, turned on as hell, seeing the guy's cock slide in and out of her. He wasn't particularly interested in the cock, but he could see how it cleaved her, opened her up. She was all sweet and pink and shiny beneath that tuft of black hair, the star of his private porno movie.

Shit. This was a business arrangement. Period. And he should feel relieved that he'd found a place to live, but he felt only sadness.

He couldn't wait to get away from Elise, but he dreaded the actual moving out, saying goodbye, knowing from now on it was just going to be legal business.

More tears. His if not hers.

How had everything gone so wrong?

Thursday evening at the station we had an on-air staff meeting, me and two full-time announcers and a handful of subs and volunteers. I filled them in on the latest station news and praised them for the quick handling of a breaking news story the previous week. I passed on information from Neil, our program director and my boss, and pretended not to notice the grins and eye rolls.

Sometimes I felt sorry for Neil. Mostly he just annoyed me. He'd come to us from television, and, snobs that we were, Kimberly and I laughed at his liking of expensive suits and haircuts and his blatant ambition. He didn't know much about music, either, which was a real problem, and mispronounced composers' names on the rare occasions when he took an air shift. He spoke longingly at staff meetings of talk shows and more news programming.

I found a garment bag on my desk; Kimberly the designer-clothes fairy had visited, leaving the skirt, the shoes and a folder with just about every detail except the inseams of our victims for the night. My date was Willis Scott III, one of our quaint local royalty, in his mid-thirties, president of a real estate company. I yawned as I scanned where he'd gone to school, his hobbies and nonprofit involvement.

On the top of the sheet, in her round, loopy, rich-girl writing, Kimberly had given me the following instructions:

Wax. Go to Azure Sky Salon and mention my name.
No garlic.
Don't say fuck too often.
Don't criticize the orchestra.
Don't cut your own hair like last time.

Just to annoy me she had put a smiley face over the *i* in her signature.

Wax? Was she kidding? I hoped she only meant my legs and armpits, something I tended to neglect at this time of year.

I took a quick look through the rest of my mail, most of it ending up in the recycle bin.

There was one envelope that must have been hand-delivered, my name neatly typed on the outside. It must be—had to be— from Mr. D. I wanted so badly to open it, but we'd hurt each other and I was afraid of what I might read. Forgiveness might be even worse than any accusation.

Inside was a single sheet of paper.

I miss you already.

Beneath it was a phone number and an email address.

I turned the paper over although I knew there was nothing on the other side. Had this really been for me? Yes, that was my name on the outside, in the same standard computer font as the letter. It had to be from Mr. D.—who else could it be from?

I could phone him. I could...

I dangled the paper between my fingertips.

There was no such thing as privacy anymore. I might have an unlisted home phone number, but my information— everyone's—was all over the place on any number of databases, easily found. I crumpled the paper and threw it into the recycling bin. Then I picked it back out, smoothed it with my palms and wished he'd written it, not typed it. There was one way I could determine it was from Mr. D.—quite simple. I could make a call to that number.

No, not now. I folded the paper and pushed it into a desk drawer, out of sight.

After all, I couldn't be sure it was him. A good proportion of the male population assumed that a woman was on the radio purely to get a man, meaning them. They sent in photos, some with their cats or dogs, and some, the anonymous ones, proudly displaying an erection but not their face. They sent their resumes, or long rambling letters explaining how we'd

been soul mates in Arthurian Britain. We attracted the sad
lonely misfits, and that was the end of it.

"You look good. Did you get into Azure Sky okay?" Kimberly bent forward and examined her lipstick in the women's
room mirror.

"Uh-huh." One of the razors Hugh had left behind had done
perfectly well.

"Now be nice to him."

"You sound like you're running the best little whorehouse
in Texas." I tucked my small silver purse under one elbow,
rearranged my shawl and willed my nipples to behave. I wasn't
wearing a bra—my top was a gray silk halter-neck, found at
a yard sale. Above my knees, the taffeta rustled. To complete
my happy-radio-hooker outfit I wore thigh-highs, black with
a seam, and a pair of large dangly fake diamond earrings.

Kimberly gripped my elbow and escorted me out of the
ladies' room.

"You have the right to remain silent. You have—"

"Smart-ass." She tugged me across the foyer, filled at inter-
mission with well-heeled, mostly middle-aged patrons, mixed
in with a few Birkenstocked old hippies, and some younger
people in jeans and hiking boots and down vests. The symphony was nothing if not diverse.

We approached a group of people with champagne glasses;
our station manager, Bill, was among them and the administrative director of the symphony. Kimberly made introduc-
tions, her mane of blond hair tossing, and I got to meet Willis
Scott III.

He was the sort of man Kimberly would go for—I preferred
them in faded blue jeans or baggy khaki shorts—dark with a
bit of gray, handsome; expensive haircut, suit, cologne.

"I'm surprised you enjoy the symphony," he said.

"Why?"

"You listen to music all day."

"I don't listen to it a whole lot. There's quite a lot to do in the studio while the music's playing." Phone sex, for example.

"Sounds interesting."

I nodded, searching for something to say. "Tell me about what you do."

He was only too happy to, running off at the mouth about prime interest rates and equity, and how this was a great time to buy up.

I drank champagne and tried to look intelligent.

"I've got a new development just north of town," he said. "Great architecture, real exclusive, beautiful setting. We've preserved the environmental integrity, lots of trees and stuff, and we're keeping it upscale, you know what I mean? Second homes, mostly—"

"If you're that concerned with environmental integrity, why develop it? It's not as though you're providing housing for people who really need it."

He frowned, his handsome brow wrinkling. "There's a demand, you wouldn't believe it. But Jo, you know, if you're in the market—"

I guess that was what happened when you wore designer clothes or possibly gave off some sort of involuntary slutty radar. "I don't have any plans to—"

"Call me." He produced a business card.

"Okay."

Like a gentleman he held my champagne glass while I opened my purse and tucked his card away.

He moved a little closer to me and tugged my shawl back on to my shoulder. His manicured fingers rested on my bare skin a little too long. "You're a very attractive woman, Jo. Maybe we could have dinner sometime?"

I stepped back. "I work most evenings, Willis."

"Lunch, then. And we could drive out to the development after. Commune with nature. How about it?"

"I'll let you know." I couldn't wait to throw away—in the recycling bin, of course—his business card.

"Great shoes."

That was all I needed, a shoe fetishist. Maybe it was an attempt at empathy.

To my great relief the chimes sounded for the second half of the concert. As we walked back into the concert hall, one of the group—a fortysomething fair-haired woman—walked beside me.

"I wanted to tell you how much I enjoy your show."

"Thanks."

"You always sound so approachable. I think a lot of people get intimidated by classical music. It's a shame."

"It is. I'm sorry, I didn't catch your name."

"I'm Liz Ferrar." She smiled and touched my arm. She whispered, "If Kimberly thinks Willis is a hot prospect for the station, she's wasting her time. He's a real tightwad. The whole family is. And he's a jerk."

"Fuck, yes. He hit on me so hard, I couldn't believe it. Liz, don't you run the women's center in town?" She was the reference Patrick had given, the one I claimed to know. "I guess you know Patrick Delaney."

"Oh, yes. He's a sweet guy. He designed our site for free. How do you know him?"

"He applied to be my tenant."

"Good. I'm glad he's leaving Elise—I mean, you hate to see a couple break up, but when they're both so unhappy…" She shrugged.

"Come visit us—me, I mean, and Patrick, too. Call me at the station." We exchanged cards.

Happy that I'd made a new friend, I shushed Kimberly so I could listen to the music.

★ ★ ★

I arrived at the radio station by cab shortly after the concert ended, and settled myself in for a quiet evening. Time to get caught up on paperwork. I had an article to write for the newsletter, programming to select for the next couple of months.

I jumped every time the phone rang.

At two in the morning I shut down, tidied up the console and reached for the phone to call a cab home.

It rang. *No data.*

I stared at the ringing phone. I had no obligation to answer—we were off air. After seven rings the caller would be transferred to the station's voice mail.

But I answered anyway.

"I've missed you," he said.

"I've missed you, too."

"I'm sorry, Jo. I pushed you too hard."

"It's okay."

He sighed. "I want honesty between us. It's been two nights and I've had time to think and…"

"And?"

"We don't need this sort of relationship. We have plenty of other things to talk about. We don't have to continue in this way. Unless you want to."

"What do *you* want?"

He laughed again. "Whatever you're willing to give. Darling, it was plenty of fun for me but I love to talk to you. It's up to you how we proceed now. By the way, you looked ravishing at the symphony tonight."

My voice shot up an octave. "Oh, my God. Please don't tell me you're that creepy Realtor. Or that you even know him. No, of course you're not. Your voice is different…sorry, I'm rambling. You were there?"

"I have my sources." He paused. "What I'm saying, Jo, is that you should be in a real relationship. I'd be jealous, of course. But I don't want you to feel…obligated to me in any way."

"You're trying to drop me, aren't you?"

"In a way, yes. I don't want to lose you. I hope I won't. That we'll be friends. I accept that you don't want to meet. This is entirely on your terms."

I dropped my head into my free hand and groaned. "I don't know that we can go back. I'm not really clear what we're arguing about."

"I'm not sure we're even arguing. I don't want you to get hurt by our…affair."

"Affair. You're so old school."

"Yes, I am. How would you define our relationship?"

"I don't know. Does it matter? It is what it is, whatever that might be." I paused. "If I did fuck someone, what then?"

"You mean, should you tell me?"

"Yes."

"If you wanted to."

"Tell you or…describe it to you?"

"Whatever you feel like doing."

He kept throwing the ball back into my court, giving me the control—or pretending to give me the control.

"I might ask you to do the same. Tell me about an encounter you had. Would you do that?"

"If you asked, yes. Gladly."

I stood, pushing my feet into my shoes and reaching for my shawl. "Let me think about it. I should go home. I'm glad you called." I was a bit scared. We seemed to have moved very fast into kink territory and what alarmed me most was how it excited me. Kimberly had once said that even ordinary people have the most bizarre sex lives, that a huge amount of kinky stuff goes on in nice normal neighborhoods between nice normal people. I'd asked her what her preferences were, not really believing her, challenging her.

She had leaned forward and whispered in my ear, "Woof. Woof."

Then we'd both collapsed in giggles. But ever since then, my mind had opened up to the possibilities. I'd wondered. I'd been curious.

And now here was my chance to go on my own voyage of discovery and storytelling and while it was exhilarating I was scared by it. Would I regret not going on the kink voyage when I was old and gray (although Kimberly assured me the old hippies were the best—or the worst—depending on how you looked at it)? Would Sinbad have regretted never taking the voyage?

"Before you go…" He cleared his throat. "Very high heels and stockings with seams, my source said. Real stockings?"

"No. Thigh-highs."

"Ah. No garter belt, then. A pity."

I smiled at the regret in his voice. "But with no panties," I lied, and pushed my ordinary white cotton pair down. Not quite a lie.

"No panties at the symphony?" He laughed.

"I'm sure I wasn't the only one. The orchestra was pretty good tonight. I don't know if your source actually listened to the music. Maybe he spent the whole night looking at my legs."

"My source also mentioned your nipples."

"Your source needs a cold shower."

"Jo?"

"Hmm?" The air had shifted, or so it felt, although the studio was perfectly warm and comfortable. My nipples were erect.

"Show me."

"Show you what?"

"Take off your top."

I turned on the speaker to the phone and untied the halter top. It slithered down my torso in a caress of satin.

"That rustling sound…"

"My skirt."

"Ah. And your nipples…"

"Erect. Very hard. Dark pink like raspberries. I'm pinching them."

"Good. Are you standing or sitting?"

"Standing."

"Spread your legs. Can you feel the air on your cunt?"

It was the first time he'd ever used the word, the first time I'd ever liked a man to say it to me. The contrast between his cultured voice and the crudeness of the word made me shiver.

"Now lift your skirt. Tuck it up, if you can, so you can keep your hands on your breasts. I want to see you exposed, the contrast of the black stockings against your skin. That rustling is supremely erotic, by the way."

"Say it again," I whispered, my skirt tucked up.

"What?"

"Talk about my cunt. Please."

"Your cunt." I could hear the smile in his voice. That's what we say in the business, when you want to convey an upbeat attitude on mic. *Put a bit of smile in it.*

"Your cunt," he repeated. "I'm imagining your hair looks very dark against the white of your legs. Quite a lot of hair. You're not the sort of woman who'd shave or wax it into submission. Is your cunt wet, Jo?"

"Yes. I want to touch myself."

"Not yet. Can you come from touching your breasts?"

I moaned and rocked my pelvis forward. I thought of the pinkness and wetness between my legs, my clit a hard splinter of nerve endings. I pressed my middle finger hard against my nipple as though it was my clit, rotating.

"That's right, darling. Get yourself off."

"Talk to me," I gasped. "I'll come if you talk to me."

The studio door banged open, and I blinked as the room flooded with light.

Jason stood there, his mouth hanging open at the sight of me.

I stood there for a moment, horrified, my fingers stilled, before I lunged forward and disconnected the call. I fumbled to pull my top up, my skirt down.

"I'm sorry—" Jason mumbled. He had an erection; I could see it distending his jeans.

"No, I'm sorry. Oh, fuck." I could get fired for this.

"I was...uh, I didn't think you were here."

"I didn't know anyone else was here." My fingers shook as I tied the halter top. "I'm leaving now."

I grabbed my shawl and purse, mortified, further embarrassed by having to scoop my panties from the floor. I'd find another phone and call a cab. I'd wait for it outside, braving the freezing temperature, rather than having to face Jason after what he'd seen.

"I'm sorry," I said again. I walked toward the door, toward him, discovering it was almost impossible not to walk with a sexy sway in the shoes.

"Uh. It's okay. It was hot." Jason blushed. He backed away from me. "You're hot."

I stopped. I needed a real man, a flesh-and-blood man. Just for tonight.

And then I can tell Mr. D. about it.

I guess I was ready for this journey, after all.

"Jason, I need a ride home."

4

HE STUTTERED AN ANSWER—SURE, YES, YEAH— and jingled his keys in the fidgety sort of way men do, particularly young, hyper guys, and led the way outside. We both fumbled around with the lock and the alarm, jerking our hands away when we made contact with each other.

I hoped Jason was as nervous as I was.

Once outside the fresh air hit my exposed and overstimulated pussy with a cold burn and I clamped my legs together. Another icy caress as I climbed into the front seat of Jason's pickup and then I squealed as the cold vinyl of the seats hit my thighs.

"You okay?" Jason looked at me with concern.

"Yeah, I'm cold."

"I'll turn the heater on when the engine's warm."

"Thanks."

We set off, me very conscious of every bump and ridge in the road, which seemed to address my clitoris with a blatant reminder of what I was about to do. As we neared the all-night drugstore in town, Jason slowed.

"Do you, ah, have, ah, you know, should I…" He looked uncertain. After all, from his point of view I hadn't exactly spelled out what I wanted him to do. Maybe he thought he was giving the radio station's eccentric squealing masturbator a ride home after which we'd say good-night to each other and he'd drive off with a merry toot of his horn.

I'd be tooting his horn for sure.

"No, it's fine, I have, uh, you know," I replied fluently. Unless he wanted to buy himself a toothbrush? I think I had a spare somewhere. "Thanks for asking," I added.

We arrived at my house before the truck had reached anywhere near normal temperature, and I eased myself from the seat, relieved that my skin did not separate from the vinyl with a loud, rude sound. Once again the shock of frigid air hit my crotch and I scuttled for the front door, with Jason behind me.

He stood very close to me as I inserted the key into the lock, not touching me, but close, and it would have been damned sexy if he hadn't been wearing a down jacket. There might actually have been some contact. But I got the door open and lunged for the lights and the thermostat.

Brady appeared, mewed and collapsed on his side in front of Jason.

"Is your cat okay? He just fell over."

"Yes, he does that to people he likes."

"Cool." Jason bent down to pet him.

"Let me take your jacket," I said, the perfect hostess, and relieved Jason of his jacket—he put his gloves carefully in the pockets, which I thought was rather sweet. He hung his messenger bag on the rack next to his jacket, removing his cell phone.

"I have to…"

"Oh, sure." I left him to make his call, wondering who it was to. Not a girlfriend, I hoped. Or his mother, which would be even worse. I went into the kitchen to feed Brady, who transferred his affection from our guest to me, weaving around my legs as I tipped kibble into his bowl.

Jason came into the kitchen. He didn't offer an explanation for his call, which was none of my business anyway, and looked around. "Nice place."

"Thanks." The perfect asexual inner hostess kicked in at this point and I asked him if he'd like something to eat—I swear the words just popped out of my mouth—while in the back of my head the slutty hostess shouted, *Get him upstairs! Remind him you're not wearing panties! Unzip him!*

"Uh, no, I'm fine."

I found myself gazing at the banana in my fruit bowl on the kitchen table—Freud would have had a field day with me—and reminded myself sternly to think about the matter at hand. While I attempted to figure out my next move, I picked up the container of cat food to replace it in the cabinet.

And then, proving that one of us had some sense, he came up close behind me—I could feel his warmth, and the nudge of his erection against my butt. His hands slid up my sides. "You are so hot," he whispered.

I grabbed the edge of the counter, weak-kneed as his mouth moved over my neck, warm and tickling. I turned my head to kiss him, whimpering a little as his hands cupped my breasts. His mouth was nice, gentle and sweet.

I turned in his arms. "Let's go upstairs." The slutty hostess had won the fight.

I led him upstairs, enjoying the swish of the taffeta skirt and the assertive clip of the high-heeled shoes on the wooden stairs, and into my room.

He was right behind me, breathing fast. I wondered if he could see up the skirt and decided that as soon as I could I'd bend over in front of him, or part my legs accidentally.

"Okay, Jason." I turned and he almost bumped into me. "You may undress."

He gave a huge grin, which made me think that maybe I hadn't sounded like as much of a dominant bitch as I'd intended. "Sure." He took off his shirt. Nice chest, a scatter of hair; not superdefined, but pleasant to look at.

I reclined on the bed, one leg outstretched, the other bent, with my wrist resting on the knee. I wanted to see whether he'd angle himself to look up my skirt.

He did, taking a couple of steps towards the end of the bed, ostensibly to put his shirt on the wooden chest at the foot of the bed. The bulge in his jeans, which seemed to be more or less permanent—or had at least been there in the twenty minutes or so since our first encounter at the radio station—seemed even more prominent. He bent to unlace his boots and kick off his socks, then put a hand to his belt buckle.

Show-off. Delicious show-off.

He snapped the button of his Levi's and unzipped, sliding the jeans down his legs and kicking them away. He wore gray knit boxers that clung to every contour and ridge. Very impressive.

He hooked a thumb into the waistband and looked at me. Then he looked up my skirt again and swallowed.

I slid off the bed and unzipped the skirt, leaving me in my heels and stockings and the silk halter-neck top. I reached into the bedside cabinet drawer for a condom and walked over to him, conscious again of the sexy sway the shoes gave me. I ran my finger down the underside of his cock, through the cotton knit.

He moaned.

I pulled his underwear down his thighs and he stepped out of them, his cock bouncing slightly as it was freed. It was gorgeous, rigid and curving, a drop of pre-come welling at the tip.

He smiled, but his breath came fast. "Can we…"

"Sure." I pushed him onto the chest at the end of the bed. It had a padded top, kind to the knees. I knew. This was how I wanted him. I stood astride his thighs and kissed him, not the gentle way he'd kissed me, but deep and carnal and wet, while his hands roamed over my breasts and thighs and butt. One hand slipped between my legs and his breath hitched when he found how wet I was and it was my turn to moan as he took a finger to my clit.

I sheathed him in the condom and placed one knee beside him, easing him into me. He gripped my hips hard. "Go slow," he said, then looked embarrassed. "I mean, I don't want it to be over too soon. I want it to be good for you."

"'S okay." I was very close to coming, as though I was a pot that had been about to boil when Jason had interrupted me at the radio station and now had full heat beneath it. My body had forgotten about the intervening embarrassment and awkwardness and now wanted to go back to where we'd left off. But Jason inside me, that unexpected, delightful presence curving inside me, jerking a little as I moved—I wanted to hold the moment, concentrate on the gorgeous slide and retreat as we fucked.

He untied the halter-neck top and let it fall, lifting a breast to his mouth to suck the nipple. The sensation shot to my clitoris. "Keep doing that. Harder."

I ground myself on him and came so hard it hurt.

"Christ! I felt that." And he thrust up as I gripped him, his eyes dark and wide, and shuddered as he came.

I collapsed on his shoulder, coming back into the present and becoming aware of my breathing, his breathing, the rapid thud of his pulse, the scent of our sweat and bodies. He sighed and nudged me. "Jo, I'd better…"

The condom. Of course. He reached to kiss me on the lips— a friendly sort of gesture, for which I was glad—as I untangled myself from him. I crawled onto the bed, leaving the shoes behind, and slid the stockings off. I resisted the temptation to ask him what he'd like to do next, in case he suggested we watch MTV or say he wanted to sleep. I was pretty much wide-awake and I wanted him again.

"Was that okay?" he asked, settling onto the bed next to me.

"Better than okay." I wondered how experienced he was.

"Cool." He grinned. "I've wanted to do that since I met you."

"You're kidding!"

"No. No, I'm not." He touched my breast, making small circles around the nipple, and gave a small sound of satisfaction as it stiffened and darkened. "You're gorgeous. Sexy. I can't believe I'm here with you."

His cock stirred. I reached down and took him in my hand, squeezing gently. I sat up and ran my hands over him, exploring his planes and surfaces. He twitched away as I kissed his nipple, then settled back, sighing. I kissed his belly and thighs, deliberately ignoring his erection, while he stroked my breasts and shoulders.

"Tell me what you want," he said after we'd kissed awhile.

I reached for another condom.

"Don't you want more foreplay?" he said earnestly, as though I wasn't conforming to some textbook of female erotic behavior.

"Sometimes I like hours of it. Right now I want to be fucked."

"Okay!" He took the condom and rolled it onto himself, then pushed me onto my back, eager to show me what he could do. And for an exercise in stamina, it wasn't bad, lots of nice sweaty thrusting and flexing and groaning from both of us.

"Have you come yet?" he asked after a while.

"I don't come like this." I rubbed my foot up and down his back.

"Shit. Why didn't you say?"

"I didn't say I wasn't enjoying it. I am."

"What should I do?"

"Keep doing what you're doing."

"But I…" His hips were moving again. "I want you to …"

"Jason, just shut up and fuck me, okay?"

He stopped, shocked, and then grinned. "You sure?"

"Yes."

"Cool."

I was a bit worried about his lack of vocabulary for a couple of seconds before he started fucking me in earnest, and hurtled to a climax before collapsing on top of me.

"That was…that was great," he said, propping himself up on his elbows. "What would you like me to do now?"

My mind wandered off onto some stuff I'd read somewhere about dominatrices who made their submissives do the laundry or clean the bathroom, but it seemed like a waste of good manpower. I had this gorgeous, unstoppable young male in my bed, all puppy eyes and eagerness, willing to do whatever I wanted, and—

"Jason, I hope you don't feel I'm using you."

He looked up from my nipples—very enterprising, while I was thinking of a reply, he had taken the initiative to start kissing his way down my body. "No. I like you. I think you're…"

Oh, please don't say I'm hot again. It's flattering but—

"You're nice. Like, when we had those third graders tour the station and you showed them around. You were really cool with them. They liked you."

"Oh. Thanks. I like you, too. And that—oh, that's nice." Perhaps everyone's vocabulary shrank when the sex was good enough. Jason lapped and nibbled at my thighs and my clit, and I came to his supple, energetic tongue, surprised, pleased, thrashing around.

"I'm hard again," he said, almost apologetically. I wasn't aware he'd deflated at any point, and I had a feeling I'd come across the used condom in the bed pretty soon.

"Then let's do something about it." I handed him a condom and watched him roll it on, kneeling above me. "And I'll go on top."

"Will you come like that?"

"Almost definitely." It was sweet how concerned he was with my orgasms, when I, or any other woman, could out-orgasm him, or any other man, until the cows came home.

And I did. Or at least, until the arrival, not of any cows, but of my new tenant.

"I guess this is it," Patrick said.

Elise leaned her head against his shoulder. "You've been so great about it all."

"Hey, stop it. Next thing you'll be inviting me back in and then we'll start all over again."

"You're right." She stepped out of his arms and he felt as though he were ripping up inside. It was a definite physical sensation, a weird tingle down his arms, adrenaline maybe, or a heart attack. He waited. Was he about to drop dead on his soon-to-be ex-wife's—or rather, his own—doorstep?

Damn, she'd get his life insurance. The merry widow.

"Yeah. Okay." He took his glasses off and pinched his nose, hard, to force the tears back. "I couldn't find the drill. It's somewhere in the house. It doesn't matter. I'll buy another. You need to have one."

"Do I?"

In Elise's world there was always someone with a drill, always someone to look after her and protect her and do things for her. Him, her father, her brothers, even Patrick's friends— God, if he thought any of his friends were screwing her or wanted to screw her, or coming around with their big drills at the ready, he'd kill them, but they'd be insane not to want to screw her....

"Patrick, just go, please." She looked waiflike and frail, clinging to the front door. She was as tough as old boots.

"I changed the furnace filter."

"Thank you. You didn't have to."

He nodded and trudged to the truck he'd rented for the move.

He drove round the corner, parked and cried for a good two minutes. Well, he thought, blowing his nose, at least he hadn't cried in front of her.

She hadn't cried in front of him, either. Shit, he should have torn the house apart and found the damned drill. He'd always despised couples who got into deathly, expensive fights over household items when they divorced, televisions or favorite bits of furniture, but now he understood that irrationality. He couldn't even bear to think what it would be like if the disputed property were a pet or a kid, but this marriage had none of the above, a thought that did not cheer him particularly.

He put his glasses back on and shoved the truck into Drive, stomping his left foot on the floor in the way he always did driving an automatic, and drove to his new apartment.

He rang the doorbell several times and eventually Jo opened the door. She wore sweats and pink slippers and her hair was on end. She looked sleepy and mussed and sexy. (Yeah, and ten minutes ago he'd been crying over another woman.)

"Sorry I woke you up," he said.

"No, it's fine. Come on in."

He didn't want to come in the house, but he did to be polite, and she gave him a set of keys.

"I'll move the pickup," she said.

Funny, he wouldn't have thought she was the sort of girl to drive a pickup, and sure enough she wasn't. A kid wandered out of the house, with "I got lucky" written all over his face—Christ, he was young—and moved the pickup. He introduced himself as Jason, asked what Patrick liked in his coffee and went back into the house. He came out again as Patrick backed the truck into the drive.

"She said I should help you."

"Thanks." Exactly how many boyfriends did Jo have?

She wandered out again with mugs of coffee for them both, which she offered with a vague, satisfied smile—heck, now he was paying attention, he saw she had "I got lucky" all over her, too, but for some reason on her he found it endearing—and then she went back into the house

"Cool. IKEA," said Jason when they got to the flat boxes in the truck. "You want some help putting these together?"

"And what happened next?" Mr. D. asked, when I told him the story at work.

"Please don't tell me you're thinking of something along the lines of a hot threesome surrounded by cardboard boxes."

He laughed. "Not until now. So how did you get rid of Jason?"

"He said he had work to do. It was easier than I expected."

"And do you think you'll do it again?"

I tucked the phone under my chin as I replaced CDs on the shelves. "We work together and it could get awkward. I enjoyed it, but it was a bit like having a well-trained puppy around—he was so eager and happy to please me. If I'd asked him to be rough or selfish—and I did, remember?—he'd defuse it by being acquiescent. Quite unintentionally…I don't think he was jerking my chain."

"Another dog metaphor?"

"Or a bitch metaphor, but you're too polite to say it. I guess that's why I have a cat—you never really know what they're thinking, although the answer to that is probably nothing at all. But back to Jason—I'd always thought I'd enjoy a hot young stud who was hard all night long, but his erection never went away, and it was boring. I wanted some variety, some textural interest."

"Did you think about me when you were fucking him?"

"No." I put the last CD on the shelf. "I thought about telling you about it. When he curled his tongue around my clitoris and put his fingers inside me, I thought, Mr. D. will enjoy this. Did I tell you I kissed him and tasted myself?"

"Go on." His voice had a dreamy, throaty quality.

"Are you hard?"

"God, yes. Tell me more."

And I did, and heard him sigh and groan and give a low laugh.

5

"BRING HIM TO BILL'S BIRTHDAY PARTY," KIMBERLY
said.

"Who?"

"The Leprechaun. I can be his rebound girl." She propped
her feet up on her desk and took another mouthful of coffee. It
was Wednesday and ostensibly we were meeting to proofread
the station newsletter and discuss the fine details of the station
manager's birthday party. She peered at the papers strewn over
her desk. "Should this really be the Erotica Symphony?"

"What? No! It's the *Eroica*, Italian for heroic. Please tell me
there isn't a *T* in the middle."

"Just kidding."

"And you can't be serious about Patrick. He's only been
separated a week. Less than a week."

She shook her head. "My sources tell me it's been six months
since they split up. He's ready." She tapped her pencil on her
desk. "And when are you going to start dating someone?"

"I don't really feel like it." I considered telling her about
Jason.

"Dating or telling me?"

At that point the phone rang. "Yeah, she's here." Kimberly winked at me with the receiver pressed to her ear.

"What is it?"

"Wait, honey," Kimberly cooed. "You just sit tight."

The door to her office swung open and a huge bunch of flowers appeared, almost masking the station receptionist.

"Ooh, who are they from?" they both squealed as I snatched the card out from the floral depths.

Mr. D., please. But these weren't his style, I hoped, and they were far too expensive to be from Jason. I ripped open the card.

"They're from Willis Scott." I stared with disbelief and fascinated horror at the phallic floral exhibition in front of me, while Kimberly and the receptionist made excited, giggly comments.

"What does he say?" Kimberly plucked the card from my hands. "'I owe you lunch. Best, Willis.' How cute."

"Is it?" I stared in fascinated horror at the flowers, some of which I was sure had been genetically engineered by a scientist with a dirty mind. Nature could not be so crass.

"Of course. He's getting ripe."

"Like a cheese?"

"Ripe to make a major gift." Kimberly reached for her Rolodex, flipped it over and began typing. "I'm emailing you his number. And his cell. He'll be a change from those bearded intellectual bores you usually date—"

"Hugh did not have a—"

"Or those muscle-bound rock-climbing types—"

"One, four years ago before I met Hugh—"

"Or those pretty dancers who couldn't decide whether they were bisexual or not—"

"I couldn't help hanging out with other dance majors and that was a long time ago, and only one was—"

"So now you can date an adult," Kimberly said with an air of

finality. "And if you give me the Leprechaun's email I'll invite
him to Bill's party."

I scribbled his email address on a Post-it. "I don't know why
I'm agreeing to let you pimp me for the station or corrupt my
tenant."

"I'm sure both of us will behave with the utmost profes-
sionalism." She handed me a paper napkin as I spluttered coffee
over her desk.

After six months of housesitting, friends' sofas and occasional
returns to Elise's bed in a house that no longer felt like home,
Patrick thought he should feel relieved to be in his own place.
If only. He felt he didn't belong in this small space, him and
the half-dozen humming computers, the clean quiet of it all.
Jo was a remarkably silent neighbor—he guessed she slept most
of the day. He met her one gloriously sunny afternoon planting
bulbs in the front yard.

"Daffodils," she said. "The squirrels eat everything else."

"Right," he said.

"Are you coming to Bill's party?"

He hesitated. "Maybe."

"It'll be fun," she said, stripping off her gardening gloves.
"Liz Ferrar's coming, probably some other people you know.
Everything okay in the apartment?"

"Yeah, it's great, thanks." He sounded wildly enthusiastic—
he really needed to get out more—as though he were commenting on an orgy.

She usually left for work in the late afternoon and out of
curiosity, and by the need to deal with his laundry, he entered
the house later that day. The doorway to the apartment opened
into the upstairs of the house—polished wood floors, white
walls, all very ascetic, like a nunnery.

Except for the bathroom. The half-open door revealed a
rack across the bathtub, with expensive underwear laid out to

dry. Christ. Was she wearing something like that under her gardening outfit? Classy stuff, too. Sexy and silky and…stockings, too. A far cry from the faded Santa Claus panties, all that exotic lace and silk and satin. Underwear made to be displayed, slowly removed (or not at all), brushed over a guy's face so he could catch her scent.

Grimly Patrick held on to his laundry basket. There was no way he was going to touch her underwear. Absolutely not. Just because he'd seen her naked once and admired her legs and liked her voice on the radio didn't mean he had to… No point in touching anything, he argued with himself. They were just scraps of fabric. Now if she, or someone, was wearing them, that would be far more interesting—a nipple poking against taut silk, or a crisp of hair against dampened satin, or… He tried to summon up some good Irish Catholic guilt, and failed.

Something brushed against his leg and he almost dropped the basket. The damn cat, of course, looking at him with solemn, reproachful eyes.

"I get it." Patrick hefted the basket. "Don't tell her."

A bloodcurdling scream came from downstairs. What the fuck… He dropped the basket and ran down the stairs and into the basement.

At first he didn't recognize her and gave a yell of fear at the faceless stranger who stood screaming in the dim light. She wore a pair of Wellington boots with her jeans tucked into them, a long-sleeved sweater with rubber gloves and something over her face that he recognized, with incredulity, as a fencing mask. In one hand she held a pair of barbecue tongs.

"What the hell?" he shouted, in relief that it was only Jo.

"Get it off my foot!"

"What?"

"It moved!"

"Why are you here in the dark?"

"I don't like to see their eyes."

He snapped on the light. "Whose eyes?"

She pointed at her feet. The cat strolled forward and sniffed at her toe.

Patrick squatted to take a better look at the small scrap of fur that lay on her foot. "It's okay. It's dead." He now saw the discarded mousetrap on the floor. "Why not just throw the whole thing out?"

"It's wasteful." She said it with a reproachful air. Then she screamed at him. "Don't use your hand! You get could sick!"

He took the tongs and retrieved the mouse. "What day does the city recycling pick up dead rodents?"

"I throw them in the backyard."

"Okay." He unlocked the back door and threw the day's catch out. "Jo, if it freaks you out so much, I could catch mice for you."

She removed her fencing mask. "You would?"

"Sure. But why doesn't the cat catch them?"

"Sometimes he does. I don't think he's much of a hunter. That's real nice of you, Patrick, but you can't use glue traps and they have their own peanut butter—"

"Consider it a term of my rental. Why do you wear a fencing mask?"

"One time a mouse wasn't dead and when Hugh found it he let it go and it ran up his leg and bit his knee."

"Inside his pants?"

"No, he wasn't wearing… I mean, it was summer. Shorts." She smiled. "I'm very grateful. Really. I have another trap over there. You'll need the flashlight. It's dark in that corner. I just hope they enjoy the peanut butter. It's not organic, but it's quite good."

"Of course." He found another small corpse with an expression of surprise on its face, or what looked like it. Under her cringing supervision he smeared more peanut butter onto the traps and reset them.

All the while he wondered what she was wearing beneath her jeans and sweater.

"Thank you for the flowers," I said to Willis.

"I'd hoped you might call me." He snatched two glasses of wine deftly from a circulating waiter and handed one to me. Around us the party was in full swing, held in the large open space in the middle of the radio station. Once the building had been a small parochial school and this had been the assembly room. I'd lost sight of Patrick, who'd been appropriated by Liz Ferrar.

I shrugged. I'd sent a polite email thank-you to Willis. I wasn't about to make up any excuses. I took a small sip of the wine—not much, I had to be on air in ten minutes.

"So, lunch," he said as though I'd made some sort of encouraging response.

"I'm flattered and all that, but you're not really my type."

He grinned. "You're very direct. I like that."

Oh, crap. I couldn't win with this guy. So much for honesty. "Oh, I think Bill is going to cut his cake. I'd better—"

"Not for a while yet. So how about it? Lunch tomorrow? I'll pick you up at twelve?"

Before I could come up with a conventional sort of response about checking my schedule, he grabbed my hand. "Look, I know you think I'm a flake because I've cut a few trees down in my time. We have different values. You're a sort of hippie—"

"No, I'm not. My mother is a hippie. Just because I work in radio—"

"Whatever. I make money. I like money. I like spending money on girls."

"Jesus, Willis, listen to yourself. I'm not a girl."

"Woman, then. Women."

"And I don't like the idea of being some sort of money pit. What's in it for you anyway?" I almost hoped he'd say *fucking* but even he wasn't that crude.

"Jo." His thumb caressed the back of my hand and to my astonishment it made me feel…well, probably more the way I should have felt during a night of fucking with Jason, the permanently erect. "I'm interested in you. I know you're going to say I don't know you, but I'd like to. We have different values. So what? It keeps things interesting. I have money and I guess you don't. So let's pool resources."

"And what do I bring to this interesting relationship?"

"Willis! So glad you could come!" Kimberly bore down on us, deftly reorganizing her wineglass, plate, purse, napkin and various other odds and ends to kiss Willis's cheek without pouring zinfandel down his pants. "Jo was just talking about y—"

"No, I wasn't," I interjected before Kimberly encouraged him any further.

"We'll talk soon, okay?" And she was off in a cloud of social fairy dust, leaving me fuming and Willis in firm possession of my hand.

"We'd have fun," he said.

My instinctive retort was to say I wasn't into fun but I hesitated. Some fun might be good. I had a serious sort of job with strange hours and a very odd sex life—and I could seduce the pants off Willis and tell Mr. D. about it. I took another look at the clock on the wall.

"Time flies?" he said.

"I have to be in the studio. Watching the clock is a major part of my job. Okay, then."

"Okay to lunch?" His face split into a huge grin.

"Sure. Pick me up here." There was no way I'd let him know where I lived.

I made my escape to the studio, where our early evening

announcer signed off and I pulled a few CDs, annoyed that I might miss the cake. I went online for the latest weather report and local news and closed the studio door but left the light on. This was one of the occasions when Neil or Bill would give guests the grand tour so they could have the pleasure of staring through the window at me.

I lined up a short piece to begin with and glanced at the phone. It was too early for him to call, but... I wasn't sure he'd approve. And that raised some uncomfortable questions. Did I need his approval? Was I using Willis the way I'd used Jason? (Except that had been entirely spontaneous...hadn't it?) And we'd parted on good terms with no expectations and... Willis was just so unlike the men I usually dated, but according to Kimberly I made bad choices in that area. I pulled out my cell phone and texted her to save me a piece of cake, and then watched the countdown on the music currently playing.

Cake was nice and simple and not sullied by issues of morality. Unless you were concerned about your weight or a wanna-be dancer obsessed with keeping yourself to bone and muscle (and probably planning to barf it up anyway), cake was a pleasure, pure and simple.

The music ended and I came on air and made a short announcement. My philosophy was that we did not have personality announcers, but a smooth flow of music and if our listeners noticed the voice had changed, that was fine. But it was the music that kept them listening.

When I flipped the mic off someone knocked at the door and I got up to answer it. To my surprise it was Patrick with a plate of cake.

"Kimberly told me to bring this to you."

"Great. Want to come in?"

"Sure." He came in and looked around. "So how does all this work?"

I gave him my usual semitechnical explanation and offered

him a seat. "Stay while I talk on air, if you like. Try not to sneeze."

"I won't."

"You'd be surprised how many visitors have a coughing fit." I took a quick bite of cake and put my headphones on.

This time I talked a little longer, giving a weather update and mentioning the music that would be coming up later, aware that I issued an invitation to Mr. D. *This is when I can talk.*

Then I hit the play button for the CD, faded the mic down and switched it off and removed my headphones.

"Do you get nervous?" Patrick asked.

"No. Some announcers imagine they're talking to one person, or their pet. I don't. If you think about how many people might be listening it's unreal, intimidating. So I just talk."

"And you like being here late at night?"

Well, yes. "I'm not always here late. I can put a show together by downloading music and recording the announcements, and that's what I usually do if I want an early night. An intern comes in to make sure everything is okay and can step in to broadcast from the other studio if something goes wrong. But generally I work live." I forked more cake into my mouth. "Thanks for bringing me this."

"No problem." He cleared his throat in the way men do when they are about to get personal. "Kimberly seems nice."

"She is."

"You've been friends for quite a while, she said."

He was asking for a character reference, in other words. I thought I'd move things along a bit for him. "She'd probably appreciate a ride home, if you're driving, that is."

"Good to know." He nodded in an emphatic sort of way. "I'll leave you to it, then. Unless you'd like more cake?"

I told him I was fine and he left me to the quiet of the studio. Now and again a group of visitors came by, and I put my headphones on and looked properly busy at the console even if I wasn't at that moment.

I was watching the clock. I was waiting for the moment when everyone left and my time with Mr. D. began.

"I'm worried I'm turning into some sort of fuck-bunny monster," I said to Mr. D. before he'd barely had a chance to say hello. "It's as though every guy I see, I'm eying up as a possible sexual partner."

"Everyone?" I could tell he was trying not to laugh.

"Well, not everyone. Not Gerard Morgan. He's one of our major supporters and I think he's about eighty. I'd probably get his wife, Marilyn, as part of the deal, too—she keeps him on a short leash. On the other hand she's a nubile seventy-five-year-old. They're both pretty frisky, now that I think about it. I'm talking myself into it. See what you've done?"

"I'm not sure people aren't eyeing each other up as sexual partners most of the time. Perhaps you're being more honest than most of us."

"I accepted a date tonight with someone I think is despicable."

"Why?"

"My friend Kimberly—I've talked about her—persuaded me it would be a good idea, and she's cultivating him for a gift to the station. She thinks I don't date the right men."

"I think she's right."

I twisted the phone cord. "And I accepted so that I could fuck him and then tell you about it. No, I know what you're going to say. It's my decision and all that. I don't have to fuck him and we can talk about something else. I know. So why am I doing this?"

A silence. "There must be something you like about him."

"He's physically attractive. Not my type, but he's handsome. And there's something about him—he's crude and materialistic but he doesn't pretend to be anything else and I admire him for it. No, the real reason I find him attractive, Mr. D., is that I want to have sex with him and then tell you about it."

"And this makes you feel—what? Guilty, sad?"

"Are you a shrink in real life?" I grinned. "No, it makes me feel excited. It makes me feel powerful and sexy, and I like that. But at the same time, it worries me."

"I don't ever want you to feel obligated to me. I love to talk with you. We can talk about whatever you like. You don't have to describe your conquests to me unless you want to."

"But I do want to."

"Then that's what we'll do. How long do we have?"

"About fifteen minutes."

"I'd like to have you talk on air seconds before you come. I'd like to hear that roughness in your voice and know you're speaking to me, something you and I share. Will you do that for me, Jo?"

I hesitated. My next recording was cued, and the notes I'd use to make my next announcement lay ready on the console. I could do it, but what would his next demand be? "If I do that, will you ask me to come on air next?"

"No. That moment is for me. I don't want to share that with anyone."

I squeezed my legs together. I was alone in the station—I'd made sure of that—but I wondered if he'd delayed calling so he could specifically ask me to do this. In which case, I'd put him on the spot, too.

"Unzip yourself," I said. I put the phone on speaker and heard a rustle, the slide of his zipper. "Are you hard?"

He gave a soft, sexy laugh. "What do you think?"

"Describe your cock for me."

It was something of a test. I didn't want bullshit about his hard eight inches because in my experience eight inches, or more, was something that existed only in men's imaginations.

Besides, who wanted a dick the size of a baseball bat pummeling their insides?

"It's hard—I mean, hard in the sense of difficult—to describe something I've seen so many times. It has a slight curve to the right—I suppose because I'm right-handed. My pubic hair is dark brown with a few gray hairs, quite tightly curled. My cock is brown, darker than my skin, but the head is dark red. It's very smooth. I'm running my fingertips up and down the ridge on the underside. Teasing myself."

"Go on." I traced my fingers lightly over my breasts. My nipples tightened.

"Now I'm cupping my balls with my other hand. They're warm and heavy. Tightening against my palm."

I listened to his labored breathing, the sound of his excitement.

"Jo? I'm touching the head of my cock with my thumb and forefinger, squeezing it. There's some seepage, now."

I traced the outline of my nipples and spread my legs. I'd worn a skirt for the party and beneath it my cunt felt full and heavy. "Tell me more. Tell me what your cock looks like now."

"Darker. Wet. I'm using lube." A gasp. "The head is swelling. Getting very sensitive. I'm using my whole hand. Sliding up and down."

I slid a hand under my skirt and into my panties. Above my head the second hand of the clock moved. "Wait!"

He groaned.

I put his call on hold and moved to the console, placing the headphones on my head. The last chords of the music died away and I slid the faders into position, slowly and smoothly.

My voice sounded calm and soothing through the headphones, announcing what we had heard, and what was coming up next. A few words about the weather, and a short statement about the sponsor of the next hour of music, the local theater company, and their next production. "I'm Jo Hutchinson and it's my pleasure to be with you for the next few hours."

My pleasure indeed. Mic off, music up, phone call off hold. I gripped the edge of the console, pressed my pubic bone against it, hard, and my orgasm roared through me.

I dropped into the chair, out of breath.

"Jo? You okay?"

"Sure. I feel like I've run a mile."

"Me, too. The way you said *pleasure*—that did it for me. You were speaking to me then. I felt it." He laughed. "God, you make me feel like a randy teenager. I'd already jerked off at work thinking about you today."

"You did? Where?"

"At my desk. I told my assistant I wasn't to be disturbed and…well, you can imagine the rest."

I could, but I also wished he'd waited for me, waited until I was off the air and I had heard him come.

"Are you disappointed?"

"At what?"

"That I do this without you?"

I shrugged before realizing he couldn't see my gesture. "I don't see that it's anything to do with what you and I have. I guess I'm flattered that you fantasize about me."

"We have such a small part of each other," he said. "I don't want to jeopardize what we have, until you decide you want more from me."

"You know my answer to that."

He sighed. I heard clothing rustle, and the sound of his zipper going up. "So how was the party tonight?"

"You knew about it?"

"I received an invitation, yes."

I sat up a little straighter. "Were you there? Was that why you called so late?"

"You know I keep a low profile."

"I can always look at the guest list," I said, although I knew I wouldn't. I wanted to keep the mystery. "I like the idea of you watching me across the room. How did you feel when you saw me flirt with other guys?"

He laughed. "If I had been there, I would have loved to have watched you. And seeing you flirt with other men—I would have felt hopeful. Excited. Because I would know I would receive the greatest and last pleasure, to be the one you would tell everything to."

"So if I don't seduce this guy tomorrow, will you be disappointed?"

"No. You can never disappoint me."

6

I DREAMED SOMETHING RANG AND RANG, PEALING in my ear. I grabbed out and reached the phone.

A giggling squeal assaulted my ears. I blinked at the numbers of my digital clock. Three in the morning. I'd been asleep less than an hour.

"What?"

This time I recognized the voice.

"Kimberly? You okay?"

Another fit of giggling.

I finally figured out what the two syllables were she kept repeating. "You woke me up to tell me he has a foreskin?"

"Shit, sorry. I thought you'd be awake." More giggling. "It's weird."

"He's Irish. It's probably normal there."

"I didn't know what to do with it."

"Where are you?"

"My place. In the bathroom. He's asleep."

"Oh, good. He might find it depressing that you're on the phone to a girlfriend giggling about his dick."

"I wouldn't say a word in front of him. It's bad manners."

"So is waking me up."

"I'm sorry. I had to tell someone about it."

I yawned. "I'm pretty sure there are AM call-in shows for this sort of situation. You sure you're okay? Not overwhelmed by foreskinned leprechaun sex?"

"He's cute. Nice. Sexy. We had a good time."

"Great. Why don't you go to sleep, too? Good night."

"Are you grouchy for any other reason than being woken up?"

"No, I'm fine. 'Bye." I disconnected the call and rolled over, dislodging Brady, who had swollen to twice his normal size and heated up to an alarming temperature, as cats will. I allowed myself a moment of self-pity. Kimberly had a guy in her bed and I had an overheated lump of fur in mine and a vibrator somewhere on the floor. I scrabbled around for it in a half-hearted sort of way, put off by the thought of the dust bunnies it might have accumulated. Sleep seemed a more wholesome alternative.

"I thought we'd have a picnic." Willis grinned with approval at me—I thought it was approval, but it might have been self-satisfaction. On the other hand my outfit of cowboy boots and a black-and-white polka-dot, knee-length skirt looked pretty good to me. "That okay with you?"

"That sounds great." It was one of those unseasonably warm days in the Rockies where half the town appears in shorts, grabbing a few rays before the temperature plummets with the setting sun.

He wore jeans and a battered leather jacket and looked slightly more human than in his expensive suits and ties, or at least slightly more like a guy I'd date. He ushered me out to his car, a sort of jeeplike thing, and I bit back the first comment that rose to my lips about its mileage. This was not the sort of vehicle acquired for its light carbon footprint.

"Like it?" he said, mistaking my interest.

"Sorry, I don't know much about cars."

To my relief, he didn't take this as an invitation to educate me, but opened the car door and once we were seated, made a fuss of selecting music, adjusting the temperature and so on. Then he drove through the town and west into the foothills.

He didn't say much and I wondered if he was shy, or maybe thinking he'd made a mistake.

"Are you seeing someone?" he asked.

"No. Are you?"

"No. You acted weird about coming out with me, so I thought…"

"I was in a fairly serious relationship for quite a long time. I haven't got the hang of dating. How about you?" I'd given up telling him he wasn't my type. He couldn't or wouldn't believe it.

"Divorced. I'm not ready for a serious relationship just yet. I like sexy, adventurous women like you."

"What do you mean by adventurous? I used to date a rock-climbing fanatic. I went climbing with him a couple of times but I was scared to death."

He shot me a glance. "You look athletic. Sure of yourself."

"I ride a bike, but doesn't everyone?" I looked at the road we were on, winding through pine trees. "This might be a good road to ride. Do you like sports?"

I'd asked for it. A lecture followed on the local football team. He stopped. "I guess you're not into football?"

"No. I meant, do you climb or run? You look like you work out."

"I lift weights, go to the gym a few times a week. Ski in the winter. Play a little golf."

Oh, God, please don't talk about golf or start comparing Brecken-ridge to Aspen.

He didn't, having turned off the road and onto an unpaved

track, probably an old logging road. The interior of the car was warm with the bright sunlight that flickered through the trees, and I hated to admit it, but I enjoyed the leather seats and the comfortable ride, the luxury of riding in an expensive car.

"I hope this wasn't too early in the day for you," he said. "I brought brunch."

"That's very thoughtful."

He pulled the jeep to a halt in a sunlit meadow. We weren't far from town but when I opened the door and stepped outside I was struck by the peace, the quiet. "Is this it? The place you're going to develop?"

He nodded. "It's still in the early stages. It may not happen."

"And if it doesn't? Won't you lose money?"

"I'll have the land. It might happen next year or in ten years. You never know." He reached into the back of the jeep for a picnic basket and cooler and led me over to an outcropping that held the heat of the sun. He was an attentive and solicitous host—he even had a plaid blanket that he spread on the rocks— and the picnic basket turned out to be one of those fancy ones with china plates and cutlery. He'd brought bagels and lox and cream cheese and champagne in the cooler.

So who was seducing whom?

"This is nice," I said, hoping the surprise didn't show in my voice. "Great bagels."

He popped the cork on the champagne, not making a big deal of it but easing it off softly. A little vapor rose from the neck of the bottle before he poured it into two glasses, pale and sparkling. Good signs—I wondered how he'd be as a lover.

"You're the first girl—I mean woman—I've brought here," he said.

"Yeah? You seem to have all the right moves." I clinked my glass against his.

He smiled and unscrewed the cap of a bottle of sparkling water. "I have to drive, but you go ahead."

I raised my face to the sun. Perhaps it was the champagne, perhaps it was the company of a handsome man who was not full of self-important chatter, as I'd feared, but I felt extraordinarily peaceful and at ease.

I finished my bagel and wondered if it would be crass to ask if I could have one for later—I decided it would be—but accepted an orange, one of those big, fat expensive ones that I hardly every bought. The rind peeled off with an easy grace and a wonderful whiff of scent.

"You're a very sensual woman," Willis said.

"Is that a euphemism for greedy?"

"No. You enjoy things. You show it." He reached to refill my champagne glass.

"This is all perfect," I said, indicating our picnic. "Other than your yearning to cut down trees and build ugly houses."

"Heck, they won't be ugly. I'm working with a green architect."

"Green with pointy ears?" I lay back on the blanket, eyes closed, and chortled at my own joke, a little drunk on champagne and sunshine.

"You're a funny girl."

"Woman."

He shifted toward me. Oh, this was so damn easy. Too easy. Without opening my eyes I separated a segment of orange and stuck it in my mouth. His face hovered over mine as I chewed and swallowed—I could feel his breath on my lips—and he moved in and licked juice from my chin. I was impressed. An enthusiastically chomping woman would not be a particular turn-on, or so I'd think, but he managed to take the moment from slightly comic to erotic with one light touch of his tongue.

His tongue touched my lips and he reached for the orange in my hand, loosening my fingers from the few segments that remained. He fed them to me before taking my hand and licking the juice from my palm.

"Nice," he murmured.

I closed my hand around his chin, smooth from a recent shave. He smelled, very faintly, of lime, something subtle and expensive. I wouldn't have expected this from the brash Willis I'd first met.

"More orange? Champagne?"

I opened my eyes. "You."

He looked surprised. Maybe he expected to have to seduce me, or maybe he didn't expect me to be quite so direct. But he didn't think too long, particularly when I sat up and stripped off the long-sleeved T-shirt I wore and began on the buttons of his shirt. His hands flew to my breasts; I wore a pink cotton bra with a little lace, what I considered suitable for a lunchtime seduction.

He reached into the picnic basket. Yes, condoms for dessert. My bra was tossed carelessly aside as he nuzzled and kissed my breasts and I pulled his shirt from his jeans.

He had enough muscle and hair that he didn't look like a pretty boy, but I noticed a certain awareness, a flexing of his pectorals, as though he was posing for my admiration. I suppose the equivalent for a woman was to suck it in.

"I like your chest," I offered, feeling that all that time at the gym should be acknowledged. I stroked his biceps and glanced down. His erection pushed against his jeans.

He dipped a hand beneath my skirt. I propped myself on my elbows to watch his mouth at my breasts, his hand working between my spread thighs and my skirt bunched up at the waist. I liked that he played around my underwear, sliding his fingers under the elastic, stroking the dampened fabric of the crotch with his thumb. He took his time and when he slid a finger inside me I clenched on him hard, my breath short.

He raised his head from my breast. I wondered for a moment if I'd burn in the warm sun. "Am I going too fast for you, honey?"

"No. It's great."

I reached for the button of his Levi's and slid his zipper down. White Jockeys, not my favorite (was there ever a more stupidly designed piece of underwear in the world?) but I didn't intend to look at them for too long. I shoved his jeans and underwear down and his cock sprang into my hand.

He lost his concentration, his hand slowing on my clit, and I bounced my hips at him. What the heck were we going to do about our cowboy boots? Mine, it appeared, were going to stay on. He paused from regarding his dick approvingly to unzip my skirt and pull it and my underwear down. He raised himself onto his knees to stroke the condom over his penis, gazing at himself with adoration, jeans and underwear lodged at his calves. I was excited but at the same time I was an observer, taking notes for later.

He levered himself over me, and I saw we were about to embark on classic missionary style. And, yes, his boots were staying on, too.

"You're gorgeous," he said, staring at my nakedness, my cowboy boots, my darkened nipples. "I want to fuck you so bad."

Willis was losing his cool a bit, I was pleased to see. His mouth was half-open, lips wet, eyes hot. His hand stroked his cock, up and down. I don't think he knew he did it, but when I reached down and touched my clit his eyes widened.

"Now," I said.

I loved the sight of his cock sliding into me, the juicy, rude sounds of our fucking, the warmth of the sun on my skin. The scent of the lime shaving product he used mingled with those of sweat and oranges and champagne. Beside my head his arms flexed as he pushed inside, withdrew, pushed again, and my hips rose to meet him. He murmured to me how good it felt, how wet and hot my pussy was, how he couldn't last, but he'd lost me. I tried to recapture my own rhythm, but it was like watching someone run away from you, and while the experience was pleasant enough, I couldn't catch up.

Willis was way ahead of me now, lost in his own excitement, sweat breaking out on his forehead and chest before he dropped onto me, out of breath.

"Wow," he said. "That was great."

He rolled off me and reached for a paper napkin. Condom disposed of, he turned back to me. "You okay, honey?"

The best answer, it seemed to me, was to take his hand and guide it to my clitoris.

"You want more?" he asked with a grin. And then he continued, "Oh. I thought you'd…you know, you seemed real close."

"Close but not quite there." I added, "It's the way I work. You were great, but the first time, with someone new, it's not always easy to figure out what they want. Don't feel offended." *Just rub my clit, you idiot.*

"No, no, I'm not offended." He shook his head with such vehemence that I didn't believe him. "It's just that generally gir—I mean women…come pretty easily with me."

"I will, too."

I pressed the great lover's hand a little more insistently where only minutes before he had dabbled and played with such skill. He looked pleased at my praise but pulled up his pants and zipped up in a way that suggested today's fun was over and his cock needed time to recover its hurt feelings.

Then he gave me an orgasm with very little effort on his part, as I'd predicted, and a lot of heaving and gasping on mine. I couldn't help thinking he saw it as the consolation prize for the girl who didn't appreciate the finer points of the Willis Scott III penis.

I rolled away from him and scrambled to my feet. "I need to pee."

He blinked at me and it occurred to me that maybe I should have said something in praise of his technique but my bladder was about to burst.

After taking advantage of the privacy of some scrub oak nearby, I stepped back out into the open meadow. Sunlight drenched and warmed me, caressed me, and the long grass brushed against my boots with a soft shushing sound. A small breeze brushed my nipples erect. I stretched out my arms and circled, taking a few dance steps, feeling the old familiar stretch, my body drawing itself up and in, taut, strong.

Willis watched, arms folded on his knees. I'd forgotten what it was like to have an audience, to see admiration and wonder. I tipped my face back to the sun, eyes closed, orange and yellow and red sparking behind my eyelids.

"I'd like to make you look like that." I heard the brush of grass against denim as Willis approached.

"Like what?"

"Ecstatic." He bent to kiss my nipples. He slid his hands down my sides, over my hips, my butt, and then knelt to kiss my mound.

I didn't need to be told to open my legs. He held me, strong gym-toned arms around my knees, and his tongue parted and flicked, small nibbles and sucks and the occasional graze of his teeth. I gripped his shoulders hard, my legs shaking, and came with the colors of the sun flaring behind my closed eyes.

"Nice?" he said, grinning up at me as I opened my eyes.

"Ecstatic," I said, trying to get my breathing under control.

He stood and reached for my hand, drawing it to the front of his jeans. "I've never seen a woman so comfortable with being naked. With being watched."

"I was a dance major."

"Yeah. You've got great muscle tone." He groaned a little

as I squeezed his erection. He put his other hand on my hip, stroking, assessing.

"What would you like me to do?"

He blinked and looked at my mouth. "Uh…"

I dropped to my knees and undid his jeans to reach his cock, and darted my tongue out to catch the drop of liquid that welled from the slit. He groaned again, and put his hands to my head, and I breathed him in and took him as deep as I could. His fingers dug into my shoulders, moved to grip my head, to guide me. This time it was he whose legs shook and who cried out, his hips jerking as he spilled warm and salty into my mouth.

I released him and wiped a dribble of semen from my chin.

"Wow," he said. "It's great in the open air."

"Like salami sandwiches," I said as we strolled back to the blanket.

"What?"

"When you get up to a high altitude—higher than this, the top of a mountain, maybe—terrible food tastes great. Salami on white bread, for instance."

"You're a funny girl. Woman." He picked up and handed me the bottle of mineral water that he'd abandoned by the picnic gear. It was a polite gesture, I suspected, that I might want to rinse out, but I took a large swallow and suppressed a belch.

"Was that better than a salami sandwich?" I asked.

"Never even thought about a sandwich of any kind," he said. "Not once."

A small breeze raised goose bumps on my arms. "Maybe I'd better put some clothes on."

He looked at me with appreciation as he fastened his jeans. "Don't want you catching cold, but it's a pity. I like looking at you. I think you like it, too."

I made a noncommittal noise as I dressed. There was a spec-ulative quality to his voice and I wondered what he was going to suggest—a strip show at the next Realtors' Association breakfast perhaps. Generally I found that once I'd admitted to my time as a dance student all sorts of odd things went through guys' minds, the first being speculation as to whether I could put my feet behind my head (easily) or what I could do with a pole (nothing out of the ordinary).

Willis, looking thoughtful, packed up the picnic basket. He tossed me another orange, which I caught with a minimum of fumbling and stowed into my purse for later, and then I finished off the champagne. Pretty soon I'd need a nap, relaxed by sunshine and good sex and good food.

"So," he said with a studied air of nonchalance as we walked back to the jeep, "I wondered if you'd like to do something on Saturday. Something special."

"He said *what?*" Mr. D. sounded, well, shocked.

"Isn't it more to the point what I said after?" I cued up my next CD. "I think you're rather like me. You've had a lot of sex but it's been fairly conventional. Vanilla. Nothing kinky. And one thing I've realized since meeting you is that there are all sorts of possibilities open to me, and maybe this is the time for a little exploration. I'm not saying I'll never fall in love again, because that's plain dumb. But I'm single and it's a good time for me to experiment. Didn't you tell me once this is one of the kinkiest things you've done? I'm sure you've done other stuff, too."

"Well, when I was younger…"

"Yes? I think you owe me a story."

"We don't know that the king told Scheherazade any stories."

"Afterward, I'm sure he did. He'd proved his point, and she would have demanded it. Three years of stories without even maternity leave? She would have wanted a story and a foot rub when she'd had a really tough day with the kids."

"I'll tell you a story another time, I promise." He paused. "And what did you say to his proposition?"

"What do you think?"

"So tell me all about it," Kimberly said. "Did you make this coffee? It's god-awful."

"He's nicer than I thought."

"Details. Details." She tapped me on the hand with a plastic spoon.

"No foreskin. How are you managing with yours?"

"It's not mine, and I'm woman enough for it. Come into my office and give me the dirt." She led the way, swaying on cowboy boots that were far sexier than mine, scarlet leather with black embroidery.

"No, you give me the dirt." I closed the office door and sat in my usual place. Her office was the only one in the station that had a decorative quality to its mess.

"Patrick's real sweet," she said. "Never thought I'd go for sweet, but he's just that. And the foreskin is actually sort of useful. Adds bulk. Never a bad thing, not that he needs bulk, but it's a nice little bonus. He's funny, too."

"I've always thought he's depressed, but I don't see much of him."

"You can be funny and depressed. A lot of people are. Did Willis take you somewhere nice yesterday?"

"We had a picnic."

"A picnic?" She stared at me. "That doesn't sound like him. Will you see him again?"

I shrugged. "Possibly."

She gave me a long searching look. "What's up with you, Jo?"

I resisted the urge to squirm in my chair. "Nothing, other than taking your advice and trying to learn how to date."

"You're different these days. Secretive. I don't mean in dick details, but you seem distracted. Are you okay?"

"I'm fine."

She frowned. "Maybe it's too soon. You were with Hugh for a long time."

"No, it's time." I hastened to reassure her. "I know I was resistant to the idea at first but I think you were right."

She leaned forward and patted my hand. "I'm saying this because I'm your friend, honey. I think you're keeping something from me and I don't want you to be hurt. Anytime you want to talk, I'll listen. Okay?"

"Thanks. You're a good friend." I was touched by her concern but there was no way I would tell her about Mr. D. or what Willis and I would be doing this weekend.

"I have an idea," she said. "Let's double-date. Patrick's taking me to the Shamrock Club Saturday night—it's some sort of Irish place with traditional music and Guinness. Why don't you and Willis join us there?"

"I'll ask him, but we're probably doing something in the evening and I'm not sure how long it will last."

"You have fun."

What an opportunity I was missing. I was badly in need of fashion advice. *Kimberly, what should I wear to an orgy?*

7

SO WHAT DO YOU WEAR TO AN ORGY? ALTHOUGH, Willis assured me, it wasn't an orgy. Oh, no, no, no. Just sex among friends.

His friends. Another couple. Great folks. I'd love them. One way or another.

The cowboy boots had been quite a hit with Willis but they were awkward to get in and out of. Not that I'd necessarily take them off. I eventually settled on kitten heels and jeans—I looked good in them and I didn't want to look as though I were dressing for an orgy even if I was. Jeans with cowboy boots, as Willis had so amply demonstrated, were not great for spontaneous sex, and I didn't want to picture myself sitting on the floor, undignified, wrenching off my boots with my jeans around my knees, and holding up the activities. ("There in a second!")

Maybe it would be the sort of house where you shucked your shoes in the hall, or, more likely, your panties.

I topped the jeans with a scoop-neck black T-shirt, and beneath everything was some of my good underwear. I was sure Mr. D. would approve. I toyed for a moment with tidying up my pubic hair, but why bother? I didn't think, if all went according to Plan A, that I'd have the panties on for long, or, if I chose Plan B—"If you like, you can watch. You don't have to do anything you don't want to," I had been assured—it wouldn't matter anyway.

Sparkly earrings, yes. Perfume, definitely; I hoped our hosts would not have an allergic reaction.

Willis eyed my living room as I grabbed my black suede jacket and a small clutch purse. "Very nice. And a cash flow with the apartment. Great neighborhood. How much equity do you have? Have you considered—"

I stopped him with a kiss. "Stop being such a Realtor."

His hands closed on my butt. "Yeah, it's time to play. Let's go."

I guessed from his hyper attitude and the slight dusting of stubble on his jaw that he'd been at work that day. His tie was loosened and shirt sleeves rolled up despite the chill of the evening, and when we got to his car, a shiny BMW this time, I saw his suit jacket folded neatly on the backseat.

The house we drove to was in the suburbs, where too many people tried to live their dream of a house in the mountains. Although the lots had pine trees you could see the neighbors' lights and hear their dogs bark.

Willis put the car in Park and turned to me. "Don't be nervous, babe."

"I'm not nervous."

"You are. Body language. I'm an expert." He leaned to kiss me and I slid down in my seat, wanting the moment to last, the sweetness of his mouth and scrape of his chin.

"Okay." Ever businesslike, he slipped off his tie, folded it and laid it on top of his jacket on the backseat. "Let's go. Relax. They're great folks. They'll make you feel right at home."

The woman who answered the doorbell was wearing jeans and a T-shirt like I was, but her breasts were probably twice the size of mine. "Willis, honey, great to see you. We've really been looking forward to this, haven't we, Jake? Jake?" she called over her shoulder and pouted. "He's watching the game. I'm Cathy. May I take your jacket?"

To my relief she didn't recognize my voice, but led us downstairs to a basement with a huge flat-screen TV and expensive-looking leather furniture.

"Hey, Willis. We're in overtime," the guy hunkered in front of the TV said without looking at us. Willis sat beside him on the couch.

Cathy made a cute face at me, the females in exile from sports, and provided the guys with beers from a bar at one end of the basement, and poured white wine for me.

"You have a lovely home," I said, since we seemed to be deep in a suburban dream rather than any sort of naked sweaty activities.

Naturally she beamed and offered to show me the rest of the house and I admired the master bathroom with the his-and-hers sinks and listened to the story of how the marble countertop had arrived cracked and the hassle of getting a replacement. The bedroom featured a huge bed with a velvet cover. Cathy darted forward, giggling, and whisked something from the bedside table and into a drawer—I think it might have been a vibrator, but I wasn't sure.

"Where do you keep your books?" I asked.

"Books? Oh, some over there—" she gestured at a cabinet that held knickknacks and a couple of books "—and some in the study." She gave me an odd look.

Several rooms later—after viewing bathrooms, spare bedrooms, a study (housing a scant half-dozen more books but many sports trophies), family room and dining room—we ended up in the kitchen, a masterpiece of granite counters, stainless-steel appliances and a beautifully polished hardwood floor, a room I truly envied. She bent to retrieve a tray of crudités from the refrigerator, treating me to an impressive display of cleavage.

As she straightened up she caught me looking and grinned. "Aren't they great? Jake's birthday present for me, but I think they're a present for him."

What was she talking about? She giggled and placed the tray on the counter. "Boob job," she explained, and hoisted up her T-shirt.

I stared at her breasts, round and solid with large pink nipples. I'd thought she was wearing a bra, but they were a masterpiece of technology, needing no support.

"Great," I said. "Were they really small before?"

"About your size," she said. "Willis is really into boobs. He'll probably want you to get yours done."

"We haven't known each other that long," I said, wanting to cross my arms protectively over my small and untouched breasts.

"It's so worth it. Jake loves them and it makes me feel so sexy." She pulled her top back over her breasts and opened the dishwasher door. At that point I realized I wasn't in Kansas anymore. She unloaded a handful of brightly colored dildos and butt-plugs into a plastic bowl—I was relieved to see they were the only items in the dishwasher, and that I wouldn't have to ditch my wineglass and switch to beer.

"Can I do anything?" I asked and immediately regretted my question. What if she asked me to get busy with a dildo?

Fortunately she took my offer at face value and set me to work arranging chips on a serving tray while she scooped various dips into bowls. Then we took the snacks down to the basement, and so far, other than the breast display and the dildos rattling around in the plastic bowl on Cathy's tray, it was just any weekend afternoon in suburbia.

"Oh, that's gross, guys," Cathy said.

The game had ended and the guys sprawled on the couch,

beer bottles in hand, while on the screen a blonde with breasts even bigger and more rigid than Cathy's divided her time between sucking a huge torpedo of a penis and glancing flirtatiously at the camera. The owner of the penis was a large hairy guy with a slight potbelly.

"That is so unreal," Cathy said, grabbing the remote from Jake and switching the set off. "Jake, this is Jo. I showed her my boobs."

"Hi," I said.

Jake, a bulkier version of Willis—clean-cut, middle-class—lurched to his feet and leered. "Hey, little lady. Does my wife have great tits, or what?"

I was so dumbfounded at being addressed as "little lady" I only managed to mutter something along the lines of "Yes, she sure does," before gulping the remains of my wine.

Willis ambled over and put his arm over my shoulders, letting his fingers fall onto my breast. "Jo's are pretty nice, too. Small, though."

"Show us your tits, honey," Jake said to me.

"What's the magic word?" I snapped at him and shook Willis's hand and arm away.

Jake stared at me.

"Oh, honey, you are such a big, bad boy," Cathy cooed and placed a hand on her husband's arm. "Where are your manners?"

Jake grinned in a way that might have been irresistibly boyish and mischievous and mumbled something apologetic in my direction. He then stuck his hand down his wife's top.

I marched over to the bar and poured myself another glass of wine. I was feeling very Puritan and uptight, instead of sexually liberated and daring, and I didn't like it. And now I could see how this room was set up for what was about to happen: the bowl of condoms on the low table near the television, another on the bar along with the dildos, a pile of soft towels, tubes of lube, the sturdy sofa, a collection of ottomans for various positions.

Willis followed me over to the bar. "You okay, Jo?"

"Yeah. Fine." I was not being the life and soul of the party, that was for sure. I glanced over at the sofa where Jake and Cathy sat, he now nuzzling between her breasts, her T-shirt up to her chin. She gave me an encouraging smile. I wondered if Jake was concerned that her breasts could snap back and injure his nose when he emerged.

"Hey," Willis said in a whisper. He kissed me, wet and tender. "You don't have to do this. Like I said, you seem an adventurous sort of woman and you have a lot of confidence in your body and I thought you might get off on it. No pressure. If you're not comfortable, well… " He stopped to leer at Cathy's breasts.

"Jerk," I said, half-meaning it, and pulled my T-shirt off.

Willis's attention shot back to my breasts as I'd intended. He examined the red satin and black lace—one of my sluttier bras—but from the expression on his face it worked. Jake withdrew his face from Cathy's cleavage without evident injury and took a good look.

"My panties match," I said.

"Right on," said Jake. He leaned back on the sofa and Cathy wriggled between his legs. I found myself staring at them, and had to remind myself that that was why I was here; we were audience, for the moment, Willis and I, but soon we'd be participants. Cathy undid Jake's pants and hoisted his semi-erect penis out, but he was looking at me, and at Willis's hands, which now moved to unfasten my bra and toss it aside.

Jake licked his lips. Cathy, her hand moving up and down his cock, looked over and smiled. "Cute," she said.

Willis took one of my nipples into his mouth and I watched Cathy bend to Jake's cock and run her tongue from balls to tip. He rolled his head back, his hands in her hair, while she deftly removed her jeans. Underneath she wore a thong—I could see it disappear into the crack of her ass.

"I want you naked," Willis said. I couldn't figure out the undercurrent here. I had a strong sense that the men had some sort of competition going—the biggest tits, the best underwear, the most compliant woman. I wasn't really sure what it was. I liked being on display, being watched, and moaned when Willis fingered the crotch of my underwear, and liked it even more when both Jake and Cathy paused to assess my half-naked state.

She released Jake's cock, shiny from her saliva, and sat back on her heels, thighs spread. The thong was tiny and sequined and she appeared to have no pubic hair.

She smiled as she saw me looking and stood to slide her thong down. A narrow strip of pubic hair, trimmed close, remained, her pubis smooth and curved.

"Didn't that hurt?" I blurted out.

"Jake likes it. So do I." She ran her hands down her belly, and passed them lightly over her crotch. Of course, everything to please Jake. "It makes me very sensitive while we're fucking."

She was naked now, and Jake sat admiring his penis and her while she turned slowly, arms raised and hands behind her head.

"Damn, you're hot," Willis said. I don't think he said it to me. He rubbed one of my nipples between his finger and thumb, but his attention was mostly on Cathy.

"Aren't you boys overdressed?" I asked, partly in revenge for the "little lady" crack earlier, and partly because I wanted to see the two men together, to compare erections and physique.

A flurry of undressing occurred as soon as I'd spoken, shirts and jeans and underpants dropped onto the floor, both men kicking their clothes away, and grinning. Willis was erect, his penis curved up, longer and more slender than Jake's, which, like his physique, was broad and powerful. Jake had more body hair; next to him Willis looked boyish and pretty.

It seemed, by some unspoken agreement, that Cathy and Jake were to perform first. I wondered if their scant collections of books included one on orgy etiquette and this is what good hosts did.

I was interested. I'd never seen people fuck before, or seen a couple so absorbed in each other and at the same time so absorbed in the impression they made. Willis stood behind me, caressing my breasts, his cock rubbing against my butt. He lowered one hand to slide down my belly and into my panties. "I'm going to make you come," he whispered.

Jake sat on the sofa, Cathy astride him, both facing us. She ground herself against his cock, while his hands pinched and squeezed her breasts. I could see her pussy shine wet with excitement, her clitoris swelled erect, everything revealed beneath that little strip of fur.

She raised herself to slide down onto his cock, steadying herself with her hands on his knees, sliding. She took Jake's fingers into her mouth and then lowered his wet hand to rub her clit. Both of them moaned.

I wondered if they'd rehearsed the routine that followed, a seamless switch from one position to another, moving from floor to sofa, from kneeling to standing, and back. They employed subtle variations of speed and intensity, both of them beautiful and absorbed, performing. They ended up on the sofa in their initial position, a nice touch, and looked at me and Willis, challenging us.

I wanted to hold up a scorecard.

"Lie down," I said to Willis.

I flexed my legs a little and kicked my panties aside as Willis eased a condom onto his penis, from the bowl our hosts had provided on the bar. When he was on the floor, I performed for them, sliding into the splits, impaling myself.

"Damn," said Jake.

Willis moaned.

I steadied myself with my hands. I couldn't really move, and neither could he; it was all for show. I bent one leg forward and planted my foot near his shoulder. I had some leverage now, some slide, all the control.

Cathy and Jake were moving faster now, noisy, their faces red.

Willis and I went into an urgent scramble, separating briefly, and then he arranged me on all fours on an ottoman so we could watch the other couple, he standing behind me, his hands on my hips. This was not performance now, this was fucking, hot and urgent, his hips slapping against mine, his balls rolling at my inner thighs, both of us groaning.

Cathy and Jake were oblivious of us now, his cock sliding in and out of her pussy, his legs flexing with each thrust. If the moment had not been so erotically charged their posture and expressions would have been comic; but they were at that point where all that mattered was the climb, the pursuit. I saw her come—I'd never seen another woman come, but I heard her voice rise and saw her strain and gasp and then go still, her mouth open, her expression far away. Jake pumped hard into her and the slickness of their joined parts became creamy with his semen as he groaned and the two of them subsided, and she slumped on his lap, her eyes sleepy and satisfied.

But not that satisfied. She pleasured herself as she watched us, smiling gently, one manicured finger circling her clit. I wanted that, too. It was our moment, me and Cathy, as we both came, me frantic against Willis's thrusting, she languid and amused, taking a lazy climax. This time she came quietly with a slow shudder, her mouth open, eyes closed, and my pussy clenched and spasmed against Willis's thrusts.

"Damn," Willis said and sagged onto me. "Oh, damn, that was good."

He released me and I collapsed onto the floor in a heap, then rolled over onto my back, my legs splayed apart. "I like you, Willis."

He shook his head. "Hey, you like my dick and Cathy's pussy, but I'm not complaining."

"Of course I like her pussy. It's a work of art."

"Maybe you girls can put on a show," Jake said. He'd tipped Cathy to one side and was investigating the chips and dip. "What is this?"

"Eggplant," Cathy said. She reached for a piece of celery. "Can I get anyone a beer? More wine, Jo?"

I stifled a giggle. We'd gone straight from X-rated to snacks with barely a pause.

Cathy strolled naked across the room to one of the trunk-style ottomans and lifted the lid. She offered us terry robes, one of which I took, although both of the men refused, preferring their discarded underwear. She put on a robe and fussed around a little, providing us with drinks and urging us to help ourselves to the snacks. What happened next? Bridge? Scrabble?

Willis kissed me. "You did good, babe. I knew you would. Enjoy it?"

I nodded and sipped my wine. We made some conversation about careers—Jake worked in IT and Cathy was the office manager for a construction company. I told them I worked in media.

Jake looked longingly at the remote but Cathy snatched it away and stored it in one of the ottomans. I wondered if she'd scoot the ottomans around the room later to frustrate Jake when he started looking for it. She perched on his knee and he put his hand on her thigh where the robe fell away.

"So, what do you think?" Willis asked Jake.

"Nice," he said. He put his beer bottle on the table. "Jo, do me a favor, honey? Come on over here."

I looked at Willis. He gave me an encouraging smile.

I walked over to the sofa and stood in front of Jake and Cathy.

Jake reached out and tugged at the belt of the terrycloth robe. It fell open, revealing me to them. There was a pause as Jake and Cathy assessed me. Their scrutiny hardly felt sexual. I was being judged, found worthy, regarded as a specimen.

Jake nodded and Willis came forward to lift the robe from my shoulders.

"Great muscle tone and flexibility," Jake said as though he was choosing me for his team. Maybe he was. He rested his elbows on his knees. "Needs some cosmetic work."

"I'm not getting my tits done," I said.

He grinned. "Not that, honey. Your bush." He touched me, then, his forefinger stirring my pubic hair.

"Heck, it suits her," Cathy said. "She's a nature girl, right?"

His finger slid down, resting on my clitoris, then scooted sideways to where hair curled at the top of my thighs. "You could get this waxed, maybe. I think that would do."

"Do for what?" They were talking about me as if I were a thing, an object, but all I was aware of was the tickle of his finger as he explored my intimate areas.

"Do you think she could hold her own with the others?" Willis asked. "Most of them are younger."

"Yeah. How old are you, honey?"

"Twenty-nine."

"You're so lucky!" Cathy cried. "You'll always look younger than your real age. I bet you get carded."

"Sometimes." I shifted my legs apart a little, hoping I wasn't being too blatant. "What are you talking about?"

Cathy stroked my side, from rib cage to hip. "You have lovely skin. What do you use?"

"Nothing in particular. Cocoa butter."

Jake was definitely paying attention to my clit now, his finger sliding and circling. "Sweet little pussy," he murmured, "under all that hair. Gets real wet."

Willis joined them on the sofa to get a better view of what was going on. "You gonna make her come, man?"

"Sure," Jake said. "Baby, you like that?"

That consisted of his thumb sliding inside me while Cathy fondled my breasts.

"Wait!" I said and wrenched myself away from them. "Look, you're working me up so I'll agree to something, right? I won't do anything involving drugs or prostitution. Or anything else illegal."

"Hey, this girl's sharp. Okay. You want to come first or after?"

I laughed, despite my aroused state, and reached for the bathrobe. I sat a little distance away from them on an ottoman. Both Jake and Willis had erections poking the fabric of their underwear and I leaned back, hands on the edges of the ottoman and parted my legs, just a little. Just enough for them to get a good view of my pussy. I wasn't sure what they wanted, but they'd played dirty pool.

Jake and Willis exchanged a glance. "You tell her, man," Jake said.

8

"WELL, NOW, THAT IS VERY INTERESTING," MR. D. said.

"I think it's sensible if you want to fool around with more than one person. That's why the club was formed, apparently, so that people could feel safe in a discreet environment. The way they described it was odd, though—as if the whole structure and all the Baroque rules were a joke, yet in a way they believed in them."

"So you signed on the dotted line?"

"Not yet. The contract looks rather more serious than I thought it would. I'm going to get someone to take a look at it."

"Very wise." He cleared his throat. "You're an amazing woman."

"Does that mean you want to know what happened next?" I was a little disappointed. Here I was about to sign away my soul—in a sense—and Mr. D. wanted the end of the story. I guess this was what Scheherazade felt like when she'd had a bad day in the harem or the eunuchs had been particularly annoying.

So I told him.

I teased him a little, making him think we'd abandoned the fooling around and sat down for a serious discussion on the Rockies Investment Association, or as they affectionately called it, the Getting Your Rocks Off Association. No pressure, they assured me, and even though there was a written agreement it was all based on trust and mutual respect.

"I can't tell you any more," I said to Mr. D. "It's confidential."

He groaned. "You're a cock-tease. So you got dressed, had a cup of coffee and polite conversation and then went home?"

"Not exactly."

"Well?"

"Okay." I relented. "As you may remember, I was busy flashing Jake and Willis. And you know I'd told you there was a collection of dildos on the coffee table?"

I told Jake he could send me a copy of the contract and allowed my legs to part a little more, leaning back onto my hands.

Cathy, who'd been sitting next to Jake, wriggled forward to take a look, too. "She's being a naughty girl, don't you think, honey?"

"Yeah. Nice girls keep their legs together."

"Then I can't be a nice girl."

Jake moved to my side and ran his hand along my collarbone. "Okay?" he said, very quietly, without any of his former crudeness, and I realized he was asking permission to kiss me; and he was asking Willis, too.

Willis, sprawled on the couch, nodded.

I turned my face to Jake's and his tongue slid along my lips, prompting me to open. Someone—I wasn't sure if it was Willis or Cathy—untied the bathrobe and pushed it back from my body, touching my nipples lightly in passing.

Jake's arm supported me as our kiss deepened and our breathing became quicker and uneven. His mouth moved to my collarbone and breast. My head fell back. Someone else stroked my belly and thighs and I felt something hard and slick nudge my pussy.

"Yeah, that's right," Willis muttered. "Oh, damn, yes."

But it wasn't flesh that pushed into me, stretching me. Something buzzed gently and I almost jumped out of my skin as the buzz became something more than a sound. I opened my eyes to see Cathy pushing a dildo inside me, while with her other hand she'd fixed a small, lipstick-size vibrator against my clitoris. I wasn't entirely surprised but at the same time I wasn't shocked, or not much. And there was such a feeling of luxury to be the center of attention, to be the one who was being done, fucked, pleasured, with no demands made that I reciprocate.

"Is that nice, honey?" she asked. "I love it when Jake does that to my breasts."

Jake's fingers stroked and pinched my nipples, moving from one breast to the other with a delicious sense of timing; he knew exactly when to make the switch, when to bring one nipple to a painful intensity of feeling as the other demanded equal attention.

Willis sat on the couch, his underwear pushed down, cock in his hand, stroking himself.

"I want to see you come," I told him. I was getting very close, watching Jake's hand on my breasts and Cathy's manipulation of the dildo and vibrator—my legs were spread wide and raised now, and as I watched she pulled out the silicone cock, gleaming with lube and my juices, and rubbed the head on my clit, briefly replacing the vibrator, then drove it back inside me.

Willis's face was flushed, and his hand moved faster. "I'm going to come," he panted. His legs flexed, his face set and driven.

"Wait for Jo, honey," Cathy said. "Grab a towel." The towel

instruction made me snort with laughter but in no way diminished my increasing excitement.

"Oh, Christ," said Willis. An arc of semen splashed onto the coffee table.

"Oh, *Willis*," Cathy said as though she were June Cleaver and he'd trodden mud over a clean kitchen floor. More semen looped and splashed, this time onto the towel he'd managed to grab, and he groaned loudly, semen dribbling from his cock onto his fist.

"You're so gorgeous," Cathy whispered. She bent her lips to the nipple that was awaiting its turn and sucked, hard, and I came, in a great lurching rush that doubled me up, and left me gasping for breath.

As the spasms subsided I sagged back against Jake's arm. Cathy slid the dildo into me more gently now, and I reached down to push away the vibrator, which was almost painful post-orgasm. Things felt very wet down below, with the lube and my juices, and I was glad Cathy's upholstery was protected by terrycloth.

"Okay, Jo?" Willis was now ready for round three, erect again in record time. I wasn't sure that I was. My legs were like jelly and I was trembling still from the intensity of my orgasm. My mouth was dry from all the gasping and I could barely move.

"Great," I managed to say, and rolled off the ottoman onto the floor in an undignified heap. I decided I'd watch this round. I managed to stagger to the bar for some more wine and settled into a huge, oversize armchair. Was it my social duty to masturbate? I really didn't have the energy and I knew that after the mindless buzz of the vibrator I'd be pretty numb. No, this was time-out.

Cathy was on Jake's lap again, her bathrobe discarded, kissing him. He kissed well, I'd found, even if I didn't like him particularly (little lady!), and I found myself grateful for his gentleness and expertise. Would Cathy get the same sort of experience?

Apparently not. She giggled as the two guys conferred over the basket of silicone goodies. "Not that one! I won't be able to go to the bathroom for a week!"

"Pretty little pink one?" Willis dangled one of the smaller butt-plugs between two fingers.

"Oh, okay." She stood and bent over, spreading her butt cheeks. "Make sure the lube is warmed up. I—ooh!"

"Gorgeous," Jake said, staring at the invasion of his wife's butt. "Hot damn, girl."

He stood and dropped his underwear.

It was sexy and funny at the same time, the two guys jostling together for a better look at the bright pink projection in Cathy's ass, their cocks bobbing in the air. It made me uncomfortable, too, in a particularly squirmy sort of way that was partly curiosity and repulsion, and yes, a bit of desire in the mix. I'd never gone in for any sort of anal play, other than a discreet, nicely lubed forefinger (and only up to the first knuckle—Hugh had large hands). Cathy, from her flushed face and parted lips, seemed to be enjoying herself immensely as Jake kneaded her (or possibly his) birthday presents, a far cry from his subtle manipulations of my breasts. She was sitting on Willis's lap and shifted onto his penis with a small whimper—oh, yes, she'd feel stretched and doubly invaded now. She and Jake kissed deeply.

I held my breath. Who would deal with Jake's erect cock? Willis's hands were on Cathy's hips, guiding her, and he could easily reach Jake. But Cathy broke the kiss and slid Jake's dark shiny cock into her mouth. All three of them swayed together, Cathy pleasuring Jake and moving on Willis's cock while he rested against the back of the sofa, eyes closed. They produced a symphony of murmurs and groans, the quiet slap of flesh, three people whose relationship I could barely attempt to understand.

I envied them their closeness at that moment, the trust between them, their unselfconsciousness.

Willis reached forward to stroke Cathy's hair and she removed her mouth from Jake's cock to turn and smile at him. There was a brief, silent exchange between them, a moment of yearning from Willis, a glimpse into something private and painful on his part, which Cathy responded to with regretful, apologetic affection.

I sipped my wine and wondered about risks I hadn't really considered before. Not the physical risks of sexual encounters but the possibility that love might come sneaking up on you, taking you unawares and leaving you powerless.

My clothes lay strewn on the floor near the bar and I moved quietly to retrieve them. I dressed at the bottom of the stairs leading to the first floor of the house; they wouldn't be able to see me if they even cared where I was. Shoes in hand, I tiptoed up the stairs and found my jacket and purse in a closet.

A magazine and some mail lay on a shelf in the hall and I found the address and called for a cab. I didn't think they even noticed that I had left.

"Are you busy?"

Jo hovered at Patrick's doorway, a large envelope in one hand and a plate of cookies in the other.

"No. Come on in."

She peered around him as though looking at a dragon's den. "It's just that Kimberly said you were a lawyer, and…"

"I'm sort of a lawyer."

"Oh. What is a sort of a lawyer? Could you take a sort of look at something for me?"

"Sure. I passed the bar and couldn't find a job. I'd put myself through law school doing web design and not sleeping, so I kept on doing it."

"Does not sleeping pay well?" She wandered in and gazed

at his panoply of computers. She was barefooted, in jeans and a sweater with a hole in one elbow, her hair on end. As though suddenly remembering the cookies, she thrust the plate at him. "For you."

"Thanks. You didn't have to—"

"I'll pay you, of course. These are a gift. It's okay, I didn't make them."

He took a bite of one. "They're good. Can't you make cookies?"

She shook her head. "Whenever the recipe says to drop them onto the sheet, they stay in little lumps. I think it might be the altitude." The cat strolled into his apartment through the open door, and she scooped him up. "I'll put him outside."

"He's okay."

As he cleared some papers from a chair for her his cell rang. He glanced at it and shut it off. She raised her eyebrows. "One of my clients has forgotten her password. She always updates on Monday afternoons and she always forgets her password. So, what is this you want me to look at?"

She handed him a contract for something called the Rockies Investment Association and sat quietly while he read, the cat on her lap purring and digging his claws into her denim-clad thighs.

"Okay," he said. "You know this is a bunch of pretentious crap, don't you?"

She smiled. "Yeah."

"It seems an odd sort of thing for an investment club to have. All this emphasis on confidentiality."

Her hand moved to stroke the cat's chin. His eyes closed, the purring getting louder. "Oh, there was some hassle with insider trading a few years back."

"And this bothers me. Look." He pointed at a paragraph. "You're being asked to agree to the rules of the club but there isn't an addendum with the rules on it. So essentially you're agreeing to something unknown. And they don't spell out the penalties for leaving the club without thirty days' notice."

"That's all they sent."

And sent by courier, too. "Well, an investment club. It's not like they're going to ask you to swing naked from the chandeliers or anything."

A quick flash of something in her eyes and the cat uncoiled and dropped to the floor with a thud. "So how legally binding is this?"

He grinned. "As legally binding as anything with your signature. But as I said, it's legalistic crap. It's meant to intimidate you, make you think you're getting into something special." He took another bite of cookie and brushed crumbs from the paper. "Don't put in any more than the initial one hundred they ask for until you see how your money does, and cross out a few things for the heck of it. This is a contract. It's the start of a negotiation, not the Ten Commandments. And keep a copy."

"Thanks." She smiled. "I should pay you for your time."

I'll take a blow job, please.

Where in God's name did that come from, with Kimberly depleting his sperm stock every night? He almost choked on his cookie.

She regarded him with mild concern. "Are you okay?"

"Fine, fine." A pen and some other small items cascaded from his desk as the cat sauntered across it with a fine disregard of property and settled on the windowsill.

She rose. "Bad cat. Come here."

"He's fine. No, for God's sake, you don't have to pay me. You'd figured out this was crap on your own. Thanks for the cookies."

She tucked the contract under her arm and scooped the cat from the windowsill. "You've been very helpful. Thanks."

She went back into the house, leaving him unsettled. He suspected the Rockies Investment Association was not all that it might seem on paper, but ultimately it was her business, her decision. If his relationship with Elise had taught him anything, it was to think twice before jumping in to protect someone when they didn't need or want rescue.

Even when every instinct you had told you that you were right.

"And so I'm invited to lunch with some sort of committee tomorrow," I told Mr. D.

"A committee. Lunch."

"Do you think they're going to screw me on a pristine white tablecloth in the private room of some tasteful, discreet restaurant?"

"You have a way of filling my mind with the most shocking images. Tell me more."

So I told him that naturally I wouldn't wear panties. I'd wear stockings and a garter belt and a severe black suit with a skirt at knee level, the jacket showing just a hint of cleavage and red lace that matched my lipstick. No bra, just a silk camisole, and the jacket thin enough to show my erect nipples.

"Lipstick?"

"Oh, yeah. Bright red lipstick, my best bitch lipstick."

Imagine it, I tell him…

We've had a careful lunch served by a pair of deferential, respectful waiters who nevertheless exchanged glances that they thought I didn't see. *So this is the latest one…* Or maybe they hoped I would see. The food was delicious and sensual, a salad of beets and goat cheese and greens that tasted of spring and sunlight, nuts scattered over all. Steak, rare, that left a smear of bloody juice on the plate. Wine, of course, something pale and expensive and complex.

For dessert, a chocolate mousse served in a martini glass with a saucy curl of dark chocolate peeking over the edge, and coffee served in exquisite, tiny porcelain cups. A plate of tiny sweet strawberries in case anyone needed an extra little nibble.

Willis and Jake were there, observing me, watching my tongue and lips as I ate, and the Chairman, a middle-aged man in a beautiful suit that had the drape of silk and the heft of a fine wool. He was handsome, powerful, his dark hair sprinkled with gray, features chiseled and masculine, with piercing, deep-set brown eyes.

"You, Mr. D."

"My dear, you flatter me. I'm not nearly so good-looking."

"So you see, Miss Hutchinson, trust is absolute. You do understand."

I dabbed at my lips with the fine linen napkin. "Of course."

"Well, then, how about—shall we say, Wednesday night? We'll send a limo for you."

I nodded in agreement. "Thank you for the delicious lunch."

"My pleasure. But before you go, Miss Hutchinson, there's one more thing." He beckoned to one of the waiters, who stepped forward. "A gesture of good faith, if you will."

I stood. I knew what he wanted. The waiter was quite young, probably a college kid putting himself through school, dark-haired, with small gold-rimmed glasses, a gold ring in one ear. He stepped past me with a word of apology and cleared the table. I took my lipstick from my purse and reapplied it. Jake nodded at me and I removed the jacket, revealing the silk and my hard, excited nipples.

The waiter brushed crumbs from the tablecloth with a small silver-handled brush into a cute little silver dustpan, then stepped aside.

"Pretty, isn't she?" the Chairman said to the waiter. "Would you like to fuck her?"

He blinked and stared at the Chairman and then at my nipples.

"Go on. Touch them."

I smiled at him encouragingly. He wore a long white apron and black pants, but a sizable bulge showed in the apron now. His hand drifted across my nipples.

"Continue." The Chairman beckoned to the other waiter, who brought brandy and glasses for the three men, the spectators, and then a small silver tray with a condom on it. He returned to his station on the opposite side of the room, watching.

I pulled my skirt above my hips, feeling cool air caress my thighs and butt. I leaned against the table, supporting myself on my hands.

"I did mention I was wearing high heels, didn't I?"

"Oh, God. Go on."

The table edge pressed into my pussy. I parted my legs, steadying myself.

Behind me the waiter untied his apron; I heard the rustle of linen, followed by the small sound of a button releasing, the hiss of a zipper. His hands grasped my hips. One hand dipped between my thighs and lingered on the wetness, dabbling, preparing me.

His finger slid into me. I watched the faces of the three men around the table, who, despite their languid poses and their glasses of brandy, radiated tension. The Chairman raised one eyebrow; he had detected a change of stance, a shift in my position.

"Is all well, Miss Hutchinson? Will you share with us what Ben is doing?"

"His finger is inside me. Now two. Three." I moaned a little.

"I assure you his cock is bigger than that. Isn't it, Ben?"

"Yes, sir."

"Show us, Ben. Miss Hutchinson, stay where you are, please."

The waiter stepped back a little and his feet shuffled on the carpet. I loved this, although I couldn't see it, the display of his erect penis to the others. Across the room the other waiter watched. He shifted and lowered his hand to his crotch, in the unselfconscious way men will when dealing with a troublesome erection. Was it Ben's display that excited him, or the prospect of the fucking that was to follow?

"Very workmanlike," the Chairman commented. "Yes, I think that will do. What do you think, gentleman? Uncut, you will notice."

The tear and snap of a condom and then something hard and slick rubbed against my butt. I caught my breath. My camisole gaped open, revealing my breasts and erect nipples to the men at the table and the waiter opposite. I raised a hand to pinch them into still harder peaks.

Small motions of their shoulders and hands below the tablecloth told me that Jake and Willis were masturbating. The Chairman, however, sat motionless, both hands on the surface of the table.

Ben continued to rub his cock against my butt for a while, occasionally dipping it between my legs. He reached one hand to pinch my nipples as I had done, his gesture bringing the faint scent of a kitchen, the aromas of oil and meat and onion and smoke to my nostrils. His fingers were faintly dusted with black hair.

He pushed inside me and I gasped. I hadn't appreciated how large he was or how eager. He took his hand from my breast and gripped my hips again, pumping into me. Opposite me the other waiter had pushed his apron aside and unzipped, his cock in his hand, rubbing frantically. Jake and Willis were both red in the face and openly excited now, but I noticed they each had a hand reached across to jerk the other off. I would have liked to watch them do it, but this was not a time for me to watch and enjoy. I was the main attraction.

Willis was the first to succumb, groaning loudly and arching back in his chair. The waiter against the wall came seconds later, catching his semen in his apron.

Ben pumped faster now, slapping against me. He hesitated, poised, gasped, his hands slick on my skin, and shuddered against me.

I ground my pussy against the table. I understood that my orgasm wasn't the point of this exercise, but that didn't stop me wanting one.

"Thank you, Ben, Miss Hutchinson," the Chairman said. Other than a certain brightness around his eyes, he seemed unmoved.

Ben slid out from me and I heard the rustle of clothing and his zip going up again.

The Chairman rolled his chair out from the table, knees spread wide. An impressive bulge showed at his crotch. "If you will, Miss Hutchinson. No, the skirt stays as it is."

I dropped to my knees and crawled over to him on all fours. My pussy was swollen and I wanted an orgasm badly. Maybe if I squeezed my knees together…

I fumbled with the Chairman's zipper and slipped my hand inside his pants. I couldn't resist teasing him a little. Yes, warm fabric—silk, of course—and a large, ridged bulge. I unsnapped the fastening at the waistband of his pants and laid the fabric aside, then delved into his silk boxers. His cock sprang out, powerful and curving, the open slit hinting at the extent of his arousal. A warm, salty scent rose to my nostrils.

I heard Jake and Willis moving around, finding better positions to watch the proceedings.

"Legs apart, Miss Hutchinson," the Chairman murmured.

Damn. My pussy and butt were exposed for their enjoyment, but not for mine. I bent to lick his cock, a little intimidated by its size, tasting him, tracing the blue veins that decorated its length. I closed my mouth over the plumlike head….

"Dark red, right, Mr. D.?"

"God, yes. Take me in your mouth now. All of me."

And I did, breathing through my nose, his pubic hairs coarse and fragrant, careful with the task to which I had been entrusted. I cupped his balls with my hand, stroking the sensitive area beyond them, and offered the occasional, delicate scratch.

He didn't make a sound. One hand moved to my head in a gentle yet commanding caress.

Behind me I heard the wet, rhythmic slap of a palm against a cock. Or maybe more than one, as the Chairman took his pleasure to the delight of the onlookers. And take his pleasure he did, maintaining that silence and self-control, with only the tightening of his calf muscles against my sides and a sudden movement of his hand on my head to exert a little more pressure. That was all. I doubt his expression changed. He sucked in a deep breath and held it, then let the air out as my mouth flooded with his warm semen.

I swallowed and withdrew with a respectful kiss to his flaccid cock. With the utmost courtesy, the Chairman handed me a napkin to wipe my mouth. He took another to pat himself dry, and then fastened his pants.

"Very good. More wine, Miss Hutchinson? Or a glass of water?"

I declined both. What I really wanted to do was come, and I think he knew that.

"Let the poor girl jerk herself off," Willis said. "You'd like that, wouldn't you, Jo?"

"Miss Hutchinson?"

I cleared my throat. "Thank you."

Ben moved forward to pull out a chair for me. With my skirt still tucked up around my waist I sat and hooked my legs over the arms, revealing my wet and swollen pussy. The room was absolutely silent. The waiter standing against the wall took his cock out again, but a glance from the Chairman

made him swallow and flush in embarrassment and quickly tuck himself away.

I licked my finger—not that I needed any more wetness, but I thought it a sexy sort of gesture all the guys would appreciate—and stroked my nipples, knowing the silk would cling to them.

And then I masturbated, rubbing myself hard and fast, while the men watched, for the most part impassive. Jake licked his lips at one point, which made me shake with lust (he knew it; he winked at me) and Willis reached down to adjust his cock then sat, legs apart, his erection pushing through his pants. The Chairman watched with a genial smile, which somehow seemed the sexiest thing in the world.

My orgasm roared through me and I moaned loudly. The Chairman raised his eyebrows, looking mildly amused, while I jerked and thrashed around in the chair, before subsiding, limp and satisfied, my arms and legs hanging.

"A delightful lunch," the Chairman pronounced. "Thank you, Miss Hutchinson."

Jake reached a hand to help me to my feet. I straightened my skirt and buttoned my jacket again, and we left the private room of the restaurant, passing a few late lunch parties. I wondered if they had any idea of what had taken place behind the closed doors.

Mr. D. enjoyed my naughty fabrication so much (The Chairman! All those outsize dicks! The waiter presenting a condom on a silver tray! I was quite proud of my inventiveness….) I didn't have the heart to tell him the next day that the Chairman was in fact a guy a few years older than me with reddish hair called Harry, who was an accountant, and that we met in a sports bar and ate hamburgers and fries.

"Oh, yeah," Harry said, "the rules. Don't worry about them,

Jo. It's more fun if you find out as you go." He winked at me. "Safe, discreet, sexy. That's all you need to know right now. Another beer?"

9

"IT'S SNOWING!"

I turned the monitor down and tucked the phone under my chin. "Kimberly, at eight thousand feet sometimes it does snow."

"You can't bicycle home. We're coming to pick you up. But not too late. Your intern's in tonight, right? So you can prerecord and we'll come get you at ten."

I glanced at the clock. "Okay. Can you make it ten-thirty?"

There was a pause. "What's up? You really want to stay later?"

"No. Yes. I mean, thanks. That's real thoughtful of you. I appreciate it."

Yes, I appreciated the offer of the ride home, but it meant I wouldn't talk to Mr. D. I'd also had to delay my first experience with the Rockies Investment Association, since Mother Nature had stopped by and I had cramps and a huge zit on my chin. An early night might be what I really needed.

Snow, the first snow of the year. I went out of the studio to the office area and looked out of a window. It was settling on grass and trees already, falling silent, with small flakes that promised a drop in temperature. I thought with anticipation of my skis and poles, and rushed back to the studio to prepare a full weather report and cue up the "Dance of the Snowflakes" from the *Nutcracker.*

Poor Kimberly. She'd never quite accepted that at this altitude sometimes it snowed, and spent every winter in an agony of anxiety about snow tires and investing heavily in cashmere and leather accessories. Her idea of skiing was hanging out at the bar at a ski lodge; I'd tried to get her to cross-country ski with me one time and she was horrified at the possibility of maybe having to go to the bathroom outdoors. I quipped that if there was a bathroom there, it would be okay. She didn't think it funny.

I programmed three hours of music and announcements into the computer and chatted with my intern for a time. It was after ten-twenty now, and I knew Kimberly would be late, so I settled in to edit sound bites for on-air fundraising. We'd invited some of our longtime listeners, and a few new ones who'd made themselves known to us by calling or emailing with enthusiastic praise, to record their thoughts about what the station meant to them. Some had dried up, tongue-tied and embarrassed, at the microphone; others had chatted with abandon.

Like this one, six minutes of a blow-by-blow description of her morning routine, and how listening to the news started her day (and her husband's, the two dogs', the cat's and her baby's), which I'd reduce to thirty seconds while keeping her enthusiasm intact. Highlight, snip. Highlight, move. Keep her breath in there so she sounded like a human being.

The phone rang, but it was an internal line. Kimberly and Patrick had arrived. I asked them to give me a few moments to finish my work and then gathered my things together.

Ann, my intern, took over in the studio, and I made my way through the dark building to the entrance. At first I didn't think Kimberly and Patrick were there because the lights weren't on, and then I heard a rustle and a soft sigh from the sofa.

I stopped dead, my hand on the light switch, considering a loud throat clear before illuminating them. As my eyes became accustomed to the dim light, a little outside light from the street made soft by the pearly quality of a falling snow, I saw what they were doing and froze.

Yes, they were making out. Kimberly's blond hair spilled over Patrick's shoulders, and her gloves and scarf lay on the floor. As I watched, he lifted his head from hers and nibbled under her ear. I heard her make a small sound of pleasure, that same soft sigh I'd heard earlier. His hands moved to her blouse, unbuttoning, her skin gleaming pale in the dim light. They looked like an old black-and-white movie, no color, just monochromatic shades, moving slowly as though underwater. Or maybe that was me, my perception of the scene slowing it down so that I noticed every move, every small noise.

Her head tipped back, eyes closed, and Patrick's mouth moved across her collarbones. And down. A rustle and the rush of nylon against skin indicated that he'd unfastened her bra. Her hand smoothed across his head and she raised one knee to rub her calf against his.

I caught a glimpse of her breast, full and white, the nipple large and darkened before he lowered his head there.

Oh, jeez, was my first thought. I couldn't possibly walk in on them now. But I didn't want to. This was far more erotic than Jake and Cathy's naked, professional fucking, possibly because I knew them both, my best friend and my number-one mouse killer. And they were unaware of my presence; they weren't performing or putting on any show; they were pleasing each other (although the thought crossed my mind that maybe they liked fooling around in places where they could get caught).

Patrick moved his arm—I couldn't see, but I think he'd held

her breast while he suckled it—and slid his hand over her thigh and then inside, pushing her skirt up. She wore stockings, the real things with garters—proof, as Kimberly had once told me, that she really liked a guy, because who'd want to end up with strange indentations on their thighs? His hand moved with a steady rhythm in the darkness.

He raised his head to watch her face. Her mouth was open. She had that same distant look we all get when we're on our way to a really good orgasm and her freed breast moved as she sucked in air. Oh, God. I was watching my best friend have an orgasm, but I couldn't stop looking or stop myself enjoying it, either. And I was listening, too, because now her breathing accelerated and she gasped a little. At the same time, they barely moved. She seemed frozen, and Patrick—I knew his hand moved, but if I hadn't known what they were doing I would have thought them a statue.

Patrick murmured something to her. I couldn't catch his words, but whatever it was sent her over the top. He fastened on to her breast again as she arched up—I felt it in my breast, between my thighs—and then she writhed, moaning in a fairly restrained way that I admired. I was fairly convinced that my orgasms were, to the viewer, an undignified thrashing about.

She subsided and reached a hand down to his, stilling it, then lifted his fingers to her mouth and licked them.

Oh, you naughty girl, Kimberly.

She reached for his zipper.

He put her hand aside, to my disappointment, and said something about the time, then leaned to kiss her on the lips. She nodded and reached behind herself to fasten her bra, while Patrick straightened her skirt (and also reached down to adjust his dick, I couldn't help noticing).

Kimberly smiled at him as he buttoned her shirt. She reached into her purse and pulled out her cell. I came back to life then as my cell buzzed against my hip and tiptoed back down the corridor. I was pretty sure they hadn't been aware of my presence and I needed a moment to collect myself, and also give the illusion that I was on the point of leaving the studio.

"I'm just finishing up." My voice sounded a bit hoarse. "Where are you?"

When I returned to the front, the light was on. Kimberly, talking and applying lipstick at the same time, complained about the weather. She was her normal lively, if angsty, self and I wondered if I'd imagined the erotic scene I'd just witnessed.

"Oh, it's so pretty!" I exclaimed. "We must have an inch or more out there already."

"It'll be a disaster driving into work tomorrow," Kimberly moaned.

"Where's your bike, Jo?" Patrick asked. "I'll drive."

He must have learned that Kimberly's idea of driving in the snow was to creep along at about walking pace, straddling two lanes.

Outside it was magical, silent and cold. Our breath puffed out in the air and snowflakes landed on my eyelashes, my lips, as I gazed up at the sky.

Behind me, Kimberly's agonized monologue on the loathsome weather continued while Patrick loaded my bicycle into the hatchback of Kimberly's car.

I scraped a handful of snow from the ground, formed it into a snowball and threw it at her.

"Not funny!" She dived into the front seat of the car.

A snowball hit me on the side of my neck. Patrick, his glasses gleaming, grinned at me. "You throw like a girl," he commented.

"I am a girl." I grabbed up some more snow and lobbed it at him.

"Let's go!" Kimberly wailed as though a pack of wolves were about to descend upon us, or we would have to resort to cannibalism to keep body and soul together.

Patrick and I exchanged a glance and returned to the car, shaking snow from our jackets.

Kimberly handed me a tissue. "You are such a mess."

"It was fun," I said, mopping at my face.

"Snow is not fun. Is it, Patrick?"

"It is, but it's not as fun as you," he said, which sent both of us into a fit of giggles. He drove through the snow with Kimberly grabbing for his arm and her seat belt every time we took a corner, but by the time we arrived at my house she was laughing, too.

"Have you eaten? I can open a bottle of wine," I said as I hoisted my bicycle out of the car.

I led them into the kitchen and fixed a grilled cheese sandwich for myself. They'd been out to eat.

"I want to see your place, Patrick," Kimberly said, looking at my wine collection, which was down to only a few bottles; Hugh was the one who bought the wine. I bought peanut butter. She plucked out a bottle and frowned. "I guess this will do."

"Shall I check the traps?" Patrick asked me.

"Gross. She has you doing that? Ask her for a reduction in rent."

"Oh, I think we live in a mouse-free zone now. Sure, come and see my place." He took the bottle and glasses and led the way upstairs and through the dividing door into his apartment.

"Where are the candles I gave you?" Kimberly asked, shedding cashmere garments onto his desk.

"Sorry, I'm not really a candle sort of guy." But he opened a cabinet and found candles and lit them, while Kimberly flitted around the room organizing things. It drove me mad when she did that, pushing a picture frame an inch or so to one side, rearranging other items—not that Patrick had many items for her to rearrange—yet her efforts mysteriously improved the room.

She folded a screen back, revealing a bed, and straightened

the cover. "You need some throw pillows. I'll get you some. Don't you think so, Jo?"

"Don't bully him," I said. I opened the bottle of wine. "Guys don't like throw pillows. They sit on them and burst the filling out or throw them on the floor. Right, Patrick?"

"Absolutely." Patrick pushed one of the glasses away, shaking his head. "Not for me, thanks."

"Are you sure?"

"I don't metabolize alcohol well. It's the Irish genes." He opened his miniscule refrigerator and grabbed a bottle of water.

"This is a really cute place!" Kimberly cried. "Very European. You've used the space so well. Did Jo help you pull it together?"

"No, her, uh, boyfriend helped."

"Hugh? But he'd moved out by then."

"No, the other one. Jason."

She gave me a questioning frown. I knew that look. She'd be all over me the next time she got me alone, cross-examining me for lurid details.

"Come sit down, darlin'," she cooed to both of us and we sat on the bed. I realized then that Kimberly had had a fair amount of wine at dinner.

Patrick smiled brightly. "Two lovely women in my bed. Have I died and gone to heaven?"

"*On* your bed," I said. "It's a major difference."

"A man can dream." He raised his bottle of water in a salute.

Kimberly giggled. "Have you ever had a threesome?"

"Not yet," Patrick said. "But ask me again in about fifteen minutes."

"Jo?"

I shook my head.

Kimberly eased a cowboy boot off and put her stockinged foot on Patrick's thigh. "I've never even kissed a girl," she said. "Not since junior high."

"Tell me more," Patrick said.

"If I were to kiss a girl now, it'd be Jo. She's so cute." She looked at me, blinking. "You have dirt on your face from your games in the snow. Honey…" She beckoned to me.

I leaned forward, wondering what she wanted, and she kissed me in a clumsy, drunken sort of way.

"Steady, cowgirl," I said, pushing her away.

She collapsed onto Patrick's lap. "You kiss her now."

"Maybe he doesn't want to." I really hoped Kimberly wouldn't remember this in the morning.

Patrick took my chin in his hand and give me a firm, brotherly kiss on the cheek. He grinned. "Time to take your kit off, girls."

"I'm on my period," I said, matching his facetiousness.

He rolled his eyes. "We can put a towel down."

"Oh, don't be gross," Kimberly said. A second later she let out a snore.

Patrick and I looked at each other. She was fast asleep on the bed, her skirt riding up, revealing the top of one stocking.

He straightened her skirt and removed her other boot.

I took the throw from the foot of the bed and folded it over her. She'd be furious when she woke in the morning and found she'd neglected her usual rigorous cleansing-and-toning routine.

I unfastened her earrings and laid them on the small bedside table. "Don't let her drive home if she wakes up."

"She's out for the night." He stood looking down at Kimberly, an odd expression on his face, tenderness and regret mixed.

"You okay?"

"What? Oh, yeah. Just disappointed that I won't be hearing more about junior high."

"Me, too." I hesitated. "You have dirt on your face, too."

"Do I?" He scrubbed at his face.

I stepped forward and rubbed his cheek with my thumb.

"Not tonight, Josephine," he said. "I've always wanted to say that. Is it Josephine?"

"Yeah. I hated it for years."

"Jo suits you better."

There was a pause. I still had my hand on his face and I stepped back, feeling like a fool. "Good night, then."

I grabbed the bottle and glasses and fled back to my side of the house, unnerved by that moment of contact and the intensity of his gaze. My thumb still held the warmth of his cheekbone.

What the hell was I doing?

"Hey, wake up."

I could smell coffee. I opened an eye to see Kimberly sitting on my bed, a cup of coffee in each hand and a bundle of clothes beneath her arms. Mascara was smeared beneath her eyes and she wore a plaid dressing gown that had to belong to Patrick.

"Thanks." I took one of the cups and sat, rubbing my face and hair. "You okay?"

"Fine. We broke up."

"What?"

"Yeah, I know it sounds real dramatic. It isn't. I was his rebound girl and other than the screwing we don't have a lot in common. He's a nice guy, though." She looked away as she said it.

"And you're okay with it?"

"I guess. He broke it off." She laughed. "I'm suffering from hurt pride. I'm the one who breaks things off. And it was after we had sex this morning."

"Jerk," I said.

"Nah. I was the one who grabbed his pecker. I was pretty insistent. I guess he was being polite. Real polite. Very considerate, very... I mean, the guy knows what he's doing, as far as fucking goes." She dropped her clothes onto my bed, cowboy boots tumbling on the floor, and wandered to the window and pulled the blinds up. "They ploughed. We got about six inches, I figure. Do you have eye-makeup remover?"

"Sure. Help yourself. You know where the towels are."

She made a move toward the bathroom but turned, her hand on the door. "So what happened last night? I was drunk as a skunk."

"Not much. You fell asleep and snored a bit."

She made a face and retreated into the bathroom. I listened to the shower run and breathed a sigh of relief.

After a half-hour she emerged, her hair wet and wrapped in a towel, her face clean and shining.

"Why didn't you tell me about Jason?"

Good question, and why did she have to remember my embarrassing revelation and not her own? I swung my legs out of bed and headed for the bathroom, muttering that I had to pee.

When I came back out she sat in front of the mirror braiding her wet hair. Her reflected eyes sought mine.

"We don't have secrets from each other," she said. "We've known each other for five years, Jo, and it's not just whatever happened with Jason. I feel left out. What's going on? You're not in any sort of trouble, are you? Is everything okay with Willis? Because you can tell me. You can tell me anything."

"I know. I'm not in trouble, Kimberly, and I don't think I'm dating Willis anymore. He hasn't called in a couple of days. He was a nice guy, but he really wasn't my type, and I wasn't his."

She pulled her cowboy boots on. From outside came the scrape of a snow shovel.

"Patrick's shoveling the drive, bless his heart," she said.

"And about Jason—technically it's sexual harassment. We decided to keep it quiet, and since he wasn't going to tell anyone, I couldn't, either. He's a lot of fun. No hidden piercings, though he has a cute tattoo on his shoulder. Lots of stamina. Pretty dick."

"Okay." She looked slightly mollified.

"Want some breakfast?"

"No, I'll get going, but thanks. I need to get home and change for work. You sure you're okay?"

"I'm fine. Are you okay?"

She shrugged. "I guess so. I'm gonna find me a nice lawyer—a real one—or an accountant."

"There's no accounting for taste," I said, which made her laugh. I was relieved.

I accompanied her downstairs and refilled our coffee mugs while she knotted her cashmere scarf around her neck.

"Kimberly," I said as she was about to leave, "have you ever felt that your fantasies were better than the real thing?"

"We are talking about sex, I assume?" She paused in pulling on a pair of beautiful leather gauntlets. Even by looking at them I could tell they were buttery soft. "Isn't that what fantasies are all about?"

"I guess so."

"Honey." She poked my shoulder. "You let me know when you're ready to drop the fantasies for a few hours and come back into the real world, you hear? There are friends out here, and real people, and it might not be so bad."

She swayed out through the front door and Patrick paused to lean on his shovel. They had a brief conversation and kissed each other on the cheek with, as far as I could tell, a fair amount of affection.

He'd kissed me on the cheek, too, last night, but it had felt like something far more intimate. I remembered the grip of his hand on my chin, followed by that overly long moment when he gazed into my eyes and my thumb slowed on his face.

The guy knows what he's doing. High praise from Kimberly.

I could believe it.

★ ★ ★

"Purse, cell phone, watch. Here's your locker combination." The woman eyed me up as she handed me a slip of paper. She looked like Mrs. Danvers in black leather.

I nodded, memorized the code and slipped the phone into my pocket.

"Want to take off your jacket, honey? They like to show off their bodies. It's very competitive. Boots off, too, we have a no-shoes rule in the house."

"Okay." I unbuttoned my denim jacket and stowed it in the locker. I wore a skimpy little camisole beneath that had cost a lot of money, supersoft cotton with a discreet lace trim.

The room had a tiled floor and white walls, lockers along one side, chilly and brightly lit. The only furniture was a wooden bench. I'd had a glimpse of the turn-of-the-century mansion as we drove by, the imposing front door flanked by panels of opulent stained glass. But the limousine had continued to drop me off at a modest side door; quite definitely where the hired help entered the house.

Mrs. Leather Danvers looked at me with a great deal of interest. "Very nice. Ah, here's Harry to go over the ground rules."

Harry entered the room. When I'd met him before he'd worn a suit, but tonight he was in jeans and a T-shirt, feet bare, and carried a clipboard and a binder under one arm. He glanced at me with approval, particularly at my nipples, which had perked up with the cold air.

"Welcome!" He kissed my cheek. "Great to have you with us, Jo. Okay, Angela, I can take over now."

Mrs. Danvers gave a regal nod and left the room, striding confidently on her spiked heels, black leather creaking. So much for the no-shoes rule.

"Silly old dyke," Harry said under his breath. And then to me, "So, ground rules. You'll be in the Great Room with the others. No penetration, no orgasms, that's the main rule. Two main rules, I should say." He consulted the clipboard. "You had your tests done yesterday, that's good—as soon as those results come back clean, you can start thinking of moving up. Unless you like it in the Great Room. You're welcome to stay there, some of them do, but if you actually want some fucking on your own terms, you need to think about progressing."

"No penetration, no orgasms?" I repeated.

He winked. "Yeah, but a heck of a lot of fooling around. Anything more, there's a punishment."

"What sort of punishment? By whom?"

He patted my rear and handed me the thick binder. "More than you ever wanted to know in here—the full set of rules. Ready?"

I placed the binder in my locker, and as we walked toward the door, I said, "What do you mean by 'fucking on your own terms'?"

"One of us may choose you as a partner. You don't have to accept, but it's a way to progress, and to be honest it's pretty serious if you turn someone down."

"Okay." We walked through a dark corridor and then up a staircase. After one flight, taking us to the first floor, he punched a code into a keypad.

"You'll do great," he said. "Remember, if you want to leave, call zero one on the phone, but I'd suggest giving it a couple of hours, until midnight at least. They might tease you a bit, but Jake and Willis tell me you can give as good as you get, and you don't have to do anything you don't want to. Believe me, this'll be one of the most interesting—and sexy—nights you've ever had. Pity you couldn't get in earlier, but, hey…" He pushed the door open. "You're one of the boys and girls, now. Have fun."

10

THE BOYS AND GIRLS.

I walked forward feeling more than ever that I had regressed back to high school, or, even worse, to dance class.

The large room held a group of mainly young and good-looking people, sprawled on comfortable furniture, chatting and drinking. A few clustered around a table with a partially constructed jigsaw puzzle, and a Scrabble game took place on the rug in front of the fireplace. One couple was immersed in a chess game at another table, but the largest group clustered around a television, a pile of DVDs nearby. A piano stood against one wall, and a woman sat at the keyboard painstakingly picking out a Scott Joplin rag.

It could have been a frat house, not that I'd ever hung out with frat boys, but its shabby, casual décor gave that sort of youthful, sloppy impression. But a frat house from an earlier, more innocent time, before fancy electronics. Although perhaps—given how people were dressed, or undressed—not particularly innocent.

One of the men uncoiled from a couch where he'd been entwined with a woman stripped down to her bra and panties.

He wore a pair of sweats, hung low on his hips, and it didn't take much in the way of powers of observation to see that he wore nothing beneath. His cock, semi-erect, swayed and pushed against the cotton knit as he walked.

"Well, well," he said. "And what do we have here? Fresh meat. Very nice."

He walked around me, staring at me, while I tried to suppress a smile. This was a kid who'd seen too many noir movies; he played the role of the boss/leader to perfection.

Others walked forward to stare at me, assess me. One of the group around the television hit Pause and the screen stilled.

The self-appointed leader continued to talk. "Nice tits. A bit small. Good legs." He leered at my breasts. "What's your name?"

"Jo. What's yours?"

I thought for a moment that he was going to bellow that he asked the questions, but he smiled and circled around me again.

"Someone dressed up fancy for tonight," the guy said.

The others crowded a little nearer. I knew they wanted to intimidate me, but I stood still and maintained my smile. As Mrs. Danvers had said, they were competitive, and I'd half expected some sort of hazing activity. Most of them were gorgeous, too, and stripped down to underwear or the sort of cotton clothing sold for sleeping or lounging around the house, which gave the whole place the atmosphere of a slumber party.

Something moved above. I looked up to see railings, and a couple of dark figures. The entire room was surrounded by a dimly lit walkway at the second-floor level.

"They watch us," the guy said, addressing me instead of his audience. "They're picking out who they want later tonight."

"And they are...?"

"You'll find out, Jo." He walked behind me and unbuttoned and unzipped my skirt, the same polka-dot one I'd worn to seduce Willis. As the fabric slithered around my ankles I stepped out of it.

"Well, well." He regarded my extremely expensive panties with approval. They were made of cotton to match the camisole, with a fairly modest yet flattering cut, high on the thighs, but the fabric was fine enough to reveal the shadow of my pubic hair. "I'm Pete. Stop staring, boys and girls. You'll have plenty of time to get to know your new playmate."

They drifted away, returning to the games and movies, to their places on couches or the large, overstuffed chairs that dotted the room.

Pete led me around the room, introducing me, pointing out the refrigerator, stocked with soft drinks and wine, the snack table with plates of cut fruit and cheese. He mostly ignored the couples making out, or in one case, the threesome of a girl and two guys.

"How does this work?" I asked.

"Work? We're all hot. We basically have boring things to occupy us, and up there—" he lifted his chin to the gallery "—they're watching. So we like to put on a show."

"But the no-orgasm, no-penetration rule?"

"Safety's sake, since not everyone here has been cleared physically. And it makes it more challenging for us. What's wrong, Jo? You don't like a challenge?" Before I could answer, he wheeled around to address a couple coiled together on a chair, "Do I detect wet panties, Monica? Uh-oh. And Allan's hand inside them?"

"Fuck off," she said. "Who made you dictator of the day?"

But the guy removed his hand with a rueful grin.

We resumed our tour of the room. "So what happens if there is an orgasm or penetration? And what sort of penetration?"

"We choose a punishment. A spanking, for example. No penetration means no penetration, although if you want to get technical, it has happened that a finger has gotten inside a pussy, or a cock inside a mouth, but usually peer pressure prevails. Now, Lindy here has been a very naughty girl."

Lindy, fair-haired and pretty, grinned in an embarrassed sort of way. She stood apart from the others at the side of the room, facing the wall.

"Tell Jo what you did, Lindy."

She turned around and fidgeted. "I went to the bathroom and I played with myself."

"Which is perfectly okay," Pete said. "But then what?"

"I had an orgasm. I didn't mean to, but I got carried away, and…"

"So we're punishing you," Pete said. "Tell Jo how."

"I don't know," she said. "I have to stand here, on my own against the wall. I'm bored, Pete. Can I go to the bathroom?"

"I don't think so," he said. "You can't be trusted in there alone."

"But I want to pee," she said.

"I'm afraid you'll have to wait," Pete said. He led me past her.

"I really do," she wailed, clutching her crotch. "Please, Pete."

"Isn't that sort of bad for her?" I asked as we walked on.

"That girl has a bladder like iron. We'll get her worried, and then…oh, a little public humiliation will be in order."

I looked back at her. "What's to stop her going to the bathroom? I mean, in the sense of just walking in there?"

"Peer pressure. Watch."

He turned me so we were no longer looking directly at Lindy. She began a slow sidle toward the door at the end of the room.

One of the Scrabble players looked up and shouted, "Where do you think you're going, Lindy?"

"Oh, you're so mean." She stomped back to her original position.

"So," Pete said, "you have to be careful. That might prove

difficult for a sexy girl like you." He drew a finger down the side of my face, down my neck and collarbone and circled a nipple. "Nice. You like that, don't you? I bet you like your tits played with when you're fucking."

I was aware of movement in the room as the others gathered around us, although the chess players remained immersed in their game and a quarrel over which video to watch next seemed to have broken out by the television.

Another man, with long brown hair tied back into a ponytail and wearing boxers and a T-shirt, knelt at my feet. He put his face against my knee and licked up my inner thigh, his nose bumping briefly against my crotch. And then the other leg. His hands clasped the backs of my knees, keeping me steady.

Pete nuzzled my neck. "Tell Ivan to lick you, Jo. He's good at it, the girls tell me."

Ivan's breath was warm and moist on my pussy. He pushed his nose to and fro against the crotch of my panties and grinned, inviting me to share the joke.

A girl vaulted over the back of a sofa to join us. "Mmm. You like girls, Jo? I'm much better than these losers." She leaned to kiss the side of my mouth. "Ooh. Nice titties. Get off, Pete. My turn."

Pete shrugged and stepped away as she lowered her mouth to my breast and bit gently through the cotton. I gave his cock, even more prominent now, a long, hungry stare and licked my lips. I could tease them, too. I rotated my hips and moaned a little as Ivan slipped a finger inside my panties, partly for show, but also because I enjoyed the attention and hunger and heat.

I beckoned to Pete. He obligingly stepped forward. I fingered the small gold ring on his nipple. "Did it hurt?" I asked. "It's so sexy. How does that feel when I tug on it?"

"Good." He cleared his throat.

Another guy slung one arm over Pete's shoulders and replaced my fingers with his own. "So it's girls tonight, lover boy?"

"Yeah. She's got a tight little ass." Pete turned me, dislodging the girl from my nipple. "See?" He gave my ass a light slap. "Tight as a drum. Nice. What do you think, guys, shall we let her come? Jennifer? Ivan? Jon?"

Jennifer pinched the large dark patch she'd created on my camisole. "Heck, why not?"

"Sure." Ivan's finger explored me. He'd barely touched me so far, just swept his finger over my pubic hair and along the crease at the top of my thigh. "Wow. She's wet."

I moaned since that's what they seemed to expect. Ivan's finger nudged my clit.

Pete leaned forward and nibbled at my ear. "You know you want to. You can come in front of us all. Much better than jerking yourself off at home. All these hands and lips and tongues just for you. I bet you're pretty when you come."

I shook them off. "Nice try, guys. And for the record, I look like a demented owl when I come."

They laughed and the group broke up, or rather, broke and reformed. I found myself on a sofa on Ivan's lap, his cock prodding me through his flannel boxers, pushing my legs apart. Jennifer was next to me; she smiled and placed my hand on her breast. Pete lay on his side on the floor, his head propped on one hand, with Jon behind him. From their small movements and the tension in Pete's legs, I suspected Jon rubbed his cock against the butt seam of Pete's pants.

Jennifer's breast lay soft and heavy in my palm, and the nipple hardened when I stroked it. She sighed and dropped her hand into her lap, cupping herself.

"Oh, look, Jennifer's playing with herself," Jon commented.

"Fuck off," she said. "You're no good at it. You wouldn't know a clit from a hole in the ground, you dumb fag."

Jon laughed and stroked Pete's hip. "And you're a dumb dyke."

"Now, now. Language. We could have an amnesty," Pete said. "How about it? An orgasm apiece for the ladies."

"Women," Jennifer and I said together.

Her breath and hair tickled my ear. "Don't believe them. If you want to come, we'll go to the bathroom together. I'd love to suck your clit. I can show you what an orgasm really is."

My clit gave a great jolt of pleasure.

"Would you like that?" she whispered. "I'll pull your panties down and do you."

"And I'll bend you over, Jennifer, and do you up the ass," Ivan said. "Hey, these two are up to no good. I'm disappointed in you, Jo. You haven't been here ten minutes and you're bending the rules." He gave me a light smack on the leg.

"She made me do it," Jennifer said in a whiney little girl voice. "She's being very naughty with my titty. My panties are all wet. It's her fault."

"Oh, sure," Pete said.

I stared at Pete and then dropped my gaze to his cock. "Do you have a ring on your cock, too? It's getting bigger by the moment."

Jon reached over and stroked Pete's cock through his pants. "No, he doesn't have a ring but he has a very nice tat. He'll show it you if you behave."

Pete pushed into Jon's hand. He closed his eyes as though in pain.

"Are you going to come?" Jon asked softly.

Ivan pushed against my ass, his hands on my hips. "Make him come, Jon. He's being an authoritarian jerk tonight. And he wants to, don't you, big boy?"

Jon lowered his mouth to Pete's and they kissed, long and slow as though they weren't on show, or surrounded by most of the people in the room, who had come over to observe. It was very quiet; the television babbled to itself, unwatched.

Jennifer pushed my hand away. We watched the two men absorbed in each other. I ground myself against Ivan's cock and he gave a tremor—I think of laughter, although it could have been tension.

Pete groaned. His legs flexed and he put his hand over Jon's, directing the action.

And then he rolled away, grinning, his pants distended. "You really thought I was going to come? Dream on. I need a beer."

Jon rolled onto his back, panting. His cock was fully erect, straining against his thin cotton drawstring pants. He reached down and fondled himself. "Damn, it might be worth it. Oh, yeah." A groan. "Oh, yeah. I'm going to— Hey, Pete, get me a beer, will you?"

We all laughed, and there was a little applause. Some of it came from the gallery above. I glanced up at the handful of dark figures clustered there. A little light reflected off sequins and sparkly fabric, and I realized that they wore masks.

"Let's go to the john," Jennifer said, tugging at my hand.

"I usually go on my own," I said, but I went with her anyway. We seemed to have regressed to grade school at this point.

We passed Lindy, who asked us if we'd tell Pete that she needed to go now, real bad. Jennifer made an extended hissing sound at her, which I thought was unkind and made poor Lindy clutch at her crotch desperately.

Oh, yes, definitely grade school. Low partitions on the toilets, a couple of urinals, but expensive Italian soap at a sink that was a black glass bowl on a pedestal and a lavishly flowered orchid in a ceramic pot. Jennifer pressed my fingers to her crotch. "Don't tell," she whispered. "Let me. Oh, please."

She jerked herself roughly against my hand and I found her clitoris, bulbous and smooth, with my thumb.

"What's going on here?" Ivan strolled in. "You dirty bitch, Jennifer. Can I watch?"

"No, you'll tell on us," Jennifer said. She strutted over to a urinal and pulled her panties aside, humming as she relieved herself.

"I'm not having a pissing contest with you," Ivan said, but he headed for the adjoining urinal. "You call that a penis? Pathetic. Jo, you want to play Scrabble? Or watch a movie?"

"Sure. In a moment." I retreated into one of the unprivate cubicles and pissed like a horse. It must have been either empathy for Lindy or all the unfulfilled below-the-belt activity.

"It sounds absolutely depraved," Mr. D. said the next night. Mahler played softly on the monitors. "And what happened? Did...Lindy, was it? Did she hold out?"

"Oh, yeah, Lindy. Pete—he was the guy who wanted to be in charge—sent for a huge pitcher of water and a bunch of glasses and made her pour us all a glass. And then she ran to the can, her hands between her legs."

Poor Lindy. The episode had been cruel but fascinating and darkly comic. She'd been close to tears but equally close to helpless giggles at her predicament, the pitcher shaking in her hand. At one point I think she had peed in her pants a little, when she slammed the pitcher onto the table, a look of horror on her face, thighs pressed close together, her face reddening. But she'd fought for control and continued to pour, while Pete and the others jeered at her.

When she'd made her run for the bathroom one of the guys had stepped out in front of her, arms outspread, as if to stop her, and she'd screamed and slapped him, quite hard. I didn't blame her.

"And did you enjoy your evening?" Mr. D. asked.

"I did. But it made me feel..." I searched for the words. "It made me tremendously horny and excited but part of the excitement was from being able to act mean. I loved watching the guys make out. I loved being on display and knowing that I could tease and torment and act like a bitch. But it's not real life. It's playing with other mean children. It's a fantasy existence." Kimberly's words came back to me. *You let me know when you're ready to drop the fantasies for a few hours and come back into the real world, you hear?*

"But it's a safe place to behave that way," Mr. D. said.

"I guess so. But what's scary is that I wanted to have an orgasm to see what they'd do."

"And come in front of everyone. I imagine that held some appeal for you."

"Yeah, there is that." I laughed.

"Did anything happen on the way home?"

I knew what he meant. "No, but it was fun being in a limo."

"You must have wanted to come quite badly."

"I did. I ached. I woke up in the middle of the night, feeling a sort of flutter in my cunt. Not an orgasm, but more of a buildup." I pressed my hand to my crotch and things tightened and contracted inside.

"You mean," he said, "you mean you haven't come yet? You've been in this condition for nearly twenty-four hours? It sounds as though you're practicing some sort of far Eastern religion."

"No. I wanted to come for you. I wanted to wait for you to ask me. To tell me what you wanted." My voice sank to a whisper.

He told me what to do and I obeyed him.

11

KIMBERLY WOULDN'T ANSWER MY TEXTS OR reply to emails and her door was closed most of the time at work. I missed her but there was so much I couldn't or wouldn't tell her. *Oh, yeah, I've been having phone sex—so eighties, right?— at the station with a guy I've refused to meet. And I've joined a sex club where hot people fool around and act mean and make out so I can tell the guy on the phone about it.*

On the other hand, if I wanted company there was someone with whom I'd played phone tag for a few days until we'd both given up, but I'd felt an immediate liking for her: Liz Ferrar, the woman I'd met at the symphony. And I was pretty sure she wouldn't invite me into the bathroom so she could pull my pants down and do me. I needed some reality, some interaction with adults, not half-dressed sex maniacs (I couldn't wait to go back).

I emailed her, inviting her to lunch or coffee, whatever her schedule would allow. She called me right away and we compared schedules; she was generally busy at lunchtime and I couldn't commit to breakfast or dinner with my late weeknights.

"Or there's this Saturday," she said. "Do you like kids?"

"Sure. But no one ever says they don't."

She laughed. "Sometimes I wish people would. I'm taking a group of kids from the shelter to the park on Saturday afternoon to give their moms a break. It's fun, and we could talk while the kids play and grab a bite to eat after. Patrick comes to play with the kids sometimes, too."

"Patrick?" I wasn't sure why this surprised me so much.

"The kids adore him. They miss their dads, however badly they've been treated, and it's good for them to have contact with a decent guy."

I accepted her invitation with enthusiasm. I couldn't think of anything more wholesome and down-to-earth, even though Patrick might be there (I'd been avoiding him, too).

Saturday was a bright sunny day and although I'd really have preferred to ride my bicycle the few miles to the park, I drove, since Liz and I planned to have dinner after. When I arrived, there were a couple of moms with kids in the playground, a fairly fancy one with elaborate climbing frames and beds of woodchips for any unlucky kids who fell, as well as swings and a slide.

I wandered into the adjoining community center to see if anyone was around. My experience with small kids was that they invariably all had to go to the bathroom upon arrival, however short a drive it might have been. The scent of chlorine from the indoor pool was strong in the air and people strolled in and out, gym bags in their hands.

One guy looked familiar, tall and lanky, with long brown hair tied back. For a moment I couldn't place him and then I recognized him as Ivan from the previous night. Our gazes locked. He gave a small smile, a hint of a wink and then walked past me, as though we were strangers. Of course, all very proper according to the rules of the Association.

A large glass window looked onto the gym area. A few

people were there working out with weights or on machines, and there was one guy working at a punching bag in the corner.

I looked again. It was Patrick, wearing a T-shirt and one of those strange combinations of shorts and pants that guys favor for exercise, sweating slightly as he stepped and swayed, his gloved fists landing on the punching bag with absolute precision. He was light on his feet and quick, and as I watched he closed in on the bag and landed a quick succession of short, fast jabs, his arms blurring. I'd never thought of him as being particularly athletic—he seemed fit enough, and I suspected he was one of those people who was naturally lean—and I liked what I saw. I admired his grace and his neat footwork, the look of concentration on his face.

He looked up, stopped and the bag swung toward him as he saw me.

I was convinced it was going to smack him in the face, but he lifted one hand and caught the bag with a precise, economical gesture. He grinned and raised the other in greeting, and let the bag spin away, gently rotating on the cable.

I heard a burst of children's voices and saw Liz and another woman and a gaggle of half a dozen children come into the community center, crowding over the tiled floor. Liz raised a hand to me and pointed to the bathroom, as I had predicted.

After a few minutes, a door banged and Patrick walked toward me, a backpack swinging in his hand. "Liz said you'd be here," he said.

"I didn't know you boxed." He had a scent of male sweat about him that I found disturbingly attractive.

"I don't, really. It's a great way of releasing tension, smacking at an inanimate object. I do a few weights, too."

I gazed with new appreciation at the muscles in his arms before he reached into the backpack and pulled on a hoodie. At that point, the children emerged from the bathroom and swarmed toward Patrick, wrapping their arms around his legs, tugging at the hem of his hoodie, and all talking at once. He scooped one little girl with a collection of pink-and-purple barrettes on her braided hair into his arms, and, surrounded by children, made his way outside.

"He's so sweet with them," Liz said as we followed him and the kids outside. "It's a pity I'm too old for him." She added, "And married. Mustn't forget that."

"And he's my tenant," I said, half joking. "He was dating my best friend Kimberly for a while."

"That was Kimberly? He's very discreet," Liz said. "Lucky girl."

She introduced me to the other woman, Sharon, who was her assistant at the shelter. Patrick dropped his backpack onto a bench outside and went to clamber on the climbing frame with the children.

We brought each other up-to-date. I mentioned I'd dated Willis, without telling her any lurid details and she laughed and made a face.

"He's not so bad when you get to know him," I said. "A lot of that bluster is just for show."

"Has Kimberly squeezed any money out of him yet?"

"I don't think so. Are you expecting someone else to arrive?" I couldn't help but notice how her eyes darted around, watching carefully if a car drew up at the community center.

"Sorry. Force of habit." She laughed. "You get so used to making sure none of the abusive parents are around. It's always a risk if you're out with the kids. Word gets out. Sometimes one of the women will actually tell her husband where the shelter is and that makes for trouble. It's so tough for the women, dealing with the breakup of their relationship and their kids' sadness and anger, too."

Patrick waved at me from the monkey bars, hanging one-handed, while the kids grabbed at his legs.

I ran over to them, jumped up to the monkey bars and hooked my legs over a rung so I could hang upside down.

"This is my friend Jo," Patrick said and rattled off the names of the children, who stared at me.

"That lady be silly," the owner of the pink-and-purple barrettes pronounced after a moment's thought.

"I want to do like that lady does!" squealed a little boy, and Patrick obligingly dropped to the ground to lift him into position.

I disentangled myself from the bars, too, to lift children up and steady them as they swung, and soon they were swarming over me with sudden, touching warmth. Whatever these kids had gone through they still had a capacity for trust and affection.

I took a couple of them over to the swing set, where Liz joined me, and we pushed a couple of squealing kids high into the air.

"Oh, shit," she said quietly.

I followed her gaze. A car had drawn up in the parking lot, stopped at an angle and with the engine still running. A couple of guys got out and for a moment I was afraid they might be armed.

But the little girl with the barrettes ran toward them. "Daddy!"

Sharon ran over to the climbing frame and rounded the kids up, while Liz and I stopped the swings.

"Call 9-1-1," she said to me. "He's breaking his restraining order. Kids! Come into the community center. Yolanda! Say hi to your daddy and then come over here, please."

As I dialed, one of the guys reached into the car and pulled out a huge stuffed toy, about as big as his daughter. "Baby," he crooned. "Look what Daddy's got for his little girl."

Yolanda stopped. I think she was alarmed at the size and the beady eyes of the toy.

The dispatcher wanted me to stay on the line, and as I talked, I walked toward the parking lot. Liz ran ahead of me, but Patrick got there first. He put a hand on Yolanda's shoulder. "Say hi and then come inside with the other kids."

"My daddy." Yolanda stuck her thumb in her mouth but now I was close enough to see she looked scared.

"Mr. Harris, you're breaking the terms of your restraining order and we've called the cops," Liz said. "If you leave now, there won't be any trouble."

"Fuck off, bitch. That's my baby girl." Harris lurched toward the little girl, the monstrous stuffed toy in one hand, and I wondered if he was high or drunk. "Daddy got a present for you, baby girl. You're gonna come for a ride in Daddy's car."

"Keep your distance." Patrick's voice was sharp and commanding. He moved in front of Yolanda, removing his glasses and tucking them into his pants pocket.

"Who the fuck are you, man?" Harris seemed to notice him for the first time.

"Daddy!" Yolanda wailed as Liz grabbed her. She struggled in Liz's arms.

"You give her back, bitch."

"Leave them alone!" Patrick ordered as Harris headed for Liz and Yolanda.

I heard the sound of sirens and willed the police to hurry. Liz, Yolanda in her arms and screaming, turned and ran toward the building, slowed by the child's attempts to escape.

Harris's head turned; he'd heard the sirens, too.

"Fuck you!" he shouted and swung one powerful arm. Patrick fell onto the surface of the parking lot and lay motionless as Harris and his companion leaped back into their car and drove off, tires squealing.

"He's hit someone! They're driving off!" I snapped my phone closed and ran toward Patrick, who struggled to sit up, his face covered in blood.

"Fuck," he said, swiping at the blood.

"Are you okay?" I said, surely one of the more stupid questions of my life.

The sirens grew louder and a police cruiser and an ambulance drew up. Another police car, sirens blaring, shot past the park, presumably in pursuit of Harris. Paramedics pushed me aside and started firing questions at Patrick, who got to his feet, refusing to get onto the gurney they'd unloaded.

Liz emerged from the building. "I need to take the kids back," she said. "Is Patrick okay?"

I glanced at him, sitting on the step of the ambulance, a cold pack pressed to his face, surrounded by paramedics. "He was walking just now. I guess so."

"I'm so sorry, Jo. We'll get together another time, okay?"

I hugged her and reassured her there was nothing to apologize for. Yolanda stood at Liz's side, clinging to her, her thumb jammed into her mouth.

Liz talked briefly to the police officer and gave him her card. Then she and Sharon and the children, many of whom were crying, trooped out to get back into their minivan.

Someone tugged at my arm. I searched for a name—Maurice, that was it, the kid who'd wanted to hang upside down. "The bad man gave Patrick an owie."

"Yeah. But he'll be fine."

"Will his momma look after him?"

"I think his momma lives a long way off. But I'm his friend. I'll make sure he's okay."

Maurice seemed reassured and ran to join the other kids.

I retrieved Patrick's backpack from the bench and went over to where he was talking to some paramedics.

"Shit, no. My nose isn't broken, I wasn't unconscious. I'm fine, and I'm not going to the hospital. My premiums will go sky-high."

"You may have a concussion, sir. That's quite a bump you

have on the back of your head and you shouldn't drive yourself home."

I laid my hand on his arm. "I'll drive you home, Patrick, but I think you should go to the hospital."

"No way."

I left him arguing with them and retreated into the community center, where I made and signed a statement, kicking myself that I hadn't had the foresight to get the car's license plate number.

"We caught them six blocks away, ma'am," the cop told me. "We know Harris. We can put him away for violating the terms of his restraining order, but he'll be out and making trouble again soon and there's nothing much we can do."

I thanked him and went outside again. Patrick now held a cold pack to the back of his head while signing a clipboard. He looked up at me. "I'm releasing them of all responsibility," he said. "So if I drop dead, no one will sue them."

"Great, I'll get to keep your rental deposit. Are you ready to go? I have your backpack."

He nodded and stood. I grasped his elbow. The paramedic handed me his copy of the release statement, on which was written a list of frightening symptoms that might indicate a concussion. "Keep an eye on your boyfriend for the next twenty-four hours, ma'am. He'll probably be fine, but we like to be cautious when it's a head injury."

"Sure. Thanks." To Patrick I said, "Wait here. I'll drive the car over."

He looked at me and blinked. "Are you kidding? It's ten yards away. I need to walk."

He shook my arm off, and reached into his pocket for his eyeglasses.

The significance of him taking off his eyeglasses now became clear. I unlocked the car door. "You knew he was going to hit you."

"I thought it likely. Eyeglasses are expensive." He settled into the seat. "Your windscreen is dirty."

"I know." I held up a hand. "How many fingers am I holding up?"

"Seven. For God's sake, woman, drive."

I giggled at his sudden lapse into Irishness. "I think I have some frozen peas in the freezer."

He blinked at me. "Why are you telling me this?"

"For a cold pack."

"Oh. Okay. Thanks."

We rode in silence until I drew up at the house a few minutes later. "I can light a fire. Do you want to lie down on the sofa? I have a whole bunch of DVDs and—"

"Are you planning on playing Florence Nightingale?"

"I don't remember telling them you were my boyfriend, but someone did."

"Right." He touched the back of his head and grimaced. "Yes, well, they would have insisted on taking me in unless I had someone with me, so I told a bit of a fib."

"A bit of a fib." I opened the door. "Why didn't you just ask me?"

He got out and stretched as though sitting in the car for a few minutes had stiffened his muscles. "Spur-of-the-moment. Sorry. It was all I could think of."

I felt ungracious then. "No, it's fine. I would have offered anyway, but I was planning on going out tonight.... I can cancel it."

"No, don't change your plans on my account. I need a shower." He grabbed his backpack and headed up the outside stairs.

"Will you... Do you think it's safe?"

He stopped. "You're welcome to come scrub my back, but I'll be okay. And the fireplace and movies sound great. Thanks for the offer."

He came back downstairs later, in clean sweats and a flannel shirt, and I settled him on the sofa with a quilt, two packs of frozen peas and my DVD and video collection. He seemed subdued, as far as I could tell, for someone who was fairly quiet anyway.

In the kitchen I rummaged in the freezer for the batch of soup I'd made a few weeks ago and a loaf of raisin bread. I didn't intend to spend all night seeing whether his pupils looked abnormally large, but the least I could do was feed him.

As I carried the tray into the living room, familiar tinkling piano music met my ears.

He looked up, one hand on Brady, whose purr I could hear across the room. "You don't mind, do you?" He motioned to the television. Of all the options he had, he'd gone for an old home video.

I shook my head and unloaded soup bowls, bread and butter onto the table. I tried not to watch the screen, but even as I sat my feet itched to turn out, point, move. My fingers moved, marking the steps.

"First-year recital," I said. And then, "Why didn't you hit him?"

He sat up, pushing cat and quilt away, fists clenched. "Because even if your dad is a jerk and an asshole and drunk as a skunk, you don't want to see him bleeding on the ground."

I'd opened a can of worms here obviously. "Sorry. I didn't mean to push a button."

He slumped back on the sofa and Brady settled on his knee, kneading his pants legs and purring. He stroked him and the purrs increased in volume.

"Chicken noodle soup." I handed him a bowl.

He smiled. "Great. You're all set up for bad-tempered invalids, I can tell. Sorry. I didn't mean to bite your head off. And yeah, it pushed a button, but you weren't to know." He hit the pause button on the remote. The small figure on the screen stilled into a blur of interrupted movement. "So, you want to hear the story?"

12

HE'D KNOWN SHE WOULD ASK, BUT LULLED INTO comfort and serenaded by the cat's purr, she'd taken him by surprise. Where to start, that was the problem, because how the story began was important; it colored the rest of it, and it definitely meant the ending might change. He wasn't even sure if there was an end, because things went on and you did what you could, and hoped you wouldn't screw anything or anyone else up.

He prodded at a piece of chicken in his bowl. "Good soup."

"Thanks."

"So, it's not *Angela's Ashes* or anything. Nice middle-class family near Dublin, we lived in a Georgian house, all decaying elegance with a ghost in the attic, and so on, with a bit of land. My sisters had ponies. My da's a fellow at Trinity, mum's a doctor, both smart, educated people. My da's a great guy except when he drinks and then he's a jerk. A violent jerk. And for all her fancy education my mother was like one of the women at the shelter, poor cows—she rationalized what he did and accepted it. I learned to fight so he wouldn't take it out on me when he was drunk. And that was a mistake."

"Why?" She paused, spoon halfway to her mouth.

"If he'd hit one of us kids, she might have left him sooner."

"You really believe that?"

"I knocked him down one time and she flew at me screaming like a crazy woman." He spread butter on a piece of bread.
"She left him, and I came to the States. I'd met Elise the year
before and we decided to marry. I thought I was making a clean
break of it, but there's never a clean break with your family."

"I'm very sorry." It was a conventional response but he felt
a deep kindness behind the words.

"Thanks."

"So that's why you do volunteer work for the shelter," she
said.

"Yeah, atoning for my da's sins. And I like the little kids. I'm
missing my nieces and nephews growing up. There are eight
of them. We're a prolific lot."

"And it's why you don't drink."

"Right. Not a smart thing to do with my genes." He put his
empty bowl on the table.

"You know, there are support groups for adult children of
alcoholics—"

"No. Absolutely not." He jabbed a finger at her. "Jo, I tried
it and there was only one other guy there, and half the women
came on to me."

She giggled. "Oh, come on."

"I thought it was obscene. And adult children— God, I hate
that term." He saw an expression he couldn't quite figure out
pass over her face. "Sometime in your life you just have to suck
it up and get over yourself. Everyone's screwed up one way or
another." He replaced the bag of peas on the back of his neck.
The cat investigated his soup bowl until Jo swatted him away,
and then climbed onto Patrick's chest, warm and heavy and
purring.

"Push him off if you like. More soup? In a clean bowl," she added. "How about some tea? I have Irish Breakfast."

He accepted the tea, not sure what he was getting into. Elise always accused him of being a tea snob, which he wasn't. One time she'd taken him to a place that had exotic teas from all over the world and he figured that the more the teas smelled like a damp basement, the more they cost. He liked the sort of tea he'd drunk all his life, strong enough to put hair on your chest, with a scant dribble of milk to give it opacity, what his grandmother called "a nice cup of tea."

Amazingly, she got it right, serving it to him with a graceful bob into a cross-legged position on the rug. The girl must have great quads.

"Ah, the Irish tea ceremony," she said as he sipped.

"Great. Thanks. Now tell me about your lurid past."

She grinned. "I believe in having a lurid present."

"No. That." He gestured at the television screen, which had long since reverted to a regular channel and now provided a little background noise. "Tell me about being a dancer."

"Ah. What makes you think it's part of my lurid past?"

"The expression on your face when you came into the room. The way you tensed up. And honest to God, I wasn't being nosy. I thought I was going to watch *Casablanca*."

She stood and took the remote from the arm of the sofa. "Shit. I wonder where *Casablanca* is." She clicked the recording back into life. The blurry figure on the screen came to life, twirled, leaped, stretched.

"You were good," he said.

"Not good enough for New York and that's what counts, but I was good enough to study here. The university has one of the better teachers outside of New York." She mimicked the figure on the screen with scaled-down movements, precise and graceful. "Dance memory. Sometimes I think it's written into my bones. I didn't have the right sort of body."

Your body looks absolutely fine to me. If he'd said that aloud, would she have been offended or thought he had a concussion?

"I'm too long-waisted. My turnout was always crap." She arranged her feet, heels together, toes out in a dancer's one-hundred-and-eighty-degree position. "And I was overweight."

"You were?" He looked at her and then at the figure on the screen.

"By about five pounds. Always. And that's why I stopped." She flowed across the room, arms arched, turned and snapped the player off. "I'd worked hard but I'd never been in this sort of community before, with girls who were so driven. All they did was dance and puke and their definition of a serious conversation was talking about toe-shoe maintenance or what brand of laxative was best. And the day after this recital I found myself looking at a bar of Swiss chocolate and thinking that if I ate it I could puke it up after."

"Did you?"

"No, but it was scary. I ate it to prove I could, and then I called home and told my family I was changing my major. I saw my advisor the next day and changed to a major in history with a minor in communications. And then—" she grinned "—I ate chocolate and bread, and my God, what a sensual experience that was after all those years of denying myself. I'm ten pounds heavier now."

"You look great to me." That came out right, not too leering.

"Thanks." She sat down again. "I responded to peer pressure, and that can be a scary thing. So we both have addiction in common. Isn't that special."

"Very."

She giggled again. "Maybe a group hug would be appropriate."

His dick woke up with a vengeance. He hastily rearranged

the quilt on his lap and waited to see what she'd do next. Christ, why did he feel like a teenager around this woman?

The phone rang. She listened for a while. "Oh, hi. No, he's here, with me." She said to Patrick, "It's Liz. She was worried because she didn't get through on your cell or your landline."

"Tell her hi and that I'm fine."

"Sure." Another pause. "She says she and Fred can come over with pizza if you're up for it, and check out the size of your pupils."

"Great." Although he enjoyed the company of Liz and her husband he was slightly disappointed that he was not to enter into a group hug, or anything else, with Jo.

"And we can watch *Pride and Prejudice*," Jo continued. "That okay, Patrick?"

He nodded his assent and wished he hadn't as both sides of his head ached.

She replaced the phone on the receiver. "That's okay, isn't it? Or were you hoping for *Casablanca?*"

"No, that's fine. I like Jane Austen. Movies, at any rate."

"Wow. A guy who likes Austen." She gave one of her sudden huge grins.

"So, do you miss it?"

"Miss what?" She bent to pick up his tea mug. She gazed into his eyes and he hoped it wasn't purely to check out the size of his pupils. "Dance? It was the greatest loss of my life, up to that point. I cried for months after, and it was the damnedest thing—I actually lost those five pounds for a while. But like you say, you suck it up and you move on."

Liz and Fred arrived shortly after, full of concern for him and for a moment it reminded him of being with his sisters and their families, a real girly evening, what with the *Pride and Prejudice* marathon ahead, but he didn't mind.

"Don't change your plans, Jo!" Liz cried. "If you have a date, go out. Have fun. We'll stay here with Patrick."

"Look, you don't have to—" he said, embarrassed, and then remembered the one thing he'd got out of that awful support group meeting: that he shouldn't be afraid to ask for help. By extension, he shouldn't turn help down; asking for it might be some way off.

Jo picked at a piece of pizza and caught him watching her. "I don't want to reek of garlic," she said with a slightly defensive air as though she regretted telling him of her flirtation with bulimia.

"So who is it, Jo? You didn't tell me you were seeing anyone," Liz said.

She shrugged. "Just some friends. Nothing special."

Shortly after she left the room and he heard the sound of water roaring in the pipes and tried not to imagine her having a shower. He yawned, feeling unaccountably tired. He supposed it was the aftereffect of shock, after having so much adrenaline run through him.

"You okay, Patrick?" Liz said, patting his hand.

"I'm fine. I'm not lapsing into a coma or anything. Just wondering whether I should press charges against Yolanda's dad. The cops wanted me to."

"You should."

"The poor bastard's in a shitload of trouble without me adding to it. If Yolanda was my kid I'd probably go berserk, too."

"You probably wouldn't be high or violent." Liz returned her attention to the screen. "Oh, I love this bit, when Mr. Collins gets into the cart."

Jo came downstairs, wearing jeans and a black T-shirt and sparkly earrings that probably weren't diamonds. For some reason he was reminded of Cinderella, the early versions where she was given jewelry by the fairy godmother, a pair of bracelets. The earrings seemed incongruous with the rest of the outfit, but what was a mere guy to know.

Her cell phone rang—some musical phrase that he didn't recognize—and she waved goodbye to them and left.

"Well, well." Fred peeked out through the blinds on the front window. "A stretch limo."

"Cinderella goes to the ball," Liz said. "She didn't look dressed for a stretch limo-type event."

"She can look after herself." Patrick knew Liz was thinking of pimps and drugs, the sort of problems the women in her shelter encountered, and for the most part, why they ended up there. And he knew that a middle-class background and education, even well-meaning supportive friends, meant nothing if a woman were involved with the wrong sort of man.

He didn't like to think of Jo in trouble. And while it might not be any of his business, he saw in himself the urge to rush in on a white charger and save her. But he wasn't going to do that anymore. He put the white charger firmly back in the stable, shut the door and immersed himself in the genteel problems of the Bennet sisters.

13

"HEY, JO."

I couldn't tell who it was in the dimness of the limo but I recognized his voice.

"Ivan?"

"That's me." He placed a hand on my knee which made me feel uncomfortable. Weren't we supposed to not acknowledge each other outside of the Great Room? We'd seen each other that afternoon and passed each other as though we were strangers. "Looking forward to tonight?"

"I guess so." I moved away from him and tried to see out of the dark tinted windows. We made one more stop to pick up a woman called Judy, who cuddled up with Ivan and talked to him in whispers for the rest of the journey. We were going west into the mountains, I knew, because my ears popped a little as we gained in altitude. I wondered if anyone had smuggled in a GPS to discover the destination; it could be done easily enough if you owned one. I'd tried with my cell but lost the signal. And what exactly went on on the second floor of the house?

The limo continued to climb and then made the turn onto a driveway and made another turn to take us to the side entrance.

We went into the chilly locker room where a few others were changing. We were mostly quiet. It was as though we assumed our snarky, bitchy personae inside the Great Room; here we merely prepared. Ivan snapped the elastic of his boxers and preened in front of a full-length mirror. Judy leaned to apply mascara at a mirror.

I stripped off my jeans and socks and sneakers. I wore a pair of my fancier underwear, red silk with black lace, and no bra beneath my black T-shirt. Part of me wanted to be home, snug on the sofa with Patrick and Liz and her husband, watching videos and laughing. I hoped Patrick was okay, that little Yolanda had recovered, for the time being at any rate, poor kid.

"Move it, Jo." The door was flung open by Pete. "If you're late, there'll be consequences."

"Bite me," I responded, already feeling the stirrings of naughty insubordination, and strolled through the door he held open, taking my time.

It was mostly the same crowd but in different combinations of twos and threes. The fire crackled invitingly and the snack table was stocked with a gorgeous cheese-and-fruit assortment. As we entered, a female staff member, dressed in black, was putting the finishing touches to it. She took no notice of us.

I helped myself to some wine and joined in the Scrabble game with Pete and Ivan and Lindy, who had been punished so humiliatingly the other night, and who wore only a thong and a skinny camisole tonight. Pete seemed to be in a heterosexual mood tonight, stroking Lindy's thighs and breasts, while she mostly ignored him and Ivan, shoving their hands away when she wanted to put pieces on the board. I wondered if it was a tactic to view their pieces, or, more likely, a conspiracy to trick someone—myself, for instance—into doing something stupid.

"You don't think Jo's feeling left out, do you?" Pete asked at random.

I smiled and used my Q on a triple word score. Sometimes a high Scrabble score was the best revenge.

"I think you'd better take care of her," Lindy said.

Ivan moved over to my side of the board and laughed when I turned my pieces facedown. "What are you worried about, babe? You're winning. And it's not your pieces I'm interested in."

He nuzzled my neck. "The best defense is to masturbate yourself senseless before you come. Come here, that is."

"You don't know much about female sexuality, do you?" I looked at the board. "That's not a word, Lindy."

"It is, too!"

Pete wriggled his fingers under her thong. "Mmm. Someone's getting wet."

"You going to challenge her, Jo?" Ivan slid his hand under my T-shirt.

"Do you think I should?" I stroked his cock through his thin cotton pants. "Perhaps I'll make you come instead."

Lindy ignored us. Pete's fingers were inside her thong, their mouths joined in a deep kiss.

A few people strolled over to watch, and Jennifer, who'd invited me into the bathroom last time, knelt to caress Lindy's breasts. Pete disengaged his mouth from Lindy's, and he and Jennifer pulled her camisole off over her head, revealing full breasts with a tattoo of a dragon curling around them.

"Pretty," Ivan said.

Lindy fell back against the Scrabble board, legs spread wide, scattering pieces as Pete and Jennifer nibbled at her breasts. Pete's fingers pushed in and out of her tiny thong, which was darkened with her juices.

Ivan's cock hardened beneath my fingers, and when he slipped his hand into my panties and rubbed my clit I didn't stop him. "Damn," he said, his breath tickling against my ear.

"Damn if they're not going to make her come. You want me to do you? Be quiet and you'll get away with it."

"I don't trust you." My hips bucked to his rhythm. "Hey, I take it back. You're not that bad at female sexuality. You'll tell. I won't come."

"You will." He licked my neck and nibbled beneath my ear. "You will, honey. Let it go, you won't get another chance like this. Look at Lindy. She's a big sexy mess."

She was. Above her, Jennifer kissed Pete while each of them manipulated one of Lindy's hard nipples. Lindy's own finger moved on her clit now, her legs raised and parted, her drenched thong pushed aside to reveal the dark pink folds of her pussy.

"Oh, God," I said. I wanted Ivan to stop, I wanted him to continue. I wanted to close my eyes and succumb to the orgasm that awaited but at the same time Lindy and Jennifer and Pete demanded my attention.

Ivan's mouth teased at mine and his tongue slipped inside, a gentle suckling. His other hand pinched my nipple while that sweet manipulation of my clit went on. And on. "Come," he whispered. "Come, I dare you."

I broke the kiss to see what the others were doing. Most of the inhabitants of the Great Room had gathered to watch. Jennifer knelt between Lindy's thighs now, thrusting her fingers into her pussy. Pete knelt over Lindy, stroking her breasts with one hand, the other pressed against his cock.

"He's going to come on her tits," Ivan murmured. "And she's going to come. She's a noisy girl. They won't notice if you do. God, you're so wet. You're dripping. You like that?" He pushed his finger inside me. "Like some more?"

His fingers moved in and out of me, his thumb grazing my clit. "Do it," he murmured. "No one will see."

My thighs tensed. I knew I shouldn't trust Ivan, any of them. I couldn't imagine what would happen if I allowed myself to come, but with every stroke of his hand, every clever pinch to my nipples, I drew closer and cared less for the consequences.

And then I came to my senses and rolled away. "You bastard!" I screeched and grabbed for the nearest missile, which was the velvet pouch that held the Scrabble tiles.

He ducked the shower of tiles, laughing, as applause broke out. 'Nearly got you, there, Jo."

Jennifer, Pete and Lindy had meanwhile disentangled themselves, all of them red in the face and out of breath, but grinning stupidly.

"And I was winning! Look what you did to the board!" I continued.

"Look what you did to the tiles, honey," Pete said. "If we've lost any, you're in for a spanking."

I got onto my hands and knees to gather tiles and wagged my butt at him. "Exactly how long am I going to be the new kid on the block? I'm tired of this already."

"Now, don't be mad," Jennifer said. "You—"

A bell rang and Pete jumped to his feet. "Okay everyone, look pretty."

People arranged themselves in sexy postures on the furniture. I sat cross-legged on the floor surrounded by the debris of the Scrabble game and finished my glass of wine. I knew I didn't look pretty—I looked bad-tempered and flushed and my hair probably stood on end.

Angela, or Mrs. Danvers in black leather, opened a door I'd barely noticed before, quite near where I sat. It wasn't the door we used that led to the locker room. This one had a keypad, and, I now realized, must have led to the main part of the house.

Pete came over to talk to her and then he beckoned to Lindy, who stood, tugging her camisole back down to cover herself. She looked excited and proud, and the room erupted into a chorus of whistles and applause.

"Go, Lindy," someone shouted, while Ivan crossed over to the piano and started to bang out an approximation of the Elgar piece used at graduation ceremonies.

Pete kissed Lindy's cheek and slapped her bottom in an affectionate sort of way. Angela fluffed Lindy's hair and straightened her camisole, frowning. "She'll do. Come along, honey."

I watched Angela as she punched in a code in the keypad and was amused to see it was the same one we used for the station library, following various disasters with people getting locked out or leaving important personal items inside, or, worse, jamming pieces of cardboard in the door. It didn't rely on a sequence of numbers but a manual pattern—diagonally top right to bottom left, and then the remaining two numbers across. That could come in useful.

Lindy waved goodbye and stuck her tongue out at Pete, and then she and Angela left.

Ivan stood to open the piano bench and pull out some music. When he sat at the keyboard again he played a Chopin nocturne, a soothing accompaniment to my task of finding, sorting and counting the Scrabble tiles. None were missing. I tipped them carefully back into the velvet pouch and saw the room had settled back into its usual routine. I strolled over to the piano and watched his hands on the keyboard, and, although I was no musician, I knew enough to follow the printed notes as he played.

I reached over his shoulder to turn the page.

He gave me a quick, surprised smile.

There was something about Ivan I liked, despite his most recent dirty trick—maybe because he was the only person I'd seen in real life, outside the Great Room, that is, and I liked his smile (and his touch, too). Before all this, the Association and Mr. D., Ivan might have been the sort of guy I'd consider dating. Besides, he played the piano well, and I'm a sucker for musicians.

He came to the end of the piece. "You play?" he asked.

"No. You're pretty good."

"Thanks."

I wondered if I could trust him, and decided to take the risk. While he had his hands on the piano and not me, that is. "So, Ivan, tell me how this works. How you get to graduate."

He played a few idle chords. "Okay, you've got to get a balance. They—" nodding up to the balcony "—will notice you if you stand out. If you're proactive, if you engage with the rest of us. They like to see us punished, but not too much. Some people really get off on getting punished and if that's what you're into, that's fine."

"How long does it take to graduate?"

He shrugged. "Some people get to go upstairs within days. A week, maybe two."

"What happens upstairs?"

"Whatever they want, at first. Then you get to be one of the decision makers."

"So if you graduate, you stay upstairs?"

"Some of us like it here. Pete likes playing boss. He'll stay down here for as long as he can, before he gets too old. They don't like anyone in the Great Room over the age of thirty and he's pushing twenty-nine." A few more chords, a riff of Ellington.

"Have you ever gone upstairs?"

"Yeah." His hands stilled on the keys. "I…I didn't have a good experience. So now I stay down here."

"I'm sorry."

"Babe, don't waste too much time feeling sorry for me. I'll be tricking you again soon enough. And you'll be doing something mean to me."

I gazed at him, wondering what sort of hurt he concealed, and whether we might ever be friends. I sat next to him on the piano bench. "I like you, Ivan."

"Hey, I like you, too, or I think I do. Thing is, are we worth breaking the rules for?"

"You know the rules are legalistic garbage," I said, borrowing Patrick's phrase.

"If you're here long enough, you'll take them very seriously," he said. "And after a while, what goes on in here seems more real than anything else outside."

I looked back over his shoulder at the room and its inhabitants. "Yeah, but it's boring down here, apart from the fooling around."

"It's set up to be boring." He gave me a sweet smile. "If we had internet access or our cells here, or even cable, we'd all ignore each other."

He flipped the pages of the book of music and started on another Chopin nocturne, while I wondered if tonight I had some sort of sign plastered on me that announced I was safe for confessions. First Patrick, now Ivan.

I wandered over to the bookshelf and chose a tattered paperback mystery, and settled myself into one of the oversize armchairs with a plate of cheese and crackers and another glass of wine. Jennifer perched on the arm.

"What are you reading?"

I showed her the cover.

"Is it good?" As I ignored her, she bent forward and touched my breast. "Let's take off our tops and make out."

"No, I want to read."

"Frigid bitch!" She flounced away while I tried not to giggle.

The way I saw it was that a blatant transgression of the rules—and I'd have to pick my moment, when a large group of onlookers was gathered on the balcony—followed by a punishment, was the best way to get upstairs. And apparently I wanted to get upstairs, to progress—some latent competitiveness, which I thought was safely dormant since my time as a dance student, had emerged. Even if I didn't know what I was getting into, I still wanted to meet the challenge. Sure, it was a game, but it was one I was beginning to take seriously.

Mr. D. would understand when I told him, but to be honest, my experiences in the Great Room seemed more real, more vivid, than what I experienced with him. So did my friendship with Liz and my...whatever it was I had with Patrick. I missed Kimberly at that moment, which was ludicrous. She was no prude, but what would she say? I'd mend the breach, I decided. One of us had to.

I stole a look at the forbidden door again, feeling like an idiot heroine in a fairy tale. First Scheherazade, now Bluebeard. I could get through. I could take a look around upstairs and see what was going on and then decide whether I really wanted to stay in the Association. What was with the masks anyway? I should have asked Ivan, while he was in a talking—rather than a foreplay—mood.

The piano music had stopped. He and Pete sat close together on the piano stool, and as I watched, Pete untied the leather band that held Ivan's hair back, so it cascaded over his shoulders.

The two men stood and, as Pete flung his arm over Ivan's shoulders, walked to a sofa at the far end of the room. I was expecting—hoping for, to be honest—some heavy making out to occur, but instead they held hands and talked quietly to each other as though no one else in the room mattered. As though they weren't surrounded by gorgeous bodies—the unsinkable Jennifer displayed herself in front of them, stretching and preening.

Her efforts paid off as another couple of guys approached her. One of them, buffed and shaved with a pierced eyebrow, yanked her unceremoniously by her thong onto another sofa, where she rode his thigh while thrusting her breasts into the other's face.

They attracted some attention, the focus of the room turning to their antics. I took a quick look at the balcony. A few dark figures stood there, and, as far as I could tell, with their attention on that end of the room.

I stood and stretched elaborately, running my hands over my breasts. On the balcony, no one moved. I was as close to being invisible as I could be.

I strolled over to the doorway, punched in the code and opened it just enough to slip through—Bluebeard's wife entering the forbidden chamber—then closed the door quietly behind me.

I found myself at the far end of what had to be the front entrance to the house. Across an expanse of beautifully polished wooden floorboards, scattered with silk rugs, was an imposing door flanked with stained-glass panels. To my right was a staircase, polished and carved woodwork gleaming, and I could hear faint sounds from upstairs. Meanwhile I stood here barefoot and in my underwear, feeling extraordinarily conspicuous, and to be honest, dumb. Did I really expect an orgy on every floor so I'd blend in?

I saw the shadows of a couple of people at the front door and the knob turned. I looked around, discovered a doorway under the stairs and darted inside. As my eyes became accustomed to the dimness I saw a coatrack, and then dived behind it as the door opened and I heard familiar voices.

"…and I told him if you don't get a surge protector you'll fry your hard drive, and what about data backups? Not a clue. Not even a thumb drive. I mean, these people are dumb." I recognized the voice as Jake's, and then heard the slithering sound of his jacket being pulled off.

"Oh, forget about work, honey. Let's try and relax." Cathy, cooing to her husband. I saw her hands, tipped with gleaming red nails, straighten his down jacket onto a hanger. I pressed myself against the wall as she hung a leather bomber jacket next to his.

"You smell so good, baby." Jake's voice lowered to a growl.

Oh, no.

Oh, yes.

"Honey." She giggled. "Don't you want to wait until we're upstairs?"

He made growling, slurping sounds that indicated that he certainly wasn't going to wait. Clothing rustled. A zipper slid down.

One of Cathy's hands emerged from between the coats and almost smacked me in the nose.

I ducked.

Her hand grasped, fluttered and grabbed the coatrack. I squeezed myself away from them.

Jake meanwhile issued instructions. "Leg around my waist, baby. Oh, God. Oh, yes, that feels so good. Uh. Uh. Hold my balls, baby. That's right."

Juicy, slapping sounds filled the darkness. I could smell them, his sweat, her juices. It was a bit too late to introduce myself to them at this point; what the heck could I say? Oh, hi, didn't hear you come in...great to see you again, guys.

Fortunately this seemed to be a quickie, from the acceleration of the sounds of fucking and Jake's hoarse grunts. Cathy let out a few whimpery whoops that reminded me of a visit to the primates in the zoo, and then Jake announced he was coming and something clattered to the floor.

A high-heeled shoe lay ominously close to my foot. I kicked it out again.

"I need a tissue, honey," Cathy said. "Where's my purse?"

"I got one." Jake's hairy hand rummaged around in the coats, inches from me.

"We're gonna be late." She dug her foot back into the shoe and I tensed up. Her hands appeared and grasped Jake's pants at his ankles to hoist them back into position. If she looked down and to the side she'd see me.

Oh, Mr. D. would love this. He'd love the details of the

hot bodies in the Great Room, and I'd get turned on when I described Pete and Ivan together (only I'd make it a lot sexier, pre-come dribbling from erect cocks, wet patches on their pants, fingers caressing balls and nipples). But this episode in the closet had the ironic quality Mr. D. enjoyed.

Jake did his zipper up, grumbling he was still hard, and didn't Cathy want to go down on him?

To my relief—I was getting a bit claustrophobic and the coats tickled my nose—she giggled and told him he'd have to wait. More fumbling around with the coats—I held my breath as his coat swayed and slithered on the hanger—as he reached for an inside pocket and drew something out. "I hate this damn thing," he muttered.

"It makes you look so sexy," said Cathy, the cheerleader of fucking. "Like Zorro."

"Yeah. You ready?"

So they were masked. Light filtered in as they opened the door—Cathy wore a tiny silver lamé dress, so tight I wondered how she got in or out of it, but it was so short I didn't think she'd need to remove it for anything. She tugged it down as they left to its full length, barely covering her ass.

I cracked the door after I heard Cathy's heels tap away and the creak of the stairs overhead as they ascended. I examined the garments on the coatrack. I needed something to wear that looked like normal clothes, since apparently you were supposed to arrive dressed, whatever you might plan for later, and found a wrap of black silk streaked with silver that I swathed around my waist like a sarong. Also, lying dusty and forlorn on the floor, a black mask, that I cleaned off with someone's scarf. A few dismal feathers floated away, but it would do.

I hoped no one would notice my bare feet.

I poked my head around the door—all clear. As though I belonged upstairs, I strode out of the coat closet and up the stairs, toward the dim sounds. At the first landing, I hesitated.

The stairs branched to right and left, but straight ahead of me was a door that I was pretty sure led to the balcony above the Great Room. I cracked open the door. Sure enough, a few figures clustered at the railings, looking at the scene below. Jennifer had launched into a pole-dancing act on one of the pillars, while Ivan, at the piano, played a parody of burlesque bump-and-grind.

I retreated back through the door and peered out at the staircase.

At the landing I hesitated and took the right staircase. I could smell food, something savory and delicious, and my stomach growled. I wished I'd had more pizza at home—I remembered Patrick's concern over my low appetite and how self-conscious and defensive I'd felt, but somehow strangely pleased, too. How long had it been since someone cared about what I ate?

A corridor led off at the top of the stairs and I peered down it. The smell of food was stronger now. As I hesitated, there was a muffled thump and a ringing sound, and two wall panels slid apart—an elevator. Waiters emerged with a rolling cart of food. They took no notice of me, but pushed the cart and its covered dishes into a room. I peered around the door. Masked people, Jake and Cathy among them, sat at a long banquet table with an elaborate centerpiece, laughing and talking.

The centerpiece. I took a second look. The centerpiece was Lindy, her skin gilded, flowers strewn over her naked body, a huge orchid between her thighs. As I watched, someone reached for a strawberry from the fruits piled around her, absently stroking her skin. My view was blocked as waiters bearing plates of food moved among the guests.

One of them stepped away and gestured to me to go inside but I shook my head.

At the table a guy wearing a mask that gave him the face of a lion stood and headed for the doorway and me, cell phone at his ear. He was tall and slender, a few threads of gray in his dark hair. As he passed me, I heard a few words, to my surprise apparently about investments.

"But of course..." He sounded slightly annoyed.

He sounded familiar. Very familiar.

"Mr. D.?" My voice rose to a squeak.

He turned and looked at me and the lion's eyes gazed at me, unreadable, in his mask. Did I imagine it, or did he hesitate?

I couldn't move. I felt as though I'd been turned to ice.

At that moment the elevator arrived with a rumble and a chime, and the man—Mr. D., I knew it was him—squeezed past a half-dozen waiters and more carts of food. They jostled to let him on, blocking the corridor, the carts of food between us, while I shouted to him, tearing off my mask. "It's me. It's Jo!"

The elevator doors closed and some of the guests, alerted by my raised voice, emerged from the dining room. One I recognized from his lanky build and reddish hair.

"Heck, Jo," said Harry the Chairman, "you're in a shitload of trouble now."

14

"YOUR PUNISHMENT WILL BE QUITE SEVERE," Angela, the leather-clad Mrs. Danvers of the Association, said. She wore a very professional black leather mask with rivets and sequins but one thing spoiled her appearance and I let out a nervous giggle.

She looked down at her fluffy pink slippers. "Those boots are hell on my bunions. Are you ready?"

"Ready for what?"

She didn't answer but held open the door of the room in which I'd spent the past hour pacing back and forth, not knowing whether I wanted to laugh or cry or rage. I'd been fooled, taken, manipulated, screwed.

Why? Why had he done it? Why had I not suspected when everything seemed to fall into place so easily? The only flaw in his plan—and I wasn't quite sure whether it was a flaw or not, maybe that had been planned, too—was that I had discovered him.

"Who is he?" I asked Angela.

She looked at the untouched plate of food and glass of wine they'd sent in—how very civilized—and shrugged. "The pigeon breast was quite exquisite. I'm sorry you didn't have an appetite. Come with me."

I followed her, past the dining room, which was now deserted except for a few waiters loading tablecloths into laundry bags, and she pressed the button for the elevator that had taken Mr. D. away from me. We traveled down in silence, the elevator taking us naturally enough to a kitchen, where a few staff members looked at us with curiosity. Angela led me through a series of corridors into the locker room.

"Am I being thrown out?" This seemed a dreadful and ignoble thing to happen and I felt tears prick at my eyes.

"Not yet." She spun the combination on a locker and reached inside. "Top off."

I removed my T-shirt and crossed my arms over my breasts as the chilly air and Angela's interested gaze hit them. She handed me a black leather bustier, partially unlaced, that I dropped over my head.

"Other way around," she said, impatient at my stupidity, and yanked it around me so the lacing was at the back.

She tugged at the laces and my breasts squashed together and up. She kept lacing and I gasped for breath.

"Nipples out," she instructed.

"What?"

She huffed with impatience at my stupidity. "Like this." She tweaked my breasts so that my nipples sat above the leather. "And we'll put these on."

These turned out to be nipple clamps, little crocodile jaws that clipped onto my engorged nipples, darkening and enlarging them. They were joined by a chain, which she tugged, and the sensation, pleasure and pain mixed, made me almost jump out of my skin. I was dying to know what was going to happen next but I was damned if I would ask Angela, who now retrieved her spike-heel boots from another locker, and with some reluctance removed her slippers.

As she huffed and puffed with the boot zippers, I saw myself in the full-length mirror, noticed how my back straightened at the sight of my reflection. My nipples stood out like pushpins, my eyes bright, my hair mussed up. The chain from the nipple clamps dangled at my crotch.

Boots on, Angela swiped a comb through my hair and, after asking whether I had any lipstick, reached into her own locker and applied dark red to my lips. She stepped back to admire her work and smeared a little lipstick on my nipples.

"Very nice," she said. "Wet panties?"

"What?" I didn't know whether she meant mine or hers, but she delved a finger into mine and nodded approval.

"Dirty little slut," she murmured. Her finger skimmed my clitoris and sensation jolted into my nipples. "They'll have fun with you."

"Who will?"

"You'll see." She removed her finger. "You'd better use the bathroom."

This sounded either ominous or dirty-minded, I wasn't sure which, but while I peed she rearranged her hair in the mirror, finishing it off with a great cloud of hairspray, and refreshed her own lipstick. After I'd washed my hands, she took the end of the chain and tugged, making me whimper with pain—but not all pain. At least it took my mind off Mr. D., whose actions hurt me much more than any state-of-the-art nipple clamps.

Angela set off at a brisk walk, the possibility of causing me pain apparently distracting from her bunions, while I trotted along behind her. As I expected, we went back into the Great Room, where I was met with a chorus of jeers, but also some fist-pumping and shouts of approval. Angela jerked the chain— strange how I'd never fully appreciated that metaphor until this moment—and abandoned me in the middle of the room.

They crowded around me and I grabbed the end of the chain before anyone else could.

"Oh, nice, very nice." Pete was purring with excitement, his dick tenting out his boxers. "Little Jo, all dressed up for the occasion. You have been a naughty girl, haven't you? Hey, Ivan, what do you think we should use?"

"Hmm." Ivan flicked one of my nipples with his fingers. "We need something to take that silly grin off her face."

"I do not have a silly grin on my face!"

Ivan raised his eyebrows. "Did I give you permission to speak? Did I, Pete? I don't think so. I think she's in enough trouble—she shouldn't be taking any chances. Because it could earn her extra punishment. Right, Jo?"

I shrugged.

Pete jerked the nipple clamp chain and I gave a yelp of pain. "When Ivan or I ask you a question, you reply. Otherwise you don't say anything. Understood?"

"Yes." And then as he frowned at me, I added, "Yes, sir."

He smiled approval.

There was something I liked about this game, in addition to the pressure on my nipples and the tingling between my thighs. I liked being at their mercy, and being aware, from the stirrings in their pants, that to some extent they were at mine. I could, as Ivan had predicted, take what happened in the Great Room very seriously; I could base my life around what happened here, everything outside fading into trivial obscurity. There was the added attraction of the unknown, that I was about to undergo some sort of humiliating punishment, but I didn't know what it was to be.

Illumination came in the form of Jennifer carrying a battered leather case. "Why do I always have to do this?" She dropped it at Ivan's feet and reached out to give the nipple clamp chain a yank. I took a quick step back.

"Be nice." Pete slapped her bottom.

She giggled. "Wait 'til they take the clips off, Jo. You'll feel it then." She delved into the bag and came up with a tattered leather slipper. "Eew. This stinks. Whose is it?"

"Mine." Pete took the slipper and slapped her ass with it. "Hands off. Go sit down. Everyone else, too."

Ivan reached into the leather bag. "How about this?" He held up a cane.

Pete took it from him and bent it between his hands, then gave it a few whistling strokes in the air. "I don't know. You have been a very bad girl, haven't you, Jo? What do you think?"

"You're asking me? Sir?"

"Mmm." He stroked one of my nipples with the cane. "It would hurt a lot. But I think you'd like it." He ran the cane down my torso, over my belly, and prodded between my legs with the tip. "You're not wet, are you?"

I parted my legs a little. "I can't help it."

He tucked the cane beneath one arm so he could stroke my clit and one of my engorged and sensitive nipples. "It would be real bad if you came at any time. It might earn you a couple of extra strokes. And we wouldn't want that, would we?"

I made some sort of breathy, excited noise.

"Would we?" he repeated and tugged the chain.

"No, sir," I managed to respond, as my legs quivered with excitement.

"Then I think you're out of luck." His finger at my clit barely moved and I guessed everyone else nearby could hear the small wet sound it made. The room was very quiet now, everyone sitting and watching, and up in the balcony, the dark shapes of motionless observers.

"Nah, it's too much," Ivan said and plucked the cane away from Pete, breaking the moment.

Pete laughed and folded his arms.

Ivan continued, "We don't want her passing out. Something less lethal. How about this?" The item he pulled from the bag looked painful enough, a small black whip. He trailed it over my nipples. "It'll hurt some, or to be honest it'll hurt enough, but you should be able to stand after. What do you think, Pete?"

Pete took the whip and slapped it against his leg. "Sure. Okay, let's get this show on the road." Then, as though speaking to an audience, he raised his voice. "Jo's been a very naughty girl, so she's getting ten strokes."

He tugged on the chain, taking me by surprise, and I let out a sound more like a squawk than anything else; it wasn't the sort of sexy moan that probably I should have produced and Ivan grinned.

"Panties off," Pete said.

In this room, where clothing was tugged aside or hands went delving inside, this was an unusual request. I slid my panties down, slowly. If I was going to be on show then I'd do my best (and try to restrain the unsexy squawks), because now I wanted to perform for the motionless onlookers on the balcony. And above all, I wanted to please Pete and Ivan, who had become my father confessors, my conspirators. I kicked my panties aside with what I hoped was an air of bravado, although I was feeling nervous now.

Pete strutted around, cracking the whip, his erection bouncing inside his shorts. Jennifer and another woman had opened a closet door (another of those doors hidden in the paneling, like the ones to the elevator upstairs) and pulled out a contraption on wheels. It reminded me of illustrations from the Inquisition and of gym equipment. Whatever it was, it could be tilted and angled to best display someone tied to it—and that someone was to be me.

Ivan ran his hands over my bare butt. "It's going to hurt, honey," he murmured in my ear. "Scream as loud as you want. I'll make you feel real good after."

Even in my present condition I wasn't that stupid. "You wish."

He delved into the bag and brought out a handful of leather straps with buckles, rather like wide bracelets.

Jennifer locked the wheels of the whipping horse and resumed her seat, cross-legged on the floor. She looked at me with greedy interest and so did the others. We'd watched Lindy in pretty much the same way as she poured water into a dozen glasses, fighting off loss of control and humiliation.

Leather straps in one hand, Ivan led me over to the whipping horse and arranged me on it. He caressed me as he did so, running his hands down the inside of my thighs to spread them and securing my ankles. My breasts poked through the wooden lattice and he secured the chain to the frame with a small clip. By the time he'd fastened my wrists above my head I realized the level of expertise he employed. I could move, some. But every time I moved my torso or arms, it put pressure on that chain and thus onto my nipples.

He messed around with the controls, to adjust the angle and tilt, and then nodded approvingly.

"Breathe deep, babe." He leaned in to kiss my mouth and stepped back out of sight.

Nothing happened. Behind me I could hear the small sounds of people shifting and the occasional whisper, and then I jumped out of my skin as something cold trailed over my butt. I twisted my head but I couldn't see—all the movement did was to put pressure on my clamped nipples. Pete had trailed the whip over my buttocks, a prelude to what was to come next.

What came next was a whistle of leather through air and the loud crack as the whip met my skin, and Christ! It hurt. It really hurt. Pete meant business. Tears sprang to my eyes and my body gave an involuntary jerk and clench. I gulped in air.

And another.

I'd promised myself I wouldn't cry, but I did. Tears burst from my eyes, to my humiliation. I wouldn't scream, I promised myself. They'd told me I could, but I wouldn't.

A pause. That wasn't good, not being able to anticipate the blow. Two down, eight to go—and then two in quick succession, exquisitely painful as the whip landed on places it had reached already.

I clenched my eyes and teeth shut.

Another vicious sting across my butt, but lower, catching untouched skin. Halfway there.

At the next one I screamed. I had some sort of absurd idea that if I made enough noise maybe Pete would change his mind and stop. I wrenched at my bonds and the pain in my nipples made me sob aloud. I tried to keep myself under control—breathe deep, as Ivan had said, breathe, relax my muscles, breathe myself beyond the pain—

Three. Two. One.

Finished. A roaring noise. Applause. For me. Once I'd been used to extreme pain followed by the ecstasy of its absence, and applause, but that now felt like a lifetime ago.

"You did good." Ivan's breath warm on my face. "Open your eyes. It's over. You did real good."

I opened my eyes to look into his gray-green ones. "I did?"

"Oh, yeah. They loved it." He dabbed at my face with a tissue.

"Oh. Great."

He kissed me again, deep and lingering, one hand stroking my nipples, and unclipped the chain. "We'll get these off, soon. Your butt has some very pretty stripes."

"I know. I can feel them."

He raised a hand to unbuckle me. "Be quiet."

"Why?" Why would I *not* be quiet? No one was whipping me.

He dropped a hand through the lattice and stroked me, small economical movements. "You're real wet. Come for me."

My legs shook. I gripped the frame of the whipping horse and he caught my mouth with his as I came, oh, God, I came with a great rush of pain as everything clenched and released, my nipples burning.

"Our secret," he murmured and set himself to untying me. "Was that good?"

I nodded. "Outrageously good. I don't know that it had anything to do with—"

"Babe, it had everything to do with being whipped. Even though it wasn't much of a beating."

"It wasn't?"

"Pete's a big softy. He went easy on you. Hold tight. I'll get your ankles."

He came around to the other side of the frame and unbuckled the straps at my ankles. He dropped a kiss on my butt, steadying me with his hands on my waist. "Slowly, now."

I needed his support. My legs shook and my butt was already stiffening up, so I cried out with pain as I moved. He scooped me into his arms, and laid me facedown on a couch, where everyone crowded round me to kiss me or make admiring comments on Pete's handiwork, even offering me a view in a small mirror.

I declined the view in the mirror, but I accepted the offer to remove the nipple clamps and let out a shriek as Ivan pressed handfuls of ice to my poor, abused breasts.

After that, it was a lovely, dreamy sequence of being fussed over and caressed. Ivan applied some sort of lotion to my sore butt that made me wince when it hit the tender skin, but after that initial tingle soothed and relaxed me. His fingers trailed into my cleft and between my thighs and I could have come again quite easily from the slightest touch, but instead I looked over my shoulder and told him to knock it off.

His wicked grin told me he knew how aroused I was, still, and that he would have no compunction at all about making me come and subjecting me to further punishment. He worked his way down my legs with the lotion, and I groaned with pleasure as he started on my feet and toes.

Pete fed me grapes and praised me. "You're a bad girl, Jo, but you did good."

"I did? Ivan said you went easy on me."

"Easier than he would have. He'd have made you scream much louder."

I found it difficult to believe of Ivan, who at this moment rubbed lotion into my feet and calves with such tenderness.

Pete kissed my cheek. "He made you come, didn't he?"

"Huh?" I think my feigned innocence fooled him. At any rate, he grinned and told Jennifer to fetch me some wine and my abandoned panties, and to find me a throw.

I dozed off for a time beneath the soft throw, warm and comfortable despite my tingling nipples and the leather bustier, which certainly wasn't an article of clothing meant for sleepwear. I turned onto my side and felt the tenderness on my butt and from my strained muscles, but awash with endorphins, I was miles away from the pain.

I could even regard Mr. D.'s betrayal with a little less anger. And possibly, yes possibly…wasn't transgression and punishment a way to advance upstairs? Tonight, maybe (I was a little concerned about my sore butt—we'd have to choose positions wisely) the king would summon Scheherazade and the story would reach its conclusion.

Someone, Ivan probably, played the piano softly.

Jennifer, who had appointed herself my guardian, sat at my side and whispered to anyone who came near, telling them I had to rest and would play Scrabble or visit with them later. "Are you okay, Jo?" she whispered to me if I moved. "Can I get you anything?"

What's in it for you? I considered asking her to peel me some grapes, but I was too warm and comfortable to pick a fight with her. I suspected that she wanted to attach herself to me while

I was in favor. Besides, she probably *would* peel me grapes if I
asked her in her current subservient mood, and I didn't want
to think where her fingers had been.

"Jennifer? When they send you upstairs, what happens?"

"It means someone's chosen you. And you get to do whatever they ask. So how did you find out the combination for the
door?"

"I guessed it."

"Wow." She looked impressed. "I don't think anyone's done
that before. What's it like up there?"

"Fancy. This is a gorgeous house. It's got to be a hundred
years old at least."

"No, I mean what were they doing?" Jennifer wasn't interested in architecture.

"Eating dinner. Lindy was stretched out on the table like a
centerpiece, covered with fruit and flowers."

"Gross." She wrinkled up her nose. "Were they eating stuff
off her?"

"No. It was just a regular formal dinner."

The doorbell rang and Jennifer snatched the throw from me
and bundled it up. "Look sexy!" she hissed at me and arranged
herself in a seductive pose.

"What difference would it make? Don't you think they know
who they're coming for?"

"Yeah, but...it's what we do."

I eased myself onto my side. Whatever had been in that lotion had eased the pain considerably.

Angela strode in and kissed Pete on the cheek when he
greeted her. She nodded in my direction. "That one," she said
in contempt. To me, she said, "You look a mess."

I stood and stretched a little while she watched me, arms
crossed, tapping one foot. "As though I don't have enough to
do," she said.

"What do you do?" I asked. "Other than run errands for the big boys?"

She addressed Pete. "Next time let Ivan whip some of that cheekiness out of her. Ready, Jo?" She held the door open and I waved to the room, walking carefully and not too fast.

The first thing Angela did when we returned to the locker room was to change her boots for her pink slippers, muttering under her breath. Then she set about cleaning me up. She used a cleanser on my face and an expensive, subtly scented moisturizer, and rummaged in a plastic basket for foundation and blusher that matched my skin, expensive European brands that I wanted to ask Kimberly about. She picked out a greenish-gray eyeshadow I'd never have dreamed of wearing and added a silvery highlight on my brows, and a dark gray eyeliner at my lashes.

"Look *up!*" She waved a mascara wand at my face.

"I don't wear mascara."

"Tonight, honey, you do. Don't blink."

She dusted my face with a powder that had sparkles in it and finished everything off with a bright red lipstick. I was appalled and thrilled when she finally allowed me to see my reflection. I looked pretty. And I didn't often look pretty, or at least, not like that. I also looked sluttier than I'd ever looked in my life.

"I suppose that will do," she said in disgust.

"Wow. You're really good," I said. "How did you learn to do all that?"

She shrugged. "I was a model. A long time ago. You learn these things. You need to change your panties."

"I like these ones."

She looked down her nose at me. "They've got to be pretty ripe by now, after what you've been up to. Besides, he specifically asked for these."

"Who?"

She ignored me and fished a pair of white panties from a

laundry basket that stood in the corner. Someone had gone to the trouble of ironing them. They weren't quite schoolgirl-fantasy briefs, but they were modest and much like the sort of underwear I favored when I wasn't being a sex slave or Mr. D.'s fantasy. I thought they looked bizarre with the leather bustier, but who was I to judge.

"What's his name?" I asked.

"It's not my place to say." She rearranged my breasts over the bustier.

"You have such a tough job," I said with fake sincerity, which raised a half smile from her.

She led me out into the kitchen, where a few staff still worked, scrubbing the work surfaces, and to the elevator. We traveled to the second floor of the house, where she led me down another dim corridor—soft carpet underfoot, dark red walls with the occasional piece of art or ornate mirror, and then tapped on a door.

Angela opened the door and pushed me forward. "She's here."

I walked into the room and stopped dead when I saw the man on the bed.

Behind me the door clicked closed.

15

THE LIMO CAME TO A STOP AT MY HOUSE AND I eased myself out of the door into the cold night air. Everything hurt now. The limo eased away with a quiet purr and I watched its taillights disappear.

An image came into my mind of my house keys, lying on the kitchen counter.

Oh, shit. I burrowed into the small purse I'd brought and confirmed my suspicion. No keys.

Upstairs over the garage a light burned. I pulled out my cell and punched in his number—still listed under "Apartment," something I should change. I hoped he was still awake, and alone, because all I wanted to do was shower and fall into bed and not have to make conversation.

He answered on the third ring. When I spoke my voice sounded scratchy. He didn't sound overjoyed to hear from me but he didn't sound pissed, either.

I breathed a sigh of relief as I saw lights go on, marking his passage through the house. The front door swung open. He wore sweats and a T-shirt, his hair ruffled.

"God in heaven, woman, what happened to you?"

I pushed past him. "I'm okay. Thanks. Sorry to disturb you."

"Should I call the cops?"

"What?" My legs were weak and heavy. I lowered myself onto the stairs.

She looked like hell. Her eyes were rimmed with black—at first he'd thought the black was bruising, but to his relief it was smeared mascara—and she moved with difficulty, as though her whole body hurt, her hands jammed into her jacket pockets. Her voice was exhausted and hoarse.

He was angry as hell, frightened for her.

"I'll call the cops," he said again.

"No. No, I'm fine. I…" She pushed herself up from the staircase and clutched the rail. Her jacket swung open and he caught a brief glimpse of her nipples above some sort of black leather corset, incongruous with her jeans, and that explained a lot.

He looked away until she had a chance to cover up. "I'll make you a cup of tea."

It was the sort of offer his gran or sisters would make and seemed ludicrous for someone who'd overdone a night of rough sex, but to his surprise she nodded with a faint smile. "Thanks."

They went into her kitchen, where she sat while he set the kettle on the range and found her canister of tea bags.

She shuffled over to the refrigerator. "Want some eggs?"

"Sure. I'll do it. Sit."

As he busied himself making scrambled eggs she left the room and he heard water running. She returned, her face scrubbed clean, wearing a bulky gray sweater he suspected was left behind by a boyfriend. She sat at the table and wrapped her hands around the mug of tea while he spooned scrambled eggs onto toast and pushed a plateful toward her.

She picked up her fork with a sigh and stared at the food

before shoveling it in, clearing her plate entirely. By then a little color had returned to her face.

"Thanks, that was great. Hit the spot."

"You're welcome. Sorry I overreacted."

"No problem. I looked a wreck." She swirled the tea at the bottom of her mug. "I'm fine. I'm sorry I scared you. And thanks for this, the food and the company."

He shrugged and gathered their plates to put them in the dishwasher. "You're welcome."

She came up beside him as he stood at the sink. "I'll do the dishes. How's your eye?"

He almost stopped breathing as she touched his cheek and temple with her cool fingers. Her face was so close to his he could see a speck of black she'd missed below one eye, smell her perfume and sweat. "Does it hurt?"

"Hardly at all. Don't worry." A knife slid from his fingers and clattered into the sink.

She grinned, breaking the moment. "We could stand here all night reassuring each other we're both okay. Leave the dishes, Patrick, I'll get them tomorrow. I'm sorry I disturbed you tonight."

"I was awake. No problem."

She nodded. "I'm going to bed now."

He followed her up the stairs, which was unnervingly erotic even though that was the way back into his apartment. He didn't want to think of Jo peeling off that black leather corset but he couldn't help speculating whether it had marked her skin. Neither did he want to think of the one quick glimpse he'd had of her nipples, as dark as the leather in the dim light. He didn't want to think of her at all in those terms; they had a business relationship, for Christ's sake. He was her tenant. She was Kimberly's best friend.

At the top of the stairs she hesitated. "Tonight I made a

mistake. That's all. It's bad, but not in the way you're probably thinking."

And she turned toward her bedroom, leaving him to ponder her cryptic remark.

I couldn't remember the last time someone had cooked for me, or when I'd had a stranger in the kitchen who had found their way around without my help, instinctively knowing where the spatula was kept and the plates, and what to do with the broken eggshells. With anyone else I might have felt invaded; with Patrick, it felt like a blessing. I didn't have to give directions or do anything but watch and feel safe.

Yes, safe. I didn't realize how bad I looked until I saw the expression on his face and his insistence we call the cops. Yet he accepted my assurance that I was okay without demanding further explanation. I think I'd flashed him, too, and he was quite the gentleman about it, although of course it wasn't the first time.

I'd left the Association very fast after rushing downstairs to the locker room, my hands shaking so badly I could barely operate the combination lock (and for one panicked moment I thought I'd forgotten the sequence). Jeans on, jacket on, T-shirt balled and stuffed into my pocket, and then I'd called for the limo and waited at the side door, terrified of pursuit and discovery.

Neither came. Twenty minutes, they'd told me to wait for a car, and it was the longest twenty minutes of my life before I heard the limo pull up. I sank into the leather seat and cried all the way back into town, frustrated, angry, betrayed, sad beyond words.

No wonder I looked like shit. I took a long shower and by the time I crawled into bed, it was almost dawn.

"Kimberly?" Balancing one latte atop the other I tapped at her office door. I knew she didn't have any appointments this morning and I was curious as to why she had the door closed.

Cautiously I opened the door. She jumped up and relieved me of the top latte.

"You'll never get a job in a circus."

"Damn. And I was planning to run away with one." I eased the top off my latte. "You busy?"

"Not for a few minutes." She smiled, almost. "You're in early for a Monday."

I sat. "How've you been?"

"Fine. Busy. And you?"

"Oh, okay. Busy." I took a deep breath. "Kimberly, I'm sorry I've been…distant. I was trying to sort out some stuff."

"And did you sort it out? Ready to come back to the real world?"

"Yes."

She frowned. "Patrick called me yesterday. He was worried about you."

"Oh."

"It was eight in the morning on a Sunday." She took a sip of latte. "I had company. It was sorta awkward."

"Sorry about that." A week ago she would have told me who the man was but I wasn't going to push this fragile truce. "What did he say?"

"Patrick? He thought you'd got in over your head on something, that you looked kind of beaten-up, and he thought you might need help." She looked at her watch. "I need to get to this meeting. Don't be a stranger, Jo. Let me know when you're free this week and we'll do something. And thanks for the coffee."

She strutted toward the door in her cowboy boots, balancing purse and briefcase and coffee, a fringed suede jacket hung over one arm.

"Is this new?" I stroked the suede. "It's gorgeous."

"Thanks. And do you need help?"

I hesitated for one moment, hoping she didn't notice. "No, I'm fine. I came home late and tired, that's all, and I think it scared Patrick."

She nodded, delving into her purse for her car keys. "See you, babes."

I watched her stride down the hall, stopping to exchange a few words with Bill the station manager, before she went into the reception area and left.

I wandered into my cubicle and sorted through some mail and new recordings we'd been sent, restless and dissatisfied. I wished I'd been able to tell Kimberly the whole story, because if I'd restricted the story to only what had happened that Saturday night it wouldn't have made sense. I wasn't ready to tell her, or anyone, the whole story: how I'd been duped and fooled.

It was only ten in the morning. There was a time I might have wanted to stay at the station the whole day and well into the night. There were always things to do, projects to work on.

But now I couldn't stay. I left the station by the back door and walked along the bike trail I rode to work. I turned over the events of Saturday night in my mind, of what had happened when I'd entered that room, Angela's hand pushing gently against my back.

I was still angry and humiliated but I felt then that I could forgive Mr. D., see in his actions the complex and baroque intricacies of human behavior that he enjoyed. I was prepared, at the very least, to listen to his explanation, and for him to listen while I poured out my anger at him. In those few seconds as I entered the room, I could see there was potential for forgiveness, for possibilities to present themselves.

The room had a faint scent of something sweet and delicate, a whisper of perfume. My feet sank into a Persian rug of minute intricacies and a lamp on a massively carved chest gave off a warm, golden glow. To the side something moved and, keyed up by anxiety and the strangeness of the evening, I started before realizing it was my reflection in a huge mirror on the wall. Of course.

Ahead of me stood a bed, wide and low. And on the bed, beneath a white sheet, a man lay, his head propped on one hand, his face shadowed.

"Hey, Jo."

"Jake?" My hands felt cold. I crossed my arms over my exposed breasts.

"Expecting someone else?"

I nodded.

"My reward for recruiting you," he said. "You need to thank me properly."

"Why should I thank you for rewarding yourself?"

"Good question. Let's think of it as an apology."

"An apology?"

"You abused my hospitality. Cathy's, too. She was upset."

"What do you think I did? I left early but you were, uh, busy and I realize I didn't thank you—"

He moved a little, bringing his face into the light, and I saw his expression. "You have no idea, do you? You should have seen yourself, the way you looked at my house. I finished that basement myself!"

"It's a great basement. I have mice in mine."

"See? There you go again. You don't even know you're doing it." He pushed the sheet down, revealing his erection as a threat. I'd never seen a guy use his dick as a weapon before and it scared me. "What the fuck makes you think you're better than us? Looking at my house and my wife with a high-and-mighty expression, like you're some sort of princess. Asking if we had any *books*." He spat the word out as though it was an obscenity. "Get your ass over here."

I looked him in the eye. "No. I don't want to."

"You agreed to abide by Association rules, and the rule here is that you do what I say."

"Seems like the only rule going is that I get told what to do and I've had enough. Sorry, Jake. I'm leaving."

He lay back, hands locked behind his head. "I wouldn't recommend that."

"Who's Mr. D.?" I asked.

"Who?"

"The guy who should be here. The guy who really did recruit me, and I think you know who I mean."

"I've no idea." He sat and swung his legs over the edge of the bed.

I turned away from him and walked to the door. I didn't want to turn my back on him but neither did I want to back away as though he were royalty or as though I was too scared to take my eyes off him. My hand shook as I closed my fingers on the handle and to my relief it was just a regular lock, nothing fancy.

"You'll wish you'd stayed," he said as I opened the door.

"I doubt it. You're not my type." I closed the door behind me and then I ran, back to the locker room, and escaped.

And that was why I now walked along a bike path, my fists clenched, muttering to myself, too, and still slightly stiff from the beating and tension. A bicyclist whizzed past me and I looked at the bare branches of the trees and beyond them the pristine whiteness of the mountains against a pure blue sky. I lifted my face to the dazzle of sunlight and the sharp, cold air. I needed to cleanse myself of disappointment and negativity.

I went back to my cubicle and sent emails to cover my shift for the next couple of days, got caught up on paperwork and future programming and tidied things up. I was going to take some of my unused vacation and comp time and get myself rested and relaxed. I checked snow depths and skiing conditions. Things were looking good. I thought fondly of my reserves of wax at home, the excitement of taking skis down and preparing them, pulling out favorite wool sweaters and down vests, gloves and hats.

"Can I help?"

I looked over my shoulder. Patrick stood behind me, a slight grin on his face, and I wondered how long he'd admired the sight of my butt as I knelt on the floor hauling stuff out of the hall closet.

"I'm fine." I found my ski boots and one mitten and tossed them out onto the hall floor.

He glanced at my skis and poles on the floor. "Where are you going?"

"Not sure yet. Somewhere over the Divide."

"Yeah, I heard they got six inches there. Snow," he added, as though suddenly aware that a double entendre lurked in his words.

"Would you like to come?" I found another mitten—not a matching one, but it would do. "Come skiing, I mean." Now he had me doing it, too.

"Sure. When?"

"Tomorrow. I'll drive."

"Great." He laid an envelope on the hall table. "Rent."

Our conversation became a little less stilted and monosyllabic as we agreed on a start time and discussed a suitable trail. While we talked I regretted my invitation—I'd wanted solitude and the chance to think and unwind, not an obligation to make conversation with someone I barely knew. But unless he backed out, and that could be awkward, too, I was stuck with him.

I felt bad about my reservations; after all, he'd come to the rescue when I locked myself out last night, and we'd gotten to know each other some. That, too, was a subject I didn't feel altogether comfortable with, thanks to the occasional flare of carnal interest between us.

Heck, I was the veteran of orgies and BDSM; why was I so bent out of shape by a little flirtation?

Bright sunlight shone in the car's windows as we toiled up the highway that led to the high country. Patrick, beside me, fiddled with the radio before we lost the signal, not saying much. We both had mugs of coffee. We'd both managed to spill them over ourselves. Neither of us looked as though we'd stepped out of an L.L. Bean catalogue, although my down vest, bought at a yard sale and fine once I'd patched it, had once belonged to someone who had bought from that supplier. I wore my bike pants and silk underwear for warmth and the sweater with the hole in the elbow that Hugh had left. Patrick wore a truly horrible plaid woolen shirt with paint stains, cord pants and a pair of bright red gaiters.

"We won't win any fashion awards," he commented.

"It's not as though we're going to hang around a bar in Aspen after," I replied. "We're losing the radio signal. Want to play a CD?"

He rummaged through my collection. "Do you have anything except opera?"

"No."

He shrugged and we listened to Verdi for the next hour. I tried not to grip the steering wheel in terror as trucks thundered by and I think Patrick noticed but tactfully refrained from commenting. When we turned off the highway he wrestled with the map.

"Okay. Your next left."

"Left?" I peered dubiously at the road.

"Right." *Roight.*

"Right?"

"No, left. Here."

We left the paved road and drove a couple of miles more to the parking lot for the trail, where we filled our pockets with trail mix and fastened our skis. We were the only people there, the trail, an old mining road, winding into the trees, pristine and untouched.

I launched myself onto the trail. Sometimes I liked to plod along, staring at the trees and looking for tracks of animals and birds in the snow. Today I wanted to move. I wanted the freedom of bounding through the snow, feeling the pull on my muscles and the sharp air on my skin. And I think there was part of me that wanted to impress Patrick, to show him I was strong and skilled.

Behind me, Patrick's skis hissed on the trail I'd created, an easier run, but he kept up with me. "I'll take over breaking the trail anytime you like," he said, barely out of breath.

"I'm fine." The trail dipped and turned and a blue jay, brilliant against the snow, flashed across my field of vision. I pushed my dark glasses up as the trail led into a shadowed area and then slowed to adjust them again as the sun dazzled my eyes.

I took the trail a little slower now, reminded that part of the pleasure of this sort of skiing (other than being able to wear your worst clothes) was to observe and enjoy the scenery, and sure enough, after a steep bit that required herringboning, the trees opened out to an open meadow. I was reminded of my picnic with Willis, only a few weeks ago, at a lower altitude, which made all the difference in temperature, when the sky was as sharp a blue as this. I slowed to a plod and saw snow-covered mountains on the horizon, their peaks wreathed in clouds, a stand of aspens, leaves gone, trunks etched against the snow.

"I'm duly impressed," Patrick said, moving alongside me. "Damn, I forgot the camera." He delved into a pocket and offered me some trail mix. "You're very fit."

"Fit enough for this." I was pleased with my body and how it had recovered from the beating. "It'll be fun coming down. How long have you skied? I can't imagine there's a whole lot of snow in Ireland."

"Since last year. These were a Christmas present from Elise."

He gestured at his poles and skis and looked sad and I wished I hadn't asked.

"You're pretty good."

"Thanks. And you?"

"Ever since I was a kid." I took a gulp from my water bottle. "My mom taught me and then she and I and the Great Abe used to go on picnics in the snow."

"Great Abe?"

"My stepdad. He's called Abe and he looks sort of simian. Long arms, hairy back. He's a nice guy."

"What do they do?"

"Mom's a potter and Abe runs an auto repair shop. Very Vermont. They moved there before I was born when land was still cheap. Mom's sort of an old hippie. Now and again she'll call and make a confession of how capitalism is corrupting her, now she sells her pots instead of trading them for goat cheese."

He laughed. "You like them, I can tell."

"Sure. I'm planning to visit them at Christmas."

Patrick slathered some more sunscreen onto his face and we set off again, gliding over the snow. I let him lead, observing his ass through his baggy cord pants, and wondered if he'd watched mine. Our pace and the quiet gentle hiss of skis on snow was hypnotic.

"Nice trail," he said after we negotiated some small hills and bends. "How did you find out about it?"

"Facebook. I'm on a cross-country-ski group."

We made another stop for trail mix and water and sunscreen and now the shadows lengthened just a little and the air had a cool tinge. We agreed to return, mostly a downhill run, and on my first attempt to telemark around a bend I made a spectacular dive into a snowbank.

Patrick leaned on his skis and laughed. "You okay?"

"Fine." I floundered in the snow and retrieved my hat. When I was back on the trail he leaned to smack snow from my back in a friendly, helpful sort of way, and I was relieved. Maybe exercise in the fresh air was the best way of dispelling unwholesome thoughts, just like the Boy Scouts taught, or used to teach.

So why was I watching his ass again?

I pushed forward, knees bent, and overtook him, building up a burst of speed, and loving the long effortless glide on the trail I'd broken earlier, poles tucked under my arms. Bliss, pure bliss.

Better than sex? At that moment, yes.

I arrived back at the car and waited for Patrick, who joined me a couple of minutes later, with a big, happy grin on his face. I'd never seen that before. I wondered if he'd been as happy skiing with Elise and I was glad his breakup hadn't tainted his enjoyment of the snow and the day.

"Excellent," he said as he unfastened his skis. "I'm going for a piss." He bounded into the snow through the trees and returned a few minutes later, brushing snow off himself.

I leaned against the car, reluctant to leave, but noting how the gray-and-violet shadows lengthened. Something moved in the trees. A dog?

"Look." I touched his arm.

A coyote emerged from the thick, stood and observed us for a moment, curious yet cautious. Then it retreated back into the trees.

"Wow," Patrick said. "Thanks for that."

"Thank *you*. I think you probably peed on his territory and he came out to complain."

16

"THE THING I LIKE ABOUT YOU," I SAID AFTER A forty-five-minute silence on the drive home, "is that I don't have to talk to you."

Patrick yawned. "I guess that was a compliment. Want to stop somewhere for dinner?"

"An observation, that's all. And, no, but thanks for asking. I've got stuff in the Crock-Pot. If I remembered to turn it on. You're welcome to have some, too."

"Look, you drove and now you're offering to feed me. Let me take you out to dinner another evening, so I don't feel totally emasculated."

"Okay." I took the turn off the highway. "We could see if some other people want to come."

He made a throat-clearing sound. "Uh. I was thinking, just you and me."

"Like a date?" Just in time I stopped at a red light.

"Well, no. But...would you have a problem with that? If I was to ask you out on a date that was really a date?"

I turned the radio on while I considered my answer. "But you weren't asking me out on a date."

"I wouldn't dream of suggesting it was a date. I plan to ask you if you want a website designed so I can write it off on my taxes."

I agreed that sounded good, and within a few minutes we were home.

We dropped skis and outerwear in the hall. A fragrance in the air announced that I had remembered to turn on the Crock-Pot and that dinner would be ready soon. I left him lighting a fire and went into the kitchen where I checked the seasoning on the beef stew—needed more salt, but not bad—and ladled it out into two bowls. I cut up some French bread, slathered it with garlic and butter and shoved it under the broiler, my mouth watering.

I smiled when I arrived back in the living room with a tray of food and drinks. The fire had caught well and Patrick lay on the rug, fast asleep like a dog tired out from a run, his glasses folded neatly on the coffee table.

"Hey." I poked him with my foot. "Wake up."

He grunted and rolled over onto his back, revealing a quite unmistakable erection beneath his pants. He curled up fast, rolling to a sitting position, possibly becoming aware of his condition at the same time I did. "Sorry," he mumbled, reaching for his glasses. "Wow, that smells good."

I placed the tray on the coffee table. "Fork or spoon? It didn't thicken much."

"Spoon. I want to shovel it in." He nodded in appreciation at the bottle of nonalcoholic beer I'd brought him and grabbed a piece of garlic bread. "And that's a compliment. You've no idea how great this is. Home cooking that isn't my own."

"You like to cook?"

"Sometimes. But not just for myself. It gets boring or you end up eating the same stuff for days."

"Yeah," I said around an uncouth mouthful. "Hugh was a

bit of a foodie. He knew about wine, too. He'd probably be real upset I used one of his precious bottles to cook with."

"Hugh was your, uh, boyfriend?" He was being very tactful.

"Yeah. And sorry. Hugh and I should have been more careful that day."

"Oh, I didn't mind that much." His eyeglasses glinted in a wicked sort of way. "I've been carried away with passion a few times myself."

"So," I said after a few more mouthfuls, "are you seeing anyone at the moment?"

"Shit, I'm not even divorced yet. Why? Are you interested? Reconsidering that date that isn't really a date?"

My spoon clinked in its bowl. He'd gone straight to the issue we'd both circled around so carefully.

"No, I—"

"There's a tingle between us," he said. "Doesn't mean we have to do anything about it, but it's there. And it's sort of awkward. Technically I'm still married, I'm your tenant and I'm flat broke, and I'm depressed quite a bit of the time. I'm not a great prospect. And you...?"

"I'm involved with someone," I said after a pause. "At least, I thought I was. Now, I'm not sure. There are unresolved issues."

"Hugh?"

"No, not Hugh."

"Ah." He scooped the last of his stew out of the bowl. "I think you have a rather complicated love life."

"And that puts you off?"

"No. You'll sort it out. I'll sort out my situation. I can sell the house at the end of the academic year, or maybe sooner if Elise buys me out, and I'll stop being depressed. I'm a naturally cheerful bloke, or I used to be. But there's one thing I don't do, and that's rescue damsels in distress. Not anymore. So you let me know when you're sorted out, and we'll talk about it some more."

I laughed. "You're very sure of yourself. Of me, too, I guess. So what happened with Elise?" I added hastily, "You don't have to tell me if you don't want to. Would you like some more stew?"

I fetched us both second helpings and Patrick stared at the fire for a time. "Elise," he said. "We fell out of love. I don't know why. Why should you expect to know why you look at someone one day and they're just a person, someone you know well, and you maybe even quite like, but there's nothing left? I don't know. I guess I was going through my knight-on-a-white-charger stage and she was letting her long blond hair down from the tower. And then I found out she was disappointed I didn't become a big-shot lawyer, and she wasn't some sort of mythical princess—just a fairly ordinary woman. She liked me in Ireland but I didn't export too well."

"You're still sad." I touched his hand.

"Oh, I will be for some time." He sounded quite cheerful as he wiped his bowl with a hunk of garlic bread. "Now, about this tingle."

"What about it?"

"I don't think you're convinced. It's a good thing we've both had garlic." He put his bowl and utensils down with a purposeful air and shifted toward me.

"What are you doing, Patrick?" I tried, without much success, to sound offended.

"Kissing you. Or I will be, shortly."

"I don't think—"

"In the spirit of scientific enquiry." And he was kissing me, and it was sweet and garlicky, his mouth closed, with a very gentle pressure that built. And built a little more, so that when his lower lip nudged between mine, despite my reservations I opened to him. Only a little, though. Only enough for my tongue to flick against his lower lip before I withdrew, shaking my head.

"Well?" He had that wicked look again, but it was deep in his eyes, nothing to do with his glasses.

"The experiment is over." I stood and gathered our bowls.

"Ah, now you can't tell me you weren't swept away with passion. That I'm not a great kisser." He stood, too, and took the bowls from me. "I'll do the dishes. It's a second best to kissing you, but at least I can prove I'm not overwhelmingly macho."

And the moment was over. I watched as he left the room and touched my fingertips to my lips, where his had been seconds before.

"Patrick? You're right. I have a complicated love life."

He looked back over his shoulder. "I know."

I followed him into the kitchen, tempted to tell him the entire truth, and decided against it. Hadn't he said he was no longer in the habit of rescuing women?

Besides, I was pretty sure I didn't need to be rescued.

The next day Kimberly and I went out to lunch, where she regaled me with an account of her most recent date, someone she'd met online.

"I shoulda known better. The dreads should have been a clue," she said. "Nothing sadder than a white, fortysomething guy with dreads. He wore leather pants, too, and I swear he had an armadillo down his pants. Wanted to talk about root canals all night."

"He went out on a date after a root canal?"

"No. He's a dentist. A new breed of dentists, rides a Harley and is into extreme winter sports, and, oh, yeah, he's a Buddhist."

"And did you tell him of your aversion to snow?"

"You bet." She dug into her salad. "And before you ask, I didn't investigate the armadillo. You seeing anyone yet? How's my buddy Patrick?"

"I'm going to ignore the fact that you just asked two totally unrelated questions. Please don't bring the dreadlocked dentist over at Thanksgiving. But bring your cranberry relish." I pushed my plate toward her. "Help yourself. Why don't you just order a side of fries and be done with it?"

"Because stolen fries are so much better." She gazed at our waiter. "I bet I could get you his phone number."

"What for?" I blinked innocently at her. The waiter, noting our interest, headed toward our table.

"We'll take a look at the dessert menu, honey," Kimberly said. "Mmm. Sweet buns," she added as he walked away.

"They're probably not on the menu. So if it wasn't the winter-sport dentist, who was staying over the other night?"

"Just this guy."

"And? Will you be bringing him at Thanksgiving? Is it anyone I know?"

She held up crossed fingers. "Maybe I'll bring him for Thanksgiving and it is someone you know, but I'm not saying. He's great, even though he's a bit older than I am, but I'm not gonna talk about it, 'cause it'll jinx it. So, about Patrick."

I thought furiously as to who the mystery man could be and gave up. Kimberly knew a lot of men. "Patrick is fine. I took him cross-country skiing yesterday. And it was just one of those things, I was getting my stuff together and we got talking and I invited him. And, yeah, I've invited him for Thanksgiving, too—I mean, he's right there in my house and I invite lots of people."

"Uh-huh."

"He's my tenant. I was being friendly. So, no, I haven't explored the joys of the Irish foreskin— Oh, thanks." The waiter, giving me a curious look, laid dessert menus on the table.

We discussed the dessert menu with great seriousness. I ordered us coffee and a carrot cake with two forks, knowing she'd eat at least half of it.

"Kimberly, do you think I'm stupid?"

"What? You? No way." She flashed a brilliant smile at the waiter as he placed the carrot cake in the center of the table. "You're a bit geeky. You don't go out clubbing or anything. You really like classical music, but you're not stupid."

"The thing is…" I turned the plate so she could gorge on the frosting. "Hugh was unfaithful to me. He deceived me. And then there was this other guy who did the same thing."

"Willis?" She stared at me, a blob of frosting on her lip. "You only had a couple of dates."

"No, not Willis." I hesitated, reluctant to tell her the whole story, or as much as I knew of it myself. "There was someone else. And no, it wasn't Jason. Someone I'd known for about six months and I liked. I thought I knew him, that there was honesty there."

"You mean while you and Hugh were living together?"

"Starting around the time things got weird with Hugh. You know, the bizarre breakup stuff, when he'd go out on an errand that would take four hours instead of ten minutes, and the late-night meetings and so on."

"You never told me you'd met someone else!"

"It wasn't like that. I didn't really know what the relationship was. It was platonic. Mostly. But my point is, what does that say about me? That two guys in a row betray me?"

"You choose the wrong guys. I've been telling you that forever." She scooped up another forkful of cake. "So, who was this mystery guy?"

"Just that. A mystery guy."

My cell rang. I glanced at the name and number and silenced it. Another call from Harry at the Association. I decided I'd oblige Kimberly with some dirt. "I had an erection sighting last night."

"Patrick's?" Kimberly grinned. "Sometimes the skinny short guys are so well-hung it's like dreamin' and goin' to heaven. How did you manage that?"

"He fell asleep in front of the fire after we came back from skiing."

"Sounds like an old hound dog. Did he slobber all over you?"

"No."

"Liar, liar, pants on fire," she chanted.

"Okay. We kissed. It was an experiment. Will you quit with the middle-school stuff?"

"And?"

"And it was nice. Sexy. But he's my tenant."

"He won't be your tenant forever. Elise has the house on the market, and guess who— Oh, my God, look. No, don't *look*. Be subtle."

But I didn't need to look. A familiar gust of aftershave announced the arrival of Willis Scott III, whom I'd last seen butt-naked fucking a woman he wouldn't or shouldn't fall in love with. God knew what I'd been doing last time he'd seen me.

"Ladies! Kimberly." He bent to kiss her cheek. "As gorgeous as ever. Hi, Jo, how are you?" He picked up a napkin and, to my mortification, wiped a smear of something off my face. I hoped it was frosting. I felt as though I were five years old. "Better give Harry a call," he said quietly. He straightened and motioned to the woman he'd come in with. "Do you know Elise Delaney?"

Elise was astonishingly gorgeous, tiny and slender, with a shiny fall of blond hair and huge blue eyes. Her hand felt like a small, fragile thing in mine, and her lips (soft, pink) quivered as though she were going to cry, instead of murmuring a greeting.

Willis laid a protective arm around her shoulders as though shielding her from the hazards of walking across a restaurant— all that china, those sharp knives, the hot substances—and to a table where our waiter and a couple of others dashed over to protect her from the brutality of the dining-out experience.

"Ain't she something," Kimberly said. "Walks through a

crowd of waving erect dicks every time she enters a room and has no idea she's doing it. Or does she?" She turned to look for our waiter and frowned as she saw him fawning at Elise and Willis's table. Elise's charms obviously offered more than my snippets of obscene conversation.

Elise rose, breaking free from the cluster of devoted waiters, and sauntered across the restaurant to the ladies' room.

I laid my credit card on the table, forestalling any claims Kimberly might make on paying. "Can you give him this when he comes back? I'm going to pee."

I doubted Elise was about to do anything so grossly human as pee, and sure enough, she stood in front of the mirror, running a brush through her amazing hair.

"Hi. Look, this could be awkward. Patrick is living above my garage."

"I know," she breathed.

"Oh. Okay, then. The other thing is, have you known Willis long?"

She blinked, beautifully. "He's my Realtor."

"Okay." I sounded really stupid. "Have you met any of his friends? Because if he mentions the Rocky Mountain Investment Association, be very careful."

"Oh, I have someone to do my investments for me," she murmured. "How's Patrick?"

"Fine." I'd tried. What more could I say?

"Poor Patrick." She sighed. "He won't make anything of himself. I'm so worried about him."

"But you're divorcing him." I knew no one could judge a relationship from the outside. I knew I was unfairly biased toward Patrick, but I thought briefly of wrapping that wonderful hair around her throat and squeezing it tight.

"I *had* to. It was for his own good." Her eyes opened wide and at any moment, I suspected, she could have released a few perfect tears.

Patrick, you idiot, I thought with a fierceness that surprised me. "Yeah, right."

I went into the stall, banging the door closed, and positioned myself for a long, loud pee. When I emerged, the only sign of Elise's presence was one long blond hair curled into the sink.

"I got it," Kimberly said and handed my card back when I returned to the table. As I uttered cries of protest, she said, "I guess I'd better go back to work. How about you? Still on vacation?"

"Yes, but I'll ride to the station. There's something I need there."

Outside the restaurant I unlocked my bike and buckled on my helmet while Kimberly fluttered her hand in a wave to me as she drove past.

The station was quiet, music playing softly through the speakers as I entered. I greeted the few people who were around, but did not linger for conversation. I knew only too well that I'd get sucked into some sort of problem-solving session or be asked for advice or information. As I went past her office, I saw Kimberly hunched over her phone, fingers tapping her computer keyboard. In my cubicle I watered my one plant, rising with green bravery among the scatter of CDs and paper on my desk, and opened the desk drawer. After some anxious searching I found the sheet of crumpled paper I had saved. I folded it and slipped it into my pocket, and then I went home.

I had to prepare myself and to do that I exercised. Long ago this killer set of warm-up aerobic exercises had been my daily routine, my religion. As I bent and stretched and sweated, in a ragged leotard and footless tights, my mind emptied and I became a purely physical being; I poured with sweat and my muscles became light and pliant.

To cool down I did a few yoga poses and my breathing deepened, bringing me to a place of calm and serenity.

A few more stretches and I was ready. I went upstairs and called Mr. D., for the first and, I hoped, last time.

He sounded surprised, slightly alarmed, at my voice. I wondered if he had someone else there and the thought didn't bother me much.

"Tell me why you wouldn't acknowledge me at the Association," I said. "Tell me the truth. I want what you should have told me all along."

"My dear, I misjudged you. My apologies, but I thought you knew long ago the role I played."

"I didn't. Not until I met you upstairs and heard your voice." My hand gripped the towel I sat on. I was too sweaty to sit directly on the sheet. "You set me up."

"I did, yes. You mean Willis and Jake never said a word? Hmm. I underestimated them. Of course, neither of them is very clever."

"I guess I'm not very clever, either. And why did you pass me on to Jake? That was the worst."

"Don't be angry. I was there."

"Where?"

"The mirror is a two-way mirror. Most of them in the house are. The plan was that—"

"Fuck the plan. Let's face it, you screwed up. I've had it. With you, with the Association, and you can tell Harry and the rest to go fuck themselves."

"I'm afraid it won't be that simple, Jo."

I'd been about to hang up, but the seriousness in his voice stopped me.

"What do you mean?"

"Talk to Harry," he said. "And, Jo, I know you're angry, but we had something, you and me. We still do. Can you trust me, for a little longer? I don't want to see you in trouble."

"I already am in trouble," I said. "I'm in trouble with you and your perverse games and I think you're bad for me. I wanted to see this through, Mr. D. I wanted a resolution to whatever we had—"

"You wouldn't meet me, I remember." I was pleased to hear a note of aggravation in his voice.

"Then, I wouldn't. Now, I probably wouldn't, either. But things change."

"I told you once I'd do anything you wanted." His tone had changed to sadness.

"But now I don't know if I can believe anything you say. I'm done with sexual experimentation, Mr. D., done with you."

"There's someone else? One of the boys in the Great Room?"

"No one you know." I took a deep breath. "We won't be talking anymore, Mr. D. You were a friend to me once—you helped me during the breakup with Hugh, and I thank you for that. I don't know if you were planning to seduce me into the Association even then, and it doesn't matter. I loved the phone sex, too. But it's over."

"I see. I won't insult you by telling you I love and admire you. It's too late, and you're right, I screwed up. Look after yourself, Jo."

So this was our last conversation. But I'd felt this before and the pain was somehow both real and a parody of itself.

I'd never even seen his face.

I clicked the phone off and laid it down. I scooped the sheet of paper with his phone number and email address into the bedside table drawer and pulled off my sweaty exercise gear so I could shower. Then I put on my pink fluffy slippers, my sweats and Hugh's sweater with the hole in the elbow, and went down to the kitchen for a snack.

Patrick was there, stirring something in a large bowl, the scent of yeast in the air.

"I'm making bread for Thanksgiving. I'll put it in the freezer so I won't be in the way on the day." He looked at me. "You okay?"

"Great, thanks." I crossed to the kitchen sink to wash my hands. "I'm going to make some girlie decaffeinated coffee. Want some?"

"Sure. Thanks." He dipped his hand into a sack of flour and sprinkled a handful on the counter.

As the coffee brewed, I watched him. He tipped a great creamy flood onto the floured surface, scraping the bowl with a wooden spoon. A bubble or two burst on the surface of the dough as it settled and spread; but it wasn't quite dough yet—too runny, too uncontrolled.

He sprinkled flour over the surface and scooped, turning the mass of stuff over itself, up to his wrists in dough. He held up hands from which ragged lumpy pieces of yeast hung, and took a clumsy step toward me.

"Flesh…flesh," he moaned.

"Irish zombies are the worst." I reached for coffee mugs.

Patrick turned back to the counter and worked the dough, scooping, folding, pressing out bubbles and sprinkling in more flour. The mass resisted him at first, spreading and bubbling, but calmed beneath his touch, assuming a soft docility. The surface dulled with flour. He reached for a spatula and scraped residue from the counter, folding the pieces inside, pressing the dough down, folding again.

He gave a pleased sigh when he lifted the dough free, turned it over and kneaded it again, working in a regular rhythm: press with the heel of his hand, fold, turn.

"It's looking like bread, now," he said.

I concentrated on pouring coffee into mugs. But I really wanted to watch his hands handle the dough with such deft assurance, and part of it was that I felt I watched a moment of intimacy, a man unveiling a mystery. "It's a bit late to be making bread, isn't it?"

"Am I disturbing you? I can put the dough into the refrigerator if you like and work on it tomorrow."

"No, no, that's fine. I just thought…well, it's going to take some time, with rising and so on."

"Yeah. I'm not sleeping that much these days. I might as well use the time." He smiled. "I find this very reassuring. You know, it works. Every time. You put yeast in warm water with a bit of sugar and it comes to life. No doubts, no uncertainties."

His sleeves were rolled above the elbow. I watched the tendons on his wrists flex, the coppery hair dusted with flour.

"I met Elise today," I blurted out and wondered whether I'd ruin his night.

"Did you, now." His fingers didn't pause in their smooth, rhythmic task. "A lovely girl, isn't she?"

Well, he had married her, after all. He'd been in love with her. I made a polite sort of noise and poured milk into the mugs of coffee.

He turned the dough over and slapped it, a juicy, ripe sound. "Sexy, eh?"

"It is?" Oh, what a liar I was. I had to keep reminding myself that this was bread-making, not some sort of sensual display for my benefit.

"Yeah. Gorgeous." Another slap. "All smooth and shiny and alive."

The phone rang and I grabbed it and turned away to hide my reddening cheeks. "Jo?" Harry's insinuating voice.

"Yeah."

"We need to talk."

"I don't think so." I hung up. To Patrick I said, "I hate telemarketers."

He looked at the clock and then at me, one hand laid on the bread dough. "Right."

He knew as well as I did that no telemarketer would call at ten in the evening.

I stepped out of his way as he headed over to the sink to rinse out his mixing bowl and clean dough off his hands.

"You look as though you've never seen anyone make bread before." He poured a little oil into the bowl and stroked it around with his fingertips. I shivered. I imagined those fingertips, slick and cool, doing other things. Doing things to me.

"Of course I have. I like to watch people who are good at doing things."

"I'm competent enough. Like I said, the yeast is the one that does the work." He tipped the large, creamy mass of dough into the bowl and flipped it around and over, before draping a dampened cloth over the top of the bowl. "And now it's going to sit here quietly and get busy. Who else is coming to Thanksgiving?"

"Mostly people from the station. Kimberly, maybe with a guy, maybe not. Liz and her husband. Everyone brings some sort of food. It's fun. If there's someone you'd like to ask, go ahead, but let me know." I spread peanut butter on a slice of bread. "I'm on air from six until one, which is why we eat early."

"You don't mind working Thanksgiving?"

"No, I like it. People tend to call in with nice comments. It's the one day they don't complain. It renews my faith in humanity."

He looked up from rinsing the spatula he'd used on the dough. "You don't strike me as a cynic. If anything I'd say you look sort of innocent."

"I'm not."

"Innocent doesn't mean dumb. You trust people. I like that."

I nodded. I did trust people, perhaps too much. I'd trusted Hugh. I'd trusted Mr. D. And Patrick…was he the next? "But if you don't trust people, you turn into some sort of paranoid crazy person. I go by my instincts. Sometimes they're wrong, but more often they're right."

He laid the spatula on the drying rack. "And what do your instincts tell you about me?"

"That you just tried to seduce me with a bowlful of bread dough." I tried to pass it off as a joke, but from the look on his face, neutral, impassive, I couldn't tell whether I succeeded. I couldn't tell him that I'd thought of his palm slapping my ass, his fingers smoothing and patting my skin, my sensitive areas.

He grinned. "If I wanted to use bread dough to seduce you, I'd bring you breakfast in bed. The finished product. Something delicious and flaky and sweet."

"Delicious, flaky and sweet. It sounds like the sort of men in my life, although the flakiness outweighed the other qualities." I finished my bread and peanut butter. "I'm going to bed. Good night."

He nodded back, arms folded. I left him there, leaning against the kitchen counter, looking at me with that expression I couldn't quite read.

I woke the next morning to delicious scents—yeast, sweetness, cinnamon, coffee. It was quite early, far earlier than I usually woke, but I hadn't drawn the curtains completely closed and light streamed through. Brady lay next to me on the pillow, an inert mass of sleeping fur. As I turned, I heard footsteps on the stairs, and Brady blinked, stretched and sat up, ears pricked.

I remembered Patrick's last statement to me. Breakfast in bed. My heart hammered and my stomach growled.

Something clinked as the footsteps halted and he knocked at the door.

Brady uncoiled, dropped to the floor and ran to the door, tail aloft. He was no fool. He knew that when people were awake there was a good chance of being fed. He put a paw on the door and eased it open, revealing Patrick and a tray, from which rose delectable scents.

He grinned. "I'm being very forward. I can leave this and

go. Or I'll take it back downstairs. Up to you. No pressure. You look like a woman who doesn't get breakfast in bed often enough."

I sat up. "Wow. I'm impressed. That's really nice. Come on in." It did cross my mind that a guy bearing a tray of breakfast, a rueful smile and an apology for appearing forward might very well expect to get laid. But I was willing to accept the offer at face value.

Brady, weaving around Patrick's ankles, was giving the impression that unlike me he'd do anything—*anything*—for someone who'd feed him, but Patrick lifted him gently out of the way with one foot. "There's food downstairs, you great dolt," he said, which I found very endearing.

I scooted over so he could lay the tray on the bed and gestured to him to sit down. I wasn't about to make a move but I didn't want him to think I was on the same level as my cat.

He handed me a mug of coffee (he'd brought two, but I put that down to general optimism that he'd be invited in). On the tray was a plate with a gorgeous golden, puffy pastry, oozing butter, studded with raisins, speckled with cinnamon.

"Bread dough tarted up," he said. "I rolled in pounds of butter and cinnamon and put in some raisins. I hope you like it."

My mouth full, flakes cascading down my chest, I nodded with enthusiasm. "You're a genius. It's wonderful. Were you up all night?"

"No, I slept for an hour or so while the bread rose. I have a business meeting quite early, so I stayed up while it baked." He reached to pinch off a corner of the pastry.

"It was very sweet of you. Thanks."

He shrugged, looking a little bashful. "Ah, you're a nice woman. I'm not saying it'll happen every day or even every week. Or that I'll always act the gentleman. I have ulterior motives but I'll wait until the time is right for you."

"And how will you know?"

"You'll tell me."

"You seem very sure of that." I broke off another piece of bread. "I don't know that I want to be finessed into any sort of decision."

"Then don't be," he said easily. "Take this for what it is. I'm interested, you're interested, but we both know the time isn't right now. I brought you breakfast in bed, I'm fully clothed and, since I have to leave in five minutes, I intend to stay that way. If I'd arrived wearing only a rose behind my ear and half an hour to spare, I might have had a different agenda. Okay?"

"Only half an hour?" The image of Patrick and his rose made me snort crumbs over the bedclothes. "This was great. Thanks. I hope your meeting goes well."

"See you later, then." Coffee cup in hand, he left, and a little later I heard his car door slam and the soft purr as it started.

17

I CONTINUED TO IGNORE HARRY'S CALLS AND I blocked his emails.

I was finished with the Association.

I handled responses for Thanksgiving dinner, I shopped for food, I cleaned the house. You'd never have thought I was once a neophyte in a sex club. Patrick and I circled around each other, friendly, a little flirtatious, both a little too aware of each other. That is, I knew I was. I found myself watching him. I'd look up and find him watching me. Significant moments over the washer/dryer or in the kitchen, or outside when I wheeled my bike out to ride to work, and he just happened to be around.

When I came home in the still frosty air I'd look forward to seeing the lights in his apartment. He rarely came down to greet me. A couple of nights when the temperature plummeted he emailed to ask if I'd like him to drive me home, but I always said no thanks. I liked the solitude, the cold air and my breath steaming in a cloud around me, the hiss of tires on the bike path. I felt invincible, speeding through the dark.

I took the night before Thanksgiving off, to get an early

start on things I'd forget otherwise—collecting napkins, making stuffing and preparing vegetables, because I knew no one would want to bring anything as mundane as steamed green beans.

Patrick wandered down to the kitchen, catching me fisting the turkey, to ask if I needed help. He'd returned from working out and I tried not to sniff the air for male pheromones.

"I invited a guy from the gym," he said. "I hope that's okay. We were doing weights at the community center together and got talking."

"Great. The more the merrier." I assaulted the turkey with another handful of stuffing.

"He says hi. Says you know him. He's called Ivan."

My spoon went clattering to the floor. "What—who?"

"Sorry, I didn't catch his last name." He picked the spoon from the floor and examined its dusting of cat hair. "Want me to mop the floor?"

"No, I've plenty more time to drop stuff." I rammed both fists into the turkey to stop my hands shaking.

Ivan. Of course, Ivan. I'd seen him that day at the community center. It wasn't a coincidence, surely. I was such an idiot. If I'd returned Harry's phone calls I'd know what was going on. I wouldn't be a mess because Patrick had invited someone who was probably a regular at the gym where they both exercised, and be jumping to all sorts of weird conspiracy theories.

I removed my hands from the turkey. Ugh.

Patrick grinned and turned on the faucet for me. "I—I have to make a phone call," I muttered, wiping my wet hands on my jeans after a quick wash. "Back soon."

I ran upstairs and found Harry's number. He answered, to my great relief.

"Hi, Jo, how are you? We've missed you."

His friendly tone put me at ease. "Sorry, I've been really hard to get hold of. I—"

"I'd love to chat but we have family over, so let's talk business next week, okay? Have a great Thanksgiving."

Well. More games, it appeared. I clicked the phone off and
went downstairs to find Patrick sewing up the turkey like a
seasoned surgeon, the table more or less clean, and Brady eating
something small and bloody on the floor.

"What's he got?" I shrieked.

"I gave him a bit of the liver. I've got the rest on the stove
for stock."

"For Christ's sake, will you stop playing fucking superchef
in my kitchen!" I was shaking with rage. I stomped over to
the range and looked at the stock he'd started—very professional, turkey flotsam, bay leaves and celery and crushed pep-
percorns—and wanted to fling it across the kitchen.

Patrick walked out without a word. I heard his footsteps
going up the stairs and across to his apartment.

I shoved the turkey into the refrigerator and tidied up in a
minor sort of way. I turned the stock off and put the pan into
the refrigerator, stepping over the bloody smears Brady's treat
left on the floor.

Patrick heard the roaring sound that indicated water running
in the house and guessed Jo was taking a bath.

He tried not to think of her naked.

He was an idiot. He should have put off that meeting and got
into bed with her last week instead of playing the jolly baker.
Was he flattering himself in thinking that her bad temper was
caused by horniness? More likely it was mysterious female
hormones, nervousness about having a houseful of guests, any
number of things. He'd told her he was waiting for her to give
the go-ahead, which had seemed logical and chivalrous and all
the rest of it at the time, but also left open the possibility that
she wasn't interested and might never summon him to her bed.

Except she was. He knew she was.

Gloomily he tapped a computer to life and opened what he referred to privately as the wank menu. It was the sort of thing guys joked about in bars. On more than one occasion Patrick had found himself giving advice about how to clear a cache or partition the computer in case wives or girlfriends snooped around.

He unzipped just as the door creaked open—Christ, that cat was strong—and Brady, defender of public and private morals, stalked in, eyes full of reproach.

"Christ," Patrick muttered, tucking himself away, zipping up, horribly embarrassed. He didn't honestly think he'd have to lock the door first, not with the atmosphere in the house as it was.

Brady fell over in front of him and flopped his tail on the carpet.

"What do you want?" Patrick said. "I expect she fixed you, so there's no wanking for you, boyo. Or did she give you a bollocking, too?"

Brady rolled onto his feet, walked across the room and deposited himself onto Patrick's bed, staring at him with those big yellow eyes.

"Go on, make yourself at home." Patrick switched off the computer. "You've persuaded me. I'll have a cup of tea instead."

Despite my anxiety about the Association and Ivan's presence later that day, I got up early with the usual sense of anticipation of a Thanksgiving Day—great food, friends, conversation and the quiet of a late-night shift to end the festivities. I hauled the enormous turkey out of the refrigerator and set it in the oven and made myself coffee. It was too early to call home, but I checked activities on Facebook, my laptop on my knees as I sat in the window seat. It was still dark. No sign of Patrick other than his foil-wrapped loaves laid on the counter to thaw, and all over again I felt bad about snapping at him the night before.

Brady wandered into the kitchen and jumped onto my lap. I stroked his fur and wondered what I should do about Patrick, and when, and if...and about the foreskin-enhanced dick with the Kimberly seal of approval. How annoying of him, walking into my bedroom and announcing he had five minutes; and he'd looked pretty good. But then a man serving you breakfast in bed always did.

The outside door to the apartment opened and closed and I heard Patrick's footsteps on the steps and then on the drive. I lifted the blind. It was a little lighter now, and I could see Patrick stretching, one foot on the step, the other leg straight. Oh, nice buns, I thought, and then I let the blind go in case he'd caught me ogling him. It snapped against the window and I was sure he would have heard.

I set the kitchen timer to remind me to baste in half an hour, and stretched out on the window seat. Brady joined me, purring and reeking of cat food. Hours to go, the house quiet and warm and filling with the scents of good food. Later, when I was about to serve the turkey, things would get frantic as I juggled gravy and serving dishes. But now I could savor the moment and anticipate the day.

People started arriving at about two for a dinner scheduled to start an hour later. Those who wanted to watch the game could drift away in the living room with plates of food, or take their place at the dining room table, augmented with a couple of card tables. It was a room I rarely used except when large groups of people were expected.

Kimberly arrived alone, to my disappointment, bearing a bowl of her relish and a huge sheaf of flowers for me. Liz and her husband brought desserts. Others came with side dishes, wine, beer, soda.

Patrick arrived in the kitchen, sliced his bread and arranged it in a basket covered with a cloth. He spread a slice with butter and offered it to me.

"I'm sorry I was a bitch," I said to him.

"That's okay." He watched as I bit into the bread.

"Great bread. Shall I warm it?"

"Jo!"

Oh, no. It was Ivan, bearing down on me. I hadn't even heard him come in, but at this point the front door was probably unlocked.

He placed a casserole dish and a bottle of wine on the counter and slipped his arm around my waist and kissed me on the lips. "You look gorgeous."

"Thanks." I handed him the corkscrew. "Help yourself. I've got to—"

"Thanks for inviting me," Ivan said. His arm was around my waist again. He clapped Patrick on the shoulder. "Or rather, thanks to Patrick. Jo and I go way back."

"Sort of." I dodged away from him. "Great to see you again. Do you want to go watch the game?"

"I'd rather stay with you and help. We've got a lot of catching up to do."

Precisely what I wanted to avoid.

"Jo was about to put me to work," Patrick said. "You know what they say about too many cooks."

Kimberly came back into the kitchen. "I need a bigger vase." She smiled winningly at Ivan and introduced herself. "You're real tall. Can you fetch me a vase from the top shelf of that cabinet?"

I whispered in her ear as Ivan reached into the cabinet, "Do me a favor. Keep him occupied."

"Gladly." Sure enough, Kimberly moved in on her prey. "Wow, you sure are tall. And look at those muscles." She felt the merchandise as she spoke. "Now, I know what a big handsome guy like you is really good at. Flower arranging. You come with me, sugar, and bring that lovely vase with you."

To my amusement Ivan allowed himself to be led out of the kitchen.

Patrick looked at me, eyebrows raised. "Little did I realize I'd be inviting a rival."

"You didn't. He's full of himself. I don't know him that well." Not the smartest thing to say—now Patrick would think I let guys I didn't know very well take all sorts of liberties with me. "We have about ten minutes before it gets insane. I'm going to change."

He nodded. He was as formally dressed as I'd ever seen him, in slacks and a shirt. No tie. He looked good. I loved the way the slacks draped around his— I tore myself away from contemplation of his package and ran upstairs. I hadn't put much thought into what I'd wear, and grabbed a silk tunic that fell to my knees, dark red with gold embroidery. "I used to have a dress like that in 1969," my mom had said when she'd seen it. I'd talked to her and the Great Abe before my guests had arrived and was very slightly homesick, and jealous of the foot of snow they already had there.

Black tights, dangly gold earrings, a quick ruffle of my hair and I was ready to go.

I ran downstairs and met Ivan, who raised his eyebrows. "You look hot."

"Thanks." I went into the kitchen, grabbed an apron and oven mitts and removed the turkey from the oven.

Patrick moved with quiet efficiency, putting items into the oven, keeping some aside for the microwave, lining up serving bowls and utensils. He and I made a good team.

I couldn't worry about Ivan or what he might say or do for at least fifteen minutes. I had gravy to make.

I looked around the table of people laughing, eating and drinking, and allowed myself to relax. This was good, great food and drink with friends—and a few people I didn't know well but who fitted right in.

"We didn't say grace," Kimberly said. She sat at my left—I was at the head of the table so I could make emergency runs out to the kitchen—with Patrick next to her. Ivan had managed to get the seat to my right, which I found annoying as I'd wanted to talk to the people I knew, but he was chatting away and not taking much notice of me.

"It's a bit late for that now," I said. Dishes of food were ending their first cycle around the table. "Besides, I think some of us are Jewish or Buddhist or both. Grace might take hours if we cover all faiths."

"Then let's do what my momma does." She beamed around the table.

Oh, no. "Every year, you try to hijack us into a Norman Rockwell painting."

But she was off. "Okay. Let's go 'round the table and we'll all say what we're thankful for this year. We can do that while we eat. Jo, you're hostess. You start."

"As hostess, I veto it. Where did the stuffing go? I don't have any yet."

Patrick stood, lunged across the table and found the beleaguered dish of stuffing. He handed it to me with a smile.

"Go on." Kimberly put on her brightest smile.

I stuck my tongue out at her. "Okay. I'm thankful for everyone's company and the food, I think in that order. Thanks to Patrick for helping in the kitchen. And I didn't get enough gravy. Where did it go? I'm thankful for friends and gravy and snow and the mountains and this really nice wine."

"I brought the wine," Ivan said.

"Thanks. Okay, Kimberly, you next."

"Well." She folded her hands and went into her usual long monologue about friends and good times and how blessed she was and how she loved her family back in Texas. The first time

I'd heard it I found it moving, and since then, in subsequent years, I noticed her level of impassioned reminiscence bore a direct relation to the amount of alcohol she'd consumed. But as cynical as I was, she was my friend, and I loved her for the way she wallowed in heartfelt sentiment.

Patrick was next. He raised his glass. "To Jo. Thanks for having us."

The table joined in raising their glasses and toasting me, and at that moment I loved them all, even though many of them had gravy stains on their fronts, or spoke with full mouths, or had put impossible grease stains on my antique drawn thread-work linen tablecloth.

Patrick continued, "I've had something of a rough year. But I'm happy to be here, and to have made new friends, some of them very dear and special to me." He looked straight at me as he said that and I was breathless. "And for the first time in months I feel optimistic about the future." He raised his glass, very slightly, in my direction, a gesture so subtle I wondered if anyone else had noticed it. For a moment the other guests faded away and Patrick and I looked at each other in a moment of profound anticipation and desire.

Then the moment was gone, and Ann, one of my volunteer announcers at the station, talked about her new kitten and her boyfriend, who'd gone home to the west coast for Thanksgiving, and how she hadn't been able to afford to go with him, but this was almost as good. Although, she added, she missed her mom and dad and sister, and burst into tears.

Patrick handed her a napkin and gave her a friendly hug. Others clustered around to embrace her, and someone else dropped a heaping spoonful of mashed potatoes, the ultimate comfort food, on her plate, in a practical gesture of support.

"I told you this wasn't a good idea," I said to Kimberly. "She'll start a chain reaction of boo-hoos."

"Bullshit. It's what Thanksgiving is all about. Football and

Americana and eating like a pig and wallowing in sentimentality. When do we get pie?"

"After we've finished your circle jerk-off."

"And I thought you were my friend," she said. "Where's the
dressing?"

And so we went around the table. There were a few tears,
but not the torrent I feared, some hard-luck stories, good news
about work and family, talk of people and friends far away.

By the time we got to Ivan I was working up quite an appetite for dessert and wondering what would happen late at night
when I returned from work and it was just me and Patrick in
the house.

Ivan raised his glass. "To Jo, a lovely lady. And to new begin-
nings, because Jo and I have a complicated history, and I think
this Thanksgiving marks the start of something very special
between us. So, Jo, you're the one I'm thankful for." He reached
for my hand and my fork clattered onto my plate.

I pulled my hand away, flushing with embarrassment as the
table erupted into a chorus of sighs and applause. Opposite me,
Patrick gave a small, sardonic smile.

"It was him? Your mystery man?" Kimberly whispered.
"He's gorgeous. So sweet. He was telling me all about—"

"Time for dessert." I sprang to my feet and my gravy-laden
knife tipped off the table and slithered all the way down my
dress. "Let's get these plates together. Pass them down to this
end of the table, please."

"Sure, honey," Ivan said, although I'd deliberately not looked
at him when I spoke.

To my annoyance, no one else offered to help, obviously
thinking that some heavy making out or misbehavior with the
whipped cream was going to take place in the kitchen. Instead,
when we got there, I slammed my load of dirty plates on the
counter and hissed at him, "What the fuck do you think you're
doing?"

"Oh, come on, Jo. Don't be mad. It was a joke."

"It was not a joke. I'm going to have to do a hell of a lot of explaining to my friends. Who put you up to this?"

"Calm down, honey. Or are you afraid lover boy will get mad?"

"Don't be ridiculous. Since you're out here, you may as well make yourself useful. The dishwasher is there to your right and the detergent is under the sink."

"Okay, okay."

Ivan whistled annoyingly as he rinsed plates and loaded the dishwasher.

I started the coffeemaker and filled a tray with cups and saucers, the best china I so rarely used. One thermos jug was already full of coffee. I added cream, sugar and teaspoons to the tray and took it out to the dining room. Some of the guys already looked antsy about missing the game.

Kimberly gave me a look that indicated she wanted full disclosure and I gave her a bright smile. "Give me a hand?"

"Sure." She came into the kitchen and, joined by Ivan, we brought the usual huge assortment of pies to the table, along with whipped cream.

Despite cries that no human being could possibly eat that much pie, we made a valiant attempt. Or at least, everyone else did. I picked at mine, finally pushing my plate away. "Too full," I explained to no one in particular.

Ivan meanwhile was being bombarded with questions about our alleged relationship, and I sat silent and let him do the talking. He was really good; he gave the impression we'd known each other for some time, until a mysterious rift had driven us apart.

"Oh, that's too bad," Liz said.

"Yeah, it was when the tentacled aliens swept me up to another solar system to be their goddess," I said, which elicited a peal of laughter.

"So this was before Hugh? Before you bought the house?" Kimberly asked. "Jo, I thought you were dating that rock-climbing guy."

"Oh, yeah, him," Ivan said. "Tell them, honey."

"I have a real talent for picking jerks," I commented.

"How lovely that you've gotten together again." That was Liz, formerly Patrick's number-one fan girl.

"Oh, it's early days yet." Ivan reached for my hand.

"Oh, my God, look at the time. I have to go to the station." I smiled at Kimberly, who'd offered to take over as hostess when I left. "Stay as long as you like, everyone. Eat everything, please. Kimberly will force leftovers upon you all."

Kimberly accompanied me to the kitchen when I left with my plate. "So you were runnin' around with our boy Ivan when you were still with Hugh."

"No."

She looked at me, cool, judgmental. "And here I was wasting all that sympathy on you. You could have told me. No big whoop. I thought this secrecy stuff was recent but perhaps it isn't."

"I first met Ivan a week or so ago."

"Oh, yeah?" She nibbled at a piece of piecrust on my plate. "Then why's he sayin' all this stuff?"

"To jerk my chain."

"So tell him to get lost. What's the matter with you? Patrick's really pissed about Ivan all over you like a cheap suit. You might have more on your hands than you want to if you keep this up."

I shook my head. "Where's your mystery man? I was hoping you'd bring him."

"With his family," she said quite calmly.

"He's married?"

"Divorced. He's with the kids and grandkids. We didn't want to spring it on them just yet."

"Oh." My feeble attempts at moral superiority had fallen flat. "I've got to change clothes."

I ran upstairs to change into my winter bike gear. When I came downstairs I spent quite a bit of time saying goodbye to my guests in the kitchen as I made myself a turkey sandwich for later.

I put the sandwich and an apple in my backpack and reached into the hall closet for my helmet and the bicycle itself. Normally I kept it in the entranceway, but with this many guests we needed the space. As I propped the bicycle against my hip to fasten the helmet, Ivan came out of the living room, where most of the guys had clustered to watch the game.

"I don't want you to be here when I come back," I said. "And I don't want you to come to my house ever again."

"Heck, Jo, I thought we did pretty well."

"Pretty well? Half my friends now think I was fooling around with you on the side when I was with my boyfriend."

"I feel we have a real connection, Jo."

"Not here. Not in real life. We're supposed to ignore each other in real life. Did Harry tell you to come here?"

He lounged against the wall. "Yeah, he said it might be a good idea."

I pulled on my gloves and wheeled the bicycle to the front door. "'Bye, Ivan. Remember what I said."

He opened the door for me with just a hint of mockery in the gesture. "Be safe, Jo. And talk to Harry."

He leaned in to kiss me but I dodged and hit his face with my helmet, a small gesture that pleased me immensely. I rode out into the quiet night, seeing the warm glow of houses where the holiday was celebrated, taking the center of the road to avoid the larger-than-usual number of parked cars. I turned off onto the bike path and the only sounds were the hiss and whirr of my tires and my breath. I stood on the pedals to build up speed, feeling the pull and stretch in my quads and calves, the sense of power and freedom that riding my bike in the dark always gave me.

The station felt like home; a different sort of home. I put my turkey sandwich and fruit into the refrigerator, and went into the studio, where the announcer was eager to leave and be with her family. I cued up music, checked for breaking news and weather and turned almost all of the lights off, so I sat in a pool of light at the board.

Of course I had work to do—paperwork, programming plans, creating schedules—but today was a holiday and I could take time off. I had a few pieces programmed, but announced that I would take requests, and spent some time answering calls and tactfully refusing to play some of the more outlandish choices. I wondered whether Mr. D. would call, or Harry, but to my relief—I think it was relief—neither did.

I shut down at one in the morning and left with a fizzing expectation in my gut. I was going home, where I had some explaining to do. I noticed a car in the parking lot as I left; parking spots were jealously guarded, as close to the campus as we were, but it must be someone who was a guest at a house nearby and had taken advantage of the space. As I glanced at the car I saw a sign of movement at the driver's side.

I swung my leg over the saddle and pushed off, rising on the pedals to accelerate, and swung across the parking lot onto the bike trail. There was nothing to be afraid of, nothing at all. I even doubted I had seen anyone in the car, and if I had, there could be a perfectly innocent explanation.

And then, as I gulped in the crisp air scented with wood smoke and sped forward, I forgot about the car and its illogical menace, because I was going home.

Home to Patrick.

18

I APPROACHED MY HOUSE AND SAW A LIGHT ON over the garage. So Patrick was still awake. I hoped he was waiting for me.

I opened the front door and pushed my bicycle inside, unsnapping my bike helmet and hanging it from the handlebars. Brady approached, making the affectionate sounds he always made when he was hungry, and I accompanied him into the kitchen to check on his food supplies. The kitchen gleamed, tidy and clean, although the scent of Thanksgiving dinner lingered in the air.

I left the house again through the front door, clicking it closed behind me, and dropped my keys into my jacket pocket. As I mounted the stairs to Patrick's apartment I could hear soft jazz playing. I tapped on the door.

Patrick opened the door. "Jesus Mary, Mother of God!" He reached out and removed my balaclava. "You look like a fucking terrorist in that thing."

So much for an erotic charge to my visit; a pity, because he looked good, in a pair of soft cotton pants and a T-shirt that showed off the muscles in his arms, all of which reminded me of the boys in the Great Room. But I didn't want to think about that now. He was barefoot and slightly tousled. He looked gorgeous and I wanted him to take off more than the balaclava. I couldn't believe I'd once referred to him as a leprechaun.

"Sorry, I forgot I had it on."

"Well, come on in, then. Don't stand there letting the cold in."

Yeah, real sexy, Patrick. But I went in anyway.

"I was having a cup of tea. I'll make you one, too."

Even worse, but at least I was inside the door. I unzipped my jacket and hung it on a hook on the back of the door, on top of one of Patrick's jackets.

"I enjoyed the show tonight," he said, his back to me, as he switched on the electric kettle in the tiny kitchen alcove.

"There was a nice, friendly vibe. I had a lot of callers. Only one got upset and that was because I wouldn't play any Charles Ives. We compromised with some Copland."

The kettle whistled. I heard the clink of the teaspoon as he stirred the tea bag in the mug and then had the opportunity to admire his ass as he bent to retrieve a carton of milk from the refrigerator.

"Sit down, woman," he said as he turned, mug in hand, and I saw why he'd kept his back to me: he had a huge erection in those loose cotton pants.

Naturally I pretended I hadn't noticed, but took the mug and settled into the armchair he indicated. I could see, beyond the screen, that his bed was mussed, as though he'd been asleep, or had gotten up recently. An electric charge zoomed between my legs as effectively as if I'd sat on a vibrator.

But I was here to talk, I reminded myself.

Patrick, mug in hand, pulled out a chair similar to mine and hooked a small ottoman forward with one foot. He lifted the top and flipped it over, converting it into a coffee table.

"Thanks for dinner tonight," he said.

"My pleasure. Thanks for your help." I really had to stop seeing innuendos in everything I said. Pretty soon I'd be incapable of having any sort of conversation with him at all. "And thanks for the kitchen cleanup."

"Kimberly organized it. She made Ivan do most of the work." He grinned.

There was my opening. "Yeah, I wanted to tell you about him."

He raised his eyebrows. "Oh, you really don't have to."

"But I think you should know."

He flapped a hand at me. "It's not necessary."

He had that sardonic twinkle in his eyes again, enjoying my discomfort. First Ivan jerking my chain, now Patrick. I ignored him and kept talking. "Whatever he said is mainly untrue. We haven't known each other that long, whatever he claimed, and we don't have any sort of long-term relationship, and certainly no commitment to each other."

"Ah." Patrick took a sip of tea. "And would Ivan possibly be connected with that night you came home looking like an extra from a porn film? Just a wild guess."

"Yes."

"Ha." He put his mug on the improvised coffee table.

I waited. I didn't want to get into the whole Association debacle with him. Not now. Should I thank him for the tea and leave? I looked at the toffee-colored brew and wondered about its caffeine content. I didn't want to lie awake, jittery and dissatisfied in all senses of the word.

"So I wanted to tell you… You said when I was ready, I… And at dinner today…" I stopped in terror, finally realizing the enormity of what I was about to do. Only a few weeks ago I'd told Mr. D. I wanted to be solitary, that I didn't need the baggage of emotional involvement in a real relationship, or want the sorrow that would inevitably follow. And now another man had made a public declaration to me—Patrick's gaze meeting

mine over the dinner table and the moment of recognition between us—and it could be too late and I was about to become
horribly embarrassed—

He pushed the ottoman aside and scooted his chair forward.
"Shh," he said as his knees bumped against mine. "You're about
to hyperventilate. Breathe."

He took the tea from my hand. I could barely move, paralyzed by lust and fear. I breathed out and sucked in a great
mouthful of air as I did when I first built up speed on my
bicycle, but this time the air was full of Patrick's scent and
warmth.

His mouth touched mine, softly, tentatively. His lips were
slightly rough and although I wanted to devour and be de-
voured I waited and let him move and press and nudge mine.
He could kiss, but I knew that. I wanted greater knowledge,
admission to his secret tastes and textures, to share breath and
wetness. His tongue darted to my lips and he made a slight
sound in his throat that made me shudder with longing for what
seemed like hours, but was only the amount of time it took for
his tongue to traverse my closed lips.

He withdrew and looked at me. "Okay?"

I nodded. I seemed to have forgotten how to speak.

"Well, then…" And he hauled me onto his lap, me straddling
him, so that I was pressed up against that glorious hardness at
his crotch. He ran a thumb up and down the outside of my
thigh and all the nerve endings below my waist zinged into life
again.

I moved then, touched his face and his neck and the muscu-
lar tenseness of his chest, until he caught my hands in his and
reached for my lips again. This kiss was wet and greedy and
clumsy, our teeth clashing, and at some point I'd guided his
hands to my breasts, his touch startling even through layers of
silk underwear (the practical winter kind, not the sexy stuff)

and a cotton turtleneck. His mouth moved down under my ear, where he nuzzled and sucked while I squirmed in delight.

"Jesus Christ," he said. He removed his eyeglasses.

"Don't stop." I was proud that I had managed a coherent sentence even if it was only two words.

"I think we need to think about this."

"Why?" I pressed myself against his erection and wondered vaguely if I had a damp patch there. I certainly felt warm and wet and excited. I wondered if he had a damp patch at this point.

His hands gripped my hips and moved me away. "You know I'm receptive, humbled, grateful—"

"Oh. I thought it was an erection."

"Smart-ass." He cleared his throat. "It happens when you're around and quite often when you're not. Nature is a wonderful thing. But we've still got the underlying problems—I'm your tenant. You have the remnants of a complicated love life. I'm still married although moving toward a divorce."

Fuck all that, let's get naked.

As if in response to my unspoken comment, he touched my spandex-clad crotch with an index finger and I nearly jumped out of my skin.

"So," he said, "I think we should take things easy. Get to know each other. Go on dates. Make out sometimes. Often."

"You didn't bother with all that with Kimberly." The whine in my voice embarrassed me horribly.

"I didn't feel this way about Kimberly. Sure, I liked her. I still like her. But we both knew it was going to be strictly sex, for a limited time, and we weren't going to have any sort of real intimacy. But with you, it's different. I want this to last and I'm superstitious about it. I don't want to screw it up."

"Okay. I'm not quite sure what to say. But what if we get to know each other and either you or I decide we don't want to fuck?"

He grinned. Without the eyeglasses he looked different, more serious, more adult. "And you think that's likely?"

"No."

"And here's a couple more things to consider. One, purely practical, I don't have any condoms at the moment."

"What?" And then the realization hit me that I didn't, either. Jason the ever-erect had depleted my stock. "Neither do I. Okay, that's tonight covered although I do know an all-night drugstore. But what's the other thing?"

He leaned back in the chair, hands behind his head. "Ah, I thought we might play a few erotic games first. I think you'd like that. Lots of fooling around and lots and lots of squishy, messy orgasms, lots of lovely damp patches for us both. Are you woman enough for it? It's a good way of getting to know someone, and we'll transition easily into the fucking, no shyness or clumsiness or, in my case, coming too soon."

"Is that a problem for you?"

"Tonight it would be." He said it quite easily without a trace of embarrassment. "You'll make me go off like a fucking volcano, Jo, and quite soon if we keep this up."

"Hmm. Like this?" I placed my hand on the considerable bulge in his pants. He was naked underneath, I was sure, and his cock jumped against my palm.

He closed his eyes as I trailed my fingertip over the head of his cock and down to the taut bulk of his balls. "Please don't. I have a shitload of laundry to do already."

I laughed and took my hand away. "Okay, then. What next?"

He grinned back at me and I felt warm. Warm from desire, physically warm, enthralled by his suggestion of lovely squishy orgasms, and excited as though the two of us were embarking on a new journey. Which I suppose we were.

"So how do you feel about me?" he asked.

"I don't know. Terrified. Elated. Curious. Affectionate."

"Affectionate!" He snorted. "You sure know how to boost

a guy's ego. And how the hell can you be affectionate and ter-rified?"

"I don't know. I'm scared of intimacy, of pain."

He shrugged. "Oh, get over yourself. It's the human condi-tion. We all crave intimacy, we're all afraid of pain. Sometimes you have to take the risk."

"And I find you very sexy."

"Finally. I find you very sexy, too." This time he trailed his fingertip from my throat to my nipple and I just about fell off his knees. "Hey," he whispered. "Would you like to get… affectionate with me?"

"Oh, yes."

He pulled me close again. "Let's take it easy."

"Yeah, we don't want to cause unnecessary laundry." I spoke virtually into his mouth. It made this mundane statement un-bearably sexy and I squirmed as his thumbs worked my nipples.

"No genital contact," he said in a prim sort of way that sounded as though he were dictating a rather inhibited sex manual.

"But your hand on my ass is allowed?"

"Absolutely." And he pulled me forward. The chair creaked.

And oh, God, the man could kiss and do amazing things through my layers of clothing with his fingertips. "Patrick, I'm hot."

"Yeah." He tipped his head back and smiled at me. "You *are* hot."

"Not like that. I have to take off a layer."

"Okay. Do it slowly."

I pulled the turtleneck over my head—as usual, the neck got stuck on my head and I had to fight my way out. "Sexy enough for you?" I asked when I emerged.

"I'll take what I can get. Better?" He stared at my nipples poking through the silk undershirt.

He ducked his head to one nipple and sucked hard, sending

more zings to my clit, which was becoming particularly well-acquainted with that delicious hard bulge in his pants. "Nice?" he asked.

"Don't stop. Do the other one. Please." I rubbed myself against him. "You'll make me come."

He muttered something and mouthed the other nipple while that clever forefinger played around my crotch, tickling me through the taut spandex. I gripped his shoulders. No condoms. It was a disaster. No it wasn't. It was—

He kissed me hard, his tongue thrusting into my mouth, his hands squeezing my breasts, as I came. That I couldn't cry out or make any sort of sound made the moment sexier, more intimate, more intense. And then he drew his head away and gave a sound that was halfway between a moan and a laugh.

"More laundry," he said with great cheerfulness. "And how was that for you?"

"Nice," I said. "Oh, God, it was nice."

"Let's have another cup of tea." He pushed me off and reached for his eyeglasses, and sure enough, there was a large wet patch on the crotch of his pants, and the bulk of his cock had decreased somewhat.

I was surprised, but not offended, by his forthrightness. It seemed he was someone who was energized by sex, and he whistled as he plugged his kettle in again. I stood and put my arms around him, resting my head beneath his chin, and he held me, without words, making tea one-handed, careful to keep the boiling water away from me.

"Most men collapse after sex," I said.

"Ha, that was just an orgasm. One I have to thank you for, it's true, but if we'd been fucking, well, I'd be comatose for days among the broken furniture and the wrecked carpet." He poked his cup with a teaspoon, his arms still around me. "But I'm not averse to a bit of a cuddle after. Let's go out on a date Saturday night. I have a project I have to finish and I expect you're working tomorrow, although you're most welcome to come fool around after. I'll be awake." He stopped messing with his mug of tea and looked at me. "God, I can't believe this. That we've dry-humped each other like teenagers and we're planning to go out on a date like adults. Come on, Jo, speak to me. You're awful quiet."

"I'm happy. I'm amazed. I didn't expect..."

"My amazing technique?"

"You talk too much." I placed my finger on his mouth.

19

HE WAS UNDER THE SAME ROOF, MORE OR LESS, and it drove me crazy, but at the same time I loved the craziness and the longing. I couldn't wait to get home from work the next night. Patrick led me to the kitchen, claiming I should eat, but the pot of pasta suffered as we found excuses to rub up against each other and kiss.

"Jesus Christ!" Patrick dropped the pan into the sink and turned the faucet on, disappearing behind a cloud of steam. He emerged, drying his eyeglasses on his shirttail. "You're a menace. We could have burned the house down."

"I am? You're the one who wanted to cook me something."

"You need to maintain your strength after slaving over that hot board in the studio." He bent to rummage in a cabinet. "Oh, get your hands off my arse, woman."

"You have a great arse."

"So do you, and I intend to get up it as soon as we begin to have sex. Unless of course we develop burned-food fetishes. Tuna?"

"A tuna fetish?" I moved my hands over his ass.

"A tuna sandwich."

"Sure, thanks."

He straightened, a can of tuna in one hand, and turned to face me. "Let's go away somewhere for our first screw."

"You're such a romantic. What's wrong with my bed? Or yours, for that matter?"

"I want it to be special."

He looked so incredibly sincere I didn't want to say how girly that sounded; besides which, his erection, pressing against my hip, wasn't at all girly, and was distracting me.

"How does that fit into your idea of easing into real sex?" I thought fondly of that remarkable appendage easing into me. "Forget the tuna. I'll have a banana."

"Excellent." Patrick propped himself on the kitchen table, a wide grin on his face.

"I *love* bananas." I caressed the banana in a lewd sort of way. "Love, love, love."

He cleared his throat.

"I bought some condoms today," I continued. I peeled the first strip down with infinite care. "Ooh, this is such a big, firm one."

"I bought some, too." His voice sounded a little tight.

"But of course it doesn't mean we're actually going to use them. Not yet." I continued my slow peel. "Mmm. I wonder if I can get the whole thing in my mouth?"

Patrick darted forward and took the banana from me, pressing me against the counter. "Fuck it, let's go to bed. Let's do something. Let's get our clothes off and fool around. Do you know how much I want to see you naked? To kiss and lick you all over?" He paused to bite the top off the banana.

"Freud would have loved that." Despite my flippancy, I was hoarse and shaking with desire, clutching at him. "Come on, then. My bed's bigger."

We ran upstairs, and as we entered my bedroom I was hor-

ribly aware of its untidy state, including an unmade bed. "I'll
change the sheets—"

"No. I want to be covered by your smell."

It was quite the sexiest thing anyone had ever said to me.
Patrick unbuttoned his shirt and dropped it on the floor next
to a pair of my socks.

I grabbed the bottom of my sweater to pull over my head.

"Stop!" Patrick unzipped his jeans, toeing off his socks. "I'm
going to undress you. Why are you giggling?"

"I love the boxers."

He glanced down at the pattern of bright green frogs. "I
knew you'd like these. Get on the bed."

Oh, God, I'd forgotten my vibrator blatantly tangled in the
sheets. I made a grab for it, but Patrick got there first. "And
what's the meaning of this, young lady? Did I not service you
adequately last night?"

"Uh, well, yes, but this morning..." I was embarrassed but
at the same time highly turned on at his discovery.

He switched it on and ran it over one finger. "We'll have
a demonstration of this implement of desire later. Now, brace
yourself."

He removed his boxers and I was treated to my first real
sight of his cock, sturdily erect, and I wanted to take him in
my mouth and kiss and lick. He swatted me away and I realized
what a master of sensuality the man was.

He took his time and caressed every square inch of skin as
he lifted up my sweater. *Just wait until you see my bra, Patrick.* It
wasn't the best item of clothing to wear on a bike, but I was
glad I had. He stopped his gentle caresses and stared, before
tracing my nipples through the lace, and finally bending to kiss
them.

After an eternity he reached behind me to unhook my
bra and then stared at my breasts with a look of reverence on
his face.

"I want to touch you," I said, but he shook his head, no.

He slid down my bike pants and then my cotton under-wear—as much as I'd have liked to wear the matching panties I knew that particular pair would give me the mother of all wedgies on the bike—and finally we were skin against skin, naked together, kissing and touching.

His skin was even paler than mine, silvery in the dim light in the bedroom, with a springy mat of reddish curls on his chest—I'd noticed that as he undressed—but at this moment it was all touch and slide of skin and delicious texture. I wrapped my hand around his cock and he reached down to guide me, showing me how he liked to be touched, unselfconscious and trusting.

"Condoms are…" I gasped when his mouth left mine to tickle deliciously along my collarbone and nip beneath my ear.

I liked what he was doing—I liked it very much—but at the same time it troubled me. The intensity of our contact, the sheer lightning of his touch, sent me way beyond what I'd considered pleasure, into a realm of unknown sensation. Fucking—whenever he decided it would take place, for it was clear the decision was not mine—would return me to safety. I thought I knew all about teasing and sexual play after my time in the Great Room, but with Patrick I was a novice, troubled and clumsy.

"What's wrong?" He had progressed downward, doing amazing things to a spot on my hip bone that I hadn't realized was an erogenous zone.

"I feel I should be doing more for you," I said feebly, his dick being out of reach at the moment.

"Ach, don't worry. This is sex, not some sort marketplace barter."

"Yeah, I had noticed." I didn't even sound sarcastic; just pathetic.

He sighed and planted his chin on my pubic mound. "Is fucking so very important? Because if it is, we'll do it."

This was the first time I'd ever had a guy reluctant to do the deed. "I don't know. I'm out of my depth with you."

"Shit," he said and returned his head to mine. "Stop worrying. Enjoy yourself. What would you like me to do?"

"I hate it when guys ask that."

"Really? Why?"

"I feel like I have to give some sort of grocery list."

"Ah. Half a pound of cunnilingus, please, and I'll take a bit of anal play, but only if it's fresh, not that nasty frozen stuff. Is that what you mean?"

"Something like that. So if I asked you what you like, what would you say?"

"I'm a guy. It's much simpler for me. Suck my dick, scratch my balls with your fingernails, but very gently, play with my arse—do you have any lube? Jo—"

I'd taken him at his word, scooting down the bed and grasping his cock. I rolled it into my mouth. This I knew I could do; I was back on familiar territory. Yes, like this, lick him from balls to tip, suck on the delicacy of his foreskin and head, and then—

Oh, yes, he groaned, and reached for my head, guiding me, showing me what he liked. I ran my fingers up the crack of his ass, the soft hair moist and warm, and relaxed my throat to gather him in. Deep tremors, the tightening of his hands on my head warned me that he was close, and sure enough his hips bucked and he flooded my mouth, warm and salty.

"Well," he said and reached a thumb to clean a drop of semen from my mouth. "Well, that was something. That was lovely. I'll reciprocate if that's all right with you."

He kissed me, my mouth still salty and my chin wet from his orgasm, and turned me over and at that point I was avid to come, by any means possible. One of his clever fingers trailed over my clit.

"Patrick, just do it. I don't want subtlety." I was mortified.

But he laughed and gathered my thighs in his arms and nibbled and licked at my clit, fingers inside me probing and my orgasm was like a bolt of lightning that left me limp and amazed. I really couldn't complain when Patrick started another long, slow delicate traverse from collarbone, down and down, culminating in another wicked orgasm.

I opened my eyes— I couldn't believe how heavy my eyelids felt and how my whole body sank into the bed. He sat back on his heels and regarded his cock with a mixture of admiration and pity, hard and dark red against his belly.

"You're gorgeous," I said.

"Shouldn't I be saying that to you?" He clasped his cock, stroked. "I'm about to be absolutely crass."

"How?"

"I want to come on you. Sorry, I'm a dirty bastard and you're damn gorgeous yourself. Think of it—" he pumped his cock with his fist "—as me marking my territory. I don't know why…it's this urge—I want to see my come on you. Okay? Say no, and I'll stop."

"Oh, no, please. Please, do it." I touched my breasts and I saw his jaw clench. "Go on. Do it."

"Yes, touch your tits. Play with them." His hand moved steadily on his cock. "Open your legs. I want to look at your pussy."

I did, proud to expose my secret flesh to him, awed at his lack of inhibition, thrilled by the expression on his face. I recognized the sounds he made, the changes in his breath, the shudder in his thighs that indicated he was about to come.

His hand blurred and a stream of warm semen splashed onto my chest and stomach. He moaned and dropped forward, one hand at my side, his face against my breast.

"God," he said. "Oh, my God, Jo. I don't know whether I should apologize or fetch a towel. That was so damn amazing."

I giggled. "We've gone all triple-X rated and it's our second night together and we haven't even fucked yet."

He gave a long sigh of contentment and settled between my legs, nibbling at my nipple in a lazy sort of way. "So what depraved act would you like to commit next? I think you should give me a demonstration with the infamous vibrator."

"Which one?"

"Which one? How many do you have?"

"A whole stable of them," I said proudly. "Look in that wooden box."

He opened the box, shaking his head. "And here I was thinking that this was where you kept your girlish mementoes, the corsage from the prom and so on."

"They *are* my girlish mementoes."

He turned one on and gave a yelp of alarm at the loud buzz. "Please don't tell me you use this with the windows open. I've had power tools quieter than this. Your neighbors must think you're really into home improvement."

"Not my choice. It was a Christmas present."

"I hope you didn't open it under the tree with your family looking on."

I picked my favorite from the box. "This one is the Rolls-Royce of vibrators, very expensive, very sexy, produces quiet purrs."

"And loud screams, I hope." He settled with his head on one arm, and scratched his chest. "You have a couple of orgasms and then we'll find some other naughty things to do."

I loved it, watching him watch me. At first. He nibbled on my ear and whispered sexy things that got me hot, but then that reminded me a little of Mr. D. And I hadn't thought of Mr. D. once until then.

I switched the vibrator off.

"What's up?"

"I think I'm all orgasmed out. Sorry."

"We'll give you a break, then." He reached for his eyeglasses from the bedside table. "What's wrong, Jo? I feel like you've faded away."

I shook my head. "I'm tired."

I was lying, and I think he knew it. Sometime I'd have to tell him about Mr. D. and how sex had become for me something in which I participated with glee, but always with that thought at the back of my mind, *Wait until I tell Mr. D., or Mr. D. will love how I spice this up when I tell him.*

But I wasn't gathering material for a story. It was just Patrick and me, and that was what scared me and now made me back off. I'd forgotten the intensity of crawling into another person's skin and how the boundaries between two bodies, two minds, dissolved.

"Sleep, then." He gathered me in his arms, my butt against his cock, his leg flung over mine. He reached over me to put his eyeglasses back on the bedside table.

"You're still hard," I murmured, wondering whether I should offer a polite hand job.

"Like I said, I usually am around you. Just ignore it. I'm sure it will go down on its own."

I reached behind me and stroked him.

He sighed. "Ah, that's nice, but you don't have to. Here, let me show you how to get me off fast." His hand clasped mine and together we pumped hard, his breathing quickening until he buried his face into my neck and warm wetness spread on my back.

"Your territory's marked again," I said.

He kissed the back of my neck. "Is it?"

I didn't answer; there was nothing I could say that did not open up a whole new dangerous area.

Then he said, "I suppose it's too soon to talk about love."

★ ★ ★

One of the advantages of wearing glasses was that particular thrill you got from seeing them on the nightstand in a woman's bedroom after your first night together. Or an approximation of a first night, since they weren't actually fucking. But there his glasses sat, along with a paperback flipped open, cover up, to keep her place—she was reading Ursula Le Guin, which he thought he'd like to talk to her about sometime, except he hadn't read this one and had some catching up to do. There was so much he'd like to talk to her about, although he knew he had to tread carefully. She was cautious around him, and that was smart; hadn't he warned her he was damaged goods? And he was being cautious around her, with his fucking embargo, which, with his dick prodding against the bedclothes, seemed an exceptionally bad idea.

He was already in deep enough that the insertion of his tab *A* into her slot *B* (or *C*) couldn't possibly make much difference to the way he felt about her. Christ, he'd mentioned love last night. No wonder she wasn't around to greet him and his morning erection with cries of delight. But he hoped she'd been asleep at that point and missed that bit of post-orgasmic idiocy.

He put his glasses on and took a look around her room. A nice, peaceful sort of place, nothing fancy. A few pictures he'd like to take a look at later, lots of candles (which they hadn't lit last night, being too interested in getting naked) and a bookcase he'd investigate to see what other writers they both liked. Her Mac sat on a small desk in one corner.

The door pushed open and he sat up, expecting Jo, but it was only her cat, who gave him a reproachful look and jumped onto the bed, kneading the quilt with its paws, tail waving in the air.

"Yeah, boyo, I slept here last night," Patrick said. "Get over it." He scratched Brady's head and the cat purred like one of Jo's quieter vibrators.

"Hey." Jo stood in the doorway wearing a bathrobe, a mug of coffee in each hand. Her hair was wet. She smiled shyly at him as she handed one of the mugs to him. "Sleep well?"

"Much better than usual. Come back to bed with me."

"Sorry, I don't have time. I'm meeting a friend for brunch."

He wondered—hoped—if she was giving Ivan his marching orders. Or some other guy.

She said, "I'd invite you, but it's sort of business stuff, so—"

"No, that's fine. I've got a few things to do." For the life of him he couldn't think what they might be. Nothing could be more important than kissing and touching Jo, making her come, watching her face…

He pulled the tie of her bathrobe. As he hoped she was naked beneath.

He touched a nipple and watched it stiffen, her breast shaping from pointed to round.

"Oh," she said softly. She put her mug of coffee on the nightstand and sat down beside him. If ever there was a hint that he should continue, that was it—and she took his mug, too.

He liked the way she sat, her body open to his gaze, his touch. "You're sure you don't have time?"

Maybe he should ask where the damned condoms were, because he wanted her, his dick drilling through the bedclothes. She smelled clean and fragrant, and that disappointed him. He'd have loved to get her naked in that shower with its handheld attachment and soap her up and make her come and come. Her skin was soft against his lips as he moved in to kiss her breasts and then her lips. "I owe you from last night," he said and touched between her thighs, where she was silky and wet.

"Oh," she said again as her thighs fell apart.

He disentangled himself from the bedclothes, his cock weighty and ready. She reached to stroke him; God, she'd

learned his preferences so well. But now it was about her pleasure and he listened to her breath hitch and catch at the slip of
his finger against her clitoris.

"Here," she murmured, and reached to guide his hand.
He liked that, her openness to pleasure—he remembered her
touching her own nipples as he jerked off over her last night (he
couldn't believe how crude he'd been, but she seemed to get off
on it). His cock jumped in her hand. He wasn't a great believer
in simultaneous orgasms, but he wondered if her orgasm would
be enough to fire him off, too. In a way, he hoped not.

"I love to see you come," he murmured and bit her nipple,
not hard, but hard enough to show her he could.

She whimpered. He'd learned she didn't make a lot of noise
until the end, when she got very noisy indeed and shook all
over. It was difficult to read her level of excitement, but he had
no doubt he could and would.

Yes, now, as her hips lifted and her face took on a look
of fierce concentration. Now, as her clitoris seemed almost
to retreat—he knew it didn't, it was engorgement, pure and
simple, the big buildup—now she was going to come. She cried
out loudly, twisting against him, and her hand gripped his cock
and slid.

Now, now. He watched semen spill blissfully from his cock,
spurting onto the sheets and her wrist— God, what a mess,
what a glorious lovely coming and coming apart it was.

"Sorry about the mess," he said.

She grinned and wiped her hand on the sheet. "Not the first
one we've made."

We. He liked that, that she regarded his errant semen as a
joint responsibility. "Elise always used to complain."

"About sperm?"

"Yes. She always ran into the shower after."

"She's crazy," Jo said and stretched. Her vulva was pink and
shiny. She reached for her coffee, turning so the bathrobe fell

away and revealed one glorious curve of butt. His hand moved there to clasp it, fitting as though made to be there.

"You're gorgeous," he said. "Beautiful. What an arse you have, woman."

"Thanks." She took a gulp of coffee. "I'd better get dressed."

He put his boxers on and watched with as much pleasure as if she were undressing for him. She wandered around naked without a hint of self-consciousness, and then put on a pair of socks, which looked strangely sexy to him. But, as he was learning, almost anything Jo wore looked sexy to him. She pulled on a pair of white cotton panties and a camisole, no bra. A sweater that looked hand-knitted over that, and then a pair of jeans. She knelt on the floor for a pair of hiking boots, and then sat to lace them up. She plucked a suede jacket and a long, soft, brightly colored scarf from the hook on the door.

"You're driving, then?"

"Yes. It's too cold to bike and not swelter in the restaurant."

He couldn't figure out whether she was dressed to seduce or to make him jealous, or, possibly, amazing though it might be, that that's what she felt like wearing that day.

"I'd better get back and do some work," he said and gathered the rest of his clothes, giving the warm fragrant bed a last, regretful look.

"You may well be invited back," she said with a grin.

He pushed her up against the wall and kissed her thoroughly to make sure she would stick to that, and she giggled and pushed him away.

"Look what you've done to yourself," she said with mock severity.

His cock prodded against the frogs on his underpants. "I'll keep it safe for you," he promised.

He watched her run down the stairs and heard the throaty

cough of her car starting up. He should remind her to get it tuned for the winter.

No, he shouldn't. It wasn't his responsibility, just as it wasn't any of his business who she was going out with.

20

"YOU'RE LOOKING GOOD," HARRY SAID.

I unwound my scarf; it was a bitterly cold, windy day, and the scarf wasn't entirely to make a fashion statement.

This restaurant wasn't the sort of place I normally came to, full of tanned people wearing ski-lift labels on their expensive jackets. The décor was vaguely Zen, a few fountains with trickling water and large rocks, orchids and ferns, a slate floor and much dark polished wood.

Harry examined his menu. "They make omelettes to order here—they're very good. Fancy a mimosa?"

After we'd ordered and were waiting for our food, Harry got down to business. "You have been a naughty girl, Jo. Record-breakingly naughty. How was your Thanksgiving?"

"Fine other than Ivan showing up, as you probably know."

"That boy certainly has a talent for mischief." He sipped his mimosa. "He told me your Irish boarder got quite bent out of shape."

"He isn't— Oh, never mind."

"You obviously haven't bothered to read your handbook."

Since my handbook—that large, intimidating folder—was

still in my locker, I shrugged. "I'm leaving the Association, Harry."

"You do need to go through the proper procedure, otherwise, as you should know, you'll be liable for a stiff—" he paused to wink "—fine."

I kept my face neutral and dug into the fruit salad I'd ordered.

Harry poured syrup over his waffles. "Resigning at this point wouldn't be a good idea, Jo, but if you have to...well, give us notice in writing. It's all in the handbook. I'm sorry we're losing you. It does happen. People pair off, become exclusive, but it's unusual to do so while you're still in the Great Room. In fact, we don't recommend it. And then there was the, ah, unfortunate episode with Jake."

"I haven't paired off with anyone."

"Yeah? According to Ivan, there were a lot of hot-and-heavy glances between you and this Patrick fellow." He forked in a mouthful of waffles. "Jake's pretty pissed off."

"I'm pretty pissed off with him."

"Well, in any case, the Association wants to make amends for any unpleasant experiences you may have had. And, all things considered," he said, tossing a white envelope onto the table, "you're a very lucky girl."

"What do you mean?" I opened the letter.

"Promotion," he said, a big grin on his face. "You're going upstairs, my dear."

"You're a real jerk," I commented. I read that now I could bring guests to open nights, I had use of the pool, locker room, gym, golf course and spa, and presumably, although this was not mentioned, my choice of hot young bodies from downstairs. A glossy brochure had photographs of the facilities, a near pornographic close-up of a plate of luxurious yet unidentifiable food garnished with an orchid, a shot of a golf course.

"Congratulations." Harry laid his fork down and dabbed

at his mouth with his napkin. He looked genuinely pleased, almost paternal, as though it were his doing. "So what do you think now? Oh, by the way, we have an open night tonight. Why don't you bring your new squeeze along?"

"Oh, sure." I could just see Patrick's contempt for the activities in the Great Room. I'd not felt shame until this moment. I wanted Patrick to think well of me. I wanted—

"No, upstairs. Bring him along tonight to dinner. Stay over if you like—in fact I'd recommend it. It'll be fun. I know you haven't had the best experiences with us, and I want to show you what you're missing—great food, good conversation, hanging out with smart, well-informed people. It's not all kinky stuff, although if you want kinky, you can find it, no problem. But that's all strictly optional. We don't force anyone into anything, and if it seemed that way with Jake, I'm sorry. Real sorry. I'll have a chat with him about it. He can come on a bit heavy, I know. How about it, Jo?"

I hesitated. "It sounds too good to be true, Harry, which means it probably is."

"We'll give you a really nice room," Harry said. Did he know Patrick and I hadn't screwed yet?

"I need to think about it. I'm not sure what he's doing tonight." I hoped he'd be doing me in some capacity. He'd mentioned going out to dinner. Well, why not going out to dinner and having our girly overnight consummation at the Association?

"Okay," I said. "So if I brought him along, it would be just that—dinner and staying over? No group sex or beatings or anything?"

"Honest to God, Jo, all that takes place in specific areas. It's a big house full of all kinds of different activities. If you want something a bit kinky, it's there. If you want romance, we'll have rose petals on the bed and scented candles and all that stuff. Have a massage—not that sort of massage, you naughty girl—in the spa. How about it? Have dinner, stay over, no strings attached."

He looked so homely and sincere I almost trusted him. Almost. "Yeah, sure."

"Think about it." Ignoring my sarcasm he patted my hand and then looked at his watch. "Oops. Gotta run. Call about tonight by three, okay, and I'll send a car for you." He signaled to our waiter to bring the check.

I wrapped my scarf around my neck as we walked outside into the bitter cold that brought with it a hint of sleet.

"Brrr. See you tonight, Jo, I hope." Harry bent to kiss my cheek. He delved inside his down jacket. "One more thing. Dress code." A couple of black masks dangled from his hand.

I took them and tucked them inside my jacket. "Thanks for brunch."

I sat for a moment in the car, thinking about this new and unexpected development, and read the letter again. It was tempting—Patrick had wanted to do something special for our first time—but I didn't trust Harry or anyone else there. I tossed the letter and brochure into the backseat and started the drive home, thinking I might as well stop at the grocery store and pick up a few essentials.

In the store I pushed my cart around a corner and came face-to-face with Angela. At first I didn't recognize her—no black leather in sight; she wore baggy jeans and a down jacket, no makeup, and most surprising of all, she had a baby seated in her cart.

"Hi!" I said, astonished, and making a major etiquette break.

A small boy ran up with a box of cereal. "Gramma, I got it."

"Nice job!" she said in the bright, overenthusiastic tone people use with small children as he dropped it into the cart. "Devlin, say hi to Ms. Jo."

The small boy became overcome with shyness and pushed his face against her down jacket.

"These are your grandchildren?" I couldn't believe it.

"Yeah. Devlin is four, and this one, Suzie, is almost a year." She waggled the foot of the baby in the cart. "Can you say 'hi,' cutie pie?"

Suzie leaned to grab the box of cereal.

"They're very cute," I said.

"So are you coming tonight?" she asked.

"I don't know. Probably not."

"Oh, you should," she said earnestly. "You'll love it. Last open house I babysat and my daughter and her husband went. They hadn't been there since the night they got engaged. And you don't have to bring a boyfriend. I sometimes take one of my girlfriends from the gardening club. The gardens are quite lovely in the summer."

I wondered if we were even talking about the same place.

She removed the box of cereal from the hands of the baby, who was chewing vigorously on a corner. "It's not often you get the chance for a nice relaxing break like that."

"I guess not," I said. "I'll think about it."

"Well, nice seeing you, Jo. We must get on with our shopping. Devlin, where's our list gone?" And she and her grandchildren continued through the store, the baby offering me a gap-toothed, happy smile as they left.

Patrick was out when I arrived home, and the house felt empty without him. I went upstairs and changed the sheets—by now they certainly needed it—and cleaned the bathroom and generally tidied up, creating the atmosphere I should have liked last night. Plan B, if Patrick didn't want to go to the Association—and I decided I wouldn't push it too much—was that I'd seduce him here. Besides, I didn't know when he'd be back; it wasn't that sort of relationship, I reminded myself. We didn't have to keep tabs on each other or report in. I didn't want that sort of relationship. Did I?

At two-thirty I gave in and called his cell.

"Yeah?" He sounded distracted.

"I have a dinner invitation tonight. I wondered if you'd like to come with me."

"Sure. Who is it? Anyone I know?"

"No, it's my investment association. We have an invite to stay overnight, if we like."

"Do we now?" His voice had changed.

"Yeah, it's a big place, a beautiful old mansion, and they have a gym and a spa."

"So you reckon tonight's the night?"

"Yes, I do. How about you?"

"Yeah." He laughed. "Oh, yeah. See you later."

I called Harry to tell him we'd come and arrange for the limo, and decided I'd spend the rest of the afternoon getting ready. I examined the contents of my underwear drawer. What would Patrick like? Tarty red and black lace? Demure pink? Snakeskin? Virginal cream and lace? Not a thong, I decided. Or should I dispense with the panties altogether, so I could flash him if necessary? The only problem was that given the dress I was planning to wear my flashing might be rather indiscriminate.

I hung the dress—black, short, slinky—in the bathroom to let the wrinkles steam out while I took a quick shower. Once my hair was washed, I wrapped myself in a towel and filled the bathtub, dropping in a generous blob of bath oil. Time to relax.

I eased myself into the steaming water. I wished I could trust Harry. If, as he said, all that was demanded of me was an appearance at dinner, and then an overnight stay (which he'd made clear was optional), there could be no harm done. The invitation and my acceptance were symbols of good faith, of civilized behavior. Far more reassuring was the revelation of

Angela's other life as a suburban matron and her endorsement of the open nights.

I heard a door open and footsteps. "Jo? Where are you?"

"In here. Come in."

Patrick entered, holding a bunch of irises. "For you. I'll put them in the sink, shall I? I was thinking—" His voice became muffled as he pulled his sweater over his head. "We need to set some ground rules. I'm living there and you're here, and—"

"Patrick, you can't walk in and start a conversation about boundaries while you're undressing. Can I smell the flowers?"

"Oh. Right." He handed the flowers to me. "May I join you in the bathtub, and we can talk?"

I took a deep breath of the subtle scent of the irises, cool and faintly sweet. "These are lovely. Thank you. And yes, you may join me."

He put the flowers back into the sink and unbuttoned his shirt. I watched with appreciation as he undressed, the dusting of coppery curls on his pale skin, the ropes and knots of his muscles, the free swing of his cock.

"Like what you see?" he said.

"Yes. Yes, I do. You look like a skinny version of Michelangelo's *David*."

"With glasses and a much bigger cock." He kicked his clothes aside. "I've been thinking about you. I had some work to do on-site this morning, but I couldn't concentrate. I kept thinking of you, your taste. What you sound like when you come."

He stepped into the bathtub.

I lay back and admired the view of his undercarriage as he straddled the rim of the bathtub. "I've been thinking about you, too," I said.

He settled himself into the foamy water, and removed his steamed-up eyeglasses, finally settling on the soap dish as an appropriate container for them.

"Nice," he said. "But I'm going to smell like a girl."

"I doubt it. Back to the topic of boundaries," I said. "I guess you mean, do we keep separate areas? And I say yes, absolutely. You need to work, and I have to sleep some in the daytime. We can eat together a few times a week if you like. It gets boring cooking for one person."

"And you'd enjoy my company occasionally, I believe you forgot to add. We can take turns cooking." He blinked at me. "That was much easier than I thought it would be."

"You thought I'd ask for more?"

"I was afraid you'd ask for less. How often should we sleep together?"

"I'll make a schedule and post it on the refrigerator door," I said, keeping my voice as serious as I could and trying not to burst into inappropriate laughter.

He frowned. "Who else is on the schedule?"

I raised a foot to poke him in the chest. "You'll have to take your turn like everyone else."

He grinned. "Right. Those breasts look like they could use a good wash."

I lay back and enjoyed his touch on my breasts, my shoulders and neck.

"What's made you so tense?"

"Anticipation," I said. I took the washcloth from him. "I'll wash your back."

He bowed his head to my shoulder and nibbled beneath my ear, along my collarbone, sighing. "I'm sweet on you, Jo."

The old-fashioned phrase made me smile. "I'm pretty sweet on you, Patrick Delaney."

"But I feel you're holding back on me."

My hand stilled on his back. "We're both holding out on each other."

"I don't mean the fucking. You pull back from me. I feel you doing it. So tell me something, Jo. Tell me something secret. Something you've never told anyone before." He straightened and kissed my lips, then wedged his shoulders between the faucet and the side of the tub, ready to listen.

"I was pregnant."

"What?"

"When Hugh and I were breaking up. He didn't know. I was on the pill but I'd missed a couple of days, and…it was a series of misjudgments and no one's fault. I'd made up my mind to have an abortion and then…I didn't need to. I bled a lot. It was messy and scary. Hugh was out of town and Kimberly came with me to the emergency room."

I dabbled my hand in a heap of foam. He was Irish, a Catholic, almost certainly. If I hadn't screwed up this relationship already, what I was about to confess would almost certainly do it.

Hell with that. I straightened up and looked him in the eye. "But here's the secret. I was relieved that I didn't have to make a decision. And I was also relieved people were sorry for me and supportive instead of being judgmental."

He grabbed me in a clumsy hug that set water sloshing in the bathtub. "Oh, you poor girl. You poor, wee thing. I'm so sorry."

I was so thankful for his reaction and so entertained at being called a "poor, wee thing" that I gave a great snort of laughter.

"Don't cry," he said.

"I'm not crying."

"Well, thank God for that. And where was your fellow in all of this?"

I shrugged. "Full of remorse, or the appearance of it, when he came back and found out what had happened. Sorry, that probably wasn't the sort of secret you were expecting to hear about."

He shook his head. "And here I was thinking I'd get a kinky story involving school uniforms or something."

"I could do that, too, but I didn't go to the sort of school Kimberly did. Remember when she kissed me?"

"Oh, yeah, her lurid lesbian past." He released me. "I'm honored you told me. Are you okay? I didn't mean to upset you."

I shook my head. "You didn't. I think I upset you more."

"Elise didn't want kids."

"And you did?"

He shrugged. "I didn't want to rule it out entirely. I don't want to talk about Elise. So you want to hear my deep, dark secret? For starters, I jerk off quite a lot."

I feigned a yawn. "That's hardly a secret. All guys do. What's a lot? Ten times a day?"

"I wouldn't have time for much else if it were ten times a day." He reached for my foot and stroked it gently, tweaking my toes. It should have tickled. Instead, it felt unbearably sexy. "Look, I don't want to be one of those guys who's always going on and on about his ex. But I'll say this. After we were married she rationed sex. She didn't like oral sex and she'd sulk for a week if I expressed any interest in her ass. So I took care of things myself and I withdrew from her. She acted like she didn't even like me anymore. So I'm something of an expert at avoiding intimacy. And that, Jo Hutchinson, is why I recognize you withdrawing from me, because I'm so good at it myself."

"Oh, yeah. Here comes the lawyer in you."

I'd meant it as a joke, but he frowned. "And that was another thing. Pressure from Elise and her family, and from my da, too, to practice law. Absolutely not. No way will I put on a suit and pontificate and spend my life acting like a jerk."

"I'm sorry. I didn't mean to hit a nerve. But you don't need to act like a jerk to practice law. Liz said you gave legal advice to women at the shelter."

"It's hardly the same. And it was pro bono. No chance of

becoming a rich jerk that way." But he frowned and I could see the tension in his arms and shoulders.

I leaned forward and reached around him to pull the plug from the drain.

He sat, hunched. "My da's coming into town in a few days, on business. You can meet him if you like."

"Is that a cry for help?" I stood and reached for a towel.

"A cry for moral support, and I'm not proud of it. He'll put on the charm and good behavior and not drink too much or harangue me if you're there."

"Sure. But don't you think it's a bit early for...for, well, meeting family?"

He stood, scattering water. "Seize the moment. He's not often on this side of the Atlantic, thank God. But you and me, we're not exactly playing this by the book, are we?"

I certainly wasn't. I wiped steam from the mirror and rubbed moisturizer onto my face as Patrick, or rather Patrick's erection, nudged against me from behind.

"I could do you right now." His hands were on my hips, guiding me. He nibbled at my ear, my neck.

I pushed back against him, wanting him, his cock sliding against my butt. In the mirror his hand closed around my breast and tweaked my nipple into a hard, dark point.

"Do you like to watch yourself come?" His other hand slid down my belly and disappeared below the level of the sink.

My eyes were dark, wide, and my gaze locked with his in our reflection. Even when my legs shook and my mouth opened wide, he held me; held me close to him, held me safe.

21

ORGASMS HAVE A WAY OF RELAXING YOU, SOMETIMES too much.

After my bath and Patrick's attentions all I could do was mumble that I was tired and let him tuck me into bed for a nap. I awoke a couple of hours later, tired and disoriented, my mind fuzzy. Another quick shower woke me up and I dressed and went downstairs to meet Patrick.

He was transformed. He wore a dark suit and a dazzling white shirt open at the neck. No tie, his hair slicked back, giving his face a stark severity. Once I'd thought him a leprechaun, then a fairly okay-looking guy, but until today I'd never thought of him as handsome. Desirable, yes, but that was from our progression from strangers to lovers. I suppose that was what we were now. After tonight we would be.

He watched me walk down the stairs and I slowed for his appreciation. The dress swished at my thighs; nylon whispered as my legs brushed it in my descent.

"And would those be stockings?"

"Possibly."

"It's with the greatest of restraint that I haven't pretended to drop a quarter on the floor so I could take a look up your skirt."

"I don't think they give medals out for that sort of thing." I twirled to give him a preview of what he would see later, then plucked my cell phone from my purse. "I'll call for our ride."

He raised his eyebrows. "Very fancy. And here we are, each other's arm candy."

When the limo arrived we spoiled the effect of our finery, Patrick with a large woolen scarf, me with a down coat that made me look hugely puffy, for the sake of keeping warm on the quick run from door to car. We also had backpacks with our overnight stuff.

I had been afraid that we might make a stop to pick up Ivan or someone else I knew, but it seemed we were to be the only passengers.

"So where are we going exactly?"

I laid a hand on Patrick's knee. "You'll find out."

"Hmm. I like to know where I am." He fiddled with his cell phone and I knew he was tracking our position via GPS; I also knew, from experience, that the signal would fade as we climbed higher into the mountains. Once again, I was going into the unknown, but this time with Patrick, and it was an adventure.

I pushed the button that would bring a screen between us and the driver. Patrick looked up from his cell, eyebrows raised. "What did you have in mind?"

"I need to tell you things."

"Go on."

"I'm obsessed with you." I was, but I'd meant to tell him about Mr. D. Here in the darkness.

"Me, too."

"I heard what you said the other night. I don't know. I want to say no, it's not too early, but I can't give you an answer yet. I have some things to resolve. Some emotional tidying up. So

I can't talk about love right now." I took a deep breath. "And I'm not into my job anymore. It used to be so important to me. I have… It's become routine. Very little thrill. I mean, the job has a lot of piddling administrative stuff, but the reward always used to be I'd go on air, and I'd feel I made a difference, that what I did was important. And now…it's not just that I think about you most of the time and want to be with you. I may have to face the possibility that I've burned out. That it's time to move on."

"Sure. Why not? Don't beat yourself up over it, Jo. Maybe it's best to leave while you're ahead of the game."

"I've been there ever since college." There was a note of panic in my voice. "Shit, I'm sorry. I don't mean to whine."

"And you're thinking what the hell else could you do, right? And how will that weird job look on a resume?"

"Yes."

He took my hand and rubbed it between his as though warming me up. "You don't have to make a decision right now. You have time, and for what it's worth, you sound great. Gives me a hard-on every time."

"Oh, that's real reassuring." Despite my anxiety about work and about the evening I giggled. "I don't think Nielsen has erection ratings."

He placed my hand on his crotch. "How does this rate?"

"Oh. Pretty high, I think. Or should that be hard? I hope you haven't had this since we had a bath. Maybe I should direct the driver to take us to the nearest emergency room."

He grinned. "No, this is a new one. I'm afraid I had to start all over again."

"You jerked off?" I increased my pressure, trailing my fingertips up and down his impressive length.

"Well, yeah. I told you I jerk off a lot."

I unzipped him and slipped my hand inside his pants, felt his silk boxers. "Tell me you thought about me when you did it."

He leaned to lick my ear and nibble my neck. "I did. I thought about what I'd do to you tonight. I think I'll tie you up and have my wicked way with you when you're spread out and helpless and naked. Mostly naked."

Oh, God. A frisson shivered through my nipples and crotch. I squeezed my legs together. "What if I don't want you to tie me up?" I rubbed the silk against his cock.

"I'll do it anyway. You'll be at my mercy." He flipped up my skirt. "Well, look at those panties. And the stockings, too, what a treat."

I looked down at my black panties for the pleasure of seeing his hand stroke the satin. My legs had spread wide of their own will; I certainly hadn't had anything to do with the decision. The skin of my thighs above the stockings looked very white in the dim light, bisected by the black garters. Yes, the real McCoy that made men such helpless, drooling idiots. Garters and black lace.

"Kimberly says it's serious if you wear a garter belt," I said. "You gladly suffer the strange indentations and indignities."

He unfastened his pants. "Brace yourself for indignities, then, because you'll be keeping that on all night."

"I love it when you go all macho on me." I stroked his cock slow and easy. Dampness coated my fingers as I drew his foreskin down.

"Turn toward me. Take your panties off. One foot on the seat. Spread your legs."

I did as he told me, thrilled by his commands. Mr. D. would love this. I'd—

I snatched my hand away as if his cock was on fire.

"What's wrong?"

"Nothing." And I truly believed I'd stopped thinking about Mr. D. Was that why the thrill had left my radio job, too— because Mr. D. wasn't there to share it?

He shook his head, tucked his cock away and zipped up.

"Sorry," I added, a second too late.

"One moment you're a sex goddess, the next you're blowing hot and cold. Precious little blowing, to think of it. What's wrong? Did you remember you left the oven on at home or something?" He reached to the floor and found my panties.

I felt embarrassed now, pulling the damp underwear on and straightening my dress. "I can—"

"No!" He sounded exasperated. "If you want to tell me whatever it is that turned you off, then tell me. If it was something I did or said, let me know, and it won't happen again." He shook his head. "Sorry, this delayed gratification thing is getting to me."

"It was your idea."

"I know." He stared out of the window and produced his iPhone again.

The irony, our first fight, albeit a very minor one, and we hadn't fucked yet; or, as we both knew, if we had fucked we'd be sated and happy. Or maybe not. We spent the rest of the trip in silence.

The driver's voice came over the intercom. "Ma'am, sir, we'll be arriving in five minutes."

Patrick looked at me and winked. "How very discreet."

I reached for my backpack. "One more thing." I handed him one of the masks Harry had given me.

"What the hell? How am I supposed to put this on with glasses?" He fiddled around, finally removing his glasses and folding them inside his jacket. "Why the secrecy?"

I shrugged. "It's sort of a tradition."

He took my hand as we got out of the limo and squeezed it. "Sorry to be a grouch."

"Me, too." We kissed and then walked up the imposing steps of the mansion, flanked by stone lions, to the massive front door.

★ ★ ★

Patrick knew something was off about the whole evening but he went along with it because it seemed important to Jo. There was definitely a hidden agenda here but he was so cock-driven at this point he would have agreed to anything. Suit? Sure. Silly black mask? Naturally. Small talk with strangers? Honey, for you, anything.

Because he was going to get laid, finally, and he'd walk through fire or jump through hoops to get there.

And she looked great in that slinky dress. If she moved fast, it twirled out and flashed garters and the tops of her stockings, dark against her pale skin. And beneath, the filigree of sexy black underwear with presumably a matching bra, both of which he'd remove, leaving her in the garter belt and stockings. Yes, he was a predictable fool, his brain settled firmly in his genitals and to hell with the consequences.

The location looked like some sort of hotel—huge and ornate, probably built by a nineteenth-century miner who'd struck it rich. He took Jo's hand as they went up the steps together and through a huge, carved front door that looked like it might have been pilfered from a medieval castle in the days when the nouveau riche swarmed around Europe buying bits and pieces for their painfully new ancestral homes.

Inside it wasn't a hotel, and it wasn't quite a private home, either. A receptionist—masked, wearing a tight, short black dress—greeted them, checking off their names on a list, and handed them a key to their room: a real brass key, not a keycard. "Cocktails are being served in the library, dinner at eight. You'll need a tie, sir."

Another minion, a slender young man with close-cropped dark hair, took his scarf and Jo's coat and their backpacks and whisked them away as if they polluted the spotless elegance of the vestibule, with its antique furniture and fancy rugs.

Patrick reached into his pocket for his tie.

"I rather like you like this. The hint of chest hair." Jo touched the open neck of his shirt, her fingertip cool against his skin.

He knotted the tie and turned his collar down. "Behave. I have other plans for this tie. I doubt they'll provide house handcuffs."

"They might." Her eyes were very bright, her lips parted. She reached to straighten his tie, a gesture that was oddly domestic.

They followed a group of people up the imposing staircase. By this time Patrick had become accustomed to everyone being masked. Most of the other guests (or whatever they were) wore the plain black masks that covered only the eyes and that served to emphasize women's lips. He'd not appreciated the subtlety, or, when you got close, the gleam of eyes through the mask. He was mostly longsighted, and could appreciate the general view, even if Jo, the woman to whom he wanted to be closest, appeared slightly blurred.

The library looked like a movie set but he suspected the floor-to-ceiling shelves of leather-bound books might be real. Waiters—unmasked, because obviously the hired help didn't count—circulated with trays of drinks and hors d'oeuvres. Jo looked around and shrugged. "I'd introduce you to people but I don't know who they are," she said. "Being mysterious and atmospheric doesn't always work."

"Jo! Darling! So this is your main squeeze." A guy with reddish hair approached and kissed Jo's cheek. Patrick watched to make sure his hand didn't linger too long on her waist. "Hi, I'm Harry. Glad you could make it. Everything okay? Let me get you a drink." He took a couple of glasses from a passing waiter. "You've got a great room. I hope you enjoy it, and we expect to see much more of you, Patrick. Catch you later."

Patrick took a sip from his glass and sensed the bite of alcohol under a tart citrus taste. No big surprise. He weighed the pros and cons of making one of his rare forays into alcohol consumption. He didn't have to drive or operate any heavy machinery (he didn't think Jo counted as such). He wanted to have every sense and nerve sharp when he got Jo alone (and naked and aroused and coming) but the buzz from a couple of drinks might be nice. It might also slow him down. Not that he was worried about his performance, and after all they had all night. And many more nights.

"I thought you didn't drink." Jo, right on the button.

"I don't. This seems pretty innocuous."

"Okay." She stared after Harry as he worked his way through the room, kissing cheeks, slapping shoulders, for all the world like a campaigning politician.

He took another sip. "Everything okay?" he asked her.

Just then a couple bore down upon them and Patrick gaped at the woman's astonishing breasts before they blurred into pink half moons above the top of her dress, a tight, silver thing that ended barely below her butt. They introduced themselves as Jake and Cathy.

Jake moved in to kiss Jo and she stepped aside, turning her face so he hit her directly on the cheek, not on her mouth. Interesting.

Patrick kissed Cathy's offered cheek, taking the opportunity to squint into her cleavage. Her breasts looked like a pair of pink melons, fascinating yet slightly repellent.

Jake elbowed him. "Aren't they great? You should make Jo get hers done."

"And wouldn't that be Jo's decision?" What the fuck did this guy know about Jo's breasts? He was torn between outrage and embarrassment at being caught peeking by the woman's husband.

"It's okay, man," Jake said, slapping his shoulder. "Take a good look. Fair's fair."

"Behave," Cathy said to her husband. She tugged her dress

down to cover her ass. "C'mon, honey, let's circulate. See you guys later."

"You bet." Jake laughed loudly. His hand at Cathy's waist, he steered her away.

"Are they friends of yours?" Patrick asked Jo, looking around for another drink.

"No. I just know them."

Another guy swooped in to kiss Jo.

"Hi. Willis Scott—oops, we're not supposed to use last names. How're you doing?" Before either of them could answer, something caught his attention. "Gotta go, I'll catch you later."

No last names. Interesting. And why these cryptic comments on something or other happening later? Patrick moved closer to Jo and slipped an arm around her waist. "I'm getting a bit tired of seeing you manhandled by every other guy here," he murmured.

"Don't exaggerate. Besides, I don't think I know anyone else here." But she looked around the room as though she was expecting another admirer. Or something. Then she reached a hand down to his butt and squeezed and he forgot all about the other guys and whether he wanted another drink because it was Jo, and she was his and he was in love with her.

A booming, tinny sound—he recognized it as a bigger version of his gran's dinner gong—summoned everyone to dinner.

It was another stately home setting in a huge room, one long table decorated with candelabra and flowers. He wanted to sit next to Jo, but they actually had place cards, which reminded him of his sister's wedding (and another memory arose, of his da drunk and weeping, full of unwholesome sentimental blather about losing his little girl). How many of those bloody drinks had he had? He couldn't remember, and that was a bad sign. His vision had a sharp, sparkling quality that he remembered from the few times he'd drunk seriously, and the sound in the room echoed and wavered. Already he was feeling thirsty, a warning that the poison should be diluted.

He downed the glass of water at his place setting and reached for a piece of bread.

"Hungry?" the woman on his right next to him murmured. Her eyes sparkled beneath her mask. Her voice reminded him of Jo's, throaty and sexy.

He raised his empty water glass to her in a toast, wondering whether he'd met her already or what he'd find to talk to her about, if he was even capable of maintaining a coherent conversation. He narrowed his eyes and looked at her place card, debating whether he should retrieve his glasses.

"Sorry, I don't remember whether we fucked," the woman said.

What? He gaped at her. She'd said "met," surely. Yes, of course, she had.

"I don't think so. It's my first time here. I'm Patrick."

"I'm Jackie. Great to meet you." She offered her hand. "Oh, you're *Patrick.*"

It must be the booze, distorting his hearing. "Yes, I'm Patrick. Is that significant?"

She giggled and put her hand on his knee. "I can't wait for later."

"Really? What do you have planned?"

"That depends on you, lover boy." She ran her fingers up and down his thigh.

He removed her hand and grabbed the bread basket. "Have some bread."

"Oh, you meanie." She pouted sexily at him. "So, what do you like?"

"Like?"

"Yes. What are you into?"

"Skiing, music. I'm just learning about classical but I like jazz. I box a bit, work out. What about you?" But she'd turned away to talk to the guy on the other side.

22

I WISHED PATRICK AND I COULD HAVE SAT together. He'd entered into an animated conversation with the woman on his left, and I was jealous she had all his attention. But later, I'd have him all to myself.

The food was delicious and I was starving. I'd managed to grab a few hors d'oeuvres in the library to sop up the deceptively strong cocktails. Patrick had downed several with no particular effect and I could see he was drinking wine now. I remembered how he'd claimed he didn't drink and it concerned me very slightly that either he'd lied, or exaggerated, or was just taking a risk. But he was an adult, and I figured he knew what he was doing.

"So you're Jo," the man next to me said. He took my hand and kissed my knuckles.

From across and several seats down the table, Patrick, as though alerted by some sort of radar, glared at me. I smiled at him. Let him sweat a little. If he was planning to play games later, I could play them now.

"Yes, I'm Jo," I said to my neighbor. "Why do I have the feeling I have some sort of notoriety here?"

"Oh, but you do. You're the bad girl of the drones in the Great Room. You're the only one who's had the smarts to invade upstairs."

"It wasn't that difficult." A plate of something delicious and beautiful appeared in front of me. The thought occurred that probably everyone in this room had seen me getting spanked and having an orgasm after and I hoped nobody would say anything indiscreet to Patrick.

"And after tonight…" He shrugged. "Rumor has it you're going places."

I nodded, wondering whether people joined the Association for its cloak-and-dagger atmosphere as much as the sex. I wanted to ask my neighbor if he knew Mr. D., but I'd long ago figured out that he wasn't known by that name here. I looked around the table for a tall slim man with dark hair, and naturally there were several candidates. With the buzz of conversation and clatter of cutlery on china I couldn't distinguish his voice. But I knew I had to stop thinking about Mr. D. because this was my night with Patrick.

Dinner lasted a long time, or maybe it only seemed that way because I wanted to be alone with Patrick. At the same time I appreciated the delay, the inevitable buildup in my mind, and that I could see him but not touch him. He was making the woman next to him laugh; I'd noticed that he talked only to this woman and not the one on his other side.

I chatted to both of my neighbors about, of all things, investments, and had the impression that I could have learned a lot if I'd taken notes.

"You sound a bit like that girl on the radio," one of them said as we paused in between courses. "You know, the one who's on late at night."

Woman on the radio, please. "Do I?"

Dessert arrived, tiny dark chocolate truffles, lemon tartlets and fresh raspberries garnished with a mint leaf and a fluffy cloud of whipped cream.

I refused coffee—I wanted to be awake, but not that awake—and ordered a green tea instead. People stood, gathered in groups to chat and drifted out of the room. I wondered if they were going to observe the Great Room or seek diversions elsewhere.

Patrick stood and looked across the table at me, his gaze sharp and compelling. He jerked his head toward the door and I stood, too, telling my companions I'd see them later. They grinned and nudged each other in a way that made me uneasy, but I forgot as Patrick walked toward me—no, he stalked, fierce and predatory—and reached to rip off his mask.

"Come on," he said, putting on his glasses. "I've had enough." He didn't seem at all drunk. He was still steady on his feet, his eyes as direct and perceptive as usual, but this was another side of Patrick I'd barely glimpsed.

What the hell had they told him? "Where are we going?"

"Upstairs." He removed the room key from his pocket, and dangled it in front of me. "I'm fed up with women who aren't you."

"You seemed to be doing pretty well."

His smile had little humor. "She was into web design, too." He looked around. "How the hell do we get to the third floor?"

"There's an elevator here." Once inside I removed my mask, very aware of Patrick fixing me with that fierce gaze.

He raised his hand and unknotted his tie, drawing it slowly from his neck. I watched his hands as he rolled it and slipped it back inside his jacket pocket.

The elevator doors opened and we stepped out into a dimly lit corridor that had the quiet anonymity of a hotel. It was very quiet and my sense of anxiety about the evening, which had lessened over dinner, increased again. But what could possibly go wrong now?

Patrick consulted the key ring for our room number and led me along the corridor, stopping to unlock a door and push it open.

I stepped into the room and saw that Harry's promise to provide romance had been serious. The room was golden with the glow of candles and the large four-poster bed was scattered with rose petals. Logs burned in the fireplace. A bottle of champagne rested in an ice bucket next to the bed. Our backpacks sat discreetly against one wall, looking shabby and out of place.

Patrick walked past me and looked around with approval, although I think his interest lay in the size of the bed and the huge mirror opposite. He shrugged off his jacket and sat in one of the armchairs. "Come here."

I made myself walk slowly. I wanted to run to him and snuggle on his lap, but that sternness in his expression told me that tonight he was to issue orders and I was to obey. I stood in front of him and he gestured for me to turn around. The zipper on the dress hissed and the silk slithered down. I turned around to see he now held the tie in his hands.

"Bra off. And panties."

So I was down to my garter belt and stockings as he'd intended and that cool, lustful gaze made me shiver.

"Can I undress you?" I asked.

"No. But you can see if there's water in the refrigerator and bring me some."

He wanted to watch me while I paraded around like a wet dream in my black stockings and garter belt and heels, so I made the most of it. I sashayed across the room and parted my legs to bend and inspect the contents of the small refrigerator, knowing he would look at my exposed cunt and butt and the position of my breasts.

I returned with a bottle of water and stood in front of him as he drank it. Again, that silent scrutiny of my body.

A log fell in the fireplace with a crackle and shower of sparks.

He placed the empty bottle on the floor. "Give me your wrists."

I held out my wrists and he stood to loop and knot the tie around them. He was close to me now and I longed to touch him, or for him to touch me. The front of his pants, distended by his erection, brushed against me and I pushed my hips against him.

"No," he said in a kind but stern voice, "I don't think so. Not yet. Only when I tell you. Do you understand?"

"Yes, Patrick."

"Get on the bed. I want you to lie diagonally across it and I want your legs open as wide as you can get them." He moved ahead of me to shove the pillows and the quilt in its creamy raw silk cover aside. "Lie down. Your arms above your head." I felt the pull and tug as he tied the silk tie around a bed post. The smooth sheets were cool and gentle against my skin and the faint scent of rose petals filled the air.

Patrick leaned against the bedpost, arms folded, and surveyed me, entirely serious and quiet. He shifted positions a couple of times and I guess he'd toed off his shoes and socks. He sat on the edge of the bed next to me but not looking at me, and unbuttoned his shirt cuffs. I might have been invisible, but I could tell from the tension in his shoulders, the pace of his breathing, that he was as aroused as I was.

He stood again and, with his gaze fixed on mine, unbuttoned his shirt with great care and infinite slowness. I think at one point I moaned. His hands stilled and he raised his eyebrows. "I need those legs to be farther apart," he commented, and resumed unbuttoning.

I spread my legs, exposing my cunt to him. He could see me, wide open, my secret parts swollen and wet, my clit erect.

He was busy at work on his pants now, or rather, busy at work at a slow, languorous unfastening. He stopped to remove a packet of condoms from his pocket and place them on a table next to the bed. He created a further delay by investigating the basket placed there, holding up items one at a time to show me: more condoms, a bottle of lube, a small vibrator in a sealed plastic bag. "Very nice," he commented.

Only then did he pull the zipper on his pants down and step out of them. His cock pushed against the black silk boxers. I wanted to see him as badly as I wanted his touch, but he left them on and stretched out beside me, resting his head next to mine.

"Jo," he breathed, and I saw then the Patrick I was used to, the Patrick I loved, not the imperious, exciting stranger who had revealed himself tonight. "Jo, you're so lovely. Give me a safe word."

"I trust you. You won't hurt me."

"You might get a terrible cramp."

"Okay, then. My safe word is…Scheherazade." I was out of breath. He still hadn't touched me and our bodies were inches apart.

His fingertips skimmed my hair and cheek and finally, thank God, we were kissing, the kisses wet and greedy and hungry, both of us murmuring incoherently of our need and lust, and possibly also of love; in that moment desire created its own language for us. He pulled his mouth from mine.

"I'm going to do what I want," he said. "And you'll do anything I ask."

"Yes," I said. I wanted him to fuck me right away, but he moved to kneel between my spread legs. The boxers had gone.

"Your cunt is beautiful," he said with a sort of reverence. He stroked his cock as he talked, lightly at first, and then more roughly. "You're so wet and shiny. Like pink silk. Plumped up for my cock." He reached to touch my breasts and dropped onto all fours over me. "But first…"

His tongue snaked over my clit and delved briefly inside me.

I writhed against him. I'd thought I would come at the slightest touch but although I tensed and quivered against his mouth and lips my body held back. He gave a murmur of appreciation and moved his hands to my thighs, clamping them open and preventing further movement.

He lunged back to my mouth. "Taste your cunt," he said, and I did. More kissing, our legs tangled, although his held mine down as soon as he realized I attempted to rub against him. I wanted him so badly I was beyond dignity—heck, I was wearing a wet dream outfit and tied up with his tie; how much dignity could I possibly possess at this point?—and heard myself, thrillingly, begging him to fuck me. Fuck me hard. Shove that lovely, intact Irish dick right into me and make me scream. Please, Patrick.

"God, yes." He reached for the condoms.

"No. Don't use one."

"What?"

"Scheherazade. Don't use a condom. I want to feel you. I'm on the pill. Please." I gulped for breath.

He paused, condom in hand. "Oh, fuck, yes."

The condom was tossed aside and he pushed against me for one lovely moment and then slid inside me, very hard, very large.

I think I let out some sort of strange squawk. He stopped moving and hesitated, cradling my face in his hands. "Okay, Jo?"

"Yes. Please, don't stop."

He retreated a little, pushed forward again. "Relax, will you. It's only a dick."

I giggled then and shifted beneath him, craving the right angle, the right friction, and found it. Oh, *yes*. He followed, adapting to my unspoken request, with another teasing withdrawal almost to the tip—he caught his breath and paused—

then back in, with a long delicious slide. His chest hair scraped
my nipples.

I couldn't use my hands but I could use my legs and my hips
to encourage him, to urge us both on, to rub my clit against
him and impose my rhythm, my wanting and heat, and build in
counterpoint to his. I bit his collarbone, snarled at him to *wait,
wait—stop, now, let me move,* and came in a great burst of wet
heat and relief. *Can you feel that? Feel me come.* And astonished
myself because it didn't happen that way too often and I was
filled with irrational, stupid gratitude and love.

"Good girl," he said and for once I didn't mind being called a
girl. "Oh, good girl, lovely girl, oh, Christ, you do such things
to my cock." He slung my legs over his shoulders and I felt real
fear that he'd do me an injury as he pumped away. I knew he'd
come soon; I could tell from his breathing, the increased speed
and urgency of his thrusts. His cock stiffened and jerked and
heat flooded me. He groaned and rested his head on my breasts.
"Oh, God. You okay, Jo? Sorry I couldn't last longer."

"I'm fine. It was wonderful."

He laughed and released my legs. His cock slid out in a gush
of fluid. He reached to unknot the tie and rub my arms. "Move
your arms, otherwise you'll be stiff as a board and there's only
one sort of stiffness we want around here."

I stretched my arms, luxuriating in the ability to move and
enjoying his weight and the dampness and scent of our mingled
sweat; even the considerable amount of fluid pooling on the
sheet and trickling down my thighs was pleasant.

A door opened and the room flooded with light and sound,
voices and applause.

"Nice job, Jo," said a familiar voice.

23

CURSING FLUENTLY, PATRICK THREW THE QUILT over me to protect what modesty I had left—very little—and leaped to his feet. Even then I noticed the beauty of his lean wiry body, the sway of his half-erect cock.

Next to the mirror was a door, which was now half-open, and a dozen or so masked people spilled into the room.

"Nice job," Harry said again. "Very nicely done, Jo. I—"

I didn't even see Patrick hit him, just heard a strange, fleshy thump and Patrick standing where Harry had been.

In some sort of gesture of support for Patrick, I rolled off the bed and moved to his side.

He turned on me. "Get away from me!" And then to the people in the room, "Get the fuck out!"

He thought I'd set him up. "Patrick, I didn't—"

"Shut up." He pulled on his pants and shirt. I looked on helplessly as he grabbed his jacket and backpack, and shoved his feet into his shoes. In a very short time he'd left the room.

Harry got to his feet and sat on the bed. One eye was swelling up. "Your boyfriend is quite the caveman, honey."

"I trusted you!" I was wearing a garter belt and stockings, I had semen trickling down my leg and I was close to tears, but so angry I didn't care. "You asshole! You lied to me!"

One of the women handed Harry a handful of ice from the ice bucket for his eye and snuggled beside him, her hand on his thigh. He shrugged. "The Association comes first, Jo. One of the things I like about you is how trusting you are. Mild bondage and no protection for your first fuck with the Irishman—nicely done. I've never heard someone use their safe word for their partner not to use a condom, though. That was a first."

Someone placed something warm and soft on my shoulders, one of the bathrobes the room had provided. The simple act of civility made my eyes sting and water. I struggled to get my arms into the sleeves, the belt tied. "Will you please all go away?"

"Come on, Jo, don't be a silly girl," Harry said.

Another couple settled on the bed, the woman on the man's lap, her skirt pulled up around her waist. Dimly, I realized they were fucking.

"Wow, look at this," Harry said, unfastening his pants and exposing his erect cock. "Who's gonna help out with this one? Jo?"

The woman who'd brought him the ice dropped to her knees to service him.

A guy settled into the armchair to watch, cock in hand.

"Harry," I said. "This is it. I'm leaving the Association. I never want to hear from you or your friends again. You've fucked me over one too many times."

"Point taken," Harry said, breathing heavily, his hands on the woman's head.

I pushed aside another couple fucking against the wall to grab my backpack and left the room. Outside the corridor was quiet and empty. The door closed behind me with a click. The next door stood open and I caught a glimpse of their viewing room, the air heavy with the scents of sweat and semen, and wineglasses and a few garments discarded on the floor. And the two-way mirror inside revealed a roiling mass of half-naked, entwined bodies.

Most of the mirrors are two-way…

Too late I remembered what Mr. D. had told me. How stupid I'd been.

I unfastened my garter belt and rolled the stockings down, kicking them away, then pulled out the jeans and sweater and underwear I'd packed for the next day from my backpack. I dropped the bathrobe and dressed, then retreated into the corridor, closing the door and shutting off the sights and sounds. As I crouched to tie the laces of my sneakers the first tear rolled from my eye.

"Jo." The voice was deep, familiar. Once it had been the dearest voice in the world to me.

"Fuck you." I swiped the tears away and stood to face him. "It was you who put the robe on me, wasn't it?"

He bowed his head in acknowledgment.

Face to face with Mr. D. The moment I'd yearned for and feared. Now I felt only a weary despair.

He handed me a handkerchief of crisp, folded cotton. Old school. I looked at him, at the man who'd fed my fantasies and kept my secrets (had he?) for so long. I knew his voice, I'd seen him that time before to know that he was tall and slender with dark hair flecked with silver. He was unmasked, his eyes deep brown under straight black brows, his skin slightly olive. He was handsome, his bones beautiful and sharp, wonderful cheekbones and a slightly aquiline nose. Not young, pushing fifty, but the lines around his eyes gave his beauty depth and mystery.

And yet, he left me unmoved.

I spoke first. "Don't tell me you thought I knew. Don't insult my intelligence."

"I've caused you pain. I cannot tell you how sorry I am."

"Then don't even try." I picked up my backpack and swung it over my shoulder. Too late, I remembered my down coat was inside the room, probably being used as a surface for some enthusiastic screwing.

"Jo," he said, "don't you even want to know how our story ends?"

His gentle words hit me where I was raw. I leaned my face against the wall and cried for all I'd lost—Mr. D. and Patrick, everything, even that blob of bloody tissue I'd bled out a year ago.

He had the sensitivity to not attempt to comfort me or touch me. He stood waiting until I'd finished and had scrubbed black smears from my eyes into his pristine handkerchief.

"Our story?" I said. "Not mine. It was your story, you were the storyteller all along but I couldn't see it. I was just a—a thing to be manipulated."

"Jo, don't." He reached out a hand to me.

"Okay," I said. "Okay, you tell me how *your* story ends. Meet me on Tuesday at four at the Brown Palace Hotel in Denver. No secrecy, no hidden agenda, no clowns tumbling out from closets or mirrors, just you and me. And that's an end to it."

I turned and walked away. I hoped he wouldn't follow. I took the elevator down to the kitchen, where I called for a ride home, the numbness settling in again. There was no sign of Patrick and I didn't feel strong enough to face him even though I hoped he'd got home safely.

The night air was freezing, the stars obscured by cloud. Too cold for snow, and dark, so dark. I stepped into the limo and was joined by three people whom I recognized from the Great Room, but whose names I didn't remember. They took little notice of me, but huddled together, whispering and kissing. I took refuge in the cowl neck of my sweater and leaned my forehead against the glass, arms wrapped around myself for comfort. I dozed a little on the drive back into town, blocking out the moans and sighs produced by my companions.

At my house a light burned in the apartment. Patrick was home. I unlocked the front door and walked into the house, dropping my backpack on the floor. I would have liked Brady to run to me so I could pick him up and hold him, take comfort in the soft touch of his fur and his purring, heavy warmth. But the house was empty and quiet.

I went into the kitchen and turned on the faucet.

"So you're home."

I was so startled to hear Patrick's voice that I almost dropped my glass in the sink. I hadn't even seen him sitting quietly on the window seat, with faithless Brady on his lap.

"Why are you sitting in the dark?" I said carefully. I hadn't expected Patrick to be around and I certainly hadn't thought he would sound so calm. I expected anger, resentment, harshness. I reached for the light switch.

"Don't turn on the light."

"Okay." I sat at the table with my glass of water. "How did you get home?"

"I asked the guys in the kitchen and they called for a ride for me."

"I'm glad you're safe."

"I'm not sure I am." I shivered at the chill in his voice. "I had unprotected sex with a woman who invited me to a sex club without telling me that's what it was."

"You're okay," I said. "I—"

"You seem very sure of that. I can't be." He shifted and Brady dropped to the floor and made his way over to his food dish.

"I didn't know they were watching. I swear it. I did not set you up, Patrick."

A long silence. "I'd like to believe it. Maybe tomorrow I

will. I don't know. What else haven't you told me about, Jo?"
I didn't get a chance to think of something to say before he
said, "Good night," and started to walk out of the kitchen. In
the doorway, he stopped. "How many of those guys have you
fucked, or can't you remember?"

And he walked out, leaving me speechless, hurt by the
venom in his voice but knowing he was right. He had no reason
to trust me, no particular reason to believe anything I might
say now, having left so much unsaid. I listened to the sound of
him going up the stairs and into the apartment, the rattle as he
locked the door.

I couldn't blame him for trying to hurt me, but I wished he
hadn't.

I didn't sleep well that night and finally at six in the morning, when it was not quite light outside, and I had tossed and
turned enough, I sent Patrick a text message.

Talk to me?

I showered and put on jeans and a long-sleeved shirt. I ached
a little from the sex with Patrick last night, which made me
feel extraordinarily sad since I didn't know whether it would
ever happen again. I hadn't realized how much I'd strained and
pulled, first against the restraint, and then to urge myself to an
orgasm.

I didn't look at my cell until after I was dressed, and to my
relief there was an answer:

OK.

Not the most eloquent response, and there was little I could
read into that terse reply, but at least he was willing to talk,

even if it was only to break up with me. I knew it was more than likely.

I went into the kitchen and brewed coffee as a peace offering, then returned upstairs with mugs and the coffeepot and cream. I wedged the tray on my hip as I knocked on the door.

"It's open. Come in."

Patrick sat at one of his computers, tapping away at the keyboard. "Let me finish this."

I unloaded the tray and sat, waiting for him to finish. When he spun around in his chair I was shocked at how tired he looked, eyes reddened and shadowed, face unshaven. I suspected I didn't look much better. I'd avoided the mirror that morning. He accepted a mug of coffee with a half smile and a nod.

I wondered what I would say to him, but he spoke first. "You look like hell."

"So do you."

"I've got a hangover. It's my own bloody fault. I shouldn't drink. Anyway." He stared into his mug and then at me. "So here's where I stand. I'm in love with you. I feel a right idiot for not realizing the Association was a sex club—can you believe a woman asked me at dinner what I was into and I told her I liked jazz? Why didn't you tell me, Jo? I might have gone along with some sort of group thing if you'd wanted me to. Your turn."

"I swear, I didn't realize we'd be the floor show and I'm sorry to have embarrassed you." I was crying again. I wiped my face on my sleeve. "I loved making love with you. I hate to think we'll never do it again. I'm so sorry. I'm leaving the Association and that's nothing to do with you and me. I'd decided the Association wasn't a smart thing for me to do even before I knew I was in love with you, but I honestly thought last night would be okay."

"Oh, for Christ's sake, don't cry." He swooped down from

his perch at the computer and put his arms around me. "Don't, you'll start me off. I'm a terrible weeper. I feel so stupid. All those hints people kept dropping about 'seeing us later' that I didn't catch on to. And I shouldn't have walked out on you."

"It's okay. Nothing happened." I sniveled against his chest. "I had—have—some unfinished business there, with the guy who got me into the Association. He's my complicated love life. He was someone I met on the phone. We used to have phone sex when I was at the station, late at night."

"Jesus Christ," Patrick said. He rubbed his face against my hair. "Please tell me it wasn't Harry or Jake."

"No. It wasn't Willis, either, though I did screw him." I felt sick just saying that. "I think Harry will have a really horrible black eye today."

"Good. About the black eye, not Willis." He continued to hold me, but reached for his coffee mug. "So what happens now?"

"I don't know. Are we breaking up?"

"Maybe we should."

"I'll tell you—" I wanted to say I'd tell him the whole story but I wasn't sure I was ready for that, not so soon after last night.

"I don't want confessions. I can't give you absolution. You figure it out on your own, Jo." He looked angry now and released me, stepped away and banged his coffee mug down onto the counter.

That riled me. I stepped forward and took his face between my hands, his stubble harsh against my palms, and we kissed and kissed. I was terrified and elated, full of desire and anger.

We drew apart and he stared at me, shaking his head. "I don't think we're breaking up, are we?"

"No."

"Come here." He drew me to him and we shared a sweet, coffee-flavored kiss that sizzled all the way through me, as though now we spoke a different language with our kisses. I stroked the columns of muscle on his back and delved beneath the waistband of his jeans to clutch his butt.

"I'm going to make you come and come." He sucked at my neck, my collarbone, while his hands cupped my breasts. His erection pressed against my belly.

He led me to his bed, where we stripped off each other's clothes with fumbling urgency. This was much more like a first time, a discovery of each other's skin and textures and sensitivities by daylight on a rumpled bed. We were clumsy and shy with each other, aware of the fragility of our truce and the damage we might have done. No fancy underwear today—both of us sported faded cotton, mine rather ragged, his boxers crumpled—and no elaborate choreography. Or not yet.

We kissed and touched and stroked. He didn't go down on me, and I didn't ask. I wanted his lips and breath, the closeness of being face-to-face, the intimacy of whispering words of love into each other's mouths. When he slipped a finger between my legs I opened to him and loved the small sound he made in his throat as he felt how wet I was. He did something magical and extraordinary with two fingers in me—I think—and his thumb on my clit. I came while he laughed softly, and as the spasms died away he put those two fingers into my mouth. I sucked his fingers, tasting myself on him.

His eyes narrowed. "I have to fuck you right now."

He was inside me in one masterful rush, while I hooked one leg over his shoulder and the other around his waist. I wasn't quite on my back, I wasn't quite on my side, either, and I reached down to rub my clit. He whispered filthily to me that I should get myself off, because I was a wee wanking slut, and I struggled not to burst into inappropriate laughter.

"Let me get on top," I gasped.

He obligingly rolled us over, still joined, and I settled on him, slowing to a smooth, careful slide. I stroked his chest and circled his nipples with my fingers.

"Nice?" I asked.

"Nice. Kiss me."

I dropped my hands to either side of his head and we kissed. I moved as I needed to, starting the slow climb to another orgasm, and directed his hands to my breasts. I drew my head back to watch his fingers pinch and tweak, and his cock slide into my mass of pubic hair. And out, gleaming slick with my juices. The tension built and stretched; now there was no return. When I came I looked into his eyes and they remained my constant, anchoring me.

"On your hands and knees, woman." He lifted me off him and I scrambled into position.

His breath came harsh behind me, his cock pressed against my ass. He stroked the inside of my thighs, my clit, my ass. I wanted him back inside me. I wanted to slide and play with his cock, and he teased me, nudging and entering a little and then withdrawing.

I moaned, my head on my folded arms. "You're mean."

"I'll be meaner yet." He reached across me to his bedside table. "Have I mentioned recently what a great ass you have?" He smacked me lightly. "It's small but it's plump and…" He drew a finger between my butt cheeks. "Yes, you want it like this, don't you?"

Something cold dripped onto me and I shrieked.

"Lube," he said. "It'll warm up." I felt a painful press at the entrance of my butt. "Relax, it's only a finger."

"Only a finger? It feels like the fucking Eiffel Tower."

"Keep breathing. You'll be fine. Didn't Kimberly tell you how good I am at this?"

"You never got up Kimberly's ass!"

He laughed and continued his gentle invasion. And after

a while it seemed less of an invasion and more of a welcome visit.

"Now, this lube is much more comfortable," he said. "I applied it to my special lube warmer."

"Ouch! Would that special lube warmer be your dick?"

He pushed, gentle but insistent. I concentrated on breathing, relaxing, opening to him. I knew how big he was and yes, it hurt, and I whimpered a little while he whispered that we could take as long as we liked, but I was going to get fucked up the ass. Well fucked. And that I'd like it, although maybe I should play with myself to help things along.

"You want me to be a wee wanking slut?" I gasped.

"Absolutely." He groaned. "And you'd better hurry."

He barely moved, not then. But I moved, taking him into that most private of places, slowing when I needed to, going beyond the pain and the shame. Patrick shuddered and gripped my hips with his hands.

We separated and Patrick handed me a towel, grinning at me with great pride, and absolutely matter-of-fact that we both needed to clean up. "Now I'm not big on simultaneous orgasms. I like to know what's going on. But that was pretty damn good."

"It was," I said, wondering whether I'd remember this event in the wrong place at the wrong time, riding my bike, for instance. "I'm not sure I'll be able to walk for a time."

"You don't have to walk anywhere. You're staying right here in my bed and I'm going to bring you a nice cup of tea."

"Irish sex is a strange and wonderful thing," I commented as he jumped out of bed. "Anal followed by a nice cup of tea."

"The church allows anal on Sunday, so long as you go to confession after." He looked at me as he held the teakettle under the faucet. "I know I said I wouldn't take your confession, but if you want to talk I'll listen."

"Not now."

He nodded.

I couldn't tell him everything about Mr. D. Not yet. Not until it was finished.

Despite the tea and coffee we napped together for a few hours, turning in each other's arms to kiss or caress. In mid-afternoon I slid out of bed.

"What's up?" Patrick muttered.

"I'd better go into the station."

He blinked awake and reached for his glasses. "It's Sunday. Do you have an air shift?"

"No. Things to catch up on."

"Okay. I'll fix dinner."

I kissed him and returned to my part of the house to shower and change into winter biking clothes. Outside it was bitterly cold again, the sky gray and a small chill wind blowing. I knew it was too cold for snow but the air had a damp tinge, quite unlike Colorado's usual winter weather.

At the radio station I stopped in at the studio and chatted with the weekend announcer, then made my way to my desk. As I passed the office of our manager, Bill, I heard a sound from inside. Bill in on the weekend? That was unusual. I tapped at the door.

"I didn't mean to disturb you," I said. "I just heard a…" My voice died away as I looked at his bare office, the boxes stacked on the floor. "Bill, what happened?"

He shook his head. "I wanted to keep it quiet. I'm retiring. Don't look so stricken, Jo. It's time, don't you think? I've been here for—well, for decades. Too long." He picked up a framed photograph of the station staff in the early seventies. Bill, recognizable by his height and bulk, held up two fingers in the peace sign, long hair flowing around his shoulders.

"Back then we had round black plastic things with holes in the middle for music. We went on air stoned. Those were the days. Ancient history," he said and laid the photograph carefully into the box. "And when you start thinking like that, it's time to go."

"I'll miss you."

"Kimberly and I decided to keep things discreet." He grinned. "And we can be less careful now."

"You and Kimberly?"

"Sure. We thought you knew."

"I didn't. Congratulations. I'm…well, I'm happy for you both, but I wish you weren't leaving. Who else knows you're going?"

"Ah." He propped himself up on his desk. "When was the last time Neil told you anything substantial?"

"I don't know. Two, three months ago, maybe. I can't even remember getting email from him recently."

"You know what it means if you're kept in the dark." He reached for the last photo from his bookcase, one of his grand-children. "Neil is taking over my job on an interim basis. Al-though there will be the usual careful selection process, you know the board will select him, and you know what he thinks of classical music. Get your resume in shape, Jo. Use me as a reference, anytime."

"You mean he's going to make a format change?"

"I think it's more than likely. He's right, in a way. This town needs a serious local news station." He taped the box shut. "Hell with this. I'm done. I'm going home. Kimberly's making her famous chili. Peace and love, Jo."

"Peace and love." We hugged each other. "Give Kimberly my love and tell her I expect to hear the dirt on your illicit relationship."

I continued on to my cubicle, my mind reeling. Bill leaving, the end of an era; and in a relationship with Kimberly. She'd told me it was someone I knew but I would never have guessed it was Bill.

I checked my email and viewed the mail on my desk, my appetite for paperwork entirely gone. Neil had sent an email, reminding me it was time for my annual assessment and suggesting several times when he was available, all of them before ten in the morning, an unworkable time of day for me anyway. With Bill's warning in mind, I decided I'd put off such a meeting for as long as possible, so I didn't bother to send any sort of reply.

I retreated into the dark quiet of a studio and put together a prerecorded show for Tuesday night. If I were smart, I wouldn't need it for Tuesday— my common sense told me I shouldn't meet up with Mr. D. But as a precaution, it couldn't hurt. It was a generic selection; if I didn't use it for Tuesday I could use it another time. I arranged for one of my temp announcers to come in and run the board, just in case. And then I put my bike gear on again and rode back through the cold windy night to the warmth of Patrick and my home.

24

"I'M GOING TO GIVE YOU A TREAT TONIGHT," I said to Patrick over dinner.

"What sort of treat would that be?" He stood to collect our plates.

I gazed lovingly at his sweats, trying to determine whether he was wearing underpants or not. "I liked being tied up. I thought you might enjoy it, too. Have you ever been tied up?"

Then I blushed because I really didn't want to remind him of his rage and humiliation at the Association, but he answered with his usual good humor.

"Not since I was eight, by my sisters, and I can't say it did a lot for me. But I'm willing to give it a try. So, am I dessert or would you like some ice cream?"

"Ice cream first. What did you do this afternoon?"

He looked up from spooning ice cream into dishes. "Worked out. Caught up on bills. What would you like on your ice cream? Nuts, chocolate sauce, raspberries, whipped cream? Or were you intending to use those on me?"

"Everything, please, but on the ice cream. I just changed the sheets."

"Fair enough." He placed a bowl of dessert in front of me. "So what's on your mind?"

"How do you know there's something on my mind?"

"You're fiddling with things."

I snatched my hands away from the paper napkin I was shredding.

In between mouthfuls of ice cream I told him about what was going on at the station and how sad I was that Bill was leaving. I didn't tell him about Mr. D. and that I had challenged him to meet me on Tuesday afternoon. I didn't know how to broach the subject, and besides I wasn't even sure he'd turn up, let alone whether I would.

Patrick listened, not saying anything until I'd finished. "It doesn't sound good. What's your strategy?"

I blinked. "I don't think I have one. Be evasive, I guess."

"Be evasive and get your resume out."

"That's what Bill said." I pushed my bowl aside.

"Anything else?"

"Well. This is embarrassing. I have a problem."

"Oh, yeah?"

I sighed and pushed my index finger around the bowl to capture the last of the ice cream. I raised my finger to my mouth and licked it slowly. "I have these…silk scarves upstairs. They're all tangled up. I need some help with them."

"Absolutely." Patrick snatched our dessert bowls and spoons and dropped them into the dishwasher. "I'm your man, honey. Untangling is my specialty. Lead the way."

I led the way upstairs, excited and a little afraid of the power Patrick was about to grant me.

We arrived in my bedroom and I turned on the bedside lamp and flung a scarf over it to mute the light.

Brady ran past us, jumped onto the bed and kneaded the quilt, purring loudly.

"Must the cat stay, or is that part of the scenario?" Patrick asked.

I giggled and put Brady outside. I turned to Patrick. I cleared my throat.

"Tell me what to do," he said quietly.

I took another glance at the front of his sweats. Oh, my. "I'd like you to...to undress."

"Yes, mistress."

We looked at each other and burst out laughing.

"Oh, shit. Let me try that again. Patrick, undress. Please." I sat on the bench at the foot of the bed. "Slowly."

He bowed his head in acquiescence and pulled off the T-shirt he wore. I wondered briefly if I should send him to put more clothes on, since he was wearing—one sock came off, and then the next—only his sweatpants.

He hooked a finger in the waistband and inched the pants down, looking at me with a wicked grin. Down another inch.

I leaped to my feet and knocked him onto the bed, where he landed with a grunt of surprise, with me on top of him, holding his wrists. "You tease!"

"I thought that's what you wanted." He blinked innocently at me. "Now, what about these things you wanted untangled?"

He still hadn't shaved though he'd showered after his workout—I could smell the peppermint shampoo he liked—and I rubbed my face against the tender roughness of his stubble.

"That might feel nice on your nipples. Just a suggestion." He hooked his calves around mine and strained up, giving me the full benefit of his erection.

"You're getting ahead. We're doing this on my time." I put my mouth to his and I controlled the kiss, the pressure, the intensity. I was the one who led and encouraged him to open, touching my tongue to his, teasing and withdrawing. He made a sound in his throat of appreciation, encouragement.

I released him, but not for long, to fetch a handful of silk scarves from the basket on my dresser, and when I turned around he'd removed his sweatpants. He was stretched out naked on my bed, on my sheets, waiting for me, willing for me to take charge. I was touched by his trust, his sinewy beauty. His cock was fully erect, dark against his belly.

I stood and looked at him. I didn't think I could simulate the cool, stern demeanor he had assumed when he tied me up; simply, it made me happy to look at him and know he was mine, and I think that showed on my face, for he smiled at me.

Affection. There it was again. And desire, too. Oh, yes, desire was very much present.

Anticipating my request, he spread his legs so I could tie his ankles to the hinges of the chest at the end of the bed—I hoped he wouldn't rip it apart.

"Do you need a safe word?" I asked.

"Do I?"

"I don't know. I don't know what's going to happen." The uncertainty had the quality of a mystery, a sailor setting off on a voyage with only stars as his guide. "So, I think, yes, you should have one."

"Ellington. Like Duke Ellington."

"Okay." I knelt between his legs and reached to secure his wrists to the headboard. I loved the trusting gravity with which he offered his wrists, his smile, the way he ducked his head to kiss my clothed breasts as I knotted the scarves.

He gave an experimental tug with his arms and attempted to flex his legs.

I pushed another pillow under his head so he wouldn't strain his neck, because I wanted him to see what I was about to do. My imagination was afire with all sorts of possibilities.

"You're mine," I said, hardly registering that I said it aloud.

"I am," he said.

I was still in my bike clothes, the turtleneck and spandex pants and a pair of woolen socks. I took the socks off, then the turtleneck and the sports bra I wore underneath. My body was tight enough that I looked good in just the pants. I touched my nipples lightly and smiled at him.

He smiled back.

I took one of my favorite toys from the box—an expensive, whimsical vibrator that featured a specific attachment for the clitoris as well as an undulating, rotating head. I touched it to my nipples and then knelt between his thighs.

When I applied it to his erect penis he started and gave an exclamation of surprise.

"Do you like that?" I asked.

"It's…interesting."

"How about this?" I circled his nipples with the head at low speed.

He squirmed. "I don't know…. I can't decide whether it's tickling me or exciting me. Put it on my dick again."

This time I ran it up and down the ridges on his cock and his hips shifted, his eyes fluttering closed. "Keep doing that and I'll come," he murmured.

I turned the vibrator off. "Too easy."

I slithered out of my spandex pants and panties. We were both naked now and I loved the way he looked at me, yearning for me to touch him, to make love to him.

And I did. I touched and stroked and kissed him, rubbing my face against his skin, exploring the textures of the springy hair on his chest, the soft fragrant hair of his armpits, the hollows of rib cage and flanks, and the earthy scents of his balls and cock. Some parts of him I knew already. Others, like the silkiness of his inner thigh, the corded tendon behind his knee, the delicate strength of his ankle, I learned. I rubbed my nipples against the masculine roughness of his chest hair and the stubble on his cheeks. His tongue flicked out to catch my nipples briefly before I moved away.

I lifted his cock, baring the head to caress my hard nipples, leaving them shining with fluid. He whimpered slightly and sighed.

"Taste yourself." I allowed him to suck my nipples while I rode his thigh.

"You're driving me mad," he murmured.

"Good." I shifted to kneel astride him. He tensed beneath me as I handled his cock, stroking him, and then applying the head to my clit. "I'm very wet. Can you feel that?"

"Oh, God, yes. Will you make yourself come?"

I did. I used his cock shamelessly as the instrument of my pleasure; no penetration, just the silky moistness rubbed on my clit. I squatted over him, knees spread, holding my vulva open so he could see every detail of my hair and folds and pink, excited flesh, and the shining coral of my clit. He thrust up and groaned and cursed. I laughed. I teased. And then I came, laughing still, and collapsed on him, his cock hot and hard against my belly.

"Will you not have mercy on me, you lovely fiend?" His voice was rough. He pressed his cock against me, seeking friction and relief.

"Oh, I'm quite happy here. Like this."

"Bitch." He sounded pretty happy. "Take all night. Do whatever you like."

"Oh, I will." I rose to my knees and shuffled astride him, positioning my crotch over his mouth. "Or, to be more specific, you'll do whatever I like. Lick me."

He groaned and set to work, his tongue circling and flicking my clit while I writhed and pressed myself against him—I had to be careful, I needed him to breathe, after all—and I came to his clever tongue and lips. I think I may have screamed. I know I was noisy and my legs shook and I collapsed to one side, curled against the headboard, one leg across his chest.

He turned his lips to my knee and kissed it, very wet around the mouth. "Having a good time?"

"Oh, yes. And you?"

"Phenomenal. Is there any chance of me coming anytime soon?"

"Maybe." I turned and reached for the vibrator where I'd abandoned it earlier. I stretched out beside him and rested my head on his thigh and ran the vibrator up and down his cock. I found where he was sensitive, beneath the head where the skin was pink and delicate and gleaming wet, and pressed the undulating tip of the vibrator there. He panted and writhed and gasped and told me yes, like that, don't stop, Jo, he was going to come. His body tensed. The head of his cock swelled, the slit widened and semen spurted onto his belly and chest.

He went completely limp and laughed. I untied him but he was so relaxed he barely moved. I went to the bathroom for a washcloth and when I returned he was holding his arms aloft, rotating his wrists. "I'm good for nothing now. Wow. That was something. Enjoy yourself?"

"Oh, yes. Yes, I did." I swabbed the semen from his belly. "Thank you."

"Anytime. Well, almost anytime. Maybe we should only do that to each other once a week or so." He yawned. "Am I a total wuss if I go to sleep?"

"That makes both of us total wusses." I pulled the quilt over us and switched the light off.

Brady jumped onto the bed and settled between us. We fell asleep to the sound of his purrs.

This time waking in her bed had a lovely sort of familiarity. Their clothes lay scattered on the floor, along with a bowl and spoons; they'd decided last night, after a nap of an hour or so, that it was time for more ice cream. And one thing led to another and it was quite late before Jo announced she needed to sleep and they got up again to clean teeth and so on. The odd thing was that his usual insomnia didn't kick in when he was with her, so he had the rare experience of waking from a deep sleep, swimming up to the surface and daylight. Maybe it was being in love, or maybe it was just utter relaxation from the great sex. And maybe the great sex came from being in love, a thought that pleased him immensely. The cat was wedged between them so that when Patrick opened his eyes he got a face full of whisker and Brady's green mindless stare.

What woke him, he realized, was the relentless chirp of his phone in his sweatpants pocket, announcing he had a text message. It was too early for a client, but he put on his glasses and stretched out from the bed to retrieve his phone. Oh, shit, his da, texting to announce that he was flying in the next day and which hotel he was staying in.

He prodded Jo with one foot. "Hey, what sort of food do you like?"

"Oatmeal," she mumbled. All that was visible of her was the top of her head, the quilt pulled over her ears.

"No, not breakfast. For dinner."

"I can't think about dinner before I've woken up." A little more of her emerged. She blinked.

"My da's coming into town tomorrow. Where shall we take him? Somewhere fancy and nouvelle."

"Oh. Okay. Gillian's."

"So you'll come, too?"

"Sure. I'll get a sub. It'll be best if we can do it early. There's a concert satellite broadcast until nine, so I could get someone to come in for a couple of hours and then go back in if they can't stay until the end of the shift." She sat up and the quilt fell away, revealing her breasts and her nipples stiffening in the cool air. "I've got to pee."

He watched with great appreciation as she wandered across the room. Even despite the threat of his father's arrival he still had a hard-on like a log.

She continued the conversation from the bathroom, the door open. "So seven or seven-thirty."

"I'm glad you'll be there. I need you to see my genetic stock so you know what you're getting into. And he can be pretty good company."

"He sounds like a jerk," she said over the sound of running water.

"He's that, too. Are you coming back here? I've something to show you."

She came back into the bedroom and stretched, watching him for his reaction. He loved how comfortable she was wandering around naked, something he'd found unusual in American women. His cock twitched beneath the quilt at the sight of her.

"You're so beautiful," he said, immediately feeling a fool after.

She glanced at herself in the mirror and he saw her stand a little straighter, raise her chin. "Thanks."

He waited for the list of her imaginary flaws that inevitably followed any compliment paid to a woman, but she climbed back into bed with him and slid her cold feet between his calves. Again, something he wasn't used to, a woman who was comfortable with her body.

"Except for your feet. They're not beautiful. They're freezing."

"And my hands." She placed them on his rib cage, making him jump. "It was too cold to wait for the water to run hot."

"Don't touch my dick with those hands. It'll drop off."

She didn't take the hint but snuggled up against him, her head tucked under his chin, which was nice, except he was getting hornier by the moment. And anxious, too, because she was thinking about something and it wasn't him, and not admitting it, either.

"Are you okay?" he asked.

She made a slight, sleepy sound, which he didn't quite believe. Her body had a tense, springy sort of feel to it, not the relaxed heaviness of someone about to fall asleep.

He moved his hand to her rib cage and tickled.

"Stop that!" She came wide-awake. "If you want to get laid, you're going about it the wrong way."

"I didn't think you were interested."

"I'm not interested in being tickled."

"What's on your mind, Jo?"

"Nothing in particular. I just woke up." Her hand traveled down his body. "Is this what you wanted me to see?"

He kicked off the quilt to fully appreciate the sight of her hand on his cock. She gave a grunt of annoyance and pulled the quilt over herself again.

"I want to see your tits."

"Stop whining."

"Okay, then." He pulled the quilt over them, enclosing them in a dim, fragrant cave, and kissed her mouth and neck and breasts.

She broke away to take his cock in her mouth and while he appreciated the effort—more than appreciated—he was ashamed, briefly, that he could be distracted so easily.

"Jo," he mumbled, "Jo, don't…"

"What?" she stopped licking to stare up at him. "Is something wrong?"

"Don't stop," he said, although it wasn't what he really wanted to say. *Don't leave me.*

25

NOTHING WAS GOING TO HAPPEN. MR. D. AND I would meet at the hotel bar, we'd have a drink, declare an end to something that had never really started and I'd drive back to meet Patrick and his father for dinner.

But if nothing was going to happen, why couldn't I tell Patrick about it? About any of it? He'd never asked about the Association, what I'd done there, and I'd never offered to tell. Otherwise things were great, sexy and sweet. In just a couple of days we'd slipped into an easy domesticity; he waited up for me to come home late on Monday night, and greeted me with another delicious meal. We shared my bathtub and laughed and fucked like a pair of demented rabbits. But now and again I caught him gazing at me with an expression of suspicion and sadness.

I'd tell him everything…after. And I hoped he'd understand why I needed to get this last piece of the puzzle resolved.

"You look nice," he said as I left the house on Tuesday. "A bit like a secretary from an old Hollywood movie, but nice."

"I'll be going to the restaurant straight from work." I'd put on high heels and a black pencil skirt. On top I wore a clingy cream cashmere sweater, a gift from Kimberly that I'd never dared wear before; it seemed to be begging to have things spilled down it.

"Hey," I said, punching his arm. "Don't look so worried."

"You're right. I don't have anything to worry about." He leaned in to kiss me. I was expecting something friendly and casual. What I received was hot and sexy with lots of tongue and a thorough exploration of what was under my skirt. "I trust the stockings are for my benefit," he said when he came up for air.

"It was meant to be a surprise for you later." I straightened the skirt out.

"So long as it isn't a surprise for everyone else when you sit down."

I sighed. "I'll keep my knees together, I promise. Go do some work."

I grabbed my down coat and a scarf and left the house. I turned to see Patrick at the doorway, looking sexy and rumpled in a pair of faded old jeans and a sweater and I was tempted, for one moment, to run back to him and tell him everything. I waved and got into my car, taking care to flash him as I stepped in.

He grinned and gave me a thumbs-up.

God, it was cold, and frigid air had whooshed up my skirt for Patrick's cheap thrill. I knew it would be a good ten minutes before the heater pumped out any warm air. Shivering, I started the car and turned as though I were heading for the radio station, in case he was watching.

I felt like an adulteress.

Just under two hours later I was edging my way through city traffic looking for a parking place, weighing the benefits of the hotel's valet parking against a possible parking ticket and arriving blue with cold to meet Mr. D. I succumbed, turning onto Tremont and into the front entrance of the venerable red sandstone hotel. I entered through the revolving doors, un-winding the scarf and unbuttoning the coat. I felt like a fool, now. I had no guarantee Mr. D. would turn up, given his history of half-truths and evasion. I also wasn't sure where he'd be—hadn't I told him to meet me in the bar?

"Jo?"

I turned to see Mr. D. rising from one of the armchairs in the lobby. He came to my side, smiling, and kissed my cheek as though we were casual acquaintances. Despite my vow that I would not allow myself to fall under his spell yet again, I was disarmed by the warmth of his greeting and his dark beauty.

"You look lovely," he said. "Would you like a drink? Something to eat? Or we could have afternoon tea—it's quite good here."

I agreed to afternoon tea and he led me to the restaurant, where a waiter took my coat and scarf and we settled in armchairs. A harpist played softly. Black tea reminded me of Patrick so I chose oolong, and Mr. D. ordered us scones and finger sandwiches.

"Very civilized," he said with a smile.

"Where are you from? I could never place your accent."

"Oh, here and there. My father was from Greece and my mother was Scottish, and I grew up mostly in the States. I'm a hybrid."

"I don't really know anything about you."

A waiter arrived with silver teapots and hot water and fussy little tea bags and china, a cake stand loaded with scones and tiny, delicate sandwiches and clotted cream and jam in bowls.

"Oh, you know a great deal about me," Mr. D. said. "Why don't you call me Dimitrios?"

"I know a lot about your fantasy life, not you." I paused. I didn't want to sound whiny or accusatory, even though I realized I shouldn't have cared what I sounded like. "When did you decide to recruit me?"

"Recruit you? That's rather a dire way of putting it, I think. I know Willis and he told me he'd dated you. It was really his idea. I was quite jealous when he suggested you. I wanted to keep you to myself, but you were so adamant about not meeting me."

"That's what I don't understand. You wanted to meet me, or so you say, and then you paired me up with Jake. You said you were planning a threesome but if you were behind that mirror, why didn't you come forward?"

He sliced open a scone with delicate precision. I had not realized before what beautiful hands he had. "This is rather embarrassing. I lost my nerve. I think you can probably identify with that."

"There's no excuse for pairing me up with a jerk who had a grudge against me. I didn't even like Jake when he wasn't acting like an asshole."

He touched my hand and I felt a tingle down my spine. "You weren't in any danger. I would never have put you in harm's way."

"So you say," I replied and snatched my hand away from his a little too late. "It didn't feel like it at the time. I think it was your sense of perverse fun to let Jake take your place—and I think you were annoyed that I recognized you when I went upstairs. Your plan went wrong."

He took a sip of tea, and as I anticipated, neither acknowledged nor challenged my assumption. His innate confidence always got me. "Games, Jo. It's all games. You weren't bad at them yourself, were you? You were quite a favorite in the Great Room."

"I'm done with the Association."

"It's a shame."

I raised a fragment of scone to my mouth, hoping I wouldn't drop jam all down my front. "I need to make sense of all this."

"To explain it to your young man?"

"I can't explain it to anyone unless I understand it myself. I don't know that you're telling the truth even now. What did you want from me, Mr. D.?"

"Love."

That took me by surprise, but then his rare moments of honesty had always disarmed me. "Well, you blew it. I can't love someone who lies to me," I said, willing myself to believe it. "And I did love you, you know, before I discovered you were playing me."

"I realize that now." He said it with such dignity and simplicity I believed him.

We sat in silence for a while. I nibbled on a finger sandwich. "I'd like to think it wasn't your idea to make me and Patrick the floor show. So I'm not even going to ask you."

"You're really quite lovely together," he said. "Very well matched. I hope he's what you want."

"He is. Thank you."

"Does he know you're here with me?"

I shook my head. "No."

"And have I answered your questions?"

"Not really, but I'm glad we met."

"Are you still angry with me?"

I shook my head. "Life's too short to carry a grudge. What's done is done."

He dipped his hand into his pocket. I thought he was going to summon the waiter to pay the bill, but instead he laid a small white plastic rectangle on the table, stark and bright against the dark polished wood.

A room key.

I stared at it a long moment, then looked up to meet his eyes. So it wasn't the end of the story—not yet.

"So where's your young lady?" his father asked. He snapped his fingers and their server appeared. He pointed at his empty

Scotch glass. "Another of these, and we'll see the wine list." He gazed at her as she retreated. "Look at the arse on that girl."

"Woman," said Patrick, checking his phone again for messages. "Behave yourself, you old sot. They'll spit in your soup if you're not more politically correct. This place is the world center of political correctness."

The concert broadcast was on the radio when he'd picked his father up from the hotel and he'd expected Jo to be at the restaurant when they'd arrived. They'd waited almost an hour, his father drinking Scotch while ignoring the starters they'd ordered. Now Patrick was getting worried.

"And how's Gran?" Patrick asked.

"Much the same, miserable old cow," his father replied. "You should phone her up."

"I do, and all she does is say how clear the line is as though I'm phoning from next door and then she talks about the weather. She also has some sort of fantasy that I'm getting back with Elise."

"Lovely girl, lovely girl," his father said. "And are you getting back with her? You could always keep this other one on the side. Have the best of both worlds. We're not genetically disposed to monogamy."

"We? The Delaneys? Irishmen? Come on, Da, don't be an idiot." He grinned at his father with affection. That was the problem. He liked the old man in a way, when he was sober, which at the moment, he was, more or less. "Back in a moment. I'm going to call Jo."

He went to the front of the restaurant, where the reception was better, and called the station. Someone would be there, even if it was only the announcer, but he knew they might not answer the phone since it was after business hours.

The phone rang and rang and he was just about to give up when someone answered; a woman, but it wasn't Jo, and she told him Jo wasn't there.

"This is Patrick, her boyfriend," he said. "When did she leave?"

"She hasn't been in at all today. She called an hour or so ago and said she was running late."

Running late from what? And for what—she was going back to the station? Why hadn't she called him? This was ridiculous. He thanked the woman and sent Jo a text message. Meanwhile his father was about to down another Scotch and probably order a bottle of wine. He went back to their table, where his father was chatting up the waitperson, staring blatantly at her breasts.

"Why don't we order?" he said.

"Would you like me to clear the other place setting, sir?"

"No, she'll be here soon. What'll you have, Da?"

They both ordered buffalo steak and Patrick told the waitperson to bring the wine his father had ordered with their meal.

His father reached into his jacket and produced photographs of Patrick's nieces and nephews. Patrick pretended he hadn't seen them already on Facebook and let his father do the proud grandfather bit.

"And when are you going to produce some grandchildren? Keep the family line going?"

"You mean my sisters' efforts have been in vain?"

"They don't carry the Delaney name," his father pronounced. "Now, you and Elise—"

"It's over, Da. Forget it. We've split up, we're selling the house."

Their food arrived, each plate a work of art, even if the flowering rosemary garnish looked rather girly. His father cut into the steak and waved the server back over. "I ordered it rare, darling. Look at this! Take it away."

She apologized and removed his plate.

Patrick's father poured himself a glass of wine. "I suppose you're not drinking," he said.

"I'll have a glass with you." Patrick took the wine bottle and poured himself a meager inch.

His father grunted. They raised glasses, clinked them. "Have you given any more thought to your career?"

"I'm doing fine as I am, thanks, Da."

"Playing with computers?"

"If you like. I make pretty good money at it. I've done some pro bono law work to keep my hand in." He surreptitiously checked his cell to see if Jo had sent him a text message.

"Pro bono! It's no wonder she left you."

"No, Da, I left Elise."

"For this Jo woman? The one who can't be bothered to meet her boyfriend's father?"

"No, I didn't know her then."

His father waved the server down again, Scotch glass in hand.

"You've been stood up, boyo."

"Looks like it," Patrick said with a cheerfulness he didn't feel.

"Bloody women, eh?"

"Right."

To his relief his father's new steak arrived, and was pronounced satisfactory after he cut into it and blood flooded the plate. The food seemed to steady his father, who talked for a time about the conference he'd just attended, and gave some wicked imitations of his fellow academics.

Patrick ordered a bottle of mineral water and tried not to look at his watch or check his cell. His father, having drunk nearly all the wine, ordered another Scotch.

Oh, shit.

Patrick called over the server and ordered coffee for them both.

His father slumped in his chair and then lurched forward, elbows on the table. Silverware clattered to the floor. He knocked his coffee, which the server had placed at his elbow, onto the floor.

"I'll get you another one, sir," she said and crouched to pick up the broken china.

"That's a beautiful arse you have, my darling," his father said.

"Shut up, Da."

"That's my son," his father said. "Can't keep a woman or a job. Fucking mother's boy."

Other diners looked up and stared. A waiter with a dustpan and brush approached the table, as did a man in a dark suit who introduced himself as the manager and enquired if there was a problem.

"He's the problem." His father pointed at Patrick. "My bloody useless son. His mother was a whoring useless bitch, it's no fucking surprise."

Patrick stood and handed his credit card to the manager. "I'll take the check." He handed two twenty-dollar bills to the waitress. "Thanks for your patience and I'm sorry. And this—" he threw a ten-dollar bill onto the table "—is for you to get a cab back to the hotel, Da, because I won't have you in my car. One day we'll have a real conversation, but it won't be tonight."

He left the restaurant, after signing the credit card receipt, appalled at the cost of the meal—the bar section was by far the highest part of the bill—and asked the restaurant staff to call a cab. They assured him they'd see his father got into it and he wished them luck. He walked outside and took a cleansing breath of the bitingly cold air and congratulated himself on surviving yet another evening of insults and embarrassments from his father. Maybe after a few days he wouldn't feel so raw and disappointed.

And speaking of disappointments, where the hell was Jo? He was angry with her for not showing up, not bothering to call and turning her cell off, and worried that something had happened to her. She'd lied to him, too. She hadn't gone to the radio station, and he had a panicky moment of imagining her car broken down somewhere isolated, of her cold and scared by the side of the road.

The night would have been entirely different if she'd been there. His father wouldn't have drunk enough to degenerate into vicious anger; he would have played the charming Irishman and raconteur and been tolerable company.

Once inside the car he tried Jo's cell again while the engine warmed. He tried the house, but there was no reply there, either.

He drove to the radio station and rang the bell on the back door, which was the only way to get in after business hours, always assuming someone was willing to open the door.

"Who is it?" He recognized the voice on the intercom as belonging to the woman he'd spoken with earlier.

"Patrick Delaney, Jo's boyfriend."

"She got here five minutes ago." The door buzzed open.

He walked in along the corridor that led around the perimeter of the building and met the announcer, whom he now recognized vaguely as the girl who'd cried at Thanksgiving, and thanked her for letting him in.

She was flustered and angry. "This isn't like Jo. She was over an hour late. My boyfriend is mad that I'm working late."

He saw ahead the flash of the red light that indicated Jo was on air, the studio door open. She sat at the board, illuminated by a lamp, the rest of the room in darkness, her voice calm and mellow, and saw him at the window, and stopped in midsentence, then recovered herself and resumed speaking.

When the music started he stepped through the open doorway and turned on a switch by the door, flooding the room with light.

"What the hell's going on, Jo?"

26

I TOOK OFF THE HEADPHONES AND TURNED THE chair to face him.

He looked mad, and rightly so, and he didn't know the half of it.

"I screwed up. I'm sorry. How was dinner with your dad?"

"Appalling. Where have you been? Why did you turn your cell off?"

I glanced at the clock. I had twenty minutes to explain what I'd done. "Tonight I told someone I couldn't love them because they'd lied to me. And I don't want to lie to you, or evade the truth. Remember I told you I had loose ends?"

He nodded, his face grim. He shoved his hands into his pants pockets. "Go on."

"I was in love, sort of, with a guy I'd never met. The guy I had phone sex with. Here. And I found out, more or less by accident, that he was the one who was behind my invitation to join the Association.

"After…after you left on Saturday night I met him for the first time. I mean, really met him in person. He wouldn't tell me why he'd lied to me and used me as a pawn in some sort of baroque game, and I wouldn't have listened at that point. I was too mad, too hurt. So I told him to meet me again today and explain. He agreed that I was entitled to an explanation. So that's where I was."

"This explanation," Patrick said. "Did it involve his dick, by any chance?"

I wished I could have lied to him but now I had to tell him anything, everything. "Yes."

"Admirable, your quest for truth. So you fucked him and the mysteries of the universe were revealed."

"I'm sorry," I said, helpless, watching his face harden, loving him more than I would have thought possible. "If I didn't love you I wouldn't have told you. I am so, so sorry."

"Of course." He walked toward me and I was frightened by the contempt and pain on his face. "Was it good, Jo?"

"Stop it. Please." I backed away.

"I'll tell you something. If you really did love me, you wouldn't have fucked another man and you wouldn't be talking yourself into why you had to do it. That's it, pure and simple." He reached out and put his hands, quite gently, on my neck, thumbs caressing my collarbone. "Did he make you come?"

"Please don't touch me, Patrick."

He dropped his hands and looked nauseous, pale. "So the stockings were for him. And the sexy red lace knickers. Christ, I actually believed you when you said they were for my benefit. Did you get wet for him, Jo?"

"Stop it!"

"Did you come?"

"I know you're mad—"

"Did you? Come on, Jo, the truth. Isn't that what this is all about? *Did you come?*"

"Yes," I whispered, humiliated.

"And did he get up your ass?"

I shook my head. I was about to cry and I didn't want him to see me break.

"Lying bitch." He turned and left.

I sank to the floor and cried when he'd gone because I knew I'd lost him, shuddering with grief and pain and hating myself for my stupidity and cruelty. When I looked up next, I saw I had ten more minutes before I had to go on air. I wiped my face dry and got to my feet and turned off the harsh overhead light, as though hiding in semidarkness could conceal the damage I'd done.

And then I noticed two things.

Both of them red, both of them flashing.

One was the entire set of incoming lines on the phone but there was a very good reason I hadn't heard any ring. If the mic was on, then the phone ringers in the studio were muted.

The other flashing red light was the one that announced someone was on air, live, the mic turned on.

I lunged over to the board, praying that I'd pulled the fader down, but it was still in its normal, announcing position. Every vitriolic, obscene word exchanged between me and Patrick had been broadcast to our entire listening area. I wrenched the fader down and turned it off, and sat, paralyzed with horror, watching those phones light, flash and darken as they rang over to an extension, listening to them ring and ring.

I couldn't know how much people had heard—we hadn't been that close to the mic—but obviously enough.

Then I very carefully took a drink of water, gargled a little and cued up my next CD. I took deep breaths and turned the mic back on and slid the fader up. I made a cool and leisurely announcement about the music we'd heard, what was coming up next and gave the time and temperature. Fader down, mic off, music up. Done.

I took my cell out of my purse and turned it on. Six calls from Patrick as well as three text messages, three calls from the station, probably from Ann, and one a couple of minutes ago from Kimberly. I deleted them all and called her.

"Honey, what the hell's going on?" Her voice was high and frantic. "I'm coming over. See you in five."

"No, you don't have to. It's late. I—" But she'd hung up and sure enough, in five minutes the back doorbell rang and I let her in. She wore a gorgeous leather coat, pajamas with a pattern of fluffy bunnies and cowboy boots, and I laughed at her appearance and then cried again.

"You are up shit creek," she said, dropping her huge leather tote bag onto the floor. "Wow, it's like they say, they just don't have that old-time radio drama anymore. It's time for damage control. Okay, you know the password for the general voice-mail box? Great. You get on there and erase every message that's been left and do your own mailbox, too. I'll do the rest."

"What about their passwords?"

"I know them. Don't ask. Bill's legacy. Then we'll do the email. We'd better stay here and check things for a while. I brought supplies." She nodded at the tote bag, which held fruit and cheese and crackers. "And don't listen to any of those messages. They won't make you feel any better."

"I'll have to quit after this, however good a cover-up job we do. It's bound to leak out."

"I know, honey. But you'll quit in your own time. This buys you a few days. I'm just glad Neil is out of town." She hugged me again. "Okay, girl, get crackin'."

The general voice-mail box was full and by this time the calls had died down. I erased all the messages in there as well as all of mine. Then I erased the emails that had come into my account and that of the general mailbox account.

Kimberly came back into the studio a little later and cut up cheese and fruit and fed them to me, tenderly and gently, which made me cry again. We checked for phone calls and for more emails—most of them had gone to Bill's mailbox, some to Neil's—and deleted them. But after an hour everything was quiet. As Kimberly said, everyone had probably gone back to internet porn or tonight's game. It was a time to be grateful for sports.

She stayed in the studio until I shut down and then took me back to her apartment, where Bill had fallen asleep on the couch waiting for us. I cried some more and told Kimberly the whole story in a messy and incoherent way. Bill woke up and made me hot milk with honey and offered me grass, his usual bedtime combination. ("And now little blue pills," Kimberly added with a wink.) I turned down the grass but accepted a big slug of liqueur in the hot milk and fell asleep in Kimberly's spare bedroom.

"Hey, sleepyhead." Kimberly sat on the bed. "How are you feeling? Want some breakfast?"

I sat up, rubbing my eyes and wondering why everything felt so strange and why I was in Kimberly's spare bedroom. I wore a huge striped flannel shirt that was probably the top half of a man's pajamas, and which probably belonged to Bill. Five seconds later memories of the previous evening flooded back.

"Don't cry," Kimberly said. "Oh, heck, cry if you want. You're entitled. You fucked up real good, honey."

"I know." I reached for my cell phone on the bedside table.

"Uh-oh! No! You are not to call him."

"I wasn't going to. I want to call my mom."

"Call her later when you're not such a mess." Kimberly placed the cell out of reach. "I'm going in to work soon to do some more damage control. You want breakfast? Bill will fix you something, or you can go back to sleep."

"Tell me about Bill." I wiped my face with my sleeve. "I want to hear about something good."

"Okay. Well, I was getting tired of internet dating—dreadlocked dentists and all the rest—and I suddenly thought, hey, there's this great-looking guy at work, and he's a bit older but heck, that means he's had time to put in some practice, so I hit on him."

"A *bit* older?" I echoed.

"Honey, I've never told you how old I am and you're too sweet to ask. I'm forty-five. I've got good genes and I've had a bit of work done." She tapped the underside of her chin and beneath her eyes. "And I take care of myself. So, yeah, he's a bit older, but so what? He's a real animal in the sack, let me tell you. Don't hardly need those blue pills at all, and he's real good about putting the toilet seat down and those other domestic details. We had to keep it quiet at the station, what with sexual harassment and favoritism and all. But now we're out of the closet."

"That's great," I said. "Do you think you'll get married?"

She shrugged. "Maybe. I'll get going, then. Bill can give you a ride back to the station for your car. You just keep your head down and come in for your air shift looking the picture of innocence. I'll check the snail mail. I tell you, it's a good thing no one who works at the station listens to it. Except for Neil and he's out of town. But Bill likes your show, always has, and that's why I heard you last night."

"Kimberly, isn't it illegal? Tampering with mail and email?"

She stood and grinned. "You bet. Remember the Alamo, honey. See you later."

I got up a bit later, dressing in a pair of Kimberly's fancy yoga pants, and let Bill feed me a huge amount of pancakes. "Heartbreak's always better on a full stomach," he said, flooding my plate with syrup. "Mind you, I would have fired you, too. But it's not the worst thing that can happen."

It wasn't, but I didn't feel good about losing my job. I felt good about very little in my life at that point. I drove home through suitably gray, bleak weather with the car radio turned on to a relentlessly cheerful rock station, listening to the comforting oldies I remembered from my childhood. As I pulled into the driveway I glanced up at the apartment. I knew, although there were no signs to tell me so, that Patrick had moved out.

As I headed for the front door I saw someone get out of a large dark car parked across the street.

"Ma'am?"

I turned. Oh, God, I was about to get mugged. Great. I slid my keys into a weapon the way I'd been taught in self-defense class, threaded between my fingers, my hand a fist. A man approached, clipboard in one hand. Maybe not. I'd never heard of a mugger carrying a clipboard.

"Ms. Hutchinson?" the guy asked. He held out a large manila envelope and a pen. "Sign here. Great. Thanks. Have a good day."

I tucked the envelope under one arm and went into the house. Brady ran toward me and weaved around my legs, making his usual affectionate, hunger-inspired crooning sounds. I followed him into the kitchen. Someone had fed him recently; a few scraps of food stuck to his bowl.

I walked upstairs and tapped on the dividing door to the apartment. No answer. I opened it and walked into a completely bare room. He'd taken the trouble of vacuuming, so the place was spotless. On the minuscule kitchen counter lay one of Patrick's cards with the post office box he used for his business mail and his cell phone number.

I turned the card over to see if he'd written anything to me, but the back was blank. He was gone.

I was beyond tears, shocked and hardly able to move or think. The envelope fell from under my arm to the floor. I picked it up and opened it.

Inside was a letter, lines of dense type, on the letterhead of a prestigious local law firm. I skimmed over it. Phrases leaped out at me. Breach of contract. A ten-thousand-dollar fine levied

by the Association. A meeting the next Monday at which I was
to present the fine in the form of a bank draft.

And I thought things couldn't get any worse. I stuffed the
letter into the backpack, left the apartment and went back to
bed, where I could sleep and cry for the rest of the day.

Sleeping and crying was about all I could do that week,
except that by some odd twist of fate, possibly because I knew
I was leaving the station soon, I did great shows. On the air I
sounded fabulous, competent yet friendly, informative and en-
tertaining, and the music flowed. I knew, because I made a few
tapes, thinking that if my name was not mud in the wonderful
world of classical music radio, it might be useful to have a few
demo tapes of my on-air style. No one would ever know that
the announcer off air dissolved into tears and lived on toast and
peanut butter and coffee.

Kimberly spent some of each evening with me, sitting in the
studio with her laptop, and bringing me leftovers from dinners
Bill had cooked that I couldn't eat. I took the plastic containers
home and fed them to Brady. Not a good idea, I found, after
stepping in Tex-Mex cat vomit.

I lay awake at nights wondering what I would do without a
job, without a tenant and if I should cash in my IRA to pay a
ten-thousand-dollar fine, or, if I ignored it, whether it might
go away. Yes, I decided, that was the best approach. And I'd
roll over in the bed that still held Patrick's scent and cry until
I fell asleep again. I saw little daylight that week.

I summoned my substitute announcers for the next week,
claiming that I had an emergency to deal with, and covered
my air shifts. I caught up on editing promos and public-service
announcements. I tidied up the music library. I, who had been
so grossly unprofessional, was leaving things in good shape.
Neil should be grateful.

On Friday I packed my few belongings into a box for Kim-

berly to take home. I had ridden my bike in, because the speed
and the burn of the cold were about the only things I enjoyed
these days. "You be careful," she said. "I think we're gonna get
an ice storm."

"We never get ice storms here. It's not humid enough."

"Humidity's high." She popped the back of her car. "You
call me if you need a ride. And..."

"And what?"

"I don't want to leave you with bad news, but Patrick's
moved back into his house, if you were wondering where he
was."

"With Elise?" I shoved the box into her car.

"Heck, I don't know. She's still there as far as I know. It's
his house, too. Doesn't mean they're knockin' boots. A lot of
people get stuck with an ex and a house and they just become
roomies." She hugged me. "It's shitty, honey, real shitty. Call
me tomorrow, and we'll do something fun on the weekend.
Go to a viewing or something, see if we can pick up guys at
the funeral home."

"Sure. Thanks." I hugged her back and started to cry again
to my disgust. Even I was getting a bit tired of it by now.
"You're my best friend. I love you so much."

"Shit, we'll go to a dyke bar and pick up girls if you want.
Get back in that studio and talk pretty now."

I went back inside the radio station, noticing as I did so that
there was another car in the parking lot, and wondered briefly
whose it was. Then I went back into the studio, blew my nose,
gargled and went on air.

I chose Bruckner as background music for writing my letter of resignation. Mournful, dignified, serious stuff. Just like
my letter, which I printed out, folded into an envelope and
deposited in Neil's mailbox. I didn't have long to go now and
I wanted to announce that this was to be my last night with the
station, but I couldn't. I thought of my listeners, the insomniacs

and lonely and sad and worried people who'd told me the music I played made their lives a little more bearable. Would they miss me? Would they call in to find where I'd gone?

I lined up material for the next air break. Sponsors, and the weather, which I'd do live. Kimberly was right, there was a warning of freezing rain after midnight.

And then I cued up the last piece of music, *Scheherazade* by Rimsky-Korsakov, as some sort of ironic tribute to my ill deeds, and I did what I so rarely did in the studio: put my headphones on and listened to every note, every swell and sigh, and lost myself in the music's story.

The music died away. I faded the mic up and signed off. *It's been a pleasure. Good night and goodbye.* I shut the studio down and left my station keys in my mailbox, making sure I had all my belongings, and then I wheeled my bike outside, letting the door slam behind me.

As I swung my leg over the saddle and pushed off, I heard sounds familiar to me from my Vermont childhood—the otherworldly, delicate patter of frozen rain and the groan and sharp screech of a branch giving way under a burden of ice— and I noticed how the bare branches of the trees shone silver in the parking lot light.

But I didn't have time to admire, or be horrified, by the effects of nature for long. A pair of headlights came on, and the lone car in the parking lot accelerated, heading straight for me, skidding out of control.

I stood on the pedals, praying the ground might be magically free of ice, and shot forward, my thigh muscles complaining, heading for the bike path and what I hoped was safety. Somehow my tires kept contact until I'd left the parking lot. I was clear of the car but I felt the bike skid beneath me, and on the path ahead of me was a branch that had succumbed to the shock and weight of ice and was directly in my way.

Curl up. Protect your head. I tried to remember everything

I'd heard about how to fall correctly from a speeding bike. Don't put your arms out. Don't—

The bike and I parted company, branches and the sky wheeling crazily around me. My helmeted head hit the ground with a horrendously loud bang and the rest of me followed, crashing onto an unyielding hard surface. But at least I'd stopped my free fall. I was quite happy to lie still. Nearby a ticking sound slowed and stopped, the wheels of the bike revolving. In the parking lot, the offending car roared, the deep sound of a vehicle reversing, then drove away. It was very quiet now apart from the snapping of branches and the icy, high-pitched staccato of freezing rain. Just me and the ice.

Oh, shit.

As soon as I moved I knew something was wrong and bits of me were letting me know that they'd been hurt, bumped or scraped or jarred. So, I'd better figure out the damage. First, I should sit up. I tried to roll to a sitting position and found I couldn't. One arm was holding me back, not cooperating, and then it hurt like hell and I stopped trying to sit, but the pain was here now, ripping through me.

Cell phone. I needed to call someone because it was so cold I could die here. And I was hurt. It wasn't fair. I'd had a shitty week and now some jerk had tried to run me off the road, or off the parking lot. I started to cry, and then reached behind me for the side pocket of the backpack, where my cell was.

No, it wasn't there. It was inside my jacket. I thought it was. Easier to get to, except I'd have to move the arm, which felt like agonizing Jell-O to reach it. I gripped my injured arm with the other and moved it and nearly threw up with the sudden, horrible pain. I'd have to get my glove off, but it was too much to do one-handed. I retrieved the cell phone and managed to flip it open, and it slithered to the ground beside me.

Oh, shit.

I lay down again. I knew I should call Kimberly—she'd

offered her services and this certainly was an occasion to take her up on it—but my mind wasn't very fond of behaving itself these days.

"Call Patrick," I said into the phone, and blessed modern technology as it did just that.

27

PATRICK'S PHONE RANG FIVE TIMES BEFORE HE answered. Those five rings were an eternity and it was a shock when he finally answered, cool and wary.

"What do you want, Jo?"

"I hurt." It seemed a sensible thing to say. Direct, to the point. Accurate.

"It's one-thirty in the fucking morning. Good night."

"No. I'm *hurt*." I made a great effort to communicate. "I think I've broken my wrist."

"What?"

I had trouble making out words. "My bike."

"You've had an accident?"

"Yes."

"Jo, where the hell are you?"

"Bike path…near the station."

"Oh, Christ." I could hear sounds now, as though he was moving and talking. "You're riding your bike on ice?"

"Was." The effort of maintaining a conversation was becoming too much trouble. I wondered vaguely if I were succumbing to the cold. I could see ridges of ice on my clothes. "I fell off."

"Hold on. I'll be right back."

I think I fell asleep for a minute because I could hear him yelling my name.

"Hello, Patrick."

"I've called an ambulance. They're dealing with some god-awful crash on the highway so I'm coming. Don't move."

"Can't move."

He talked and I heard him. Now and again he'd shout at me and I'd have to drag myself up from where I really wanted to go—some seductive, dark, insensible place—and tell him I was still listening.

And suddenly he was no longer on the phone but next to me, touching me, and the falling ice gleamed in the headlights of his car. "Where are you hurt? Left arm? Where else?"

"I'm tired."

"I know you are, but I've got to get you in the car." He eased me up into a sitting position, leaning against him, and the effort and pain made me cry. "Keep holding your arm. I'm going to get you to stand. And then we'll take a few steps and you'll be warm and safe."

It hurt, particularly when we both slid and Patrick cursed and held me upright. Getting into the car was difficult, but we managed it, and Patrick took off his down jacket and laid it over me after he'd buckled me in. He reached into the backseat and pulled a large, bulky item over me, a down sleeping bag.

"This isn't your car," I said with a fine grasp of the irrelevant.

"It's Elise's. It has four-wheel drive."

"Tell Elise I'm sorry if I throw up."

"Don't worry about it." He took a hand off the steering wheel to tuck the sleeping bag around me. "Are you warming up?"

I closed my eyes, fighting back the nausea and the pain. Beside me he muttered and I felt the vehicle slow down. Through my closed eyelids I saw the flash of emergency vehicle lights.

"Roads are a mess," he commented. "You're not the only idiot, but probably the only one on a bike. Hey, Jo. Jo? Say something."

"Sorry."

His hand skimmed along my knee. "I don't know which part of you to touch. Stay here."

I'd decided I wasn't going to move ever again, but I opened my eyes to see more flashing lights and the entrance to the emergency room, which looked like it was having a busy night. Patrick came through the doors with a wheelchair, and as he opened the car door a nurse ran out, telling him to wait, that he couldn't do that.

He lifted me into the wheelchair and I cried again. I was warming up and it made everything hurt, even the few bits of me that hadn't got scraped or bruised.

"Jo, where's your insurance card?" I was lying down now in a bright, noisy space. Things clattered and banged. How on earth were people supposed to get better here?

"What's your name, sir?" someone bellowed.

"She's a girl," Patrick said. He unbuckled my bike helmet and took off the face mask.

"Woman," I said. "In my backpack."

Patrick put the backpack on the gurney next to me and delved into it. He produced a couple of battered tampons, a paperback, an apple, and then stilled, the letter in his hand. "What the hell is this, Jo?"

"Nothing."

"We'll talk about it later." He found the plastic folder that held my credit cards and handed over my insurance card.

Someone tugged at my sleeve and I heard the sharp snap of scissors cutting my super expensive lightweight insulated jacket off. I faded in and out as people did things, some of them quite painful and uncomfortable. Now and again I'd wake up in a different white, noisy space or find myself watching ceiling tiles fly by overhead as they wheeled me around and expensive medical equipment beeped and whirred.

Patrick sat and watched Jo sleep and knew he still loved her.

He was sure, with a shiver of fear, that if he had not answered his cell she might have died in the intense cold. His rescue of her was the act of one decent human being to another, and he thanked God (or something, not the deity of his Catholic upbringing) that he hadn't hung up on her. That was the sort of Good Samaritan role he didn't mind playing. He had never seen anyone so pale, so blue around the lips, when they finally got that balaclava off her head, and they'd shoved him out of the way and put warm packs around her and put in an IV, working fast and using that medical jargon everyone recognized from TV and he was frightened then that he'd lose her.

Wasn't there that saying that if you saved someone's life you were then responsible for them? He yawned, scratched the stubble on his face and thought longingly of sleep, comfort, quiet, while the sounds and cries and weeping of the emergency room continued around them and she slept on.

She looked tiny on the gurney, pale and helpless, and it frightened him.

I'm hurt.

But so was he and he knew he should get out, now, finally, get away from her. What other sorts of rescues would she need from him in the future, what other dramas and late-night phone calls and lies could he expect? He'd had time to read that ludicrous letter over, the one that lay tattered in the bottom of her bag, and he wondered whether she'd suckered someone else into rescuing her from that yet. Maybe she really did owe someone ten grand. Maybe she was in trouble he couldn't even imagine.

He should have been smarter, always an easy realization in retrospect. The night at the sex club or whatever it was should

have sent him running to sanity, not climbing back into bed
with her as soon as possible. But even before that, there had
been plenty of hints: the strange nighttime outings in the limo,
the time she'd come home after a night of rough sex; the impression he'd always had that she had secrets. But he thought
about her smile, her scent, her laugh, the way she looked when
she came, and none of the bad stuff mattered. None of it.

Was he out of his mind?

Jesus.

He leaned forward to touch her hand.

No question, but he was in it for the long haul.

He'd vowed he'd never rescue a woman again (unless she
was freezing to death with a broken arm in an ice storm: there
were some exceptions to the rule), but now he had to rescue
himself.

I awoke really needing to pee.

"What are you doing?" Patrick rose from a plastic chair at
the side of the bed. We were in a curtained cubicle, under that
fierce fluorescent light and ugly ceiling tiles, with the smell of
something peculiarly hospital-like in the air.

"I need to go to the bathroom."

He helped me off the bed and grabbed my IV stand. My
broken arm was in a sling and one knee felt sore and stiff. As I
moved I noticed that almost everything hurt. "Wait," he said.
"You're flashing your arse in that gown." Holding me up with
one arm, he rummaged in a drawer and found another gown
to drape over my shoulders, and then we left the cubicle, my
legs weak and sore, and staggered—I staggered, he steadied
me—to a bathroom nearby.

"Don't lock the door," he said.

After I'd peed I caught a glimpse of myself in the mirror. I
looked truly awful, shadows under my eyes and very pale, and
I felt about a hundred years old.

"Are you okay in there, Jo?" Patrick called.

"Coming out." I splashed water onto my face and shuffled to the door. Patrick helped me back into the bed, where I fell asleep again.

He was still there when I woke, and I found out that I was to go home as soon as the doctor returned to sign the necessary paperwork. It was now nine in the morning and I discovered an inventory of damage in addition to my fractured arm. A knee that sported an ice pack, and strained muscles and scrapes. After another hour or so, armed with a list of instructions and a bottle of painkillers, we left.

"I told them I'd look after you," Patrick said, helping me into the car.

"Why?"

He shrugged and didn't say a word until we reached the house. The storm had passed and the sky was a miraculous bright blue, burning the ice away. "It's so beautiful," I said, overcome with happiness and relief. Across the road, my neighbors, installing a string of lights around the eaves of the house, waved. "And look, holiday decorations already!"

"Glad you're enjoying the pain med," Patrick said. He unlocked the front door. "Do you want to lie on the sofa or would you like to go to bed?" He looked away as he said it.

"I want a shower."

He nodded and went into the kitchen muttering about plastic wrap.

The benefits of the shower—cleanliness, heat—were outweighed by my clumsiness and the discovery that even simple tasks were complicated and painful. By the time I'd managed to put on about the only thing I could wear—a short-sleeved cotton shirt and a pair of sweatpants (no way would I parade around in my skivvies with Patrick in the house)—I was exhausted again.

Patrick had changed the sheets, to my chagrin; the bedroom was a mess, with clothes dropped where I'd removed them that week and various plates and mugs around the room. He presented me with a bowl of oatmeal and brown sugar but all I wanted to do was sleep, my injured arm resting on its own pillow. He was reserved but kind in a way that made me think he'd much rather be elsewhere, and I woke up later in the day, horrified at how much my arm hurt, to find Kimberly there.

She handed me pain pills and a glass of water. "Why didn't you call me for a ride home? I would have driven in the ice for you."

"You won't even drive in snow," I said.

"For you, I would. You scared me half to death!"

"I'm sorry. And thanks. Thanks for everything this week."

"When I said we should do something fun this weekend I didn't mean this." She gestured at my arm. "I'll fix you something to eat."

"You don't have to. I'll be real happy when the pain med kicks in, but it makes me a little nauseated and I can't eat."

"You must eat. Don't be dumb. And before you ask, Patrick went home. He'll be back tomorrow. Now you come downstairs with me and I'll fix us dinner and we'll watch a movie. I've brought us ice cream because you need the calcium for your arm."

I obeyed. I didn't have much choice and although I fell asleep halfway through the movie, I liked having her there.

But I was tired of hurting and being looked after and the prospect of several days of being helpless and needing assistance with such simple tasks as squeezing the toothpaste out of the tube made me feel even worse. And I hated the idea of Patrick seeing me helpless and needy and miserable; he hadn't been Mr. Sunshine himself, and I could hardly blame him.

He arrived the next morning after Kimberly had loaded me and my arm—I was beginning to think of it as an entity in its own right—into the bathtub to wash my hair. I was appalled at my bruises, sporting all the colors of the rainbow, which I was able to see in the bright morning light coming in through the skylights. I'd never appreciated those skylights before, since I was so rarely awake at this time of day, and I suspect the pain med added to my appreciation.

I retired to bed with ginger ale and a book and Brady asleep next to me. Downstairs Kimberly and Patrick talked and then I heard the front door open and close.

Patrick came up the stairs bearing a briefcase and a bouquet of Shasta daisies. "Oh, those are pretty," I said. "Thanks."

"From Elise. Can I get you anything?" He put the vase of flowers down and shifted from one foot to another.

"No thanks."

"I brought some work." He nodded at the briefcase.

"Use my desk if you like."

"Thanks." He sat down and opened his laptop, putting a thumb drive in the side.

"What are you working on?"

He stopped and looked at me. "Where's your purse?"

"Over there. Why?"

He brought the purse over to me. "Okay. Give me a dollar."

"Why?" I asked again.

"If I'm to represent you I need a retainer."

"Represent me?"

He pulled the Association's letter, now battered and creased from its sojourn in the bottom of my backpack, from a manila folder. "This is total bullshit as you probably know, but you need someone who can speak their language to get them off your back. Now give me a dollar."

I fumbled my billfold open and handed him a dollar. "Thank you."

I should have sounded more grateful. He nodded and shoved the dollar into his jeans pocket. "I'll be coming to that meeting tomorrow although I'll try to get them to postpone it until you're feeling a bit better."

"I feel fine," I lied.

He reached for a yellow legal pad and a pen from his brief-case and sat on the chair at my desk. "Tell me about it. Tell me everything."

"About the Association?"

"Yes. How you got involved. Who, when, where. Every-thing."

I talked. I told him what I probably should have told him when we were first involved, only now I was a client talking to her lawyer and that made me tremendously sad. At the same time I was ashamed, having to recite a list of my adventures.

Now and again he would stop me and ask a question. *With your consent? The names of the people watching? Did they warn you what would happen if you refused? How many times? Whose sugges-tion was that?*

His pen moved across the pad, paper rustling as he flipped to another page.

He stopped writing. "The binder of rules. Do you have it here?"

"No, it's in my locker."

"Ah, that's a pity. Go on."

I finished at the point where he and I had been invited to dinner.

He nodded, and flipped back through his notes. "You men-tioned a car outside the radio station, several times, and last night you said a car ran you off the parking lot. I don't suppose you know what sort of car it is? Color? You don't happen to have a photographic memory and can tell me the license plate number?"

"Sorry, no. You don't think they were threatening me, do you?"

"It's a possibility. Showing their muscle. Probably nothing I can use." He laid the yellow pad down. "Why did you do it, Jo?"

He meant Mr. D. "It was like a journey or a story. It had to have an ending. We'd been very close and it was a farewell. That sounds dumb but it made sense at the time."

He was quiet for a time. Then, back to being brisk and impartial again, "Okay, is there anything more?"

I shook my head. "I need to take my pain med."

I gripped the bottle of pills between my knees so I could open it with one hand, picked one out and spilled them over the bed.

"Oh, Jesus," Patrick said and sat on the bed, the vibration traveling straight up my arm.

"Stop it!" I said, reacting to yet another helping hand, but immediately regretted it.

He ignored me and retrieved the pills. His hands shook.

"Patrick, I'm sorry. Are you okay?"

He shook his head, took off his glasses and pinched the bridge of his nose. His voice was strained when he spoke. "I can't bear to be around you but there's nowhere else I'd rather be. It hurts so damn much, Jo, and that's the truth."

"Patrick." I touched his shoulder and he flinched.

"I—I'm sorry," I said. "You've been so generous and I'm grateful and…"

"But you don't love me."

"Is that really what you think?"

"I don't know." His eyes were reddened and he scrubbed at them fiercely. He sat, elbows on his knees, staring at nothing.

I leaned back against my pillows and forced myself not to cry. Yes, I loved him, but it was too late. Maybe.

I touched his shoulder again. "Patrick, make love to me."

28

"ARE YOU INSANE?" PATRICK SAID.

My face grew hot. "Oh, forget it. I—"

"You're out of your mind on narcotics. You can barely walk. You have a broken wrist in a cast you're supposed to keep in that sling."

"So?" I pushed. "You have something against sex with people with handicaps, or is it just me?"

To my relief his mouth turned up into a reluctant smile. "Heck, I suppose we could manage."

Thank God. I didn't realize how tense I'd been. "That's real big of you, counselor, although I should warn you I have some spectacular bruises."

"This is grossly improper professional behavior." My lawyer pulled his sweater over his head. He unzipped his jeans. "Do you need some help with your clothes?"

I wriggled out of my sweatpants and began the arduous, delicate task of unfastening the sling and easing off my shirt. I settled my wrist on a pillow. "Will you kiss me? Please?"

Kissing him was like coming home, sweet and poignant and then hot and sexy, and my whole body, despite the drugs, fired into life, every nerve ending flaring. It did occur to me that the painkillers, which I was enjoying despite the vaguely seasick sensation that accompanied them, might well be helping things along. But mostly it was Patrick, Patrick kissing me and exclaiming over my bruises and touching me only the way he could.

"Wait." He reached into my bedside table, a lucky guess, and found my supply of condoms.

I didn't argue with him as he ripped open a foil package. Mr. D. and I had used protection but Patrick was justified in not asking me, or worse, not believing me. Not with my track record.

We settled on an awkward sideways spooning position, which, as Patrick pointed out, would hardly bother me at all.

I gasped, caught between pain and desire, and yelped as he slid home. He barely moved, but let me set the pace.

"Do you like this?" He touched my breasts.

"Yes, more."

"This?" He reached for my clit. Then, "Did he do this, Jo? Did you like it?"

"Don't." I couldn't bear the sadness in his voice.

"Did he stroke your nipples? Pinch them?" His face was wet against my shoulder. "Did he tell you how pretty your breasts are?"

"Please don't." I started to cry, too.

Somehow I expected him to be rough—as punishment or just deserts or something—but he wasn't. We moved together very gently at first, but restraint and caution added an erotic charge and we broke through into a place where nothing else mattered but touch and friction and heat.

I told him I loved him when I came.

He slid his cock out of me and reached for a tissue. "I'm not sure whether that was the best or the worst sex I've ever had."

"Thanks."

He sighed and rested his face against the back of my neck. "There's something I should tell you. I slept with Elise again."

"You bastard," I said, without much conviction. "I suppose you're telling me to hurt me? What's good for the goose, or whatever?"

"I guess so. It was pretty bad. I don't think we'll ever do it again. She faked an orgasm."

"Too much information, Patrick."

"I faked an orgasm, too."

I started to laugh and wished I hadn't as it vibrated down my arm and wrist. "That's pathetic, Patrick. If you were going to screw someone else you should have enjoyed it."

"You should know," he said.

"Listen." I turned to face him as much as I could without moving my arm. "I know what I did was unforgivable. I'm sorry. But I can't keep on apologizing forever and you can't keep sniping at me forever."

"I know." He cleared his throat. "You know, I'm jealous. Not of this Mr. D. guy so much, but of all the stuff you did. The group sex and so on. I don't know whether I could be that adventurous or brave."

"Or dumb."

"I suppose so. I mean, the kinkiest thing I've ever done is jerk off over you and I feel embarrassed about that still. I've never even had phone sex. That's why I held off on real fucking with you, because I suspected you were way more advanced than I was."

"There was the anal and the mild bondage with you, if it makes you feel better."

He scowled. "Yeah. *Mild.* I feel inadequate."

"You've no need to feel inadequate," I said, and now I was the one sniping at him. "And when you ask me for reassurance about your sexual prowess, I feel like you're setting me up, so cut it out."

"Okay." He moved away from me and we lay in silence for a little while.

"I think I'll make us a bacon sandwich," Patrick said.

I wasn't hungry but I accepted. We had a truce; a fragile one, but I had no idea what would happen next. Maybe it was too late.

Neil called me first thing the next morning and sounded almost like a human being—too little, too late. I had the distinct impression Kimberly was standing in front of him, holding up cue cards. He knew about my massive indiscretion, of course.

"You're on YouTube," he said.

"Really?" I hoped he'd tell me what sort of video footage they'd used but he didn't go into details.

"I'm sorry to see you go, but it's really best under the circumstances, even though we seem to have had very little listener feedback, and not all of it was negative. Some listeners suggested we have more radio drama."

I made a neutral noise.

"Or call-in shows," Neil continued. He cleared his throat. The "show sympathy" cue card seemed to be on display. "I'm very sorry to hear about your accident."

"I'm doing fine. The doctor said it's a clean break and should heal well." I ignored the mean thought that Neil was probably immensely relieved the accident had not happened on station property.

"And we're giving you three months' severance pay. You've been with the station a long time and you've done a stellar job. I appreciate you leaving things in such good shape. Your numbers were remarkably good for a late-night classical music show."

"Thanks. That's very generous." I hung up the phone and limped into the bathroom to clean up for the Association meeting, which Patrick had managed to postpone until four that afternoon. I was getting better, it was true. I no longer walked like a ninety-year-old. I walked like a sixty-year-old with a bad knee. In addition, looking at Patrick, who was wearing only boxers and sporting a burgeoning erection, I feared we were both developing an odd sort of fetish for plastic wrap.

He washed my hair with gentle efficiency and helped me dry off. All quite friendly and asexual apart from his hard-on, which we both ignored.

Back in the bedroom I viewed the black skirt suit he'd picked out for me with some trepidation. How on earth would I manage the zipper? And a bra? I rummaged one-handed in my underwear drawer and picked out some nice conservative underwear—cream lace—and a matching bra. And pantyhose, I'd need pantyhose, but the only pair in there had a massive hole. I threw them into the trash and picked out a pair of black thigh-highs.

"I'm afraid I'll need some help dressing."

Patrick, in shirt and boxers, sighed heavily. "If I must."

"Look, I'm halfway there."

"You are? You look pretty much naked to me."

"I am wearing panties. That's not naked. You need to fasten the bra and I can do the stockings but the zipper on the skirt—"

"Okay, okay. In less than an hour I have to play attorney and I'd rather not do it in this condition."

"Is that some kind of hint?"

"Cover up and I should be fine." He stepped into his pants and zipped them up.

I'd never realized how sexy being dressed could be. Undressing, well, that was obvious, but this had the mild perversity of covering up rather than revealing. I noticed Patrick's hands lingered on my thighs as he pulled up the stockings, although he lectured me about not flashing anyone. "And you must keep your mouth shut, please. Let me talk. No smart-ass comments and no smiling." He frowned at my high heels. "No, not fuck-me shoes. What else do you have?"

Flying high on painkillers, I attempted a serious expression. But as we drove to the office where we were to meet I became nervous. "What if this doesn't work?"

"It will."

"What are you going to say?"

"It depends."

"On what?"

"We're here." He pulled the car over to a venerable red sandstone building that reminded me a little of the Association mansion. "Wait for me in the foyer and do not talk to anyone."

"I want another painkiller."

"You do not." He got out of the car to open my door. "I need you conscious, on your feet and with your mouth shut. Got it? And limp a bit more, will you? And if they offer you water, don't accept it."

"Why? Do you think they're going to drug me?" But I went inside, my suit jacket and a shawl draped over my shoulders, and turned down the glossy receptionist's offer of water or coffee.

When Patrick joined me he looked different, stern and distant, although I was amused to see he was fastening a tie, his briefcase tucked under his arm.

"Miss Hutchinson?" He nodded coolly at me as though half an hour ago he hadn't knelt in front of me pulling up my stockings. "How are you feeling?"

"Okay," I said in a pathetic voice.

"Mr. Berg and Mr. Seales are ready for you now," the receptionist said. She flashed Patrick a brilliant smile. He looked her up and down, his expression not changing. We followed her through the office to a conference room. As we entered and the door closed behind us, Patrick took my good arm and helped me into a seat.

The two men who stood by the window chatting joined me and Patrick at the large oval table and introduced themselves.

They were both youngish, successful-looking and wearing expensive suits.

Patrick took a chair next to mine and they sat on the opposite side of the large shiny oval table. I didn't recognize them, but I was fairly sure they hadn't seen me before. There was nothing lewd in their expressions when they looked at me, but they could have been acting, just as Patrick and I were.

Patrick took a fat manila folder from his briefcase, a legal pad and a fancy gold pen. He laid them on the table and sat back and waited.

"If you could hand over the check, Miss Hutchinson, we won't need to take up any more of your or your attorney's time," said Berg. "We have the papers ready for you to sign."

"My client will not be handing over a check," Patrick said.

"Ms. Hutchinson signed a contract with the Association, Mr. Delaney. It's pretty clear-cut."

"On the contrary, gentlemen, the only clear-cut issue is that Miss Hutchinson has been grossly misled by the Association, lied to on several occasions and signed a contract in good faith that said very little, but which you are now using against her. If anyone should be handing over a check to anyone, I suggest it might be Miss Hutchinson who should be the recipient." He opened the manila folder and referred to a typed sheet of paper.

And then he began talking.

I was impressed. I had to stop myself grinning as he riffed and improvised, calling upon this case or that case, while Berg and Seales became increasingly uneasy. I had no idea what he was talking about but I had the impression he had the right stuff. God, it was sexy.

Berg and Seales rallied, offering arguments that sounded like gibberish to me, but Patrick considered, discussed and rejected all of them.

In midsentence he trod rather heavily on my foot and stopped. "Miss Hutchinson? My client needs a glass of water."

Seales rushed to the credenza at the side of the room and poured iced water from a pitcher into a heavy crystal glass, handing it to me with a napkin, while Patrick fussed over me, asking if I needed a break. I said I was fine.

Seales and Berg meanwhile had returned to the window, where Patrick joined them, the three of them talking in low voices. At one point, I had the impression that things were settled, but Patrick brought up another point and they bickered for a little longer.

"It's probably not a deal breaker," Patrick said. "Let me ask my client."

He came to my side and said in a whisper that was loud enough to be heard across the room, "I'm afraid they won't return your initial investment, Miss Hutchinson, but they've agreed to drop the demand for ten thousand dollars. Is that acceptable?"

"I suppose so," I said as seriously as I could. We were talking about one hundred dollars, after all.

"We have a deal," Patrick said, and manly hand-shaking ensued. "Please messenger over copies of the new agreement to me and Miss Hutchinson." He handed them a very plain cream-colored business card that I suspect he'd run off on a laser printer that morning.

He helped me from my chair and supported me as we left the conference room, and led me to the reception area. As we left the building he loosened his tie and undid the top button of his shirt, and by the time his car drew up outside the tie was completely discarded.

He helped me back into the car and then slapped his hands on the steering wheel. "Free and clear, Jo."

"What did you say to them? It sounded like legalese garbage to me."

He fastened my seat belt. "It was. It was all about billable hours."

"What?"

"They knew I was prepared to talk them to death and they were losing money. So they caved."

"You mean, it wasn't the brilliance of your legal reasoning?"

"About five percent, perhaps."

"I thought you were brilliant. We should celebrate."

"You're celebrating quite nicely with your painkillers." He turned his car into the parking lot of the grocery store where I bought peanut butter for the mice. "You need some groceries, things you can prepare and eat one-handed."

"Great idea," I said, my heart sinking. He sounded friendly and affectionate but he was making it clear that he wasn't going to be around. He pushed the cart in the store and I picked up a few things, but my heart wasn't in it, and he ended up choosing them for me. I apologized for my lack of interest and blamed it on my broken wrist.

He drove me home and carried the bags into the house. I sat on the kitchen window seat with Brady on my lap and watched him put things away. Kimberly was due to arrive in half an hour or so and Patrick couldn't make it clearer that he was anxious to leave.

"How are you feeling?" he asked.

"Okay. Well, not really, but I've an hour to go before the next painkiller." I hesitated. "Remember how in *Pride and Prejudice* Mr. Bennet goes into shock when he finds out that Darcy has saved the family from ruin? That's how I feel. Like I can never repay you for what you've done."

"Oh, yeah. I remember that in the movie. Can you reach this cabinet? You probably shouldn't be climbing onto chairs."

"I have a step stool."

"Okay, then. I'll get my stuff." I heard him run upstairs and when he came down again he was in jeans and sweater once more, his suit in a bag and his backpack slung over one shoulder. "Say hi to Kimberly from me."

I followed him to the front door. "Patrick, what happens next? With you and me? Will anything happen?"

He opened the door. "I rather think that's up to you, Jo. You'll figure it out." He gave me a quick, friendly kiss on the lips and left. I watched him drive away and wandered back into the house to discover, rather messily, how difficult it was opening containers of yogurt one-handed.

And then things began happening to take my mind off Patrick.

First, because I enjoyed the painkillers so much but was getting tired of the nausea, I switched to ibuprofen and found my mind cleared remarkably. I wasn't unhappy, although I did feel a pang every time I remembered how Patrick had strolled to his car and deposited his suit and backpack in the backseat without a backward glance. He hadn't been unfriendly or bitter but I was at a loss. I owed him so much and I didn't know how I could possibly reciprocate. I loved him and I was absolutely certain he loved me back but I didn't know what to do next.

My one-hand typing skills were abysmal, so I abandoned email and Facebook and phoned people and discovered what a joy real conversation was again. I called my mom and the Great Abe, and told them I'd broken my wrist and had decided to leave my job at the radio station. I didn't go into any lurid details, but my mom was shocked and concerned and said all the right sort of things to make me feel better. She offered to pay my fare home for my Christmas visit and I began to look forward to the holidays.

Then Kimberly invited me to lunch with her and Liz Ferrar, and after we'd caught up, Kimberly dropped her bombshell.

"I'm leaving the station," she said. "It's not so much fun without Bill there and I've been there long enough."

"What are you going to do?" I asked.

Kimberly and Liz looked at each other and giggled. "I'm

gonna fundraise for the shelter," Kimberly said. "And that's
where you come in."

"Me?"

Liz leaned forward. "I need somebody who understands media and marketing and can work with Kimberly to coordinate
those efforts with fundraising, and I hear you're available."

"Yes, I am, but I'm—I was—a classical music radio announcer. It's not—"

"Oh, give me a break," said Kimberly, eating fries from my
plate. "You've done news. You've handled press conferences for
the station. The times I've seen you take apart press releases and
rewrite them—"

"But I—"

"Liz, you ever heard someone talk their way out of a job
offer so hard? When it's being offered to her on a plate? Jo,
you email your resume to Liz right away when you get home,
you hear? And no excuses about not being able to type. You're
already using that hand a bit now that you're not wearing the
sling."

Liz smiled at me. "Jo, I'd love to have you think about it.
Maybe you could start when Kimberly does, at the new year?
There's not a lot of money, but you're already in a nonprofit so
you know what it's like."

"I'm overwhelmed," I said. "I'd love to. Really. It's a great
opportunity. Thank you. Thank you both."

"Don't cry," Kimberly said. "I don't think I'll have any, but
what do you want for dessert?"

When I reached home again I walked barefoot through the
house, marveling at how things had turned out better than
I could possibly have hoped for. I wasn't going to starve or
lose the house or beg on the streets. I still missed being on air
fiercely, but maybe, in a few weeks, I might want to turn the
radio on and be able to listen to the music and not just what the

announcer did in between the pieces. I went into the apartment above the garage—Patrick's apartment—and appreciated anew what a great space it was. I remembered, without bitterness, what fun Hugh and I had had when we worked on it. And the first time Patrick and I had kissed properly here.

I should put word out that I was looking for a tenant. Soon.

I was lucky. I had wonderful friends, a loving family, the prospect of interesting work for a good cause and a great place to live.

The sun streamed through the windows, creating bright warm rectangles on the carpet, the sort of places that Brady liked to stretch out in and sleep in for hours. I moved into the sunlight and removed my sweater. I thought again about Patrick kissing me, making me come here for the first time, and lay on the carpet, enjoying the stretch and strength of my body, the return to wholeness I could feel in my wrist and knee.

Brady had the right idea. I took off my jeans and saw I was wearing the battered Christmas panties that I'd worn, or, more accurately hadn't worn, the first time I'd met Patrick. And then, since my socks were gray, dismal things that were probably about as old as the panties, I slid them off. My T-shirt came off, too. I wasn't wearing a bra, because the cast and my lack of manual dexterity made it too awkward.

I stretched out and reached for my cell phone in my jeans pocket.

"Call Patrick," I said, and lifted my hips to remove the panties. I laid the phone down next to my ear on the carpet.

He picked up his phone. "Hi, Jo."

"What are you up to?" I said, mentally kicking myself for not telling him I was naked first thing.

"Oh, not much. Look, I'm sorry I left like that. It's that I enjoyed being a jerk in a suit and I needed to think things over. I'm doing some legal work for Liz now, for a pittance. It's a beginning. So, actually, yes, I'm up to quite a lot."

"Oh, that's great. It's so nice to hear your voice." I considered telling him I'd be working for Liz, too, but then we'd never get to the point.

"It's nice to hear you, too. How are you? How's the wrist?"

"I'm great. Are you alone?"

"Well, yeah." He sounded puzzled.

"I'm in your apartment. I'm lying in a sunny patch."

"Like Brady does."

"Yes." I took a deep breath. "What are you wearing, Patrick?"

"What? Jeans and stuff. Why?"

"Patrick," I said, lowering my voice to a sultry growl, *"what are you wearing?"*

"Oh." Now he understood.

"I'm naked," I said.

And I heard a sound that filled my heart with relief and love and joy—the metallic sound of a zipper going down.

He said, "Tell me more."

★ ★ ★ ★ ★